Against his chest, Rysa's breath hitched. Her lip fluttered and her eyes grew huge. And Ladon knew all the pain he felt moving through her body was his fault....

Games of Fate
BOOK ONE
FATE · FIRE · SHIFTER · DRAGON

Games of Fate

of Fate

FATE ◆ FIRE ◆ SHIFTER ◆ DRAGON
BOOK ONE

BY

KRIS AUSTEN RADCLIFFE

Published by Six Talon Sign Media LLC
Minneapolis, MN

Copyright 2013 by Kris Austen Radcliffe
Second Edition copyright 2015 by Kris Austen Radcliffe

Edited by Annetta Ribken
Copyedited by Terry Koch
Cover designed by Lou Harper
Series dragon design and art by Joseph Garcia and Luchito Inzunza

ISBN: 978-1-939730-27-5
First Printing

Six Talon Sign Media LLC
www.sixtalonsign.com

THE
FATE ✦ FIRE ✦ SHIFTER ✦ DRAGON
SERIES

GAMES OF FATE
FLUX OF SKIN
FIFTH OF BLOOD
BONDS BROKEN & SILENT
ALL BUT HUMAN

Coming Soon:
MEN AND BEASTS

1

Rysa's attention deficit meds weren't in her backpack. She fished through the lint under her laptop, catching only a pen and the corner of her wallet. Wads of paper and a few stray coins filled the bag's recesses, but her pills were nowhere to be found.

If she was going to dig in her bag without getting too many stares, one of the back tables in the Continuing Education Building's basement coffee shop was a good place to do it. The café had bright, warm lighting and a bright, earthy scent, and was fairly secluded.

Not that she trusted herself to be thorough. No meds equaled a super-sized portion of "flighty" and a bottomless cup of "hyperactive." The headache ratcheting from her eyebrows, over her scalp, and to the base of her auburn ponytail wasn't helping, either.

She dug her hand into her stupid pack again even though she knew she was wasting her time.

Her friend Gavin sat on the other side of the table tapping a pencil against an assignment. They'd known each other since her freshman year and he'd long been more accommodating with her attention issues than most of her other friends, probably because he wanted to become a doctor. She was, after all, good "patience with a patient" practice.

Still hoping to find her meds, Rysa pulled a notebook out of her bag and slapped it harder against the table than she meant to. The table wobbled, a loud *clunk* popping from its uneven feet.

Gavin's hand jerked up and he leaned back.

Do you want help with your chemistry or not? he signed, his hands moving through the American Sign Language with quick precision. He wore hearing aids, but they signed, too.

"Yes." Rysa looked directly at him so he could read her lips clearly, knowing full well she'd also narrowed her eyes, even though she didn't mean to. Her head throbbed and was adding an edge to her already annoying issues.

She rubbed her forehead. "Sorry."

She did need his help. This close to finals, if she didn't figure out her assignments, she'd fail another class. The University would kick her out. She knew it.

Gavin's shoulders slumped and he crossed his arms—his way of giving her the silent treatment. He'd frowned about twenty minutes into the first problem when it became clear that helping her would take all night.

But how was she supposed to focus on homework without her attention meds? One more dip into the bag produced only a crumpled five dollar bill. She dropped it next to her notebooks.

Gavin scowled this time, his gaze following her hand as it dipped into the bag again.

It's not like he always understood his classwork. She'd helped him with Human and Environmental Policies last semester. He'd been a chore, no matter how much she tried.

Did I mess up your evening? she signed, her hands working as fast as his through the ASL. She scraped her stuff into her bag and plopped it onto the floor next to her feet.

"Were you sexting with that sophomore again?" she asked. This time she didn't look at him. His hearing aids worked just fine.

Gavin sighed, his expression flat. He usually had the laidback calm of someone who'd just finished a good workout. Women found it charming. The boy had more contacts in his phone than the University had numbers in its database.

Gavin's finger twitched as he pointed at her bag next to her feet. *Isn't it a little late to be popping stim meds?*

The headache flared, a semi-nauseating ping that made her bump the table. Her calculator slipped off a book, jarring her chai. A splash plopped onto her Chemistry Principles syllabus.

Steam rose off the course description as if she'd dropped acid on it, not hot tea.

A yellow stain spread across the syllabus and her attention snapped to the paper. The liquid ate away the words and they bled onto the tabletop, destroyed by her impulsiveness. She blotted at them, blinking.

"Rysa?" Gavin signed something, too. She didn't catch it.

He sniffed and the titanium in his ears flickered with the light from the television behind her head. She'd sat with her back to the little café's screen for a reason. News crawls and no meds didn't mix well.

This morning, when she'd come down to the kitchen, her mom had been watching the news. A suburban Chicago mall exploded last night.

Later, on the drive to campus, the radio announcers had been on and on about big fires in several of the towns along Interstate 94, between Chicago and Minneapolis.

At school, pundits had infested the news channels blaring in the student unions, bobbing their heads and pushing up their glasses, ranting about terrorists or gas leaks or 911 calls that may or may not have indicated a suicide bomb—

"I'm sure you left your meds at home." Gavin leaned back as he spoke.

Rysa usually didn't get this flustered. Or this... distracted. *Must be the headache*, she thought.

Why don't you breathe so you can drive home? Gavin signed.

Breathe? Her syllabus disintegrated on the table, ruined by a splash of hot and random, much like her academic career. She stared at it even though she didn't want to. Her mind hyper-focused on the one perfect representation of her time at the U and it wasn't going to let it go.

"You should talk to Disability Services." His chair groaned as he shifted around again.

A new rainbow of reflections danced across his hearing aids and her attention honed in on the brilliance in his ears. She stared like a deer caught in headlights.

Gavin's gaze jerked up to the screen behind her.

The images must have changed.

Rysa closed her eyes, refusing to turn around and be caught by the news. She'd spent her last class staring out the window toward the east, her anxiety creeping up for no obvious reason.

Whatever stalked the states east felt like it was about to burst from the horizon and scorch all of campus—and her in particular. The effort it took not to freak out was what probably triggered the headache, and was as big a contributor to her inattention as anything else.

Today was not a good day to forget her meds.

Gavin said something again. Her face scrunched up as she tried to parse it.

"Rysa, did you hear me?"

He'd said something about Disability Services.

What are they going to do? she signed back. *Follow me around and nag me all day?*

They'd turned her down for a translator position when she applied last year even though she'd aced the exam and had no hearing difficulties of her own. Her damned ADHD reared its head during the interview.

His jaw tightened. *Pulling ninety-ninth percentile on all three parts of the GRE will only get you so far with grad school admissions.*

She pressed on her forehead again. School, the fires—and to make things worse, her mom's obvious pain this morning before she left the house—all combined to make the perfect Storm Rysa.

At breakfast, her mother had held out a glass of orange juice, her hand shaking and her joints swollen and red. Rysa downed the juice in three gulps, more to keep her mom from worrying than because she wanted it.

The juice had distracted her, which was why she'd forgotten her meds. They were probably on the kitchen counter between the empty glass and her mom's prescription pain killers.

"I'm going home." She needed to get away from all the campus television screens. The blinking made her squint.

Gavin touched her wrist. "I just want to make sure you're alright before you go off to graduate school. I can't help you with your courses if I'm in Boston and you're somewhere in the Rockies."

She stared at his fingers until he let go. Her head throbbed in short, intense pulses and his exasperation wasn't making it better. She reached for her damned bag again. Maybe she had some acetaminophen. At least it would take the edge off the pain for the drive home.

Get some sleep. That helps, Gavin signed.

She pressed her temple. Her head felt as if every muscle on her scalp was about to fight-club her sinuses.

The pain hadn't been this bad a moment ago. The war raging inside her skull flared into her vision. The coffee shop's lights blasted down as if she sat under a hot spotlight. The slick counters glinted as if fire popped off their surfaces. The scent of coffee filled her nose with a bitterness that made her sneeze and the smell of scones coated her tongue with gag-worthy sweetness.

In one sudden moment all the chaos about school and the world and her mom fell away.

Nausea rushed in.

Her mouth opened. Blades of blinding light stabbed behind her left eye. Terrible, hideous light coming out of nowhere and burning like she'd looked directly at the sun.

"What the hell?" she gasped. A real gasp, one that, in a split second, forced air all the way down into the base of her lungs. Her hands clutched her forehead.

This wasn't withdrawal symptoms because she missed her meds. Her brain just exploded. She was going to keel over in this little coffee shop under the Continuing Education Building and that would be the end of everything and she'd die.

Spots appeared in front of her eyes and floated like wiggly balloons between her and Gavin. They churned, full of heat and glare and fire, each one its own burning, liquid universe. The spots didn't look real but she knew if she reached out, if she touched one, it would ignite and she would feel it burn her hand.

One of the weird, liquidy fire spots ruptured. Her nose filled with an acid stench so overpowering she stopped breathing.

I'm having an aneurism, she thought. She must be having an aneurism. Only an aneurism explained hallucinations she could smell and feel.

"Gavin…" She choked out the whisper. Her gut mirrored the pain behind her left eye, squirming with an infestation of the fire bubbles. Her hallucinations burst in her stomach and ate her flesh. She'd have retched but the muscles of her belly and chest wouldn't move. They wouldn't respond.

Gavin stood up and pointed at the screen behind her head. He hadn't noticed her panic. "A gas station in Stillwater exploded!"

Half an hour from campus. Her chair fell over when she turned toward the screen. The seatback scraped against the concrete floor and a nauseating metallic screech filled the coffee shop. The sound rasped against her ears, solid and seemingly touchable, like the spots.

Gavin stared at the screen behind her head. The freshman server behind the counter stared at her.

"What's happening?" Rysa's lips formed the words, but no vocalizations left her throat.

Gavin's gaze jumped from the screen to her and his face blanched. He shouted at the freshman. His mouth moved but she didn't understand.

He seemed to yell something about calling 911.

Gavin, the freshman who stared at her with terror-filled eyes, the coffee shop's now grating halogen lighting, the darkening evening outside, all spun as if the planet got on a carnival ride and left her standing alone in the void.

Warm air hit Rysa's nose as she pushed through the shop's door. The spots that weren't real—couldn't be real—took on a sharpness that would slice her open. Monsters would come out of her wounds. Fiends that would eat her whole.

A word whispered through the haze of pain. A word that sounded not like her thoughts, but also like her at the same time. Like she heard an echo of herself. Like her future self—the Rysa who was about to land fully inside of whatever hell caused the aneurysm and hallucinations—was yelling backward in time trying to warn her present, freaked-out self.

Ghouls.

Rysa screamed. She had to run. The spots chased her. *Ghouls* chased her, but the world fuzzed out as if someone had slapped a dirty bandage over her eyes.

Another spot burst, but this time a memory flashed: Her mother at the kitchen counter watching the television. She'd rubbed her knuckles and

Rysa had wrapped her arm around her shoulder. "Go to class," her mom said. "I'll be fine."

The evening gloom slammed down on Rysa again. Shadows swam. The scent of the humid summer air managed to push through the phantom burning in her nose.

Her hand hurt. Her nails dug into the real skin of her real palm.

Gavin, his nose bloody, staggered along the path toward the parking lots down the hill from the Continuing Education Building. "Don't hit me again!" he yelled.

She hit him? He glared at her like she was some kind of monster.

"I don't... I d-don't understand," she stuttered. They stood on the hill, half way between the coffee shop and the student parking lot, under the streetlight where the path intersected the walk from one of the campus barns. But she didn't remember—

Another spot ruptured. Orange and hot yellow dropped over the world like a curtain.

She stood alone in the glaring yellow bullseye of a different streetlight. This one flickered like a strobe, buzzing and popping as if it was about to explode. Her eyelids fluttered rapidly as her eyes adjusted to the pulsing shadows.

How the hell did she get into the student parking lot three blocks from the café?

She was losing time. Losing her sense of space.

She really was in the middle of an aneurysm. Nothing else explained what was happening. Not the blackouts. Not the weird, whispered warnings about... ghouls.

Why was her brain whispering about not-real monsters?

She felt like she was dying. She had to be. Her body dragged her out here to commit suicide and she couldn't stop it.

A man, tall and lanky like Gavin, walked toward her between the hand-me-down cars, his step bouncing as if he was about to break into a tango. He wore bright red running shoes and a black nylon jacket over a blaze orange t-shirt—the fabric version of the damned fire-spots eating her mind.

He stopped a few feet away, a deep inhale bowing out his chest. His hand swept in front of his nose and he sniffed the air like some cartoon character breathing in fancy perfume. Another inhale and his head tilted at an angle that should have popped every vertebra in his neck.

"Who…" she stammered. Where was Gavin? "What…"

"Right where you're supposed to be." The man's thick British accent made his words almost unrecognizable.

The same caustic stench from the spots rose off his skin.

Real stench. She gagged, her lips and nose curling in a futile attempt to keep the chemical sewage rolling off this creature out of her lungs.

His teeth gleamed in the dim parking lot light. "Calling yourselves Fates." He shook his head, tisking. "You see the future but you know nothing." He grabbed her arm.

The weirdness in her head bled into the real world and this man was its manifestation. All the spots, all the phantom smells—they were about to kidnap her. For *real*.

"Let go of me!" The man made no sense and she hyper-focused on his fluorescing mouth, ignoring everything else. His teeth glinted, sharp and too bright like they'd rip her apart if they got near her skin.

Her vision jigged like she'd changed the channel for a microsecond and then switched back to what she had been watching before. But in that microsecond, in that very brief flash when she saw something she knew wasn't really there, she saw the man lean forward to bite her shoulder.

Bite and rip flesh and eat himself a right good snack.

Because he was a ghoul. A burning, stinking ghoul.

Somehow, some part of her mind had known. It had told her.

Her chest tried to fill with air and her throat tried to constrict to make as loud a high-pitched noise as it could because the man was a *ghoul*.

He grinned at her with his razor-sharp teeth. A loud sniff rushed into his nose. "You smell tasty, luv. I might take myself a nip now, before you finish activating." He licked his lips.

"Activating?" She wasn't dying of a brain aneurism. She didn't know what *activating* meant, but the word held truth in the same way that *ghoul* held truth.

He clamped a ratty fingerless gloves-clad hand over her mouth and nose. "You're a bit of a freak, aren't you? Can't hold still. Stay normal for a moment longer, darling."

"Let her go!" Thirty feet away, Gavin jumped the lot fence, his feet pumping as he landed.

New panic flooded in, different from what she felt for herself. A scene played through the pressure behind her eyes: The ghoul was about to lock onto her friend's throat. The fiend would feel a surge of hunger and he'd salivate like an animal. Then his hands would cook Gavin's flesh.

Run! she signed. *Go*!

A new, slow dread of certainty fizzled through her consciousness from the same source as her knowledge of *ghouls* and *activating*: Something bad was about to happen. Something as terrible as the fiend gripping her arm.

A couple of car lengths away, Gavin halted like he'd run into a wall. He gagged and bent forward. The stench must have hit his nose.

"He your boyfriend?" The hand over her mouth loosened.

"Please don't hurt him." The ghoul could take her, but Gavin had a life ahead of him. He'd do good. Become a wonderful doctor.

She knew the truth of his future with the same inner-understanding she knew something horrid was coming.

The ghoul's eyes narrowed and he tilted his head again as he peered at Gavin. He flicked his chin toward campus. "You better listen, little normal. Better run. Before my mates find you."

Gavin stepped back, both his mouth and his hands working but not making sense.

"Run!" Rysa screamed. He had to get away. She'd make sure—

Then the world flickered hot yellow again and Gavin was gone. The ghoul stood on her other side, anger dancing through his eyes.

"Do *not* do that again!" He slapped and caustic chemicals burned her cheek.

He dragged her toward the break in the fence framing the walk to the road. "Claw me one more time and you'll be lucky if you keep your arm, you stupid cow."

She didn't remember clawing him. She didn't remember Gavin running away, either.

She'd had another blackout and lost more time.

How was she supposed to get away if nothing made sense?

The man dragged her through the lot gate and into the street between the University parking lots and the ones owned by the State Fair. He pushed her forward with one hand, the fingers of his other tapping in the air as if he played an invisible piano. His fingertips glowed and smoldered one at a time, turning on and off as he pressed each imaginary key. "Quiet now, luv."

A dark-gold hatchback with rusted side panels and blistered paint weaved down the street. A blue van, just as ratty, rushed from the other direction.

The man inhaled, his chin up. "Time to meet the family, princess."

2

They tumbled out of the vehicles. Ten, twelve, maybe more, their stench so thick it hung in the air like a sick yellow-green mist. They lurched around, some moving toward Rysa and the man holding her by the neck, some away.

Rysa coughed. The man laughed.

The smallest of the group lunged out of the hatchback. Slight and willowy, he—*she*—Rysa couldn't tell for sure—wore tattered sweats low on her ass and a baseball cap twisted to the side. She stopped close and tapped her foot on the asphalt as she leaned forward, her little fists pushing into her hips.

"Billy! You found her, huh?" the little ghoul said. The air whistled into her scrunched-up nose. "Yep, she's one of them, alright. Pricks!"

This thing in front of Rysa was a *child*, no older than ten.

The kid jumped straight up into the air and spun in a half-circle, landing on the precise spot she'd launched herself from but with her back to Rysa. "Bring'em out!" she yelled. Another bounce and she faced Rysa again. "Party time, skankadoodle." Little sparks popped out from between her fingers when she clapped.

Billy waved his hand in the air, his fingers skittering like they had a mind of their own. "We're too visible. He'll find us again, like at the park with the rollercoaster. That way." He pointed east, toward Wisconsin. "The Fells. Kells."

"The *Dells*, dickweed." The child shrugged.

A woman with dirty hair jerked out of the van, a balled up blanket in her arms. She staggered backward into the bumper—the weight she carried obviously throwing her balance—and she dropped the bundle.

Chains unfurled. Shackles bounced against the van's door.

Metal clinked across the pavement.

Rysa had been able to keep some wits about her. She'd sent Gavin away. But the pressure behind her eyes screamed and these people had chains and she needed to get away before—

Time hiccupped again.

Rysa had her hand around the neck of the dirty-haired woman. The skin of her palm burned as if she'd touched a hot stove and she shrieked, pitching backward.

How did she get away from Billy? She must have slammed the female ghoul against the van. They'd kill her now. Chained or not, no way would they let her live.

"Bitch!" the woman shouted.

The woman's teeth glowed like miniature, bright-white scalpels. She gripped Rysa's arms and heat pushed toward her skin and the panic wouldn't stop.

"Lizzy!" Billy caught the woman's elbows. "Hush now." Wisps of something—smoke, dust, ash, Rysa didn't know—rose from the woman's skin when he touched her cheek.

The child skipped over, her little finger poking at Rysa's chest. "Get her up!"

Lizzy let go and another ghoul snatched Rysa's head backward. Disorientation overrode all sense of up or down. A raw scream erupted from her throat as sound finally pushed out.

Hands lifted her hips into the air. More held her legs. The ghouls flung her up high above the pavement and giggled when they caught her on the way down.

The chains rattled and the child's harsh laugh hissed through the air. Billy's grip on Rysa's thigh tightened. The heat from Lizzy's palms burned through Rysa's shirt to her skin.

The sky above glowed. Reflections of Minneapolis set the cloud deck ablaze and the sky swam in yellow-green, like the haze from the monsters.

The ghouls muttered as they carried her away from the vehicles. One clamped shackles onto her wrists—big, thick manacles like she'd seen in bad movies. She thrashed, but another set clamped onto her ankles.

They held her above their heads but the heavy chains pulled down her limbs. Her back arched as her shoulders and hips wrenched downward.

She couldn't turn her head but she felt what the child did. She saw the sky but a finger melted resin into a shackle lock and bonded the metal around her wrist.

Burning seared across Rysa's right wrist. Pain jolted her mind as bright bolts and white noise. Maybe she'd blackout again. Maybe she'd blink and be on top of the blue van, her body turning ninja again the way she'd gone after Lizzy. Maybe she'd rain death down onto the ghouls.

But they held her tight.

"Stop! Please stop!" Tears blurred her eyes. Her voice rasped. The acid haze lifting off the ghouls burned away every thought in her mind.

One of the ghouls screamed and the heat at her ankle stopped. A loud crack puffed next to her head. More screams, and the hands under her back and hips let go.

Rysa fell.

Her back tensed as her instincts pulled her knees toward her chest. The shackles' weight wrenched. She rolled. Her vision lost the glow of the sky and filled instead with the blackness of the pavement.

She knew what was about to happen, felt the anguish play across her muscles and bones. She was about to hit the ground. Snap ribs. Her head would bounce, blinding her with colorless flashes. Blood pool in her mouth. A hip crack. And her forearm shatter.

But it didn't.

Huge hand-like claws—long, dexterous digits ending in vicious-looking talons—scooped under her shoulders and hips.

She bounced upward, her free-fall countered.

Every hair on her body stood up. The talons retracted in a wave that moved from finger to finger across each hand. The hands pushed her gently and she rolled again, facing upward once more.

Nothing stood over her. The cloud deck swirled in the sky, open and visible. Both giant hands vanished to nothing as well, though she felt them curl tighter.

A ghost held her inches off the ground, yet it felt warm and real and alive. Invisible muscles coiled and powerful limbs adjusted position. She rocked and a massive chest pressed against her side.

She should feel terrified. She should scream at this new impossibility and fight and flounder in its arms. But the weird whispering returned and she knew what held her wouldn't hurt her. Ever.

Carefully, she touched what she couldn't see. The energy crackling from whatever caught her left the distinct impression that it was as amazed by her as she was by it.

The creature let go and her feet hit the ground. It altered its stance and the position of its chest dropped. Weight shifted. Something strong that felt like it might be a neck rubbed her shoulder.

Across the lot, near the van the woman had pulled the shackles from, another crack thundered through the air. A black-haired man wearing black jeans and a black jacket zipped tight around his neck smashed his gloved fist into the nose of one of the ghouls.

The fiend staggered back and pulled a knife from his belt. He grimaced and his face reddened. The blade flashed, and he cut down his arm.

The acid stink increased and Rysa covered her mouth and nose. Whiffs of smoke rose from the ghoul's clothes but he continued to slice.

The man in black cursed and slashed a whip at the ghoul's arm. The tip stripped the knife and the man bolted into the lot before the blade hit the ground. The ghoul danced around, swearing, until he looked at the blade next to his foot.

It glowed red. A whine, high-pitched like a wind-up toy about to be released, reverberated between the van and the hatchback.

The knife exploded. The ghoul's leg below his knee burst into a red haze.

The ghouls didn't just burn. They didn't just eat people, either. Their blood made knives explode.

And shopping malls. They had to be responsible for all the explosions. All the fires.

Maybe she *was* having an aneurism. Maybe none of this was real. How could it be real? She stumbled backward. Maybe—

The invisible chest of the creature who had saved her from her fall blocked her way. It pressed against her back, gentle and *real*.

Her terror lessened, driven away by this giant she couldn't see but felt wrap itself around her body.

Next to the hatchback, the man in the black jacket smashed an elbow into another ghoul's chest. "Damned cockroaches!" he growled.

His voice, even filled with anger, sent a shiver up her spine and melted more of her terror.

"Fuck you!" the child shrieked. She and two others ran for the van. Billy and Lizzy snuck around and hid alongside the hatchback.

The man dropped his whip and pulled a gun as long as his forearm from a holster on his leg. The barrel recoiled as a poof blasted a barbed spike through another ghoul's heart and spine. It popped through cleanly, no blood or gore, just more of the red glow. Then hooks spread from its tip.

The man yanked on the rope and the ghoul fell forward.

Whatever pressed against Rysa's back moved away but stayed next to her. She felt its presence, but still couldn't see it—until a shimmering ghost-line of rich yellows and oranges rolled through the air. A snout and an elongated head appeared. Golden light erupted across the creature's flank in swirling dots, lines, and hard-edged patterns. Her first thought was *dinosaur*, but the creature had a vaguely canine set to its limbs. Whatever it was, it looked strong and agile, and as if it could stop every single attack the ghouls threw at it.

It reared onto its hind legs when the man tossed it the gun. Every muscle along the creature's ridged back undulated when it caught the weapon and flicked the attached cable.

The ghoul's body flew straight up, high above the fight.

For an instant, the ghoul floated still and lifeless in midair like a helium balloon on a tether. Then the body crystallized, little sparkles rapidly spreading outward from the wound in its chest. Without a sound, the shards vaporized and became a person-shaped, red dust cloud.

The red dust rippled with menace. The ghoul was dead, but the dust wasn't. It embodied something far worse than mindless rampaging. The red dust was chaos unfettered.

Rysa backed against the creature's side.

The cloud imploded. The limbs pulled in first, the dust shaping into a red ball. Flutters rippled the surface like a puff of smoke or a drop of blood.

The entire sphere sucked into a tiny point in space.

A blinding flash ripped through the street and parking lot. The creature curled around Rysa, its talons gouging the asphalt as it blocked the shockwave from throwing her to the ground.

Next to the blue van, a high-pitched screech erupted from the child. "I *hate* you, dragon boy!" She stomped her feet.

The creature was a *dragon*?

The kid ran straight for Rysa. "Give us the Fate!"

All Rysa's panic returned, clawing through the chill on her spine left by the exploding dust.

She was a *Fate*?

Billy called her the same thing when he snatched her. She pressed against the dragon's chest once again, grasping for the calm she'd felt before, but the chains attached to the shackles restricting her wrists and ankles knotted and she tripped. Her palms came down hard on the pavement, her hands wrenching inside the cuffs, and she dropped to her elbows.

Dust pillowed off the ground when forelimbs slammed down on each side of her body. A dragon neck appeared over her head and bright, glimmering reds flashed from the dragon's hide.

The beast blocked the child. The little ghoul couldn't get close.

Next to the hatchback, the man in black tipped his head as if listening to someone whisper in his ear—and above her, so did the dragon.

Energy crackled over her skin as if it moved across a bond between the man and the beast.

Their connection wove itself into her senses, brightening her perception and calming both her panic and the pain in her arms.

Every cell in her body tingled.

The dragon dropped its head next to hers. It sniffed her hair and touched her face with its snout. Warmth spread across her belly as it coiled its tail around her waist and legs.

The flavor of the energy between the man and the beast changed and a distinct sense of *dismay* flowed across their connection. Rysa leaned into the beast doing her best to soothe, feeling that she was supposed to, and flared her fingers over the swirls and patterns moving across the creature's hide.

The man in black snarled and pointed at the ghouls. "We can stop this!"

Flame burst from the dragon's mouth.

Real flame, warm and bright and scented with frankincense and spices. Real fire, not the chemical acid death released by the ghouls. It flooded the area between it, the man, and the kid.

The kid pulled up short. "You think so, huh?" She flipped off the man as she ran for the van. "Prick!"

The man glanced at Rysa, then the child, then back to Rysa again. A surge moved through the energy flow connecting him and the dragon. The beast flamed in response.

"Why are you so stubborn?" The man pulled off his gloves as he ran to Rysa, his head tipped again as if he listened. "A Fate?"

Lifting his goggles, he looked down at her with golden-brown eyes. "They *shackled* you? What kind of Fate are you that you couldn't get away from Burners?"

The dragon nudged the man at the same time as one of its hands curled around Rysa's belly.

The man's brow furrowed as he squinted at the beast. "What?"

More energy pulsed between them.

"He says you're activating." The man looked around. "Why the hell are you alone?"

"I..." She didn't know what "activate" meant, or why everyone kept calling her a Fate, even though she knew both labels were correct.

She also knew she wasn't alone. The dragon enveloped her and their energy connection cascaded over her mind. A calmness she shouldn't have settled in. She felt right, centered, and for first time in her life, she didn't feel alone.

The man lifted the chain and peered at it in the dim light. "Burndust in the metal? Can you get your hands out?" He yanked on the cuff, the furrow between his eyes changing from exasperation to concern. "Hey! Can you hear me? Try!" He blinked, his eyes wide.

Rysa blinked, too.

Her eyes saw more than was possible. More than she could handle. In her vision, several versions of the man pulled and twisted and ripped at the shackles, as he tried, but failed, to pull them off. All versions were not quite the same but all possible, as if she watched multiple takes of the same scene overlaid onto each other.

Each rendering of the man understood what was happening, even if she didn't. Each iteration worked to stop her from becoming something as terrible as the ghouls who now peeled away in their hatchback and van.

She felt a need to help pulse along the energy connecting the man and the beast and she knew even if she panicked again, she was safe with them.

A sense of separation washed over her. She'd taken a step to the side no one else had, or could. Her angle on the world reformed and she saw things clearly that had been obscured before—things that *should* be obscured. Things she wasn't supposed to see.

Possibility took on weight. Portions of time became threads. The universe had a weave and Rysa now saw its fabric.

Saw it, even if she didn't understand what she saw.

Ladon. The man and the beast share the name and it danced through her mind, a separate voice, one that, once again, was her but not her. Their names were Ladon-Human and Ladon-Dragon—called by most Ladon and Dragon—and some of their possible futures were more probable than others.

She grasped her throat, the chains dragging across her chest. No air entered her lungs. Dragon lifted her into its forelimbs and held her close to its body.

When what she knew moved sideways, the world burned hot and cold, her fingers frostbitten as her core boiled. Did the fire ghouls do something to her? Except her hands looked fine, not blue and frozen.

Her perception of Dragon fanned out, multiple takes playing at the same time again. She felt the physical edges of each possibility slide along her skin while they flared through her vision.

She held tight, feeling this big beast's intent. Knowing, understanding, seeing it all for a fraction of a second as a multi-dimensional blossom. For the moment, it—*he*—was all colors and shapes and textures at once. He gleamed with the stars themselves.

Ladon's gold-flecked eyes, warm and full of life, anchored the spinning and the world slammed back to normal. She felt better, stronger, with both of them next to her, as if they'd get her through this. They stabilized *what-is* and *what-will-be*—the present and the future—and understanding the process of "activation" wasn't important. Only that she activated now, with them.

She touched the man's chest, still in the forelimbs of the dragon. Ladon's steady and perfect heart beat strong under her fingers.

She whispered, "You are Human. He is Dragon. Together, you are Ladon." She knew, but she didn't understand. Their energy curled around her like Dragon had when he protected her from the explosion. Everything forward—every moment in the future *what-will-be*—reverberated with them. With Dragon's colors. With Ladon's speed and strength. She would be fine.

She clasped Ladon's palm. "Thank you."

She would be fine.

Ladon glanced at Dragon and his expression loosened into a wide-eyed roundness. His attention diverted from the shackles still binding her wrists, he stroked her forehead. "You're burning up."

With nothing—with everything—Rysa activated as a Fate. Her mind stepped through the rabbit hole into Wonderland. Stepped through while her body was held in the forelimbs of a beast she didn't know, but would. All while holding the hand of a man whose strength calmed the raging whirlwinds behind her eyes.

Hot-cold power burst from her skin, leaving her new, transformed. She felt Ladon brace himself but he didn't falter. He didn't let go.

He took her from the beast and carried her down the street. Dragon followed and Rysa felt what was to come.

She sucked in her breath, not because she couldn't breathe, but because the future exploded in her head.

3

Two nights before, when Ladon and Dragon backed their huge, delivery-style van toward the rear door of his cousin-in-law's bar in Branson, Missouri, they hadn't planned on chasing Burners. They hadn't planned on rescuing an activating Fate, either. They'd planned to pick up supplies: the two Israeli assault rifles Ladon's sister wanted, the new Burner harpoon—the one he lost tonight saving the Fate—plus a couple of cases of premium vodka and a new smartphone with more damned apps than Ladon could ever want.

Then the East Chicago Shifter clan called. Ladon's cousin-in-law, Dmitri, held out his own phone, a drink in his other hand and a scowl on his Russian face. A particularly virulent Burner gang moved west from Ohio. They burned libraries and churches and ate every Shifter they found, taking some directly from their homes.

The Shifters, for all their mercurial abilities, had yet to develop a talent for evading Burners. Their breed morphed, healed, enthralled—plus a host of other annoying traits Ladon didn't care to remember—but they still pleaded for help. And Ladon and Dragon still responded.

So Dmitri stood in the parking lot of The Land of Milk and Honey and watched Ladon cram rifles and vodka into the storage compartments under the floor of their big van. Both Ladon and Dragon found this vehicle more comfortable than the military transport they used to drive. And less obvious. If normals weren't paying attention, they'd think the van was a truck used by overnight parcel delivery services.

His cousin-in-law slapped the side of the vehicle and waved them off, his perpetual Russian gloom the same as it was when Ladon met him over a half-century ago.

So Ladon drove away, as tired as when he'd pulled into the parking lot of Dmitri's expansive bar-slash-entertainment complex. As tired and fed up as he'd feel twelve hours later, when he dealt with the Burners in The Dells.

And just as tired as he now felt as he drove away from the St. Paul campus of the University of Minnesota, where he'd tracked the Burners for what he'd thought—he'd hoped—would be the last time.

Tracked them and let them go so he could protect the lone Fate who now lay unconscious in the back of his van.

He pulled the parking brake and turned off the ignition. He'd found a lonely retail complex with a shadow-filled parking lot seven miles north of the campus—a secluded place where they could deal with the problem moaning on Dragon's blankets.

Ladon looked back at the young woman. Only dim light filtered in through the roof vents but he saw her twitch. The chains rattled and a hollow clink resounded through his van.

A jolt of worry pulsed from Dragon.

Ladon did his best to ignore it. Fates weren't Shifters. They were a completely different issue, one requiring caution.

He unbuckled and crouched on the step up to the back of the vehicle. Fates never had problems with Burners. Fates never had problems, period. Past, present, or future, one member of their triad always knew what the hell was going on.

Except maybe this Fate.

She is injured, Dragon pushed into his mind. The beast hovered over the girl, nuzzling her hair and sniffing her chest. He'd covered her with a blanket and now fussed with its edges, tucking and untucking every time the slightest whimper crossed her lips.

Ladon squeezed the side of the passenger seat and the leather deformed under his fingers. They wouldn't have chased those damned Burners across Wisconsin if they had known Fates were involved.

That is not true. Dragon snorted out a small curl of flame.

"Yes, it is." They stayed away from Fates, even beautiful ones who'd just activated.

How many Shifters did those Burners eat? They murdered over a dozen normals when they attacked that mall. You would have helped, even if you knew a Fate was involved. The beast sniffed at the girl's hair again. *She needs our help as much as the Shifters.*

Her chest rose and fell in shallow inhales. She moaned again, still unconscious. Ladon stared, unwilling to move closer. Best to be careful and keep his distance.

The beast lifted one of her wrists. *Her burns are not bad.* The chains bounced against the floor and filled the van with a discordant rasp. *She will not blister.*

Ladon crossed his arms. The plating on his jacket rattled when he rolled his shoulders.

She may be hurt and unconscious, but she was still a Fate. "Quit clucking over her like a damned hen."

Dragon waved his head side-to-side. *Do not yell.*

"I am not yelling! We need to get rid of her." Fast, before her family showed up.

Dragon draped his talons over her hip. His irritation poked at the edges of Ladon's mind like nettle spines rubbing his skin.

The patterns on the beast's hide sped up and he dropped his head low, one big cat eye glaring at Ladon. *She needs our help.*

Ladon knelt next to the girl. Terror still contorted her face but it didn't hide her beauty. The lush roundness of her body and the warm glow of her skin indicated Spanish somewhere in her ancestry. The enticing tones of her thick hair suggested something else mixed in as well—maybe Irish. Yet the planes of her face seemed Germanic.

And her eyes…

Did he see what he thought he'd seen in the street next to the campus parking lot? The way she'd looked at him right before she passed out had held more openness than he'd seen from a woman in a very long time, if ever.

He sat back. The smooth curves of her breasts and hips might entice, but gaining control of the situation had to be his priority. He'd long ago had his fill of women and their demands. And their disappointed looks and their leaving. He didn't need aggravation from one with the ability to see either the past, the present, or the future.

Ladon stared out into the parking lot as he unzipped his jacket. Dragon's nascent attachment was influencing his responses. It had to be. Fates caused more problems than they solved.

Most of the time. Except when they wanted to help.

"She can't stay with us," he said. Whichever Fate ability she had— seeing the past, the present, or the future—wasn't enough to justify keeping her around.

Ladon threw his jacket at the van wall. Giving in was not an option. Not with a Fate.

The jacket's plating caught the back of the passenger seat and a loud rip screeched through the van as the armor opened a hole in the seat's leather.

Ladon slapped the seat. First the Burners escape. Then a Fate in his van. Now damage to his seats?

The top of an empty vodka bottle poked out from under a stray t-shirt. The weight rolled around his wrist as his fingers maneuvered the glass. He threw the bottle at the rip, neck first. It hit and lodged in the frame, the body angled toward the van's roof.

A low grumble rolled from Dragon.

Grumbling back, Ladon kicked a pile of magazines and clothes into the corner. "So what do we do with her?"

She must come with us. The beast began cleaning her wounds. He fully retracted his talons and flattened his digits, his plate-sized claw-hands taking on an almost human-like shape. Even after all the centuries they'd shared, Ladon still didn't understand how Dragon manipulated his bones to create such changes.

Or how he managed to do such delicate work.

The beast gently wrapped the burns in bandages and tucked the material between her skin and the cuffs. Stubborn as he was, he'd continue to minister to the girl until he felt she was safe. He'd ignore all of Ladon's words and every pulse of annoyance he pushed to the beast. Dragon saw an injured young woman and not a Fate, and he was going to treat her as such, no matter how vigorously Ladon objected.

Ladon knelt next to her again and peered at the perfect contours of her face. She'd been unconscious for longer than she should be.

Fates were supposed to activate as a bonded triad of three seers. Activating alone might have done some hidden damage. "Are you sure she's okay?"

What were they going to do with a sick Fate?

He touched her forehead. Did the boys see her beauty? Or did they keep their distance? Most normals sidestepped around Fates, both the activated and the unactivated. They muttered words like "odd" and "untrustworthy." Then they pointed fingers and screamed "Witch!" and burned the Fate at the stake.

The beast sniffed her hair and shoulders. *I do not know*. He paused. *You must cut the chains.*

Dragon pulled the bolt cutters from the tool storage under the floor. At thirteen feet from snout to tip-of-tail and twice Ladon's width, Dragon *was* cramped. The beast's body alone was the size of a table capable of seating six people. But the van provided room enough for him to at least turn and stretch his neck and tail.

Ladon refused to take the cutters when the beast held them out. "You do it. You're the one fretting."

You fret as well.

"No, I do not." Perfect breasts under a tight t-shirt, perfect hips under tight jeans—she'd continue to be a distraction.

Not all Fates are bad. Dragon nuzzled her again. *No one deserves to be locked to Burners.*

Ladon's jaw tightened. The beast was correct—not all Fates were bad. This one didn't seem to be. Though good ones were few and far between.

And she'd never be part of a triad. Never understand the bond that came with it. And because of the burndust in the shackles, her Fate's seer was now and forever locked to the chaos of the Burners.

He sat back on his heels. She did need their help.

Dragon nudged Ladon's shoulder. *This is not her fault.*

Ladon nodded, touching the girl's elbow. Like them, she'd been caught in this disaster. Unlike them, though, she couldn't walk away from its consequences.

He picked up the bolt cutters to snap the links connected to the cuffs.

They'd need to cut off the restraints, but if he cut the chains now she could move when she woke up. He leaned forward, the cutters ready.

Her eyes flew open.

Surprise bent him backward. Her Fate's seer reverberated through the van, rich and oscillating and as beautiful as the moonlight color of her irises. It washed over him, warming the connection he shared with Dragon as it sensed for information about either the past, the present, or the future.

Feeling a seer normally made Ladon groan and crunch his nose as if he smelled something foul. But not hers. It felt incredible.

She is not awake. Dragon poked her with his snout, first on her left cheek, then her right. She ignored him. *A vision takes her.*

"Uncalled?" A Fate used her ability to harness the seer inside. The seer didn't use the Fate.

At least for every Fate he'd ever known.

Dragon grabbed for her waist but she dodged, the chains rattling. Her hand splayed on the blankets and her hips twisted. One foot planted and the other pushed.

Ladon fell flat on his back, the girl holding his arms against the floor, her chains spread over his chest. The strength of her limbs held him firm as she straddled his hips, her thighs tight around his waist.

Dragon snorted.

Shut up, Ladon pushed. *Are you going to help?*

Why? the beast pushed back. *You do not want help. She is lovely.*

The way her pelvis ground in slow waves against his shoved aside his anger and a new emotion coursed from his belly.

A grin worked across his face. "Well, now." Dragon might be right. Maybe they should keep her around. He could use some distraction.

She stared down at him, her expression open and inviting.

A lock of her hair dropped to his cheek and glided like silk over his skin. It kissed his lips when more fell across his chin, a touch more intimate than he'd felt in centuries.

Her eyes, soft yet intense, held his purpose. Her touch, gentle where she grasped his arms, made him want to weave his fingers into hers. The beat of her heart moved from her skin to his and his own pulse steadied.

He breathed in her sweet, complex scent.

"Lovely" didn't come close to describing the woman who pinned him to the floor.

But a blankness fluctuated with her openness. Nothing and everything reverberated across her features. Ladon guessed she saw only her Fate's seer playing through her mind's eye.

Ladon's grin vanished. "Pretty Fate, can you hear me?"

4

Whatever caused the whispering thoughts sucked at Rysa's skull. It wiggled burning and… nasty. She felt as if someone had grafted a new limb to her forehead. Her brain tried to figure out how to control the new extension of her consciousness but the grafted on *thing* wouldn't listen.

It kept turning on her, slapping inner, whispered thought versions of Burner chemicals across first one cheek and then the other, then flailing around like an energy rope out in the real air, like some horrific sea monster's tentacle.

Or *tentacles*—she couldn't tell. This new nasty thing fuzzed out like Dragon had when he turned invisible. She couldn't perceive the nasty tentacles, even though she knew they were there. Maybe she had an entire Burner octopus in her head.

A big, squishy, nasty octopus that burned sat on her mind.

Spoken words cut through her energy-tentacle-caused haze. "Pretty Fate, can you hear me?"

Ladon. The man, richly voiced and as warm as the sun.

"Wake up." *Pretty, lovely Fate*. Golden-brown eyes watched her with more attention than she'd ever seen from a man.

The nasty thing in her head whipped and memories dropped into her vision: One afternoon about a year ago, Gavin had called her pretty. He didn't speak to her again for the rest of their lunch as they sat in the student union eating peanut butter sandwiches and stale chips.

Her ex-boyfriend Tom use to call her pretty. The nasty thing in her head formed a new vision: Tom spoke, but no sound came out. His shoulders thrust forward and he dug his fingers into her back.

In the real world, the world *right now*, the energy flowing around her carried a different word—*beautiful*. It smoothed over her skin and she knew Ladon would never dig his fingers into her back.

He lifted her off his hips and set her against Dragon's chest. Stars looped along the beast's hide, filling her eyes with the music of shape and color.

Another memory: When she was a child, her father placed a kaleidoscope nightlight under her bed, the kind that threw planets and moons and comets and shooting stars onto her walls. The patterns and colors danced out from under her bed, stretched by the angle of light to the floor into funhouse shapes five times the length of her hand, and she knew she was safe from the monsters.

In the real world, she splayed her fingers over the colors dancing on Dragon's hide.

Ladon's firm but gentle touch stroked her arm. "What are you seeing? You need to wake up."

The nasty thing whipped another memory: Her father said "pretty girl" with a wink and a grin. Then he left, disappearing one day while she toiled at school, almost crying when she didn't finish the math test because she couldn't pay attention to the numbers on the page.

A bottle appeared. "Drink some water."

She sipped, hoping to wash away the other memories pressing against the inside of her head.

"What's your name?" Ladon watched every muscle-twitch, every glance her eyes made, every expression. "Can you hear me?"

"You are Ladon," she whispered.

His hand rested on her shoulder. "That's right. What's your name?"

"Rysa Torres."

"That's a pretty name. It's Latin. It means 'laughter.' Did you know that?"

"I thought it meant 'tower.'"

A smile, as brilliant as the dragon's hide, lit Ladon's face. "Laughter of the Tower, you are."

"In your eyes, I see. It stops the nasty thing in my skull." The words drifted out, a weird-vision truth set free into the river of energy flowing between man and beast.

His smile transformed into something bright and perfect. "What are you seeing?" But then his lips rounded and confusion spread across his features.

She'd see the light again. It would fill his eyes and he'd touch all of her and everything would be fine.

Her hand lifted to touch his cheek.

The normal parts of her brain, the parts the nasty thing had hijacked with its whipping tentacles and its blanketing vision-memories, those real parts released a firestorm of *Danger! Terror!*

Scream now!

The real world slammed down and the visions burst like the fire bubbles had when she first activated. On her wrists, iron twisted over bandages. When did they bandage her skin? She jiggled her arm and the dull, thick shackles sucked away all her body's heat.

The chemical stench of the ghouls hung around her, drifting from her clothes. It mixed with hints of engine oil, strong liquor, and day-old pizza.

She shrieked. "Get them off me! Please—" The ghouls shackled her. "Please!"

Ladon grabbed the chains and pulled her to him, snapping the link connected to her left wrist. Repeating the action, he locked the cutters onto the link on her right. The chains fell away.

"Legs." He scooped a hand under her thigh, pulling her foot around. The cutter snapped another link and he rolled her to the left, lifting her other foot, then snapped the last link. "Better?"

Dragon tossed the chains into the corner.

She yanked on the cuffs. If she curled her thumb maybe this time she could pull out her hand. She gripped the iron and yanked again, but agony fired up her arm and into her neck.

Rysa doubled over and shrieked into the blankets under her body.

Ladon gripped her shoulders. "We'll cut them off. When we have you someplace safe. But you need to stop screaming."

"Take them off me now!" She yelled louder than she meant to. "Please! Take them off."

"We will. But I need to saw through them and I can't do that in a parking lot. I won't chance cutting you." A slight pout pushed out his lip. "We won't hurt you. I promise."

He glanced at Dragon. Her eyes narrowed. A pulse moved between the man and the beast and she had a distinct sense that he wasn't being completely honest.

"What aren't you telling me?" She wrapped her arms around her chest and tried very hard not to rock back and forth. "Why did this happen to me?"

"You really don't know, do you?" Ladon massaged her shoulder, his fingers moving in little circles and arches. Powerful but sensitive, the strength of his touch somehow grounded the horror. Calm flowed from his muscles into hers and for the first time since she woke up this morning, she breathed deeply.

Her gaze moved from his fingers up his arm to where his black t-shirt sleeve stretched around his bicep. Even in the dim light, she saw the definition of his arms and wide shoulders.

She'd been rescued by the most distracting man on the planet.

When he let go, a sigh escaped before she could stop it. He smirked and looked away, scratching the back of his head. The youthful messiness of his wavy black hair juxtaposed with the shadow of stubble covering his square jaw and made her want to stroke his face. She wanted to feel the contrast, to understand why it worked so well to frame the olive tones of his skin.

When he looked at her again, his fingers twitched as if he wanted to touch her once more.

The damned wiggling nasty thing dropped a realization into her perception: He read the world with his hands. She knew the same way she knew their name. Energy connected him to the beast, but touching was how he learned. He wanted to dance his fingers on her shoulders so he could listen the way another man might move his head to better hear her voice.

Those hands could hold the world steady.

They could hold *her* steady. She saw it: He'd pick her up, his face buried against her collarbone and his strong arms holding her more steady than she'd ever felt in her life. Then he'd lay her down along Dragon's side.

She gasped, her hand coming up to her mouth. The nasty new addition to her mind flung the scene into her mind's eye in vivid detail—they were going to end up naked together, and soon.

But then her nasty dropped something else into her perception: A memory, but not *her* memory. Ladon throwing his jacket against the wall of the van. A distinct sense of *grumble* moving between him and the beast.

Ladon didn't like Fates. And she was now a Fate, whatever that meant.

He didn't like her kind, but he'd have sex with her.

5

The sob came out of nowhere. It yanked on her throat on its way out, twisting and contracting everything between her lips and chest at the same time she tried to inhale. Rysa felt like she'd swallowed a bowling ball.

Every single cell in her heart said she could trust him. But she'd believed that with Tom, too.

She rolled under Dragon's forelimb and jumped down to the van's back door. She didn't look at Ladon. She couldn't.

The door popped open and she dropped out the back. They were in the lot of the sporting goods store south of Highway 36, in a back corner, away from the doors. Traffic flowed by less than a block away and filled the air with a dull hiss. Trees rustled, crisp and unhappy this close to a freeway. The inky night siphoned off every hint of friendly light and the lot crawled with ugly shadows.

Rysa staggered away from the vehicle into the lot's potholes. The weight of the shackles made her stumble, but she walked anyway.

"Don't run away!"

She turned around. From the outside, their van loomed over the corner of the lot, bigger than any delivery truck she'd seen, and black and mean-looking. Some sort of faded and unreadable lettering ran along one side, and looked like an ominous warning to anyone who dared to scrutinize the vehicle.

Dragon hopped onto the pavement, a line of invisibility running down his neck and back as he passed over the van's threshold. Ladon followed, landing in front of her, a good six feet from the bumper, and reached for her elbow. "Don't call your seer until you get your bearings."

"Seer?" Was that what the nasty thing in her had was? Did she have a seer because she was a Fate?

Her body pulled in on itself. Ladon didn't like Fates like her, no matter how he acted, and Rysa's nasty seer-thing wasn't going to let her forget it. "Don't touch me."

"I'm sorry." He pulled back abruptly, his hands in the air. "If you don't want our help, that's fine. We'll drop you somewhere. Your family can deal with those..." He pointed at the shackles on her wrists. "... and whatever those Burners did to you."

He frowned and thrust his hands into his pockets. "But we think you should be careful. Your seer feels as if it's turning on and off by itself. Right?" He nodded over her shoulder.

Warm breath blew against her ear and the invisible Dragon nudged her side.

"He agrees."

Calm pulsed toward her from the big beast. Her body leaned against his neck without her willing it to. She probably looked ridiculous, slanted into thin air, but Dragon didn't care that she'd become a horrible creature with a nasty in her head.

She glanced at Ladon. Was he making those little calculations men always made? He wasn't staring at her breasts. He watched her expression instead.

Tom never watched her face when she was upset. He always looked away.

Men were so confusing.

The shackles scraped her shirt and dug into her skin. She'd pull the damned things off, no matter how much it hurt. Throw them into the Mississippi River and run away. Maybe she'd disappear into the mountains out west. No men. No Burners. No Fates.

"Rysa?" Ladon had moved closer when she wasn't paying attention— close enough she could throw her arms around his neck, bury her face against his chest, and cry until she couldn't cry anymore.

He really was distracting. And confusing.

"I can't think," she whispered. Not that she could ever think. All these thoughts about sex with a man she just met made it worse. Things might get weird between them in the future, but now, in the present, she needed his help.

So she should quit her blubbering, no matter how overwhelmed she felt.

Rysa wiped away a tear, careful not to scrape her cheek with the shackle, and stood up straight. "Why was everyone calling me a Fate?" She was just a college student, not some old world god.

Ladon glanced at Dragon. "You're a Parcae. A Fate. Not a *real* Fate, like the old cultures believed. Your kind's been calling themselves Fates since your Progenitor realized it both terrified the normals and made them reverent. You're supposed to activate as part of a bonded triad of three: One sees the past. One the present. The other the future."

But she'd been alone. "Others?"

Did the Burners eat them? Her stomach knotted again. What did she cause?

"Hey, hey, don't make that face." This time, he took her elbow, even though she'd told him to stay back.

She didn't pull away. She couldn't. He touched her and calm cascaded over her and she leaned into Dragon again. Why did she respond to him that way? Maybe Dragon calmed her, not Ladon. The beast sure seemed more accepting of Fates.

The questions whipping around inside her head felt as nasty as the new thing he called her "seer," but having Dragon pressed against her back and Ladon holding her steady kept her at least a little grounded.

"We'd been tracking the Burners a full day. You're the only Fate they went after." He nodded to Dragon again. "So no one else's been hurt. And even if they were, this isn't your fault."

He didn't know that. Didn't "fate" mean inevitable? Maybe just being *her* was enough to cause all this.

She didn't say it out loud. She had enough problems without adding a man and dragon pity party to her life. "What happened?"

He peered at her through narrowed eyes. "Do you have two mothers and a father? Or two fathers and a mother? One must have spit out your activation ten, maybe twelve hours ago."

"Spit? That's disgusting." She shook her head. "My mom was watching the news this morning. I think she'd been watching all night, to be honest. She wouldn't turn off the TV after the mall in Chicago exploded. She looked so distraught I almost stayed home, but she handed me a glass of orange juice and said to go—oh, my goodness."

Rysa touched her mouth and the damned shackle smacked against her chin.

He didn't say any words, though his expression said *uh-huh*.

"Why would she spit in my orange juice? Why would she do that and not tell me? Those ghouls almost—" The same pressure behind her eye that she'd felt in the café expanded and contracted, pulsing like a tire pump.

Ladon took her other elbow. "Sit down before you fall over." He nodded toward the van's bumper.

Dragon climbed in first and Ladon sat next to her, his arm behind her back, but not touching. "We'll help you figure out what's—"

Words blurted out of her mouth, interrupting his assurances: "But you don't like Fates." Her nasty or her attention issues, she didn't know which, motivated the outburst.

Her back stiffened. "Sorry!"

His mouth opened, then snapped shut. After a moment, he scratched the back of his head. "So *that's* what you saw."

Part of what she saw. But she was determined to ignore the other part, at least for now. She might not be able to shut up, but she could act like an adult around men. Even this one.

"It's true that we don't trust most Fates." Ladon watched a father and two teenagers leave the store. "We've had bad dealings in the past. Even good people who can see the future can be… difficult."

Ladon glanced over his shoulder at Dragon again. Equal parts of what felt to her to be regret, anger, and resignation flowed across the energy connecting them. "But that has nothing to do with you."

A new vision came out of nowhere and hit her hard: Burner fire, vomit orange and acid strong, flowed in front of her eyes. She saw it, tasted it, but didn't hear or feel it. She buckled forward anyway, her gut rolling, and dropped her head between her knees.

"What the hell?" Would her visions always be this chaotic? They came out of nowhere, like random partiers throwing beer bottles.

Then the vision dropped back into the recesses of her brain.

"You're not calling the visions, are you?" He didn't touch her. He sat next to her, his arms and neck rigid, staring at her face.

"They come out of nowhere and take over what I'm seeing and—"

"Your talisman is chaos." He said it like someone had just dropped a rotting fruit onto his palm. *Oh, that's gross.*

"Talisman?" What did *that* mean?

"Your family should explain." His gaze dropped to her wrists. "It's a Fate thing and we don't fully understand it ourselves."

He meant the shackles. This was the real reason he hadn't dug out a saw and cut them off her arms and legs. "I have to wear them, don't I? I can never take them off."

The Burners did something to the metal. Made it part of them. And now it was part of her, because she'd become a Fate wearing *them.*

Ladon said something about cutting off the cuffs anyway, but she didn't follow. All she could think about was that she was as much Burner as she was Fate.

"What if I have a vision while I'm driving?" Rysa felt herself sway back and forth even though she didn't want to. "Oh my God what if they start and don't stop? I don't want to die."

"Rysa!" He gripped her elbows again. "Metal locks a Fate to a purpose. It's like… like…" He looked up at Dragon, then nodded. "It's like a filter. My brother-in-law has these covers he puts on his camera lens sometimes. He says they're to polarize the light. It's like that. Your talisman is a filter on your abilities."

"I don't want this filter! It's the worst filter ever!" She pulled away and dropped her head between her knees again. "Can't I get a new one?"

He shook his head. "It doesn't work that way. It's set when you activate."

"So I'm doomed to see the world through flesh-eating stupidity for the rest of my life?" No wonder her seer felt like a nasty monster ripping apart her brain. "Does this mean my 'filter' is 'crap that randomly blows up?'"

Ladon chuckled. "We don't know. A talisman's context isn't always obvious, even to the triad bound by it. When is the complete context of anything clear?"

She jumped off the bumper and yanked on the cuffs. Pain ratcheted up her arm, worse than the first time she tried to pull them off, and she groaned. "I don't care if I need them! Get them off me! I don't need a filter that doesn't work!" She'd start panting if she wasn't careful.

"You can't! It's worse without a talisman." He followed her off the bumper. "It's like looking at the sun. You get everything. At least that's what I've been told."

"I don't care." The panting started. Maybe she'd die of a panic attack. That'd be ironic.

"Rysa."

She blinked, caught by the warmth of his eyes. His golden-brown irises edged toward uncanny. Still a real color, but brighter than they should be, as if a touch of Dragon's lights played through them. His black hair and warm skin were the same. His eyes just showed it more.

Her vision jigged, like it had when Billy grabbed her. Rysa felt Ladon's arms, but she saw her house through her mother's eyes: Mira Torres gripped a sword with both hands. The blade, long and bright, cut with sharp precision.

Burners paused, watching, determined.

The ghouls knew who activated Rysa: A parent, tastier than the pup.

Rysa wasn't their only quarry.

"Burners!" she coughed. "They found my mom!"

Ladon pulled her into the van.

6

"Where?" Ladon pushed garbage off the passenger seat into a plastic bag before offering to help her down the step from the raised back floor to the front of the van. Behind them, Dragon closed the back door and the roof vents.

Avoiding the gearshift, she maneuvered to the passenger seat and brushed away crumbs before buckling in.

"North," she said. The quickest way was Interstate 35W, visible through the windshield.

She pulled her phone from her pocket and dialed the house. The call rolled to voice mail. "Mom! Something's happened. I know—damn it, Mom, why didn't you tell me? Burners are coming for you! I see it. I know what they are! They know what I am. Damn it!" She disconnected the call.

"What am I supposed to say?" She should have called right away. She should have called the police and sent them to her house. The ghouls were going to hurt her mom. "Why didn't you stop them on campus? Why—"

"Because they eat people!" Ladon slapped the steering wheel. "Or you would have been blown up in the crossfire. Or—" He stopped in midsentence.

She'd distracted them. Pure and simple, she'd drawn away their attention and the damned Burners were going to eat her mom because of it.

Her mother's cell phone went to voice mail, too. "Mom! Someone found me." She glanced at Ladon, but decided not to leave his name. "He says he's going to help. Mom!"

She cut the call, not knowing what else to do. "Hurry! Please. I don't know what to tell her. Stay home, don't stay home."

Why didn't her mother answer the phone? "I'm sorry!" burst from her throat. "This is my fault. You could have——"

Dragon's big hand wrapped around the seat and stroked her belly. The strength she felt flowing from him silenced her outburst.

"This is *not* your fault." Ladon put the key in the ignition. "What's your mother's name?"

"Mira."

Ladon's hand stopped just before he turned the key.

"*Mira*? What's her last name?" His entire body stopped moving and his shoulders cinched up. His neck tensed to hard cords.

He wouldn't look at her.

"Why?" But she already knew. The Fates he'd had bad dealings with were her family. Or her mother's family, whoever they were. It's not like Rysa had met them. "It's been my mom and me since my dad left—"

"What is her last name?" His fists clenched so tight his knuckles turned white.

Dragon swung his head low. Sharp patterns burst across his hide.

"Torres."

Angry energy reverberated between Ladon and Dragon, but the beast threw back an overwhelming and complex wave. It made no sense to Rysa, and it only made Ladon angrier.

Her panic gushed up from her stomach into her throat. "You're not going to help us, are you?"

His cheek twitched. He tried to cover his irritation with a stone face, one signaling "badass warrior," but it didn't quite work.

She turned to plead with Dragon. "My mom works for the school district. She does curriculum planning. She doesn't… She's not *bad*. I swear to you. We moved here from California after my dad left. To get a fresh start. It's just us. My mom doesn't even date! She's—"

Ladon started the engine as another burst fired between him and Dragon. "Tell me her given name."

She didn't have a choice. Mad or not, he'd already figured it out. "Januson."

Ladon hit the steering wheel. He slammed on the brakes and the van skidded down the hill of the store's driveway. "Of course," he muttered.

"Is my mom some sort of war criminal? Did she free Nazis or bomb villages?" Because the way he responded, the Fates must have had a hand in all the horrors humans inflicted on each other. "Tell me!" This was too much. Not her mom.

Ladon released the brakes. "Your mother is Mira of the Jani Prime." He looked back at Dragon. "Most likely."

Not that Rysa understood what the name meant. Or why it felt ominous. An image of her mother as an old-time silent movie villain popped into her mind, complete with a top hat and a huge mustache to twirl. Her mother cackled, but since she was in black and white, a dialog card appeared instead: *Bwa-ha-ha*!

What the hell was her nasty showing her now? "What does *that* mean?" she yelled. She slapped the seat. The Burners were bad enough, but now her mother was some sort of super-villain?

Rysa Torres, the subpar Fate, locked to ghouls and unable to control the flaming visions pirouetting behind her eyes, with a super-villain mother in a top hat and a handlebar mustache.

Ladon slapped the steering wheel again. "Are you always like this? So volatile? Because it's getting on my—" He stopped suddenly when a wave of light pulsed across Dragon's hide.

"I…" What should she say? Gosh, looks like I'm a super-villain, too? But me, I'm a spaz! "Sometimes I can't pay attention. I get worked up. I don't have my meds."

Ladon grunted. "You don't need to yell."

She didn't answer. How many times in her life had she run off a boy or a friend or teacher because she couldn't calm down?

"Do you know anything about your family? The Jani?"

She shook her head. How many Fates could there be? What if the planet teemed with super-villains?

"There aren't many of your kind." Ladon leaned forward slightly and peered at the road. "Most triads aren't Prime. Often, a new Prime triad will break off and start a new family line. But not always. Your family doesn't. They consolidate power. It's their context." He looked her over. "Mostly."

"So my mom's part of one of these Primes?" Who the hell called themselves *Prime* anyway? It sounded autocratic. Something despots did.

"Your mother can read *what-is*. Make choices to optimize outcomes in the present situation." He switched lanes. "Your aunt Ismene is their past-seer. You can't hide anything from a past-seer. They know *what-was*. How you got to where you are. Your uncle Faustus is their future-seer. He's—"

Ladon grumbled. "They are not… nice, Rysa. They were once the Prime triad of the Roman Empire, until the Christian emperors decided they were satanic."

Dragon snorted.

Her mother's gold eagle. Her talisman. "My mom always wears this little eagle. Or I think it's an eagle. It looks old. And well-worn, like it had been handed down to her. She said it was a family heirloom and one day I'd inherit it."

Ladon's grip on the steering wheel intensified again. "The talisman of empire. The Jani Prime knew how to manipulate and control the flow of political information. They were very powerful, in their time. Kingmakers at a time when making a king meant controlling the civilized world."

Her mother controlled kings. And emperors. "Wait." The implications of what Ladon said about Rome sank in. "How old is my mom?" She looked old enough to be Rysa's mother, but just barely. People asked if they were sisters all the time.

"How old are you?" She looked back at Dragon. Were they immortal? "Am I going to spend eternity with randomized burning visions?" Would she be sitting in some old age home in five hundred years, her brain totally fried?

Ladon's brow furrowed. "You ask a lot of questions."

What did he expect her to do? "That exit." Rysa pointed at the off-ramp.

He pulled onto the county road, heading east.

"Am I going to turn into a Burner?" She bounced in her seat, unable to stop herself. "I don't want to be a Burner."

Ladon exhaled and glanced into the mirror. Another surge burst between him and Dragon. "You're not going to turn into a Burner."

"Are you sure?"

He didn't answer. Instead, he peered down her street when they turned.

"That house, up there. The gray one." Rysa bounced again, the need to run for the front door and pull out her mother almost overwhelming what little control she had left.

They slowed, Ladon's gaze steady on her home. His posture changed—his anger about the Jani resurfaced as he stared at the front door. "Your mother will not be happy to see me."

His words vanished before she caught them, disappearing from her consciousness. Her mom was alone with monsters and the man who said he'd help was having second thoughts. Again.

"It's dark. Maybe she left. Maybe she's okay." Rysa pointed at the house. Maybe she wasn't inside and Ladon's oscillating attitude didn't matter. "Do you think she's okay?"

He stopped the van a few houses away, up the cross street but still in view. "Please be quiet. No more questions. Let me concentrate. We need to know if Burners are about."

Was she still talking that much? "Can she get away from them? They caught me. Will she black out, too?"

Ladon grimaced.

"Do you feel Mom's seer? Should I be able—"

"Be quiet. Please." A blast moved between him and Dragon. "We're not close enough for me to feel her seer. I'm not sure about you." He scrutinized every inch of the house and yard, and pointed at the front door. "The power's been cut. The house isn't on, like the neighbors'. No residual lights. No humming."

Rysa blinked. The nasty thing in her head sat up like a dog, sniffing around. She felt a distinct need for caution. "They're here."

His stone face didn't change, but his gaze darted over the windows and the areas on either side of the house. "You need to stay calm. Don't run off. And try not to fire random seer bursts at us. Not when we're dealing with Burners in close quarters. We know this is new to you, but if you focus, you can hold it in check."

She watched the house, not really listening. She'd heard this all before: Concentrate, Rysa. You can do it. It's not that hard. You're a smart girl. Use some of those smarts to pay attention.

"Rysa? Did you hear me?"

When she looked back, he'd started to slip on his armored jacket.

"There's another one in the back." Ladon flipped a sleeve toward Dragon as if commanding her to put on the other jacket. As if she was just another problem he needed to corral.

"Just because my mom's part of this Jani Prime, you decided not to be civil?"

"Civil? You're the one yelling." He finished pulling on the jacket. "When this is done, you and your mother can go your own way."

Ladon had no desire to use her. She realized that now. He'd been friendly because helping was what he did. But she'd become the new face of this Jani family he detested and he clicked off any possibility to connect with her, as a friend or otherwise, no matter how much Dragon badgered him about it.

She told him she had problems paying attention. She didn't have her medication. With everything happening, he shouldn't expect the most iron-willed person to hold it together, much less her.

She'd try anyway. Her mom was in trouble. But Ladon's words hurt more than his anger or his annoyance. They hurt worse than any time Tom rolled his eyes. Worse than any teasing by a classmate. Worse than her elementary school counselor's disappointed sighs. More than her mother's exasperations or the arguments between her parents. Worse than anything.

The words shouldn't hurt. They'd just met. But a connection to Ladon and Dragon vibrated from the future and made the hurt echo.

Light burst from Dragon and he touched her shoulder.

She was twenty years old, for Heaven's sake. Twenty. She screwed up all the time. This path through her life was well-worn. Her soul should be hardened and she should threaten him with some plucky comeback and a Fate ninja ass-kicking because he acted like a jerk.

But it wasn't in her. Not with this man and this beast.

Ladon's eyes widened. His fingers grazed her forearm. "I know this is hard for you. I'm—"

She didn't hear the rest. The weird visions happened again: The sky stained sick with Burner fire. She felt disconnected, disoriented, like the shackles anchored her body to the underside of the clouds. She drowned in a wispy sea of acid rain.

And so did her mother.

A loud pop rocked the house. The entire building shook, the windows rattling. The house was about to burn, a fireball ripping through the entire block.

Just like that mall in Chicago.

"Mom!" Rysa sprinted for the front step before either Ladon or Dragon could stop her.

7

Rysa's childhood memory, long cherished, overrode her present: Her mommy stood outside the patio door of their California house and stared over the dry grass at the tent her daddy set up. "I don't know about a fire, Sandro."

When her mom got this way, Rysa always thought of wind chimes. She didn't hear them. She felt them. Her mom stared at the tent and Rysa felt angry chimes smashing together like they were trying to kill each other. Like the bells over the patio clanked when the Santa Ana winds blew.

"Please?" Rysa hugged her stuffed dragon and made her best second grade pleading face even though she wanted to frown. Mommy's chimes felt loud tonight.

Her daddy stopped in the open patio door, one foot inside and the other out, his neck cranked to the side as if he was afraid that he'd smash his forehead on the top of the door frame. He was taller than all the other dads at school. Taller even than Mr. Donovan, and Mr. D was *tall*.

Mommy made a face at her little dragon. "You know, honey, your other toys might like some attention." She'd piled her blonde hair on her head today in a twisty-braidy way that made Rysa think of all the statues at the museum her class visited on her school field trip last week.

She hadn't run off, mostly because her daddy came along. He took the day off work, which was really special, and made sure she didn't get left behind. She'd get too interested in the statues of people who stood like 'S's and held fruit or arrows or wore funny helmets. When Rysa pointed at one statue with no arms and an eagle necklace and said she looked like Mommy, her dad almost laughed himself silly.

Then he carried her back to her class and the other kids stared at him and his big arms and his brown eyes striped with the same green-like-a-leaf that striped the gray in hers. *Sunburst*, he'd said. Sunburst was a better description than striped. Then he chuckled and spoke to her teacher in Spanish.

"Mira, she likes that toy."

Her mom blinked, frowning again at the little dragon, and pointed at the backyard. "Fires attract attention."

Her dad had promised a camping trip but Mommy frowned like she was frowning now and said not this weekend, Sandro. Please. It's important. So her dad had hugged Rysa tight and said they'd camp in the backyard. He had lots of Spanish to teach her anyway, and lots of stories about Argentina. And, maybe if she was good, he'd tell her about Spain, too.

She wanted to learn about Spain. It was in *Europe*. And Daddy came from a place called Cordoba in Argentina and Spain had another city with the same name, which was really neat. They were like junior and senior cities. And Argentina had a *huge* city called Buenos Aires that was as big as Los Angeles but everyone was packed tighter together, like the crayons in her coloring box. And it was much bigger than San Diego or any other place they'd lived. Rysa had thought Los Angeles was the biggest city in the whole world, but it wasn't. She learned in school that—

"It's not good to attract attention." Her mom pointed at the tent again.

Her dad's concentration snapped to her mom at the same time Rysa's did. He winked and she giggled.

"What kind of attention?" Her dad always asked her mom questions like that. What do you mean? What is happening? Please be more specific.

"But Mom, we're *camping*." Rysa tried not to whine. Sometimes it happened anyway. She hugged her dragon.

The chimes-in-a-storm flowed from her mom again and she knelt so they'd be eye to eye. The chimes *always* happened before her mom wanted to say something important.

Mommy glanced over Rysa's shoulder at her dad. "Camping with your father is precisely what you need to do tonight."

"Can we have the fire?"

Her mom frowned again and her eyes went all distant like she was staring at the mountains. "A fire? What if the whole world burns?"

Her father frowned too, but didn't look at her mother. He'd been doing a lot of that lately. Rysa noticed. They didn't think she paid attention, but she did. They didn't touch each other much anymore, either. They used to touch all the time. Their elbows, fingers, toes. They danced in the kitchen and Rysa laughed and clapped and sang. Then her father picked her up and she danced with them, too.

"*Mom*-my! You're silly! The *whole* world won't burn! That can't happen. The ocean is over there." She pointed over her shoulder. "Besides, we watched a movie about grassfires and how to be careful and Daddy knows what to do and we'll put a bucket right next to it." She stood up straight. "I promise."

Her mother scratched at her twisty-braidy hair and mumbled something that sounded like Spanish but Rysa knew it wasn't. "Sweetie." She still stared and didn't look at Rysa. "One day you'll remember this, so what I say and what your father says to you *right now* is very important."

She touched Rysa's chest. "Always remember that your mommy and daddy love you, my dearest heart."

Rysa hugged her mom. Her dragon bounced against her mom's shoulder because she held him by his back leg and her mommy sighed really deep when Rysa kissed her cheek. Sometimes her mom was weird.

Mommy touched the toy's head. "He's a good dragon." Her gaze focused on the seams where his wings used to be. Wings on a dragon were *stupid*. Real dragons didn't have wings. She knew it. Her daddy helped sew up the holes.

"But you knew that already, didn't you?"

Rysa nodded. "He's the best dragon *ever*."

Her mom nodded again. "Always remember that, okay?"

Daddy sniffed and shook his shoulders like he did when he was surprised. The look vanished and he smiled, but he still seemed sad, like the surprise reminded him of fun times that he'd gotten in trouble for.

"We can hope." Dad winked at Rysa again as he lifted her up. "Well, I have something very important to say: Do you want s'mores, *mi risa*?"

She clapped so hard she lost her grip on her dragon's leg. "Oh!"

Her dad caught the little beast before he hit the ground. "Have you

given him a name?" He carried her toward the tent and the log he'd set out
for their camp.

"*Dad*-dy!" she said. "You know his name is in *dragon*. No one can
say dragon!"

Her dad laughed. "Well, I wouldn't know. I've never met one."

"And he's *special*."

Her dad stopped halfway between the house and the tent. "Both
dragons are special, aren't they, honey?"

Dragons. The concept of *beasts* reverberated within Rysa's memory,
overriding what had been, always, an instance of family love. A younger
time when she had both parents; a time when they wove her world together.

The texture of the memory changed: Tentacles grabbed its edges and
stretched. Depth flattened. Sound vanished. And what had been for Rysa a
treasured moment became something wholly different.

Memory was a jigsaw of vision and hearing and touch and emotion.
Sometimes pieces were enhanced, sometimes minimized. Recall bowed to
the story.

Not now. Rysa's memory of camping with her dad took on an
intelligence a simple story could never have. It carried more in her mind's
eye than it had before she activated.

Much more.

Her childhood clicked over to high definition and she felt the
increased pixel density, and the new information.

But she didn't understand.

In her vision, Rysa was sure her father asked her mother his question
about dragons, not her. She stared over his shoulder at the fire ring next to
the tent as an adult, no longer a child in his arms.

The fire will blaze all night, hot and blistering and acidic.

Her mother muttered something from her place in the patio door. *He's
special because he's Rysa's dragon*. Mira stared into space, her eyes wild
and angry and very scary.

Fear crept into Rysa's throat, like when she thought the monsters
would get in, before her father put the nightlight in her room, long, long ago.

In the vision, she hugged her toy dragon closer.

She looked first at her mother, standing in the patio door of their

California house, then at her father, standing between her and the fire ring. Her mother's eyes darted from the toy Rysa clutched to the fire ring, then back. Each flick of her gaze cinched her face tighter. Her cheeks tensed. The corners of her mouth pulled farther back.

Something was wrong with her mother.

Rysa tried to speak, to make a sound, to tell her father she needed his help, but he didn't hear. He left, but not until she started middle school, and then her mother hurt every day. She hurt so bad that she rubbed her knuckles every morning when making Rysa's breakfast. And she cried a little bit, but not so much Rysa noticed.

But she did, even if she couldn't pay attention. She saw it in high school, before she ran to catch the early bus outside their new home where it snowed.

She'd always know. She knew.

In the vision, her mom blinked, her twisty-braidy hair a sudden halo of chaos.

One parent blinked. The other vanished.

And somewhere behind Rysa, in the real heat, the real Mira of the Jani Prime screamed.

8

"Mom!" Rysa tasted ash and acid. Her body rebelled, demanding she run as fast as she could from the smoky inside of her house.

Her Minnesota home crackled and groaned as if some part of it had turned Burner.

The nasty thing in her head woke up the moment her foot dropped out the passenger side door of Ladon's van. Its tentacles burst from her mind like some terrible hybrid child of Athena and Cthulhu.

She'd blacked out again.

But this time, she remembered the vision: Her mom. Her dad. A fire. Her toy dragon, the one she'd lost when she was little, when she and her mom moved here, to Minnesota. She'd put it in her suitcase, the purple bag with the silver handle her mom bought her for the move, between her jeans and her pajamas with the stars and comets looping through the fabric.

But when she opened the case in her new bedroom, her dragon had vanished. Gone, like her dad.

Now, in her living room, she dropped to her knees on her mom's special rug. The burgundy one, with the abstracts—the one her dad had brought from Argentina as a gift. Mira had rolled it up herself, tied it herself, and dragged it on her own out to their moving van the day before they left California.

It had been the last thing she'd pulled from their old house.

Where was her mom? "Oh God oh God oh God," she mumbled, not thinking about her words. Or her body. Or the random flickering of images behind her eyes. Memories, not memories, visions, not visions—the nasty thing's tentacles pierced her life.

And squeezed.

Her stomach felt as confused as her head. Paying attention had never been this hard. The nasty dropped a whole new other reality into her brain and she had to parse both it and the real world.

The building groaned again, a body in the throes of a death fever. She smelled Burners. Fire crept through the walls of her house.

Where was her mom?

The ceiling boomed. She looked up as the house rocked.

Rysa knew: In the attic, her mom swung a sword, one bright and smooth and older than America. A brilliant blade made for a Prime Fate by the hands of an artisan of unparalleled character.

Rysa tried desperately to keep down her stomach's contents. She knew *what-is* plus other things she shouldn't, like the vision-memories of *what-was.*

She'd become… omniscient, even if she couldn't remember anything or make sense of it. She really was a Fate. A *monster.*

Ladon interrupted her scattered vision when he skidded across the carpet and dropped to his knees next to her. She hadn't seen him come around the corner from the kitchen. Hadn't heard him call her name, even though she knew he had.

More information she shouldn't know popped into her mind: Her meds were in the inside pocket of his armored jacket. He'd seen them on the counter and scooped them up, just like he scooped her up, now.

Above them, in the attic, her mom swung her blade. The ceiling buckled upward, snapping and groaning in pain.

A Burner must have imploded.

Rysa curled her arms around Ladon's neck, the only movement her body would make, as all thoughts of her meds disappeared.

"Rysa!" His voice flowed over her and his strong arms enveloped her body. Strong arms lifted her to her feet. "The fire's spreading. We need to leave."

"My mom's in the attic. With Burners." Everything inside Rysa screamed to run for the steps to the upper floor of their split level. Ladon held her on the entry level, in the living room equidistant from the front door, the patio door to the backyard behind the dining table, and the kitchen wall. Right in the middle of the most open area in the house. Under the vaulted ceiling rising a story and a half to the attic above. In perfect view of the open sitting room at the top of the steps.

In the one place in the house they couldn't hide from Burners.

Rysa crunched against Ladon, even though he didn't want to help her.

"What did you see?" But as he spoke, his chest shifted. He pulled her flush against his side.

A sprinkled sense of *safety* dusted her tremoring mind. She could snuggle warm and calm with this man, safe from every Burner on the planet. Even if he didn't care about her mom or any other Fate.

Why would she think such things?

"You're crying." Ladon's fingers spread over her lower back.

Ladon's head jerked toward the open banister between them and the upper sitting room, and his hand moved to her hip. His fingers splayed a little up, then slightly forward—he positioned his hand so he could move her quickly if he needed to.

She looked up at his face. His goggles hung around his neck, the muscles of which tensed, along with his jaw. Every movement, every adjustment was meant for one purpose—to keep her safe.

The house popped. The imploding Burner in the attic must have taken part of the roof. A grating noise followed, then the sounds of boots dropping out of the attic access and into the hallway.

Still out of sight, her mom screamed.

Rysa's focus swung from Ladon and locked onto the shrillness of her mother's voice as it rolled from the upper floor. The fluttering of her attention issues—the shifting from her visions to the house then to Ladon's hard muscles with no break or conscious connection—stopped. Everything but her mom grayed out. The world became background.

The Burners were going to take her mom. "Ladon! They'll eat her! Please! Please—"

A Burner fell out of the hallway entrance and onto the landing at the top of the stairs. An unbroken stream of expletives jabbered from her little mouth as she jumped up, her tiny finger poking the air in Rysa's general direction. Her dirty clothes, her matted hair, her backward baseball cap only dressed her malicious Cheshire grin beaming down at Rysa.

"Skankadoodle!" the child hissed.

Ladon held Rysa's arms around his torso as he stepped in front of her. He splayed her fingers over his stomach, his hand over hers. His palm and fingers cupped her entire hand, his skin warm and dry and rough like she'd expect of a man who worked with his body.

"They won't touch you." His words reverberated through his chest to the cheek she pressed against his back.

He told the truth. Nothing got by this man. Nothing at all.

A Burner she didn't recognize flew down the hallway and landed next to the child.

The child laughed and jigged around on one foot.

"Your mother must have breathed burndust. She's frantic." Ladon leaned back enough to block her sightlines to the Burners. "She's taken some of their chaos into herself."

"What?" Her mother breathed the same stuff that was in the shackles?

A massive pulse of energy burst from Ladon, the transfer stronger than any she'd felt so far between him and Dragon.

Rysa's breath caught. She couldn't see around Ladon. Where was the beast?

Still out of sight, still down the hallway, Mira screeched.

The rage in her mother's voice gouged holes in Rysa's already fractured attention. Many times, she'd heard her mother angry. Seen her face squish as if she plotted revenge. But she never sounded like she wanted to *kill*.

Mira's foot stomped onto the head of the Burner lying on the landing. The child danced backward into the sitting room and out of range of Mira's sword.

A flash reflected off Mira's raised blade and her finger jabbed the air toward Ladon's head. "Why did you bring her here?" Mira snarled. "You were supposed to—"

Her mother vanished. Her sword bounced down the steps, stripped from her hands.

The invisible Dragon had her mom. He jumped off the upstairs landing, her mother enfolded in his forelimbs. Rysa saw her mother's leg kick, her shoulder thrust, her fist strike the parts of Dragon she could reach.

Dragon landed on his feet, her mother gripped tightly and his big head curling around Ladon. Another pulse washed over Rysa as the man and the beast communicated.

Ladon scooped his arm under Rysa's backside and lifted her against his waist. "We leave."

Disoriented by the lift, Rysa held tight anyway, doing her best to track the vanishing and reappearing parts of her mother.

Dragon bellowed and her mother rolled away, her hand finding the hilt of her dropped sword before she came up to a crouch. "Touch me again, you damned beast, and I'll cut you!" She waved the sword.

"Mom! Stop! They're helping!"

Ladon jerked back when Rysa yelled, but he didn't let go. She twisted against his torso, reaching for her mom.

"Put me down!" She slapped his shoulder.

"No! We go!" With his free hand, he pointed at the child on the landing. "They'll take the house." His jaw set. "Why are Fates so stubborn?"

"I told mammaskank she's ours!" The child danced around her unconscious companion. She stopped suddenly, her little body holding a mid-jig pose, and kicked the Burner laying on the landing in the neck. "Asswipe!"

Mira swung the sword. The blade sliced and the end rail of the stair banister split in two. "You let them bind her with their talisman!"

"He tried to get them off me." Rysa held out her cuffed arm. "He tried to help! The Burners would have eaten me. Mom!" She slapped Ladon's shoulder again. "Let me down! I can help her. Please!"

Ladon glanced over her shoulder at the child. His face crunched like he thought putting Rysa down was the worst idea ever, but he dropped her anyway.

Mira swung the sword and Dragon's outline momentarily blazed in the air.

"They were never going to eat you, daughter!" she swung again. "Why didn't you stop them in Wisconsin? You are the Dracos! Why didn't you cause—" And again. "—enough distraction she could activate on something *else*?"

Another swing. "Anything else. Her cell phone. The grommets in her damned shoes. It didn't matter! My present-seer showed me *dragon* and I can't hide her any longer and you should have been enough."

Mira dropped to her knees. "Why weren't you enough?"

A sob lurched from her mother's throat, raw and evil-sounding and full of scorching pain like she'd swallowed fire.

Rysa tried to haul her mother to her feet. "Why didn't you tell me? Why didn't—"

Mira leaned forward, her eyes glassy with chaos, and screamed directly into Rysa's face. "Stay away from me!"

The sword in Mira's hand glistened.

Rysa should have ducked. She should have squirmed or screamed or done something, but the woman in front of her, the woman screaming hatred into her face, was her mom. The woman she'd cooked dinner for when her joints hurt too much.

The woman she'd put her adult life on hold for so she'd be here when her mom needed her.

The real reason Rysa fretted about leaving for graduate school. Her attention issues ate her life, but her mom, she gave to willingly. What else was she to do?

The sword passed by the top of Rysa's head. Her mom wouldn't have cut her. She didn't mean—

Mira lifted into the air.

Dragon threw her mom at the patio door. She hit hard and dropped, landing on her feet, her sword still in her hand.

"Momma don't want you no more, skankadoodle!" The child laughed from the top step and jumped up and down like she rode on a pogo stick. "But wwwweeee looooovvvveeee yyyooouuu."

She blew Rysa a kiss.

Mira's body jerked and jolted as if she stood on a fault line and an earthquake moved the world under her feet. Her eyes flitted from Rysa to Ladon to the child, and back in a random pattern, at random intervals.

And her hair, usually smooth and braided, flared around her face like a jumbled ball of yarn. Mira, this woman Ladon had told her was not nice, who, as he said, was a kingmaker, this woman, her mother, looked like she'd catch rats with her bare hands.

Then eat them raw.

Mira's back straightened. Her spine elongated and her chin lifted. She stood tall for the first time since they found her—for the first time, Rysa thought, since they'd moved to Minnesota.

"Have you figured it out yet, Ladon-Human?" The tip of her sword scraped across the tile floor at the base of the patio door. "She's a singular."

Ladon helped Rysa up off the floor, his face a mask of confusion. He placed a hand on either side of her waist, but he didn't look at her. He watched the Burner child. "You have all three Fate abilities," he said to Rysa.

Past, present, and future chased each other around in her head, but they looked the same—flat and tentacled and nasty. She was her own inattentive triad.

"Can you see the Burners, daughter?" her mom whispered. Rysa barely caught her words. They seemed to bounce off the patio door glass, amplifying on their own as they smacked against Rysa's eardrums.

"No one can read Burners," Mira continued. "Too much chaos. Burners—monsters without fate." She chortled, a rough noise that sounded as if ash was about to come out of her nose. "Except now. They have you. They have purpose. They'll be unstoppable."

Rysa looked down at the cuffs around her wrists. Her biceps ached, tired from carrying around the metal's weight. Chaos weighed more than people knew. Yet she carried more randomness on her shoulders every day than a normal person without her issues carried in a lifetime. So she should be used to it.

But this was too much. Was she as much Burner as she was Fate? Would she end up like she feared, her mind burned away?

"Mira!" Ladon roared. His big arms encircled Rysa. "Why do you do this?"

At the top of the stairs, the child clapped, an evil look of boredom on her tiny features. "Are you done yet?" she asked. "The roof's burning. You set it on fire when you popped that dickwad dumbass putz from Indiana in the attic."

Her face wrinkled into a sour mask. "Indiana. Full of idiots." She turned in a circle, then pointed at the threshold between the kitchen and the dining area in front of the patio door. "Don't know where he's from, but it ain't Indiana."

Billy moved so fast he managed to duck under Dragon's lunge.

He punched her mom in the face.

Mira bounced against the plate glass, a new screech ripping from her throat. She swung her blade but it missed its target.

Billy snickered.

Mira stepped forward, closer to the dining room table, her sword up and ready to strike.

For the briefest moment, for an instant so fast split-second was too long, the room dropped into total silence.

The walls and the furniture and the people—Dragon and Ladon—defined in Rysa's perception as if outlined by a black marker.

The Burners vanished, cloaked in their chaos, but they left a smudge on the present, points where the universe crisped and withered.

Her nasty Fate's abilities whipped, uncalled, between all of them, sensing, looking, licking. Seeing.

And within that absolute essence of *right now*, Rysa knew. She saw Dragon's intent—to get her out. She felt the fractured disconnect of Ladon's need to help and his desire to leave the Fates to their fate.

But she knew nothing of her mother. Like the Burners, she saw only a crisped shadow.

Then her mind flashed as if someone had set off a firecracker behind her left eye.

Something new took over her vision: The house gone. The walls reduced to ash. The moon traveled the sky filling and emptying, and trees behind the house grew dry, their leaves dropping for winter.

Reflecting off the bottom of roiling clouds, south of what was her home, she saw *what-will-be*: both downtowns burned, St. Paul to the left and Minneapolis to the right. She looked to the east: suburbs burned. To the west: flames licked the sky.

"You see it, don't you, daughter? The future? Your future-seeing uncle warned me. He said the world will burn and burn and burn and a singular would be the key."

What-is crackled into Rysa's vision again, but this time the tentacles of her nasty flickered like the flames used in her chemistry class to heat gas to glowing.

Rysa's mother pointed at her again. "The moment I realized I was pregnant with you I knew he spoke the truth."

Now Rysa knew it too: She'd set fire to the world.

"You're the Ambusti Prime, daughter. The Prime Fate of the Burners."

9

In front of Ladon, from the shadows by the patio door, the burndust-addled Mira accused her daughter of future terrible deeds. She glared at Rysa, her features twisted and evil, and tipped her sword toward Rysa's cheek.

Against his chest, her breath hitched. Her lip fluttered and her eyes grew huge. And Ladon knew all the pain he felt moving through her body was his fault.

He should have tried harder to get off the shackles when she activated. He should have ran more lights on the way to campus. They should have gotten to Rysa sooner.

Twenty-three centuries he and Dragon had fought battles and dealt with Burners. Twenty-three sets of one hundred year intervals, a meaningless measure of time for someone who'd lived through so many of them. Yet, they'd persevered and done what they were supposed to do.

Every single one of those actions and reactions dropped onto their heads like a grain of sand blown in from the desert. Twenty-three centuries and sometimes Ladon wondered if he still had the strength to move through the dunes of his life.

"Mom," Rysa whispered.

The young woman clinging to his arm carried no such weight. Yet the boulder of her new existence would smear her flat if he and Dragon did nothing—or worst, the minimum necessary to finish this job.

He'd been annoyed by her questions in the van. Irritated when he realized she was Jani. But she didn't deserve this. No one deserved vile insults hurled at them, especially from a parent.

So Ladon folded her tighter against his ribcage, his arm around her back and his hand spread protectively across her shoulder blades.

Rysa wasn't the terrible things Mira spat from her Burner-confused mouth. The beautiful, overwhelmed woman he held cared more for her mother than he'd ever seen a Fate show. More than her mother had earned, now or ever.

More than he would merit, if she cared for him.

Another Burner appeared. Mira attacked, and the implosion blasted the patio door outward in a hail of shards. Glass peppered the backyard, but Dragon rolled out through the burning flower beds, a snatched Mira thrashing in his forelimbs.

He'd climbed the wall and hung from the ceiling, waiting for an opportunity to lift Mira. Dragon had hung upside down, transferring to Ladon the discomfort in his talons caused by the fire creeping through the ceiling, as much to punctuate Rysa's pain as his own.

Ladon carried Rysa out of the house and onto the burning grass. She gasped, unable to breathe. Her soul melted in front of Ladon's eyes.

Mira clawed and bit, and Dragon dropped her before backing away. Her sword had blown out with the door and now poked out of the deck's wood cross pieces.

She lunged for it.

"Mira!" Ladon bellowed. The house burned behind her, hot enough now she glistened with sweat and effort.

"Come with us." He reached out his hand.

She'd stop the ranting when the burndust wore out of her system. And then he'd make sure she apologized to her daughter.

Mira's gaze landed on Rysa and she stared, her eyes blank but her brow furrowed, and she tilted her head to the side, like a Burner.

Her seer blasted through the backyard and Ladon winced, the jarring clanging of her ability smacking against his mind.

Like her future-seeing brother and her past-seeing sister, Mira had always been slightly musical, like an instrument left in the wind. The Jani Prime could have been good, if good had been their talisman.

Their fate.

"It's going to kill her." Mira continued to stare, her head tilting farther. "Her talisman. It'll cover her mind with thicker and thicker coats of ash and fire."

Mira would blister if she didn't move away from the house.

"Come away." Ladon held out his hand again. "You can help. Make sure that doesn't happen."

Rysa would not die. Nor was she going to face a future full of agony or lies. He'd make sure. This time, he'd respond fast enough.

"Before, when I blacked out, I saw my dad," Rysa whispered.

Ladon bent closer. "You're safe. We're here."

She'd suffered enough.

"He vanished one day. I don't know where he is." Rysa pulled away. The brilliance of her seers washed over him and, dazzled by the full beauty of her potential, his hold on her loosened.

Her arms dropped and the damned shackles slid down her wrists.

She didn't move.

"Mira!" Ladon didn't know what to do.

How was he supposed to help a singular Fate? He barely understood the workings of a triad.

Though he should. After centuries, he should.

Human!

Another Burner burst out of the patio door. Mira swung, her sword slicing with vengeance. The neck of the Burner split. Mira screamed and the blade dropped from her curled fingers.

Behind Ladon, Dragon dodged the crafty Burner who'd punched Mira—the one with the British accent.

The Burner Mira sliced imploded into a writhing red ball.

She leaned back, her body countering the pull. Then she leaned forward, her eyes narrow.

Her hand rose, her head still tilted, and her finger slid across the implosion's surface.

Dragon slapped the British Burner into the woods behind the house and pivoted, his intent to grab Mira.

Her eyelids drooped. She stared at her finger tip, her face slack like she'd given up. She didn't look at Ladon. She didn't look at Rysa.

Next to him, Rysa's foot planted and her body tensed in preparation to leap. "Mom!"

Ladon lifted Rysa into the air. If she moved closer to her mother, she'd get hurt when the ball exploded. She might die.

Mira licked the liquid from her finger.

Dragon lunged across the deck. Mira vanished just as the Burner ball exploded.

Ladon curled around Rysa, his hand on her head to protect her eyes.

He'd seen other Fates breathe burndust. Take it in to cloak themselves in its randomness. It hid them from all seers and made them invisible to their own kind. But he'd never seen a Fate take from an implosion.

She rips at my coat. The beast let go and Mira tumbled through the grassfires spreading across the lawn. *I cannot hold her.*

"Mom!" Rysa thrashed like her mother and pummeled Ladon's shoulder. "No no no!"

Something he'd never experienced happened. Something so utterly brand new he didn't know how to respond: Her seers latched onto his connection to Dragon.

Ladon stopped cold in his tracks. Dragon rolled onto his back, his hide sparking with wild, mixed-up flame patterns. Rysa connected to them—how, neither he nor the beast could fathom.

No Fate had ever felt their connection before, much less touched it. Only once had a Shifter heard Dragon, and that was long, long ago. And they never saw the woman again.

But Rysa's seers curled around their connection in what felt like long, finger-like waves, and caressed both his and the beast's minds.

Her world lurched and his perception followed, flat-lining. Everything turned a single radiance. It all held the same importance. Sparkles ignited along the tree's bark, the fire heating their sap to bursting.

The remains of the house sparkled as well, and strange chemicals lifted from the debris as a colored haze.

People filled the streets, robes pulled tight around thick waists as they backed away from the hell pouring into their neighborhood.

He saw it, but he didn't hear.

He blinked, the roar of the real world suddenly snapping back. He couldn't know about the people. The normals were on the other side of the house, blocked from his vision.

Rysa's seers had backwashed into his mind.

But how was it they carried no sound?

Ladon dropped to his knees, Rysa against his chest. He'd never been connected to a seer before, felt its power from the inside. Seers danced on the edges of his consciousness, mostly grinding against his mind. Sometimes they filled his head with music, from the few Fates whose souls weren't polluted.

Musical seers, like Rysa's. But the Burner chaos disrupted her abilities and made a cacophony, not a symphony. Maybe that was why wrongness backwashed with her seers.

Her siphoning flipped and pushed toward him. The world oscillated from too dim to too bright.

We must leave, Dragon pushed.

Ladon didn't hear. He didn't understand. He missed the beast's words, the vision pulling him in too many directions.

Rysa tightened her arms around his neck. Her terror flickered through his mind, a dancing clown flailing its arms and cackling for her attention.

And his too, now.

Mira ran for the trees behind the house. The British Burner followed.

Ladon spun, Rysa in his arms, his mind in a desperate spiral as he tried to parse where each individual Burner was located. They danced like idiots through the backyard and surrounded the thrashing Mira.

He let go of Rysa. Mira needed—

Human!

Rysa coughed. She stepped toward Mira and away from him. She moved toward the Burners.

Dragon's tail swished across the burning grass, a great arc of shadow through the flickering. *Protect Rysa!*

By the trees, the British Burner grinned, his teeth as hot as the fire. Mira swung at his head but he dodged and clamped his fist around her elbow. He yanked her closer and the fingers of his other hand skipped over her flesh as if he played a tune.

Mira screamed.

The ghoul licked the skin from Mira's forearm.

"Mom!" Rysa fought against Ladon's grip, her seers sparking. Her body shook as Mira's agony echoed in her limbs.

Ladon had seen such attachment before with children, even as adults, whose family was their core. Attachments to parents who soothed tears and celebrated achievements.

He never expected to see it between Fates, and especially not between Jani Fates.

Mira wrenched away from the Burner. Blood coated her arm and the talisman bracelet around her damaged wrist slid onto her palm. The Burner grabbed for her again but she threw the talisman of the Jani Prime at Ladon's head.

He caught it, the gold eagle clinking against a wedding band looped onto the heavy chain. Rysa clutched the bracelet before he could wipe away her mother's blood.

Mira yelled again, but her words disappeared into the thunder of the fire.

She said 'Keep her safe.' The Burners had formed a wall between Dragon and the trees. *I cannot get close.*

"Mom…" Rysa slumped against Ladon's chest.

The beast's head swung around and a pulse washed over Rysa to Ladon. *A new vision takes her.*

Dragon rolled between Ladon and the Burners, his concern flooding through their connection. He staggered slightly, the images of flames covering his hide danced out of sync with the real fire surrounding them.

Rysa's siphoning disoriented the beast as much as it disoriented the man.

"My mother's wedding ring. My mother's charm. My mother is gone. Vanished like Dragon." Her breath rushed in stuttered breaks. "Gone invisible to mimic the burning world."

What was she seeing to speak in such riddles?

Mira screamed one last time. Even through the haze and the heat mirages, Ladon saw a sudden regret take her body. Her shoulders slumped. She pointed at Rysa but yelled something at the British Burner, something Ladon did not hear.

The ghoul swung to slap, but she bolted into the trees. The other Burners watched, their heads swiveling between Mira's escape and Dragon standing between them and Rysa.

They ran after Mira.

We must leave. Dragon pushed Ladon toward the neighbor's yard. *She distracts them. We must protect Rysa.*

"But—" What would happen to Rysa if they abandoned her mother? Even after all Mira said, Rysa trembled in his arms.

The Jani will retaliate. The Burners are no longer our problem. The beast ran behind the houses toward their van.

The familiar stretching ache, as the distance between him and Dragon grew, twisted inside Ladon's muscles. He had no choice but to scoop up Rysa and follow.

Her ice cold arms sucked away his warmth though her skin flushed from the fire.

He ran across a picnic table, jumping up and over a fence.

Her mother's blood streaked her cheek. He stopped, Dragon skidding across the lawn next to him. The blood dripped down her jaw, thicker than it should be from a simple fingerprint. He dropped her feet and she teetered, grasping for his arms.

His gut clenched like he'd been punched. A tongue-shaped streak colored the sleeve of her shirt.

"Did one of them bite you?" Ladon asked. But none had gotten close enough.

He pulled up the fabric and peered into the space between her wrist and the shackle and saw a bite identical to the wound Billy inflicted on Mira.

He lifted Rysa's other arm. Another one, under her sleeve, but higher up.

She was manifesting the Burner's attacks on her mother.

How can this be? Ladon pushed to Dragon. They'd never seen anything like it. Even members of a triad were not connected with such strength.

A porch light flicked on. Ladon lifted Rysa again and darted toward the van.

"Everything burns." Her voice all but vanished into the fire's roar.

The siphoning ceased, but he still felt the defeat pushing from deep inside her mind.

Over the course of his long life, he'd seen death and terror and anguish. He'd caused his fair share. He'd seen Fates and Shifters cause more. Sometimes, every few centuries, it got to him. He'd wake in a cold sweat, an overwhelming dread that he'd lost Dragon destroying all other thoughts.

When it happened, his limbs turned to ice, as Rysa's did in his arms.

He'd been cruel when she first woke, his words gruff. He'd shut out her concerns with his anger. The hurt had washed across her face before she opened the van's door. He'd seen it magnified in her eyes when he followed her into the house.

She ran from him.

She'd tried to save the one person who, until moments before, had treated her with kindness.

He held her closer, a new resolve taking hold.

He'd never be heartless with her again.

Rysa clutched the bracelet and the ring. The shackles scraped his neck, her tears dampening his hair below his ear. She breathed in shallow inhales, each intake tight and constricted.

"When I hurt you, please forgive me." Her lips grazed the collar of his jacket. "Please come for me."

Forgive *her*? What was she seeing? "Rysa?"

Her eyes didn't focus. She saw only this new vision. Yet her face showed openness again, like it had in the lot when she activated. Open and happy, wide-eyed and calm, for him.

Even though the Burners dragged away Mira. Though he'd been callous. Though she bled from wounds that were not her own.

Her face held no edge of fear. No undercurrent of sharp tension because, deep in her gut, she thought him a threat. She offered only a future he didn't deserve.

"Beautiful." How could she give him such trust? If she knew him, she'd think better of it.

He carried her around another house to the van. Dragon set her on the blankets as Ladon pulled the door closed.

We must dress her wounds. Dragon dabbed at the blood.

Her chest heaved. She pulled herself into a tight ball, still not aware of where she was. Ladon touched her elbow and her shoulder.

Mira's ramblings about a burning world meant nothing—Fates, as a breed, constantly issued dire warnings about one apocalypse or another, mostly to scare the normals into submission.

No person as good as Rysa would set fire to the world.

Dragon stroked her forehead. *Her fever has returned.*

Ladon touched her cheek. "Maybe it's from the house." But a new fear crept into his mind: The present-seer of the Jani Prime had uttered one truth.

Rysa's talisman might do as Mira prophesied and as the layers of ash solidified, she'd solidify with them.

She'd die.

Marcus will know what to do.

Ladon's core squeezed. Daniel, Timothy, and Marcus, the only Fates Ladon had ever called ally. Now only one brother remained.

"That's not a good idea." Marcus would not be happy if Ladon appeared on the past-seer's doorstep, Rysa in his arms. Not happy at all. Ladon had ceased to be a true friend a century and a half ago.

She should not have uncalled visions, Human.

"I know." Her skin did feel hot to the touch.

On the edges of his mind, her three seers twined into an indistinguishable knot. It disguised their resonance, which was why he hadn't noticed before and why he'd thought she had one that slipped and darted. They overlaid each other and he couldn't tease apart which one played and when. She probably couldn't, either.

Damned Burners had hobbled a very rare Fate.

"Ladon." She caressed his arm to his palm and settled her fingers into his.

Agony still contorted her face and body. Ladon looked up at Dragon as the beast settled next to her, his huge hand splayed over her hip.

We must hurry, the beast pushed.

10

L adon's memory, long distant with time:
        He stepped back as the blast from the forge rushed over
his protective leathers. The new blade glowed with the perfect temperature,
the exact brilliance and malleability he needed. Satisfied, he lifted his work
to the anvil.

He swung his hammer. Metal met metal and he listened to the clang—
and for the changes that would bring superior balance and strength to this
new sword.

Clang! Ladon's back and arm fell into the perfect rhythm to make a
perfect blade.

Requests for tools had been placed—tilling implements, some
fasteners—and he'd start those next. They'd lived in this part of Gaul
for more than four decades—long enough for the offspring of his *Legio
Draconis* men to produce their own offspring.

Stones had been placed and walls erected. Their encampment had
grown into a settlement and now *Legio* grandchildren overran everything,
climbing on wagons, stockades—and dragon haunches.

Ladon smiled as his hammer descended. He'd not have it any other
way.

The blade formed true. He let his thoughts follow, dropping into the
swing of his muscles. This life, away from the dying carcass of Rome, had
finally brought calm to him and his sister.

Alarms sounded. Ladon stopped mid-swing, his attention jerked to
just outside the smithy entrance. Jarring patterns oscillated over Dragon's
hide as the beast reared up. *Parcae!*

Sister-Dragon sprinted by outside, Sister following as she buckled into her armor. They'd be through the gate and into the forest before Ladon pulled his leathers over his head.

He dropped the new blade into the quench. Throwing his gauntlets at the wall, he pushed through the door and into the courtyard. "Armor! Now!"

Dragon pranced, his head up as he listened to his sister. *More than one triad approaches.*

What could they want? Fates came near at their own peril. All the families knew to stay away from Ladon and his sister.

His Second appeared, armor draped over the big man's elbow and Ladon's stallion saddled and in tow. Ladon threaded his arms through the breastplate as he swung up to the saddle. "Pull in everyone."

The man glowered, his gaze darting to the others yelling and arming themselves throughout their fortification. They were fighters unparalleled by any Roman military unit, but they were normals and Shifters.

Fates would shred them.

"Do as I say." Ladon's stallion lurched, agitated by the flames curling from Dragon's mouth. "You are not to engage Fates."

His Second listened, thank the gods, and would keep their people safe.

Dragon undulated through the gate and Ladon's stretching connection to the beast raked hot coals over his nerves. The beast stopped outside, his head swinging back and forth as he waited for Ladon's stallion to catch up.

Undergrowth and forest started three dragon lengths from his stallion's pawing hooves, brambles less so.

Fates' seers flowed like blood between the trees, but Ladon's connection to Sister-Dragon quieted—they had already moved too deep into the timbers for him to hear the other dragon.

A bush moved, punctuated by panting, and a lad burst from the underbrush. "Our mother!"

A second young man, his build and face identical to the first's, stumbled out of the trees behind his brother, a woman limp in his arms. He dropped to his knees in front of Ladon's stallion, his chest heaving.

The woman's present-seer sputtered, as if she'd lost control. It cried out like a rasp against wood and Ladon felt the hole gouged into her mind.

She'd lost a triad mate. In front of him, the woman's mind bled onto the dirt with the words babbling from her mouth.

The first lad swung his arms at the trees. "They killed our father, but our papa holds them off. Father told him to. Father said—"

The woman screamed and the lad dropped her with a thud. She ceased suddenly, the lad falling over her body. He shook as violently as his mother.

Far into the forest, the woman's other triad mate died. A Fate's life flared through the trees, a wave of power not unlike what followed a catapult's heave of Greek Fire.

Her triad-mate's death smothered her in her own, lone present.

Ladon dropped from his saddle and straightened her neck.

Maybe she could survive this. Give her boys a few more years. Sister might seethe, but he'd give this family shelter.

Fate or not, no lad deserved to see his parents murdered.

"Mama!" The second lad shoved Ladon aside. His ear dropped to her chest. Only a single hiccup left his throat when he sat up.

"They came for us," he croaked. "They claim we are part of their family. That we are to be a tribute."

The other lad closed his mother's eyes. "For the new Emperor. But our fathers spit into our mouths this morning. Both in turn, in each of ours."

"They said to run."

"So we ran," they said in unison.

These lads' parents sacrificed their lives to protect their boys from yet another insane Emperor. They gave their children something Fates never extended to each other—a chance.

The lads' eyes glazed. They both blinked and both their mouths slacked—at the same time, in the same way, synchronized.

Human!

Ladon stepped back. The beast saw the new motion first, but Ladon felt the power of a third lad flare from the trees. His brothers, in front of Ladon, moved mirror-opposite each other, their arms out.

The new lad leaped, pushed high by his brother's added momentum.

Ladon countered but the young man's abilities compensated.

He fell onto his back, the lad's knee in his throat.

Ladon roared—he offered these children help and this is how they responded?

He punched but the lad dodged and ripped Ladon's *Legio Draconis* insignia from his armor's straps. He leaped away as quickly as he had charged.

The lads gripped the entwined dragons of the insignia as one being. They did not acknowledge Ladon, nor did they pay heed to Dragon. They stared at the metal they held as all remaining normalcy blasted from their bodies.

Seven hundred years walking this earth and neither he nor his sister had witnessed a triad activate. Now a new Prime triad activated in front of him.

Holding a *Legio* emblem.

Sister emerged from the trees. "I told you they'd come for us! They still believe us part of the—" She stopped, her sword half sheathed, her gaze darting from one lad to the next.

The internal growl from Sister-Dragon set Ladon's teeth rattling.

Sister snatched their emblem from the lads. "You let Fates activate holding our insignia?"

He stepped between her and the lads.

He'd had enough of killing. "I will not cut down children."

Especially the killing of Fates.

Her sword clinked against her scabbard. "They are men! And active."

Slight, their hands and feet large for their frame, they hadn't reached their full height. They were men only because they were now parentless.

The lad who had stolen the insignia sat up. "We mean you no harm, Dracas. Of this we swear." His eyes were a different color than his brothers', and his face rounder, but his body carried the same lean strength. "I am Timothy."

The lad who had burst from the trees first pushed himself up. "I am Marcus."

The lad who had carried their mother bowed his head. "I am Daniel."

"Not all of our kind is in league with the devil." Marcus stood. "Not every Fate dances with the Sins."

Timothy held out his hand. "Please return our talisman."

They did not falter, nor did they cower. They faced the dragons, tall and strong, even if they all shook down to their bones.

Sister could destroy them now, if she wanted. Take from them what they needed so their triad could never use their abilities. But potential flowed from the young men, great in both power and soul.

So Ladon pried the insignia from his sister's hand.

Daniel laid it on his palm, then closed his fingers over the two metal dragons. He glanced over his shoulder at the trees, his seer sputtering to life for the first time. "They will return with reinforcements in two weeks' time. Their leader wants a fight with you, Dracos." He handed the pin to his brother.

"You have always won," Marcus intoned.

Timothy took the pin as he watched Sister. "Our fate may yet be death."

He walked forward and stopped within striking range, but he did not shrink. He bowed his head and dropped to one knee, his core remaining erect. "We serve only the Dracae, benevolent Dracas."

Ladon repressed a grin.

"We serve you. We serve your brother. We serve the beasts who circle us now, their hides as clear as the waters of the river." Timothy's gaze, strong and true, turned to Ladon.

"We are now and forever the Draki Prime."

11

Sixteen centuries the Draki Prime lived among Ladon's men. Sister never completely accepted them, though many times over the years she took Timothy into her bed.

Sixteen centuries through losses so horrible they overpowered Daniel's unmatched ability to see *what-will-be*. Through gains so brilliant Ladon and his sister still lived off the riches acquired. Through wars and deaths and births and the inception of a Fate family who wove themselves through much of Europe's technological innovations.

Until the night Daniel and Timothy bled to death on the shores of the North Sea. Ladon and Dragon purchased a steam ship and crossed the Atlantic the next day. The entire trip they vomited, Dragon unable to sleep on the waves of the ocean. They retched for months afterward.

A light penance for the failures that drove them from their home and destroyed the only Fates who had ever treated Ladon and Dragon as anything other than a blight on the world.

Marcus crossed the ocean as well, chasing after Shifter healers. Ladon visited twice, the first time to help build the house in the then-bustling town on the Minnesota River. They'd sawed wood and nailed the boards, but barely spoke. He and Dragon left shortly after they set the roof.

Seeing Marcus without his brothers pained them both, the memory of Daniel's and Timothy's deaths a cloud that never dissipated.

Staying away was the least Ladon could do.

Yet here he was, inching his van down the driveway of the little house outside of St. Peter.

The gravel spread into a large parking area between the house and two outbuildings. The detached garage must have been added in the fifties or sixties. Ladon didn't recognize it as he peered through the deep gloom. It looked solid but old, the peeling paint popping in high relief in the van's headlights.

The house also needed painting. Cracks riddled the ornate gingerbread. But the structure stood true, as it had in 1884, when Marcus set the foundation with his own hands.

The Parcae sickness had already started to cripple his joints. Not that Marcus complained about the pain.

In the back of the van, Dragon lifted his head. He'd curled around Rysa the entire drive, cycling the area of his hide near her face in calming patterns. The beast hoped to use his lights to bring her out of her stupor. She didn't wake, but she didn't drop deeper into her vision, either.

"Are you sensing him?" Ladon had sped to St. Peter and it was now shortly after midnight. He backed the van toward the front porch and turned off the ignition.

He sleeps. Dragon nuzzled Rysa's cheek.

The beast's agitation tensed Ladon's neck and jaw. His fingers strained. He'd gripped the steering wheel the entire drive from Rysa's home.

Ladon's new phone sat on the passenger seat, silent except for the whine all electronics produced. The app mining cell phone calls for words such as "fire" and "chemical spill" and "smell" showed no hits. It had led him to the theme park in Wisconsin, but nothing appeared now.

Ladon suspected that the beast was correct—the Jani family would inflict a swift vengeance and pull their Prime present-seer from the Burners. The ghouls were unlikely to attack anyone else, Fate or Shifter, once the Jani had taken their revenge.

He'd put out a call anyway. Every Shifter within four hundred miles was on high alert, but nothing. No indication of Fate activity, either.

He'd called Sister, asked her to drive east. Take over hunting the Burners, just in case. She'd agreed, until he told her about Mira and Rysa.

She hung up on him.

Rysa had started trembling about ten miles outside St. Peter. She didn't open her eyes. Dragon stroked her hair.

The beast raised his head. *The front porch light is on.*

Ladon checked the mirror. Harold, who had long been Marcus's companion, pushed through the screen door.

Ladon's boots hit the gravel. He slammed the driver's door.

Tall and lean, Harold stood on the porch in plaid sleep pants. He squared his shoulders, pointing at Ladon. "You decide to show up now, in the middle of the night?"

"I need Marcus's help."

"Of course you do. Why else would you come around? Huh? To visit maybe, you know, the last remaining member of your Parcae triad?" He threw his hands in the air. "Because that *couldn't* be the reason!"

Harold called them Parcae. Ladon didn't understand why. The only Fates who had ever been good to him were the Draki Prime.

Ladon ran his fingers through his hair before pointing over his shoulder at the van's rear door. "A vision has Rysa. She won't wake up. She's trembling."

Harold gritted his teeth. His expression hardened and he flipped Ladon a rude gesture as he ran down the steps. He crossed the gravel on bare feet, his heels dancing on the sharp rocks, and hopped into the back of the van.

Ladon followed.

"Ladon-Dragon." Harold nodded to the beast as he crawled toward Rysa. "Where did you find her?" He felt her forehead. "She's got a fever."

It has decreased. Dragon signed the words. He balanced himself on his haunches and lifted both of his six-fingered claw-hands off the floor. Then he flattened and elongated his digits, retracting his talons, to accommodate human gesturing.

They'd both learned sign language before leaving Europe. Ladon had never seen Dragon so proud as the day he first communicated without his human's help. He'd long tried to create text on his hide, occasionally even attempting to write, but it never made sense.

Signing, though, the beast could do.

Harold frowned. "I don't remember my signs, Great Sir. I apologize."

"He says it's decreased." Ladon ran his hand through his hair again.

Sweat glinted on Rysa's forehead. If she fell back into her activation, she'd die, no matter how frantically Dragon tried to cool her down.

Die and leave forever before Ladon had a chance to apologize for his behavior.

Harold ducked his head out the door. "Where's her triad?"

"She's a singular."

Harold balked. "A singular? And her family didn't protect her?" He touched a shackle. "Who the hell put these on her?" His face heated as he poked Ladon in the chest. "You better not have done this! She activated tonight, didn't she? She wouldn't be like this if she hadn't just activated."

Ladon grabbed Harold's throat so fast the other man jolted in surprise. "She needs help. You will help her. Do you understand me, *pedes*?" He would not tolerate Harold's usual behavior. Not now. Not with Rysa in danger.

Harold swung at Ladon's head, but Dragon caught his arm.

Please help Rysa, the beast signed.

"I understood 'help', Great Sir," Harold choked out. "I can't help if your human throttles the life out of me."

Ladon let go. His fingers constricted, lurching in little spasms. Hitting Harold wasn't the way to better the situation.

Harold rubbed his neck. "Don't call me *pedes*. I was never one of your men."

"Where is Marcus?" Ladon would muzzle Harold anyway if he continued to cause more problems than he solved.

Harold pressed his palm against Rysa's forehead and then the side of her neck. "Get her inside."

She felt too warm and her arms trembled when Ladon picked her up. Cradling her close to his chest, he jumped to the driveway. Dragon followed, his hide dark. He sparked though, his concern for Rysa flashing as minute points of light along his sides.

Harold held the screen door. Dragon squeezed across the threshold, first his head, then each shoulder, and turned on his side and contracted his ribcage to fit his body through. The beast moved fast and looked as if he flowed through the opening.

Harold stepped in behind the beast and flipped on the lights, Ladon following with Rysa. The clean lines of the house's modern interior stood in stark contrast to the grillwork coating the outside. A huge painting, abstract and distracting, hung over the fireplace.

"Still tasteful, I see." Ladon set Rysa on the perfectly proportioned couch.

Harold ignored him and ducked into a darkened passageway, vanishing around a corner. Muffled voices wafted into the living room.

Marcus, Dragon pushed.

Ladon nodded as he squatted next to Rysa. "She stopped twitching." He touched her arms, checking the bites she had manifested at the house. No blood seeped through the bandages, but dirt crusted the ones under the cuffs.

They'd get the damned shackles off her. He'd shape a talisman bracelet or necklace from the chains, something small and unobtrusive. Or he'd cut down a cuff, round it smooth so she could wear it without difficulty. Then he'd stud it with jewels, to counter the Burner ugliness that had bitten into her life. Or maybe braid fine gold and silver around it, if she preferred.

Whatever he did, he'd make sure it didn't weigh her down. She needed her talisman, but by the gods he'd make sure she wasn't a slave to it.

Dragon leaned his head over the back of the couch. *Marcus comes.*

The sickness began eating at Marcus when his brothers passed. Since 1862, he'd been looking for Shifter healers to calm the inflammation ravaging his joints and organs since the loss of his triad mates.

Ladon gripped Rysa's fingers. He'd find her a healer, if he needed to. But as a singular, she might not get sick. He didn't know. They may not know for years.

The voices grew louder and Dragon's head pivoted toward the door behind the couch. Ladon stood, dusting his knees.

Marcus shuffled out of the shadows. He stopped in the harsh light of the living room, his iron eyes squinting. The sickness had worked its horrors and his balance betrayed him, distorting his stance with subtle shakes.

He'd aged. At the end of World War Two, the second time Ladon visited, Marcus had looked to be in his mid-thirties. He'd stood on the porch leaning on his cane as he watched Ladon and Dragon back their truck toward the house. Ladon's girlfriend had kicked him out. Marcus waited for Harold to return from the Pacific theater. They drank enough whiskey that night to drown a mule.

Now, light streaked his dark hair and lines creased his face. Marcus had become a man who could be Rysa's grandfather.

The past-seer inhaled and stood up as straight as he could. "Dracos," he said, using the Roman honorific for both Human and Dragon.

"Hello, Marcus." Ladon moved around the couch and took his elbow.

Harold frowned but didn't argue. Dragon pulled a chair close to Rysa. The beast sniffed Marcus's head as Harold and Ladon helped him descend onto the cushions.

"I have a considerable amount of medication in my system." Marcus waved his swollen knuckles at Ladon. Pain etched creases around his mouth. "They interfere. But I will do what I can for the young lady."

"Thank you." Ladon squeezed his arm. Marcus had always been a man of honor who offered assistance to anyone in need. He'd helped his share of Shifters over the centuries, to the dismay of his brothers.

Ladon squatted next to Rysa. She breathed quicker and shallower than he liked. "She's been like this since we left her home. Dragon says she's still in a vision."

Marcus's mouth twitched. "Not good." His past-seer reverberated through the room, a brilliant and practiced music produced by an instrument honed from centuries of use.

It had slowed since Ladon last visited, dulled by both pain and drugs.

"This may take a moment. I need to find the edges of her seers," Marcus said.

The past-seer sat back, surprise rounding his expression. "She's Jani."

Dragon dropped his head over Rysa, a protective shield between her and the men.

Ladon and the beast should have realized Rysa's family would be a problem for Marcus. A terrible problem. How had he not thought the situation through? How could he have been—

His mouth rounded and he glanced up at Dragon. *Did she infect us when she was siphoning?* She'd said something about not being able to pay attention. The disorientation he'd felt at the house burst back into his mind. Did she always see the world in such a fractured way? How did she live missing connections? She was bright—both he and Dragon felt her intelligence—but she missed information. Lost perceptions. Forgot things.

And he had, as well, when his focus had constricted so tightly to her.

Harold jabbed his finger at Ladon. "*Jani?* You brought a *Juni* into my home? What the hell were you thinking?" He yanked open a cabinet next to the fireplace.

Infect is not the right word. She is connected. The beast nuzzled her hair, ignoring Harold. *It is strange.*

Inside the cabinet, Harold's katana and other swords sparkled in the light. He pulled out a handgun and a box of ammunition. "Are you trying to kill Marcus, too?"

Ladon's attention jumped from the weapons to Harold's tight face. The man dare not imply negligence on Ladon's part.

Ladon vaulted across the room and slammed Harold against the wall. "What happened to Daniel and Timothy was not my fault. They told me nothing! I had no idea that *Les Enfants de Guerre* had come for them."

Rysa spasmed.

Ladon felt it, a bit of sensing picked up from Dragon. He dropped Harold, his attention pulled back to her scent, her shape. He knelt again, stroking her arm.

"Harold." Marcus beckoned for him to calm down. "Please get me a glass of water. And some for the young lady. She's been thirsty since they left The Cities." He stroked Rysa's forehead, the melody of his past-seer playing through the room.

"But—"

Marcus's past-seer flared and Ladon held in a wince.

"We all must follow the thread fate has set for us. Letting it upset you helps no one. Besides, she's Mira's daughter. Not Faustus's. She means us no harm." Marcus crinkled his nose.

Les Enfants, the War Babies as the Shifters called them, were destined to become the next Jani Prime. Their father, Faustus, Rysa's uncle and Mira's triad-mate, had groomed them as such for six centuries, to the annoyance of his sisters. Or so the rumors said.

"Mira never told her about her heritage. She has no idea who she is. Or what she can do." Marcus waved at Harold. "Please get the water." He leaned over Rysa. "Her mother vanished from her life tonight."

Ladon tapped the edge of the cushion. "Mira—" He stopped speaking, wondering how to phrase what he needed to say. "Mira called her terrible things, Marcus. Accused her of being a monster." Which Rysa wasn't. "Then she touched an implosion."

Marcus scoffed. "That is why she's vanished so thoroughly. I see nothing of her. Not even a wisp of a trail."

Ladon nodded. He'd seen Marcus track other Fates who thought themselves hidden. They'd been wrong.

Marcus shook his head. "Damned burndust will do permanent damage, Ladon-Human. Harm Mira's heart and lungs." He kneaded the knuckles of his right hand. "She submerged herself in their chaos. Risky." He sat back, his face drawn. "So Mira of the Jani Prime hides."

He laid his palm on Rysa's forehead. "We had better wake the young lady."

12

Quick and lovely music wafted to Rysa. The weave and warp of the universe vibrated with its notes. It sang, touching *what-was*.

"Rysa, can you hear me? Wake up, beautiful." A pause. "She's still not opening her eyes."

"The vision calms." The music of the past played through *what-is*. "I've never seen such power. She's Prime, Ladon-Human. *Oh—*"

"Marcus!"

"I'm fine."

A new voice: "I want you out of my house!"

"I said I'm fine."

The music fatigued. It faltered, only a little, but enough that pain scratched at the delicate parts of Rysa's mind.

New burning would soon flow in through a gash at the back of her mind, like cockroaches swarming through floorboards.

Her body thrashed and her eyes flew open. She sucked in air through a wide open mouth, her lungs filling to capacity. The world. The real world.

No fire. She had to heal the gash. Heal, or—

"Hold still, beautiful. Don't hit anyone with those cuffs."

She'd had a vision. The Cities burned. She saw it in the sky, on the underside of the clouds. The whole world burned. She hadn't heard it, or felt it, or smelled the acid and smoke and ash she should have. But the vision had popped into the back of her mind like the reflection of a television screen on a window.

She felt more confused than terrified.

Shouldn't she be screaming? Didn't sociopaths act this way?

Unfeeling in the face of horror? What was wrong with her?

But something did coil itself around her gut. Something causing fear. It felt separate, and small, as if little bugs had moved in under her mind. Then the feeling vaporized, like a bubble popping.

Or a Burner.

She truly was a subpar Fate. Terrible and stupid and she'd set the world on fire and not care.

She gulped, trying desperately to pull in her arms, but nothing moved.

Dragon's head descended from above, the side of his jaw and a cat-like eye inches from her nose. His talons wrapped around the metal engulfing her wrists.

He let go and her arms dropped, but her legs didn't move.

"Are you okay?" Ladon's hands gripped her knees.

They'd get her through this. They'd make sure she was okay, no matter what happened. She blinked, realizing she was staring into his uncanny eyes.

But she'd burn the world. Set it on fire. She looked away.

"You were unconscious for a long time. It might take a moment to get your bearings." Ladon glanced between her and an older man sitting in a chair next to the couch. "Correct?"

The man shifted and the fabric of the comfortable but modern chair whiffed against his clothes. "Yes." He offered his hand. "I am Marcus, past-seer of the Draki Prime. It is good to meet you, Ms. Torres, daughter of Mira of the Jani."

They didn't know. Marcus was a past-seer and he didn't read the *burn burn burn* that must be pouring off her soul like a chemical spill. He didn't see it.

Maybe she was overreacting. Maybe, again, her God-awful hyperactivity made the world look worse than it was.

Ladon released her knees and she bent forward, holding her stomach. She sat on a chocolate-colored couch in a small but inviting living room. Soft sounds filtered in from outside. The remote cottage she'd awoken in looked like the mirror opposite of her home in Shoreview. She'd stepped through the looking glass into a comfortable corner of a world full of handsome men and brilliant beasts.

Men and a beast who could stand against anything.

Maybe she'd be okay.

She took Marcus's still extended hand. His grip was firm, despite his swollen knuckles.

Swollen, like her mom's.

"Do all Fates get rheumatoid arthritis?" she blurted out. What if that Burner concentrate in her mom's body made it worse? Her mother would moan and throw up because the pain was so bad and—

Pressure flared behind her left eye and she flinched. The cuffs smacked her cheeks when she pressed her temples. Her mom had yelled at her. Rysa had done something stupid again, not paid attention, the child who bumbled through life and couldn't even activate on the right talisman. And now look, she was going to set the world on fire!

Rysa Torres, the Burner-Fate. "Where's my mom!" It came out too loud, but—

Ladon dropped onto the couch next to her and curled his arm around her shoulder. "We don't know where she is and we won't be able to track her until her body sheds the burndust in her system. So we take care of your safety first, okay? We make sure these uncontrolled visions stop. I think that's what she'd want, anyway. Right?"

Behind her, Dragon nodded.

The Burners might eat her mom. "But…"

"We'll get her back. I promise. She probably escaped and is sleeping it off under a tree right now."

This man who had been mean to her earlier sat right next to her with his arm around her shoulder. He sat with their bodies parallel, though, like they were drinking buddies.

"One should never underestimate a Prime present-seer, even one crazy from dust."

Behind them, Dragon snorted. Rysa picked up a distinct sense of *affirmation*.

She flopped under Ladon's arm and against the couch. Tears started but she gritted her teeth. She'd be strong, for her mom, even though her world was disintegrating. Home, school, everything fell apart around her.

She felt like a toddler, terrified and alone in the grocery store because she'd lost her mom. And now some weirdo with a flamethrower was chasing her through the aisles.

"I see fire." More gritting of her teeth, this time to repress a hiccup.

Marcus pointed at Ladon. "The good Dracos will rid the world of the vermin who did this to you, will you not?"

Ladon shrugged. "These particular Burners." He plucked at his t-shirt and pulled it up to his nose. "The bastards smell *terrible*."

Rysa snorted, the tiniest smile edging out from under her anxiety. At least they were confident men and not spazzes, like her.

Ladon chuckled and smoothed a hair from her forehead.

She stiffened. She didn't mean to, but such an intimate touch surprised her. Tom never touched her hair. Not once.

Ladon pulled back. Shock played across his face, followed by something she never expected to see—his shoulders slumping in disappointment.

His gaze settled on the man standing behind Marcus. He didn't look at her again.

At the house, he'd held her against his side. Picked her up and carried her out. So to him, touching her face must have been the most natural thing in the world. Though he'd been a jerk earlier and should have felt she wouldn't appreciate it, natural or not.

"We'll cut off those cuffs in the morning. Right, Harold?" Disappointment still knotted Ladon's shoulders. "And make you a talisman you can wear." He still refused to look at her.

All she wanted to do was to apologize, though he should apologize to her.

Behind Marcus, Harold's eyes hardened, drawing her attention away from Ladon. The tall man held a glass of water in each hand. Annoyance hummed from his coiled muscles as he offered one to Marcus and the other to her.

"That's right. In the morning." Scowling at Ladon, he adjusted the holster under his left arm. A gun poked out. A big gun.

"Thanks for the water." Rysa's throat grated like she'd swallowed sand. The water helped, despite Harold huffing like he'd shared his last drop with the Devil himself.

He leaned close to Marcus's ear. "Don't tax yourself."

Marcus frowned. "I'm fine." He nodded toward Rysa. "She has only the shirt on her back."

Harold's back stiffened. "What do you know about your family? Tell me the truth." He pinched his lips together and poked out his chest. "I may not be Parcae but I can tell if you're lying."

Ladon's arm snaked around her shoulder again. Dragon nudged the nape of her neck, his snout next to her ear. They shored up her strength, but Harold's antagonism pressed on her like a weight.

She didn't know anything about the Jani. And the way he glared at her, it took all her self-control not to curl up on Ladon's lap.

Harold grunted. "Just like a Jani."

"Leave her alone." Ladon's arm tightened. He sounded like a cop, or a teacher, or maybe a general. He'd infused the authority of war into those three words.

Neither Ladon nor Dragon looked at her, but Ladon leaned forward. Dragon's forelimb moved over the back of the couch and wrapped around her other side. They insulated her with a warmth completely the opposite of the ice she heard in Ladon's voice—and in Harold's bitterness.

"She doesn't know anything. If she did, I would have seen it." Marcus set down his glass. "And I didn't. Yet someone saw you before you activated, young lady, even though Mira's been hiding you. The events of your entire twenty years are muddled." He inhaled, rubbing the bridge of his nose. "Timothy could do that. Stitch up the present so that a past-seer couldn't read it. It takes considerable skill and willpower. But to hold it for twenty years? Your mother is formidable, Ms. Torres." He shrugged. "Though we knew that already."

"Then how do you know she isn't lying?" The question hissed from Harold, low and menacing.

Marcus turned his head, his dark gray eyes more resigned than angry. "Because I am the past-seer of the Draki Prime, that is why. Even for the time I have left, I am better at what I do than any other Prime." He pushed himself to standing. "Justinian would not have failed to hold the Empire if we had become his tribute. This—" He waved. "This *all* would have been Rome. All of it."

Marcus teetered.

Harold grasped his arms. "Marcus, I'm sorry. I'm—"

"I can read the edges of your past, Ms. Torres, but only your aunt Ismene can undo the stitching." Marcus pulled away from Harold and pointed at Rysa. "*Everything* around you is muddled. I cannot see the Jani." He rubbed his temple. "I will try again in the morning."

Ladon pulled his arm from behind Rysa and stood up, taking Marcus's elbow. They whispered, Harold on the other side of Marcus glowering first at Ladon, then over his shoulder at Rysa.

Dragon touched Marcus's shoulder. He nodded, then stood straight. "We do what we must, Ladon-Human," he said.

Ladon looked at Rysa and grinned.

Smiles like that only crossed people's faces right before they said things like "buck up" or "it could be worse" or "at least we have food to eat and a roof over our heads."

"There's a spare room upstairs." Ladon pointed at the stairwell along the outer wall of the house, but didn't say anything more.

Harold helped Marcus vanish into the gloom of the dark hallway behind the couch, glancing over his shoulder before the shadows took him.

13

R ysa sat on the edge of the huge bed in the center of the tiny
room. Moonlight trickled in through the dormered window
tucked into a corner of the little house.

When she brushed her fingers along the white-painted headboard, her
seers flared, the image flickering on the outer edge of Rysa's abilities: Dark
hair and warm skin. The woman laid hands on Marcus and her touch helped
for decades.

Rysa pulled back her hand. The past was more obvious than the
present or the future. She distinguished it only because the people or the
technology made it obvious. Otherwise, it looked the same as *what-is* and
what-will-be.

Dragon wedged himself between her feet and the wall, his head
draped over the blankets, next to her side. He kept his colors muted but
bright enough she saw the furnishings clearly. The kaleidoscope of patterns
dancing on his hide reflected off the dresser against the wall and the small
chair in the corner.

"So it's called Parcae sickness?" Rysa asked Dragon. Not rheumatoid
arthritis. Something distinctly Fate attacked both Marcus and her mother.

Ladon had followed her up the stairs and she'd asked about it while
he stood in the doorframe. She faked calm and he'd gone off, presumably
to sleep. But she heard rattling and electronic noises coming from the porch
swing below the window.

He'd let it slip that the sickness struck Fates who'd lost a member—
or members—of their triad, like Marcus had lost his brothers. Her mom's
knuckles were as swollen as Marcus's, too. And her pain had been bad for

many years. Did this mean her mother's triad were dead?

They had to be. Her mom must be the only Jani Prime left. Maybe Rysa's seers could show her the truth, but she didn't know how to use them for simple questions like "What am I going to eat for breakfast?" much less complicated stuff about people she didn't even know. And if she did see some aunt or uncle she didn't know die, how would she know if it was in the past, present, or future? It all looked the same.

Dragon rolled toward Rysa, his patterns flowing in calming blues and greens, and puffed out a small flame.

A noise from the hallway caught her attention.

"I brought you a t-shirt and sweats." Harold stood in the door holding a stack of clothes. He pointed at her wrists. "We'll get those off tomorrow."

He was being nice?

An apologetic smile jumped awkwardly across his face as he set the clothes on the foot of the bed. "Marcus scolded me for a full ten minutes." He shrugged. "Sometimes I don't think. But if anyone can judge character, it's a past-seer. He says you're okay."

She nodded and tried to smile back. "It's alright." He was only trying to protect Marcus.

He'd changed into street clothes but the gun still poked out from under his arm. "The sweats will be too big." He shrugged again. "They'll do until you get clothes that fit."

"Thanks." She patted the t-shirt.

A micro-vision bounced through her mind's eye, a sudden little squirm of one of the tentacles: The half-built house silhouetted against a sunset. Chainmail in a wooden crate. Army fatigues.

It dissipated as fast as it appeared. At least this time nothing burned. And it didn't disorient. She breathed deep, thankful the vision hadn't taken over.

Harold watched her from the foot of the bed. "You just had a vision, didn't you?" He frowned and tapped the mattress.

"Can you feel it?" She sat up straight. "Ladon and Dragon can feel it. Will everyone know when it happens?" If she had an uncontrolled vision somewhere public, would all the passersby stop and stare? "What if someone calls the cops?"

Harold chuckled. "You're full of questions, aren't you?" He wiggled between the bed and Dragon to sit next to her. "Normals can't feel seers, so don't worry too much about it."

"What are you? You're not a Fate, but you were here when Marcus built the house." She'd seen something she was pretty sure had happened before the invention of automobiles. The clothes had all looked uncomfortable.

"I'm a normal." He shrugged. "Mostly normal. A Mutatae made me like this."

"Mutatae? Mutants? Like eye blasts and telekinesis?" Shifters were bad enough.

"No, no. Nothing like that. That's silly, anyway."

"No sillier than dragons." She leaned against the beast when he snorted.

Harold scooted back on the bed. "True. The Mutatae call themselves Shifters now. Most can morph their bodies."

"Oh, Ladon told me about them." Parcae. Mutatae. "The Burners are called Ambustae, aren't they?"

Harold nodded. "Yep."

Which was why her mom called her the Ambusti Prime. She suspected the naming rules had little to do with Latin grammar and everything to do with Fate arrogance. Anything to make themselves sound grand and imposing.

Harold scratched Dragon's eye ridge. "There's only two Dracae, though. Right, Great Sir?"

Dragon snorted again and rubbed against Rysa. She'd sensed something about a sister. Something dark hidden so deep in the past her seer couldn't find it.

"The Shifters breed like rabbits." Harold snorted too, an impressive mimic of Dragon. "Or rabbits breed like Shifters."

"What about you?" He didn't look any older than her.

"I was born in 1544." His voice dropped into a British accent similar to Billy's. "In the hills outside Manchester. Lived under Tudor rule, I did." His nose crinkled and his voice changed back to the southern Minnesota accent he used earlier. "An insane Shifter cursed me."

"*Cursed* you? Seriously?"

He waved his arms like a magician. "'Upon thy head I leave a scourge so foul, so torturous, that thou shalt walk this Earth always!' She kissed me right on the lips—" He pointed to his mouth. "—before yelling, 'You will now and forever annoy the dragons!' Then she ran off, cackling like a fairy tale witch."

Rysa grunted, trying not to laugh. "Annoy?"

"I said she was insane." Harold grinned, but his eyes filled with surrender. He hadn't asked to be made immortal.

"Shifters can do that?"

"They've got enthrallers who can make you do things and morphers who can do crazy shit with their bodies and a couple of healers who can kill just as easily as they can make you like me." He shook his head. "She must have been class-one or I would have been maggot chow long, long ago."

"Wow." Then Shifters were more than simple shapeshifters. A lot more.

"You be careful if you run into one. They're a slippery lot." But he smiled and patted her thigh. "Don't worry too much about it. The Great Sir won't let any Shifters near you, will you?"

Dragon blew out a little flame and rubbed Rysa's side again. She chuckled, feeling better than she had in a long while, and wrapped an arm around his neck.

Harold leaned close and winked. "I've made an art of annoying Ladon-Human. I'm very, very good at it. Anna-Human ignores me."

She squeezed his fingers with her free hand, smiling too, happy that he seemed to have accepted her. "Hopefully, I won't be annoying."

His eyebrow arched. "I don't think you have to worry about that, either."

Until they spent time with her. "Thanks for the clothes."

He squeezed back. "You sleep. We'll get those damned things off tomorrow. I think he's got a plan for making you a talisman that won't, you know, be so obvious." He scratched Dragon's crest. "Ladon-Human's always got a plan."

Dragon nodded.

"They're good at what they do, Rysa." He traced a little star flowing by on the beast's hide. "Only idiots mess with the Dracae."

Dragon rolled onto his back. Squiggly lines burst across his belly.

Harold laughed. "See? He can be scary when he wants."

The squiggly lines turned into tiny sword-shapes.

"He's a big mimicking lug, that's what he is." Harold stood. He stopped in the door and grasped the frame. "You're a rare find, if you didn't know. A Fate with all three abilities. Doesn't happen very often." With that, he closed down the door and walked away.

Dragon touched her cheek, unease rippling across his hide.

"I'll go to sleep." Things might be clearer in the morning.

Dragon dimmed to a soft shimmer. She stripped off her dirty clothes, folding her jeans and setting them on the floor next to Dragon's front limbs. Pulling a fresh t-shirt over her head, she crawled into the bed, watching reflected stars and squiggles and glowing triangles glide across the walls.

14

"How long has it been since you've slept?"

Ladon steadied the porch swing with one hand, his vodka in the other, as Harold dropped onto the slats next to him. The chains creaked and the bolts in the porch's ceiling groaned. Harold paid no heed. Ladon looked up, checking the sagging roof anyway.

"Why the sudden concern?" His relationship with Harold had never been good. The man bristled at what he called "the arrogance of the long immortal." Perhaps Harold had softened, now that he approached five centuries of his own feet walking the earth.

Harold scowled. "Marcus and I talked."

Ladon glanced at his phone. Nothing on the app. Jani vengeance had probably already descended on the Burners. The War Babies were cruel enough to slice bits off that British Burner and use his flesh to detonate the others. They'd take his limbs and leave his torso, then dump him in a field to fizzle to dust.

Not a good death for anyone, even a Burner.

All these years, the War Babies had stayed in Europe and kept a low profile away from Ladon and his sister. Ladon didn't pretend to understand Fate machinations or their convoluted justifications for allowing the murdering scum to continue to breathe. Nor did he care. He'd vowed long ago to peel their skulls if they ever again came near the people he cared about.

He took a swig of vodka. It helped him tolerate the terrible world and the whine of his damned phone. Landlines weren't noisy. He took another swig and shifted the assault rifle on his lap. He'd picked the large one with a scope that could hit anything within three hundred feet of the house. He couldn't be too careful, down here by himself. "I had a nap before the Chicago incident."

Harold shook his head. "How long has it been since the Great Sir slept?"

Ladon glanced at the porch roof and the room above. "We left Wyoming seven days ago."

"A week?"

"Yes."

Harold scratched his ear. "He can't go much longer."

Ladon stopped a mouthful of the vodka in mid tip. "I know my own dragon."

Harold sat back on the swing. "Since when is he yours? You're his."

The whine from the phone was bad enough without Harold's opinions adding to the noise. "You know nothing."

"I know he's *hers*, now." Harold nodded upward.

Ladon and Dragon would keep Rysa safe. They'd help her find her way. But her reaction earlier when Ladon touched her hair made it clear she didn't trust him. Though she seemed to trust Dragon.

He took another sip. The beast *was* showing a strong attachment. He'd be inconsolable when she went her own way. He'd mope and his hide would dull to shadows for months. Maybe a full year. "She's a Fate."

"That she is." Harold grabbed the vodka and took a swig. Coughing, he shook his head. "Jesus, man, what are you drinking?"

Ladon shrugged. This case of vodka did have an abrasive edge. He didn't mind. It helped him stay awake.

"Where the hell did you get this?" Harold held the bottle out and scrutinized the Cyrillic on the label.

Ladon shrugged again. "Derek's cousin." His brother- and cousin-in-law didn't get along half the time, but Dmitri's business holdings were a connection to the modern world Ladon and his sister could not live without.

Plus, Dmitri supplied the best weapons. And vodka.

Harold returned the bottle. "Pavlovich's providing you with booze? And it hasn't started a Shifter civil war?"

"Dmitri does what he wants. No one dare tell him otherwise."

The offending Shifter "disappeared." Ladon never asked about Dmitri's practices. Not knowing seemed the best course of action.

Harold laughed. "Right. I'm sure." He took the bottle and gulped another drink. Whistling, he handed it back. "That's going to kill you. All these centuries and bad Russian vodka is what's going to do you in."

"Can't die." He pointed up at the room above. "What would Dragon do?"

Harold laughed and the swing jiggled. "I'm going to stamp WWDD on one of those stupid rubber bracelets." He tapped across his wrist.

The odd cultural references should make Harold endearing. They didn't. "What the hell are you on about?"

Laughter roared out of the other man. "Still clueless about the wider world, I see?" He shook his head. "The more things change, the more you stay the same."

Ladon and the wider world didn't get along. "The more things change, the more annoying you become."

Harold pulled the bottle away and lifted it high. "Thank you for noticing, oh great Ladon-Human, leader of both men and beasts." A loud grunt followed a swallow.

Still nothing on the damned phone. Ladon took back the bottle. "How is Marcus?" If the healers had stopped helping…

Harold's face fell. "He's convinced his time is up. What Daniel predicted is about to come to pass." He gestured at the sky. "Damned Parcae and their stupid beliefs! Fate this. Fate that. I told him that I'd sell my swords. Pay that damned healer on the Boundary Waters, but the son of a bitch's got no medical training. He can only give Marcus some comfort."

"Dmitri's a healer. I'll pay." Ladon took another swig. "Whatever he wants. I'll pay."

Harold stared at him for a long moment. "Pavlovich won't touch Marcus. He's too high profile to help a Parcae. The other Shifters would drop on him like Sputnik from the sky." He pointed upward.

"Dmitri will do what he is paid to do." Though he might enjoy the challenge of fixing Parcae sickness more than the money he'd make. Not that he'd admit it.

Harold watched the clouds. "You could have told me this when I returned from The War."

"You didn't ask." Ladon rubbed at his hair. "Besides, Dmitri hadn't entered the States the last time I saw you."

"Derek had."

Ladon's brother-in-law's relationship with the Shifters was complicated, Dmitri's buffering notwithstanding. "If you sell your swords, I want them. I'll give you a fair price."

Harold shook his head. "This winter's going to be hard."

One quick nod and Ladon set the rifle against the railing. "Derek will take care of it."

"Ladon, you don't have to—"

"Yes I do, Harold, and you know it." He should have fixed this problem long ago.

You need to sleep, Human.

Harold scowled and pointed at Ladon's nose. "It's creepy when you two talk to each other. Your face does odd things."

"He says I need sleep." The beast's fatigue fanned his own.

"He's right. So does he." Harold nodded toward their van in the drive, a dark monolith in the gloom.

I cannot sleep. I will not leave Rysa unguarded.

"He says he has work to do." If Dragon slept, they'd be locked in one location for a full twenty-four hours. The beast would be vulnerable. So would Rysa.

"Go upstairs. Get a few hours. I'll stay up." Harold pointed at the door before wiggling his fingers for the rifle.

I will go up to the roof and keep watch.

Ladon stood, rubbing his face. "He's going up to the roof."

Harold nodded and set the rifle against the porch rail.

They may not be able to fetch Mira and give Rysa back her mother, but Ladon could help Marcus. "Dmitri will cooperate."

Harold slumped in the swing, the same unconscious response Ladon always saw when Harold fought against his ever-present need to sit tall in Ladon's presence.

"We used to be comfortable," Harold said. "Even with the sickness, we were okay." He lifted the rifle and laid it across his knees, his fingers tapping the stock. "It's been hard to travel to Sweet Lake and that damned bastard won't come down here without extra payment. He hides up north."

Harold raised the vodka to the sky with his other hand. The swing creaked as he pushed absently with his foot. "He takes our money and he drinks himself into a coma. Just so he can hide."

Ladon looked at the phone. Still nothing. "I'll pay him a visit."

Harold shook his head. "Send the Dracas. AnnaBelinda and Anna-Dragon have always been scarier than you." His hand bounced against his chest in a Roman salute.

"If I can get Sister away from home." She hadn't let Derek out of her sight since the last time Shifters came looking for him. His brother-in-law chafed, feeling as if under house arrest, but he'd never tell that to his wife.

Nor had she listened to Ladon, either, when he mentioned it.

"Fresh northern Minnesota air would do both her and the husband good." Harold slumped forward, his elbows dropping over the rifle to his knees. "And she can beat up a Shifter. Always a good time, I'm sure."

Sister did enjoy smacking around bad Shifters. Ladon looked up at the southern Minnesota sky. It glowed bright and beautiful, like Rysa's eyes, not hard, like his sister's. He glanced at the ground. He'd have to watch himself with Rysa.

"I've been working at the grocery store." The swing creaked. "Stocking shelves. A couple of the local teenagers come by when I'm at work and keep an eye on him. He tells them stories about Europe and sword fighting and the Black Death and they love it. But we could use the help."

All this time, and they'd never asked. They wouldn't. Ladon wouldn't either, if he'd been in the same position. Still, he felt like an idiot for abandoning the last of the Draki Prime the way he had. All because how it ended made him unhappy.

Ladon handed the phone to Harold. "If the app indicates a hit, yell. Dragon will wake me."

Harold held up the phone. "It's low on juice."

Ladon pulled the van keys from his pocket. Harold annoyed him but he was the most trustworthy normal he knew. "The charger's in the glove compartment."

The phone's screen cast an eerie glow onto Harold's face. "What the hell is this app, anyway?"

"Dmitri loaded it onto the phone." But he knew what it was—a bit of Shifter armor against the hellhounds stalking the innocent among their people.

A few movements of his finger and Harold's eyes widened. "Damned Mutatae," Harold grumbled. "How long has their cold war with the rest of the planet been going on?"

Ladon rattled the handle on the sticking screen door. He'd get a crew out here to repair the house. "Since the Inquisition. They're still angry."

Harold shook his head. "No one holds a grudge like a Shifter."

No one but his sister. He glanced at the normal sitting on the porch swing. He'd never been kind to Harold. Not when Marcus brought him home and not after, either, when Daniel and Timothy died. "We okay now, Harold?"

The app held the other man's attention. "Yeah. We're good. For now. I promised Marcus I'd be nice." Harold sniffed and his voice dropped into a pitch-perfect imitation of the past-seer. "First, we see who is behind this. Then we tame her fire."

Ladon nodded. Marcus never stopped until he completed a task, no matter how fatiguing—or dangerous—it might be.

Harold took another sip from the bottle. "You'd think he's Yoda or something."

"Who?" Ladon didn't need someone else to worry about.

Harold laughed and waved Ladon off. "Go on. Get some sleep. Marcus will see to your new darling in the morning."

I want a bath.

How a Fate would react to being called "his new darling," Ladon didn't know. "He wants a bath first. And she's not my new darling."

Harold snorted. "You all need baths. And yes, she is your new darling." He pointed into the house. "Go on, you idiot."

Dragon lay on the floor of the little room, his bulk filling the space between the bed and the closets fitted into the sloped walls. He shifted as Ladon entered and his head tugged on the blankets at the foot of the bed.

She's sleeping? Ladon pushed.

Anxious sparks played along Dragon's back. *Yes.*

I'll go down the hall. Next to the bathroom, the other bedroom's door stood open. He'd be respectful and do the decent thing.

No. Dragon undulated over the bed. *You will not.*

Ladon stepped back as the beast squeezed through the door. *Why are you being stubborn? I can't stay in there with her. You saw how she reacted when I touched her downstairs.*

Women didn't pull away from a friendly gesture like his touch to her hair after they'd spent hours sleeping next to Dragon.

Ladon drummed his fingers on the doorframe, his fatigue muddling his attempts to understand her response.

He thrust his hands into his pockets. He'd apologize in the morning. Make it right.

You must stay with her. What if she has another vision? I will be on the roof. Dragon tapped his snout on the ceiling.

In the little room, the only seating besides the top of the dresser and the bed was a wooden chair in the corner. *I'm tired.*

Then sleep. The beast moved toward the stairs.

But—

Do not complain. She is pretty.

Reflections from Dragon's hide danced over the walls and a few made their way into the bedroom and over Rysa.

She was more than pretty. She was stunning. He could get lost in the curves of her body and the moonlight of her eyes. *I smell bad.*

She smells of Burner. The beast's head swung around. *You were good to offer Harold help.* He disappeared into the living room.

The screen door opened and Harold spoke to the beast. Ladon would apologize to Marcus in the morning, as well.

Make everything right. Harold said something else to the beast and the outside walls of the house creaked. Dragon moved to the roof.

On the bed, Rysa breathed in the slow rhythm of sleep.

Ladon wanted to make things right. More than he'd wanted to any time in the past.

Perhaps something else had moved across their connection when she connected to their energy at the house. Perhaps her youthful view of the world had loosened a part of him he'd thought long calcified.

It felt good, as if he'd awakened with the warmth of the sun touching his face.

Let her siphon. She gave them a gift much greater in return. They'd help her hold in check the Burner randomness, if she wanted. It would be their payment.

The bed squeaked when she shuffled her legs. Ladon listened carefully to her breathing, making sure she hadn't slipped back into a vision. She sighed, content, and he exhaled.

And maybe, someday, she wouldn't recoil when he offered a touch.

At his feet in a neat pile on the rug were her ripped-up shirt, her socks, and her jeans. He stared, trying not to picture her bare hips.

Dragon had been sitting on her clothes the entire time he'd wedged himself between the bed and the wall. He'd done the same thing several times over the centuries. Staked his claim. Showed Ladon what he wanted by caressing a hip and marking a woman with his scent. Ladon always went along with it, enjoying the company and the attention and the sex, mostly to make the beast happy.

He rarely had the chance to choose a woman on his own.

He pulled off his socks. Best not to allow his emotions to attach themselves to a Fate. The sun would rise in a few hours and until then, he'd sleep, happy for a moment to feel the warmth from her body.

He dropped his t-shirt next to his socks and lay down on top of the blankets. The bed creaked and she rolled over, her nose inches from his shoulder. Dazed, he took in her complex scent of warm blossoms and mist-under-the-moon.

Her hand moved toward her chin but stopped when her nails grazed his elbow. Fingers moving in the small jerks of sleep, she curled her hand around his arm.

He kissed her forehead. When he pulled back, the taste of her skin lingered, sweet as he suspected it would be. Sweet and lovely and as dazzling as her scent.

She'd fallen into his life accidentally, unintentionally. He couldn't be swayed by the promise he'd seen in her eyes. They had boundaries to consider. Edges to delineate.

What did she see when her eyes shined and she bared her soul to him? Did she see a man and a beast, or did she see *his* soul, with its marks and scars and shriveled attempts to be human?

Would she be willing to take his hand and lean against his shoulder and be patient enough to see him as something other than an anachronism?

When she sighed, he closed his eyes. Best not to think of such things. He and Dragon had a job to do. Then they'd return to their quiet life. Entertaining fantasies of a new voice in their silent world would lead nowhere.

But tonight, he'd give her comfort. He drifted into the few remaining hours of sleep left to him, his fingers wrapped around hers.

15

Rysa never dreamed like this. She should be pondering how to find her mother, or how to deal with the shackles, or how to avoid a burning fate. Yet her dream hands threaded under Ladon's dream t-shirt and over the hard muscles of his abdomen and chest.

She dreamed of the heat of his body and the shelter of the space between the man and the beast. Of calmed seers and lights and strong hands soothing her fears. Of his dream breath, intense and full of desire, tickling her neck.

Then he was inside her, moving with slow determination, his arms twined in a tight embrace around her body. Solid arms, his fingers learning every curve and line of her hips and thighs. Arms that would never let her fall.

They moaned, but no sound filled her dream ears. She knew only the deep rumbles pushing from his body into hers. She felt his mouth. His tongue. Curls wrapped around her fingers as she stroked his hair. He smiled. Gave a kiss.

She'd never felt this good. She couldn't, in real space. No one wanted her like this in real space. Yet here, this man—this beautiful, perfect man—wanted to spend his life with her.

Consciousness flickered, the dream fading. Images, tactile and visual, vanished, but her body ached. The dream retreated into a desire. Maybe a hope. She floated in the space between sensing what she wanted and knowing what was real.

She began to reintegrate information from the world. Her front felt hot. Her back tingled cold and uncomfortable. The blanket wound around her hips and compressed her legs. Squirming, she yanked, but something large held it down.

Distant now, the dream beckoned. She wanted to find it, to remember, but only the ache in her belly and a lingering sense of happiness remained. If she held it close, maybe she wouldn't forget.

She opened her eyes, knowing she'd have to, sooner or later.

Ladon grinned, his mouth inches from hers. "Good morning, beautiful."

One of his thighs lay between her legs. Her head rested on his shoulder. He stroked down her arm, gentle but firm.

Shock hit hard and she flung herself backward.

"Careful!" He reached for her but she flopped off the edge.

When had he come in? She didn't remember Dragon leaving. Did she black out? Why had she cuddled against him in the middle of the night? She'd wrapped her entire body around his. "What—"

"Dragon didn't want you alone. And I needed sleep."

"Umm…" What had he seen? She wore only a t-shirt and her panties.

"Nothing happened. I swear you'd sleep through a tornado. Or a volcano. Or a wrecking ball coming through the window." He pointed at the curtains fluttering in the breeze.

"Oh!" Her attention snapped to outside. Did she sleep through an attack? Ladon wouldn't be here with her if she had. He'd be beating up Burners. Punching them with all the strength in those arms.

Diffuse images popped into her mind, more physical sensations than anything she saw. Did she dream about him?

"It's okay." He sat up.

No shirt covered his torso. Or his shoulders. Or those arms. Every muscle skirting his core defined, his chest sculpted, he moved with a fluid grace no man should possess.

He grinned again. "You're nice to look at, too."

She snatched the blanket off the bed and held it under her chin. It pulled between her breasts and she kicked at it, fanning it out to cover her front.

His eyes traveled over every curve and plane of her body, but he wasn't doing the terrible calculations guys always did. He looked happy, like she'd expect him to look when he watched Dragon play. Tom never looked at her with such reverence.

She pulled the blanket tighter. "How long have you been awake?"

"A while." His grin widened to a smile and he picked up his t-shirt off the floor. He sniffed it, frowned, and flicked it like he was airing it out.

"A while? And you let me…" She waved and the blanket dropped across her legs. Grabbing it again, she pulled it tight around her neck.

He laughed as he twisted his torso into the black shirt. Was everything he owned black? His jeans were dark gray. His boots had once been black. That jacket with the plating on the sleeves was black, too. So was the van. He probably owned sunglasses with black lenses.

"You were asleep. And obviously happy." He winked and sat back on the bed, weaving his fingers together behind his head.

Aware that her mouth was open, she snapped it shut. "You're *terrible!*"

His smugness vanished and he gestured at the ceiling. "I'm sorry! I'm a jerk, okay? I was a jerk when I was callous about your… your… attention issues and I was a jerk when I touched you downstairs and I'm a jerk right now." He paused. "Dragon didn't want you alone and damn it, you can hate me for it, but I'm going to make sure you're okay."

He stared at her with his incredible golden-brown eyes, his brows and mouth both frowning. She'd made him feel bad and he sat on the bed, all handsome and pouting with the most kissable lips she'd ever seen.

Rysa gulped air into her lungs and she stepped back against the dresser, her fingers fumbling. She shouldn't think of him that way. They didn't know each other. But he apologized for being a jerk and he wasn't treating her as if only her boobs mattered. And he did have kissable—

The blanket fell to the floor.

His mouth opened enough that she glimpsed his teeth.

He hurdled from the bed and lifted her up in one smooth motion. She floated for a moment, held in the air by solid muscles, her body as weightless as the morning sun warming her back.

Her bottom came to rest on the dresser. He leaned toward her, his gaze locked to hers until his chest pressed against her breasts and his breath tickled her cheek. His lips hovered just above her temple.

What had she dreamed? Touching him this way, feeling him this close, overrode all the *but but but* thoughts that any sane woman should have. He was a jerk who didn't like Fates. Except the ones he considered friends. And he apologized.

It took all her effort not to moan.

His breath grazed her ear, his lips moving along its edge. "Your seers are rich and beautiful and very distracting." He didn't back away.

Like you. Whether the thought came from her nasty or from him, she didn't know.

She fought her own body as her arms enfolded his waist. The need to tuck her fingers under his shirt and feel his skin blotted out everything else.

A groan rolled from deep inside his chest, more a low boom than any sound a human should be able to make. "I think they're affecting me. They did in Minneapolis." His body felt like a bow about to snap, but he didn't move. He held her without gliding his touch over her skin. His lips pressed into her hair but he didn't kiss. Nor did he press his obvious erection against her belly.

She tried to breathe through it but her deep inhales only thrust her breasts harder against his chest.

"I know your seers showed you something about us when we found you. Something physical. Your eyes dilated. Your hips swayed and your cheeks colored. The same responses happened just now."

Even with the stench of Burner clinging to him, he smelled of sunshine. It mingled with the texture of his skin. She pulled him closer. The metal around her wrists dug into his back, but he didn't recoil. He continued to hold her thighs.

"When I touched you last night, it made you angry. You shouldn't be angry, Rysa."

She heard the words but they slipped by, lost in her hyper-focus on a spot on his chest just below his heart. She wanted to kiss it, to lick it. To experience in the *what-is* what she knew would be a brilliant, bone-melting reaction.

Her hand glided up his torso.

He grabbed her wrist. A pause and he kissed her knuckles. "Say something."

Her body didn't want to talk.

Another groan boomed from his chest but she leaned toward him, holding tight to his waist with the hand he didn't grasp. His tension rearranged itself, moving from a uniform tightness to a rock in his lower back.

"We can't do this." He kissed the bridge of her nose before he pried himself away enough to see her eyes. "You deserve more respect than a jerk like me can give you."

He wanted her, but he wanted her to want him more.

"You're not a jerk."

He almost touched her cheek. His fingers stopped a hair's breadth from her skin before his hand vanished to his side. She wouldn't have pulled away this time. She would have concentrated on the feel of his fingertips as he traced the line of her jaw.

He tilted his head, his eyes distant. "Maybe someday I'll be worth that look in your eyes."

A tentacle whipped. *What-is*, the real present, sank below her seers' vision of *what-will-be*:

His palm glides over her naked breast, his fingers pinching her nipple. Their bodies entwine, as much of their naked skin touching as possible.

Dragon's colors. Dragon, with them.

Then *what-was*: Tom, her first love, on top of her, moving faster and harder than he should have her first time. He was completely involved in his own pleasure. Not thinking about her. She could tell. He didn't look at her.

But Ladon's eyes will gleam, happier than she thought possible.

It all heaved through her, her back arching. A cry tore from her throat. "Rysa!"

The real world snapped back. She wasn't on the dresser. She was on the floor straddling Ladon's hips, a knee on each of his wrists. Her arms tightened around her chest and her hands burrowed in her underarms. The damned shackles scraped through Harold's old t-shirt.

They were still dressed. They hadn't—

"What did he do to you?" Ladon's eyes narrowed to slits. His cheek twitched, his neck muscles tensing so tight the line of his jaw turned white.

"What?" She'd pinned him, but her actions weren't the focus of his anger.

"Someone hurt you. I felt it. Just now. I—" The concern in his eyes worked down his features and loosened his jaw. "I see it on your face."

She touched her cheek. Tears.

"No one will *ever* treat you that way again." He smacked his shoulders against the floor. "Damned normals." Then he turned his face away and muttered something that sounded vaguely like "snap his neck."

"What happened?" She didn't know. Did she black out again? Ladon's anger caught her off guard. They didn't know each other. Why did he care about Tom?

Everything reeled. She couldn't think.

"You don't remember? You flipped me and started crying." He nodded toward his hands. "Will you let me up?"

"Oh." Lifting her knees, she released his wrists.

He sat up and pulled her close in one motion, a protective shield against any pain another man might dare think toward her, much less inflict.

"I'm sorry, Ladon. I didn't mean to lead you on. I... I don't do that. I'm not like that. I—" She babbled but she didn't want him to let go. She felt safe for the first time since she activated. Safe against his chest. Safe from Tom's meanness. Safe like maybe she'd find her way through the hell of her fated future.

"I need to learn how to handle this connection we have." He shook his head. "I shouldn't have picked you up. You're—" He stopped suddenly, holding his breath. "I've never dealt with anything like this before. It's disorienting."

"*Disorienting* is one way to describe it." Most people didn't get first-hand knowledge of what it meant to greet the day with a head full of attention deficit.

He shook his head. "But by the gods, you are hard to resist."

She snorted. It snuck out her closed mouth. Sure, she was hard to resist. She was a spaz who clung to him like some pathetic sea creature.

He held her away so she could see his eyes. "You are exquisite, Rysa."

Her mouth dropped open. Men didn't say things like that to her and mean it. They said it to soften her up so she wouldn't pay attention when

they did their little mental calculations. And they never used words like
"exquisite." Always "sweet" and "nice" and "doable."

"Has no one told you so?"

She shook her head.

He hugged her close again. "Modern men do not understand true
beauty, even when it sits on their laps wearing nothing more than a t-shirt
and lace panties."

She covered her still open mouth. "Oh!" Her cheeks warmed and she
bit her lip, though she knew she shouldn't be ashamed. They hadn't done
anything.

"You're adorable when you're embarrassed." He lifted her off, but he
didn't revel in her awkwardness. "Dragon's with Marcus anyway."

She realized he'd never leave out Dragon. Not with her. She was
too important to the beast. Her mouth dropped open again. She hadn't
considered *that*. "Oh."

He exhaled hard and scratched the back of his head. "I apologize.
Again."

"How can this be happening?" She'd reacted the same way to
Tom. Four days and they were having sex in his dorm room. Like it was
inevitable.

Ladon smirked, running his fingers through his hair. "I think your
seers are pushing the future into the present." He smirked again and looked
away.

A buzz vibrated from under the bed, followed by a chirp. When they
dropped to the floor, they kicked her clothes. Now only one leg of her jeans
was still on the rug next to the bed. Her phone was in a pocket.

Her phone's battery had been low yesterday. It must be about to run
out of power. And she'd forgotten to check on Gavin. How many times had
he texted her since last night? She reached under the bed, happy for the
distraction, and pulled out her phone.

Nineteen. He'd texted her nineteen times.

"So the whine was from your phone," Ladon muttered.

"My friend Gavin." She cycled through his messages. *Where are you?
Are you okay? I can't find you. Rysa, please text me back. Please. I know
your phone is on. The cops are looking for you and your mom.*

He was okay. The Burners hadn't eaten him.

Ladon stared, unblinking, at her phone. "Is he the one who hurt you?"

"He's my friend. The Burners chased him and—"

"You were in danger and he ran away?" Annoyance, anger, and something distinctly male Rysa didn't understand pulsed off Ladon. He continued to stare at her phone.

Ladon acted as if her impulsiveness had infected him. "He's my friend, Ladon. I told him to run."

He shook, an intense micro-moment accompanied by a blink, and stared at her for another moment.

Then he sprang to his feet, not looking at her again. "I'll go downstairs." He grabbed his boots so fast his motion blurred.

The door banged against the wall when he stalked out.

She watched him go. Were her emotions backwashing to him? They had to be. And Ladon couldn't tell the difference between Tom and Gavin.

In her hand, the phone's screen went dark, the battery now completely drained.

She'd gone to counseling after Tom. The woman had sat on the other side of the room, nodding and saying obvious things like "How do you feel?" and "Write down your thoughts. We'll go over them next week." Rysa had. Diligently. She'd learned three things: She was mad. Sad.

And bad.

She never told the therapist. Saying it out loud made it sound even stupider than it did when it rattled around in her head. Even then, before she knew she was a Fate, she knew her Fate's soul wreaked havoc on the men in her life.

She set down her dead phone. She shouldn't involve Gavin in any more of her problems anyway.

Involving Ladon and Dragon was bad enough.

16

You must not drink. Dragon seized Ladon's vodka and poured it on the driveway. *Rysa will smell the liquor. She will not be happy.*

"Give that back." Ladon snatched at the bottle but Dragon threw it over the garage. The morning sun hit the glass as it sailed through the air and Ladon squinted at the glare. "All the damned phones and wifi in the house are giving me a headache."

That is not why you drink. His patterns jarring and vivid, the beast snorted flame into the sky. Waves trailed through the dew and clung to the side of the van when he swiped the vehicle with his tail.

"Yes, it is." Ladon did have a headache. It pounded against his temples and Dragon's reprimands weren't helping.

You could shower.

"She's showering." Naked, the spray running down the curve of her back and over her breasts. Those damned cuffs sliding along her damp skin. Ladon tried to force back the image by tapping his knuckles against his forehead. He'd rein in these thoughts. Give her the space she needed.

He hadn't done so upstairs. He'd seen it on her face after her phone buzzed. She'd looked at him the same way she had the night before, when he touched her hair.

Modern women were confusing. "You're a pain in the ass, you know that?"

You will show her respect. You will not drink and make her leave. Dragon dropped his head and set his forelimbs, and wild pulses rebounded across his shoulders. *She is not afraid of me and I want her to stay.*

The beast hopped around Ladon like a giant glowing dog and made his head hurt more. Behind them, the van's door stood open and the morning sun flooded the interior. He could get another bottle. He needed clean clothes, anyway. And he'd left out their tools.

You have no right to act this way with me. I am not the one who almost had sex with Rysa.

"I did not!" He yelled louder than he meant to. Three sparrows in the front yard took wing. "I wasn't going to." Though he would have, if the circumstances had been right. Are right. Will be right. He grimaced, knocking his knuckles against his forehead again. He'd sworn to give her distance but his desire for her hips wouldn't leave him alone.

Dragon pranced sideways, his entire body between Ladon and the vehicle. *She is upset about her mother. The shackles frighten her. She does not understand what it means to be a Fate. You will make her feel less in control if you give in to your base desires.*

Ladon stepped forward and stopped inches from Dragon's snout. He wanted to yell "You're not my sister!" and drop into the van's driver's seat with a bottle in each hand but he sniffed and slapped the beast's neck instead. "She's affecting me. I can't think."

Do not blame Rysa.

"I'm not blaming her!" *We didn't even kiss*, he pushed.

You are acting like the Draki Prime when they were teenagers. Dragon raised his head and blew more flame into the sky. *You want her to stay as much as I do. Yet you behave like an idiot.*

Ladon whipped a pebble down the driveway. It skipped across the gravel before slamming into the mailbox post next to the road. A crow sitting on the box took flight, cawing the avian form of "Idiot!" If the bird had a middle finger, it would have made a grand gesture at Ladon.

He'd awoken this morning with a beautiful woman wrapped around him. Beautiful and without the usual disdain heaped on him by Fates and Shifters.

Though *disdain* wasn't the correct word. They showed more of a reverent and terrible awe. It manifested as the nervous stare of someone afraid of a beating.

All the wars, all the battles. How did he justify five centuries as a Roman *legatus*? All the killing. Sooner or later, the disdain would dart through Rysa's eyes. No matter how he detailed his life, or explained his reasons and the context of his history, it would raise its head and nothing else would matter.

In the eyes of modern women, how could he be anything other than a monster? "She's a Fate. She's not going to stay with us. You have to understand that."

She will do as she pleases. I will not drive her away because I am afraid she will leave. Dragon flicked Ladon's shoulder, his irritation swarming through their connection like a full hive of bees. *We have lived long enough for you to understand this, Human.*

Ladon slapped the beast's neck again. "You're the idiot! I'm realistic." The beast may be right, though. Both dragons had a sense of the world as it was. Better sense than his. Better than the Draki Primes'.

His brother-in-law chuckled and said they saw better than any human. If they couldn't see the world, how could they mimic it?

"She was sleeping right next to me." Wiggling her thigh against his crotch. Ladon rolled his shoulders, stretching the ligaments. *And she smells nice*, he pushed.

Dragon snorted, ignoring him. *I want a bath.*

"Then take one. No one's stopping you." Dirty dragons were surly dragons. Perhaps the beast might stop chastising him if his back wasn't covered with soot. "You look like a giant lint ball when you mimic to invisibility."

Dragon pushed Ladon toward the porch.

Behind them, Harold walked out of the shed carrying two sawhorses. "There are shammies in the garage. I'll get the hose when we're done." He set the sawhorses next to the van but thought better of it. He tapped his chin and moved them to the side, into better light.

Dragon ducked into the vehicle and reappeared with his jug of baby shampoo. *Scrub my ridges.*

"Looks like now's the time. I'll go get it, then." Harold pointed over his shoulder.

Ladon slapped the beast's tail. "Only if you stop complaining." He'd had enough badgering for the day. He stripped off his t-shirt and boots. No use getting his clothes soaked. "You hold still this time. And don't dowse me."

I will dowse you if I want to. You were going to have sex with Rysa.

"Let it go!" Twenty-three centuries and the beast picked now to drive him insane. "She's had enough hurt in her life. I won't add to it."

Harold walked out of the garage, shammies and hose in hand. He hooked the hose to the water feed by the porch. "You better not. Hell hath no fury like a pissed off Fate."

Ladon grabbed the hose with more force than he intended. Fates stewed and planned and vengeance often ended up piercing his left shoulder above his clavicle with an arrow poisoned with the blood of a Burner. Ladon shuddered, wishing he hadn't pulled up *that* memory.

Harold took a step back as he gestured surrender. "I just think you need to talk to her about what it means when the Great Sir takes a shine." He pointed at Dragon.

Ladon sprayed the beast's side, ignoring Harold. Why were women complicated? It used to be that all he had to do was smile and run his finger down an arm and he'd have himself a companion.

Until she got sick of him.

Sooty water splashed off of Dragon's haunch.

The water is cold. The beast rolled away from Ladon's shammy.

"I'm going in." Harold waved in Ladon's general direction. "She's Jani. You treat her well. If you don't, you put all our lives in danger, you son of a bitch." Harold flipped off Ladon as he walked into the house. The screen door slammed behind him.

What did Harold care? The Jani had ignored Marcus for a century and a half and weren't likely to start caring now.

Ladon scrubbed at Dragon's shoulder, harder than he should, and tried to ignore the beast's complaints about the water's temperature. "How many rivers have you bathed in? It's no worse than that." *You're acting like a baby*, he pushed.

I have bathed in many rivers. They were also cold.

The bath would take forever if the beast kept rolling around like a hedgehog. "Why don't you wash yourself? You can hold the shammy."

My ridges are dirty. The beast presented the bumps along his back.

They ran his entire length, interweaving in an intricate plaited pattern.

Ladon had seen both dragons rub trees bare of bark to clean their backs. He sprayed Dragon and scrubbed between two particularly dirty bumps. Best to wash the grumpy beast and save Marcus's oak.

Dragon's coat didn't wave under the water and it appeared duller than it should. Ladon rinsed off the shampoo and the beast's ultra-fine, transparent down rebounded, but not as well as it should have.

"Someone needs a salt scrub."

I need to sleep.

"We'll get you home." And Sister would act like an adult. She'd help protect Rysa so they could rest.

Dragon snorted. *Sister and Sister-Human are stubborn.*

Yes, they were. Thank the gods for Derek. Ladon hoped his brother-in-law could talk some sense into his sister.

Rysa watched through the screen door. The mesh pixelated Dragon's hide as Ladon sprayed water over the beast. Her eyes attempted to compensate but his colors looked like they'd been visually autotuned. A new headache threatened.

Or maybe she had a drumbeat against her temples because of what had happened upstairs. In the shower, phantoms of the dream had played across her skin as the warm water ran down her thighs. She'd caught herself moaning once, her fingers spread on the shower wall tile. If she went outside right now, she'd fall over dead from embarrassment before her foot hit the porch steps.

Outside, Ladon scrubbed soot off Dragon's flank. They bickered. She couldn't hear it, but she felt it through their connection and saw it in Ladon's body language. Rysa watched as Ladon's arm rubbed, then stopped. His shoulders stiffened before he sprayed more water.

Confusion latched onto her proto-headache and clamped tight the muscles at the base of her skull. Her seers knew they'd get physical, and soon, too. It didn't matter if involvement in her issues complicated his life. And Dragon's.

It wasn't like she had impulse control. Running away and talking too much telegraphed her problems. And that stupid bounce she did when she felt enthusiastic made everyone around her sigh. How long before Ladon got sick of watching her do that? Last semester, a guy she liked and who seemed to like her started pinching his lips when she became excited. Two dates, the relationship lasted. Less than a week.

But that was her life. No control.

And her mother abandoned her with a nasty thing in her head—and a very nasty accusation.

She wasn't going to think about it now. It couldn't be true. She'd never—*never*—do anything to hurt anyone. She'd never hurt Ladon and Dragon.

Outside, Ladon walked around Dragon's side. He fluctuated between finding her attractive and stomping around because she was a Fate. Navigating his mood swings was as confusing as navigating her own.

Behind her, Harold cleared his throat. She spun around. He stood in the hallway to the kitchen holding a prescription bottle and a coffee mug. "He may look your age—and honest to God he's acting like a kid right now—but he's not."

She blinked, half pulled from her focus by Harold's comment. Yet she couldn't stop looking out the door. Smooth and agile, Ladon moved like he knew where everything was—his own body, Dragon, the ground, the van, trees, handholds. Everything. She could watch him run, jump, and climb all day long.

"Rysa." Harold had moved next to her when she wasn't paying attention. "Did you hear me?"

"Sorry." She didn't feel hyper, but she did feel overwhelmed and paying attention to anyone other than Ladon was difficult.

"It's okay. With all that's happened, I'd have a hard time focusing, too." He held out a bottle. "Ladon-Dragon brought these in this morning before running light therapy with Marcus." He glanced at the ceiling. "When you and Ladon-Human were still sleeping."

Her meds. They'd grabbed her meds from her kitchen counter? A flash of a memory burst into her vision, then vanished just as fast: Her seers had known at the house that Ladon had tucked them into his pocket.

She stared at the bottle. How was she supposed to get a handle on using her abilities? She didn't know if what she knew was something she should *know*. "They rescued my meds?"

Harold shrugged and the pills inside the bottle rattled. "Looks that way."

The damned cuff smacked his wrist when she took her meds. "Sorry!"

He patted the back of her hand and handed over the mug. "Water. He'll be done with the Great Sir soon." He nodded toward Ladon and Dragon. "Marcus is mediating. He's looking for who's behind all this." He frowned when he glanced at the hallway. "I wish he wouldn't."

Rysa opened her meds and downed a pill. Maybe they'd help calm her seers. They helped her attention, even if they did make her nauseated. She figured it was a trade-off she'd have to live with, if she was going to function in the modern world.

She pointed with the mug toward Marcus's study/ bedroom down the hallway. "He doesn't have to look." But all she saw was fire. If they were going to get answers, Marcus needed to find them, not her.

Harold didn't respond. He took the mug and stood for a moment, watching Ladon and Dragon. "Go out and give him a hand. He's been sulking since he came downstairs. Seeing your lovely face will make him feel better." Harold raised the mug and winked before vanishing into the kitchen.

She set down her meds. Outside, Ladon swaggered around Dragon.

He jumped against the corner of the van, one bare foot hitting the bumper and the other about halfway up the vehicle, a shammy in hand. A twist and he landed gently—how, Rysa could not fathom—with one foot on Dragon's shoulder and a knee on the base of his neck.

When he leaned over, lovingly scrubbing the beast's back ridges, the sun hit the water clinging to his shoulders.

Rysa moaned. She couldn't stop it before it passed her tongue and she wasn't sure she wanted to, anyway. Every inch of her skin tingled. Her breasts wanted to be touched. Her thighs pressed together. Her lips parted.

The dream flitted through her senses once again.

She pinched her eyes closed. How the hell was she supposed to handle this? Did all new Fates go through the future and past interfering with the present? Or was this just because she was singular? Hopefully,

Marcus could help.

"It's no colder than it was ten minutes ago!" Ladon yelled as he dropped off the beast's back.

Dragon grabbed the shammy. He wiped his head and his chest, his big tail flicking across the gravel.

"Fine!" Ladon stalked away and stopped next to his t-shirt and boots. "Don't waste the water."

They'd started bickering again.

Dragon flicked one arm over the top of his head, his six fingers forming the American Sign Language 'V' hand-shape with his palm toward his head. Then he flicked his wrist over, rotating the 'V' upward.

The door banged shut behind Rysa, the loud clap echoing off the van and the garage as she skidded across the porch to the top step. "He called you an idiot!" she yelled. "Dragon signed *idiot* at you!" Bouncing, she ran to the gravel, Harold's too-big sweats sliding down her hips. "What other signs do you know?" Her hands worked as she spoke the words.

Could Dragon sign? She hitched up the sweats as she ran barefoot across the gravel. "Ouch!" A stone poked her heel and she grabbed her foot, wincing.

You can sign? the beast signed. Vivid, wonderful colors and reflections of place and proportion and emotions washed into her perception. Her entire body responded, her back arching, and a moan ripping from her throat. She dropped to her knees on the gravel, stunned by the intimacy cascading over her mind.

17

Overwhelmed by the intensity flooding from Dragon, Rysa teetered against Ladon when he helped her to her feet. She glanced up—all the depth and excitement moving across the beast's hide also filled Ladon's expression. Dragon's lights danced on his human's skin.

Do you know many signs? Dragon ducked to the other side of Ladon. *I will teach you more. I know most signs.* He ducked back. *Derek signs with me. Marcus remembers some, but Harold does not.*

Ladon grinned. "He's excited."

You are Rysa. Dragon combined the 'R' hand-shape with the sign for 'laughter.'

"Is that my new name sign?"

Yes.

Joy shot from the beast. A tactile sense of a color flashed: wine, roses, the warmth of a fireplace, moved across her skin like a smooth, tightly woven velvet.

It merged into Ladon's fingers as they danced over her hips.

Her body responded again, parts heating and limbs wanting to entangle with both the man and the beast. If Ladon started massaging like he did when he found her, she'd have an orgasm right here on the gravel. A full-on, blinding orgasm like Tom never gave her, fully clothed with this man she'd just met.

She shuffled backward, a blush rising up her neck, and stopped about three feet away, her hands smoothing over her thighs on their own.

Ladon's gaze dropped to her hips.

"Don't do that!" He'd stare at her body and distract her from everything but his.

His eyes traveled up, stopping at her breasts.

But he didn't ogle. He looked at her as if she was the most beautiful woman in the world and by God he wasn't going to miss *that*.

He stood holding his t-shirt, bare-chested and mouth-watering, wearing an expression that said all he wanted to do was to pick her up and kiss her and touch her body and say how sorry he was for running out mad.

She couldn't be angry with him. His reactions were her fault. She'd brought the inevitability of sex to the forefront this morning, not him.

Rysa closed her eyes and turned around. "Quit distracting me!" How was she supposed to pay attention to what needed to be done? "Put on your stupid shirt."

A chuckle mixed with the sounds of him pulling the shirt over his head. Then his arms enclosed her waist, his chest and shoulders against her back. "I'm sorry. I didn't realize I was distracting. And here I thought Dragon was—"

She pulled away, holding up her hands. They couldn't do this. No more of him stroking her waist with his gentle-but-firm touch. She'd melt. She'd lick the spot below his diamond of chest hair the inevitability of sex would become a reality.

She'd ruin everything.

They needed to cut off the cuffs and find her mom and figure out what to do about the Burners and—

Hurt played through his eyes and his neck tensed. But he caught it and his expression turned stony. Then he caught that look, too.

She shuffled her bare feet on the gravel. "We don't know each other," she whispered. They didn't, no matter how entwined they felt.

His neck tensed again. "You're right. We don't know each other." He jammed his hands into his pockets. "I should think before being so forward. I have no right to touch you as if our time's been decided."

He stepped back. Only a couple of inches, but it felt as if he'd moved into a different time zone. "I apologize. Again."

Nodding, she wrapped her arms around her chest. She felt cold, like the sun had gone under storm clouds. Rain fell on her life at the same time she rejected the only umbrella available.

Human is sorry, Dragon signed.

"Dragon!" She'd been so distracted by Ladon's closeness that she'd forgotten the beast's questions. "I'm fluent. I took the translator's exam last year. I was going to work for Disability Services but my attention issues got in the way."

Rysa can sign with me. The beast knocked Ladon's shoulder. *She is fluent*. He knocked Ladon's shoulder again.

He shrugged, ignoring the beast, and pointed at her wrists. "Burndust makes metal brittle so Dragon's been testing the chains. He thinks he can heat a link and make you a bracelet."

Dragon signed *yes*.

"But we cut you a length you can carry just in case." He pointed at the sweats, then over his shoulder. "It's in the van."

She looked down. No pockets.

"I'll find a pouch. Or we'll make one. Don't worry."

He'd stuck his hands in his pockets again. And he watched her wide-eyed, like a puppy.

"Thank you," she said.

He nodded, a quick grin appearing then vanishing off his lips. "Let's get those off." He motioned to the side of the van. "I found the hacksaw. Don't use it much. It was under the theodolite, of all places." He shrugged again as Dragon nuzzled her hair. "Next to the duct tape."

"Wait." She stared at the back of the van. Tripods, a theodolite, a compass, and other surveying instruments she couldn't identify littered Dragon's blankets. Distracted again, she stepped forward, peering around the beast's bulk. "Why do you have a theodolite?"

The old-school brass and steel instrument rested next to the door. Sunlight hit the level bars and green glinted off the glass tubes. The love child of a microscope and a pirate's spyglass, its gyroscopic wheels gave it a vaguely science fiction aura.

Ladon walked backward toward the van. "There's more to life than killing Burners. Sometimes we need to measure elevations. Those cabins in Jackson Hole don't pick their own views."

The theodolite, the tripods, the licensing number on the back corner of the van—Ladon and Dragon worked a job. "You survey?" She bounced a little, unable to stop herself. "In Wyoming? In the mountains? I'm studying natural resources management. Fragile ecosystems. Caves mostly. I want to go to the *Caverna de las Brujas* in Argentina. My dad's from Cordoba. Are there caves where you live? My parents took me to Carlsbad when I was a kid and—"

She stopped midsentence when he smiled. It wasn't some "aren't you cute" or "that's nice" smile. His entire face smiled. His mouth, his cheeks, his eyes all drew upward. Every guy she'd gone out with grinned and looked at her breasts, running through their mental calculations weighing horniness verses uneasiness. Not Ladon. He smiled because of her.

When she was a kid, she'd walk off grids in the backyard and pretend they were different ecosystems with different plants and animals for her to explore. She'd asked her dad for a theodolite to help her mark elevations, but he said he'd have to look up what it was first. Then he moved out and she never saw him again.

Ladon had a real theodolite in the back of his van. He wasn't just some god sent to earth to kill Burners. He was a real man with a real job and real skills beyond fighting and he could teach her how to measure the angles of the land.

"Will you show me how to use the theodolite?"

The smile turned into something deeper. Dragon flashed behind him and Ladon laid his fingers on the beast's neck. A complex wave blazed across Dragon's hide. It overrode her pain and anxiety. They all stood on the gravel, Dragon nuzzling Ladon, then her, then Ladon again.

"Yes." He didn't say anything else. Didn't repeat the word. He offered a simple yes that filled the space between them. Yes, beautiful. Yes, for you.

Yes.

"Let's cut off those cuffs." He extended his hand and nodded toward the plank suspended between the sawhorses.

She sat on the back of the van while Ladon held the shackle. He sawed, his gaze never leaving the line he cut through the resin binding the cuff together. Dragon lounged on top of the van, the talons of one of his claw-hands dangling over the edge and his big head resting on the other. He looked quite clean and comfortable with the sun bouncing off his shimmering hide.

"Not many people know what a theodolite is." The saw ground into the joint and filings scattered across the plank. "Maybe you can work with us when you're done with your schooling. My contracts are always asking about environmental management and water features." He stopped and blew on the cuff.

"I'd like that." A job, in this economy, and one in the mountains. A smile bubbled up and it took all her effort not to bounce. Which she shouldn't do, anyway. The med was giving her a tummy ache.

A bad one, too, probably because she'd missed her dose yesterday. She rubbed her midsection with her free hand.

Ladon yanked the cuff apart and she lifted out her wrist. The burns weren't bad. Her skin looked sunburned. When she unwrapped the bandages before her shower, the bites had healed to scrapes, too.

"You heal faster than any Fate we've ever met." Ladon worked at the other cuff until it popped off, too.

"I've always healed fast. I don't get sick, either, though I do get side effects sometimes." She rubbed her stomach. "My mom said it was because of my hyperactivity. My body's speedy."

"You okay? You look pale." He lifted her leg to the plank.

Being both a spaz and a wuss wouldn't help anything. She sat up straight. "It'll pass. I took one of my meds."

Ladon positioned her leg, careful of her knee, and rotated the cuff so the joint was up.

"Thank you, by the way. For helping me. And finding my meds."

Ladon nodded toward Dragon. "He found them."

The beast's hand dropped down and he signed *Yes*.

Ladon chuckled as he worked on an ankle cuff. "We've been watching for Burner activity. They've been quiet." He dusted the filings off her foot.

She nodded toward the house. "Marcus is meditating. Maybe he'll give us some direction."

The cuff popped off and he switched to her other ankle. "Your safety comes first." He nodded for emphasis. "We'll get the visions under control. He'll help."

"The world's going to burn." It dropped off her tongue and slapped aside the brief moments of happiness she'd felt earlier.

Ladon set the saw next to her ankle. "You don't know that. It could mean anything." He glanced up at Dragon's perch on top of the van as he returned to sawing the cuff. "We don't believe it anyway. You're one of the best people we've ever met."

He didn't know that, either. He couldn't. They'd just met.

Dragon's head and hands swung over the side of the van. *We know. We are connected.*

Ladon cut through the last cuff, but didn't pull it apart. He glanced up at Dragon and a pulse moved between them.

A wave of nausea pulsed through her gut, mimicking their energy flow.

"He's going to get the piece he cut earlier. So you're not without your talisman." Ladon looked sad, like he'd just told a child she'd never be an astronaut. Or a firefighter. Or a decent human being.

The beast hopped off the side of the van and disappeared around the front.

Ladon pulled the final cuff apart.

Pain ratcheted from her kidneys and roared through every joint in her body. A gasp pushed between her lips.

She leaned over the planks and vomited up her med, the water, and the little bit of bagel she'd eaten after getting out of the shower. Her body rejected what it once tolerated. Her nasty did not like stim meds. Not at all.

Harold yelled from the house. Something about Marcus having a seizure. He wouldn't wake up. The words ran past Rysa's ears so fast she couldn't catch them.

She fell off the bumper and her arm scraped along the gravel. Her shoulder hit hard. Her nasty growled, coupling itself to Marcus's ability, and she felt the Parcae sickness eating away at his body. He'd done so much for her. She couldn't let him die this way.

"Dragon!" His name croaked from her throat.

18

When Rysa was little, before school lasted the whole day and she played on the patio under the olive tree for hours with her plastic forest and her animals, she'd hear the neighbor's dog bark. Huge and black as the monsters her father scared away with her nightlight, he'd growl and snarl. But she wasn't afraid. He couldn't get over the wall between her yard and his.

Until the day he did.

His front paws hit the top of the painted blocks, his teeth bare, his back paws scraping away chunks of concrete. He tore for her and her toy horses and the juice box Mommy gave her for a snack.

Her mouth opened, but no words, no sounds, came out. Just her little body needing to throw up and run and curl into a ball all at the same time.

That's how Rysa felt when the vision's jaws clamped down and she screamed "Dragon!"

Only desert, dust, and low buildings the same beige-gray as the earth existed here, in this isolated bubble of time. The sky burned as blue as a wall of plasma flame. The square fence of razor wire could rip apart anything that might climb over it. Unknowable boundaries cut it off from the universe, but somehow Rysa got in.

No insects buzzed. The sun scorched and Rysa's skin should prickle, but this unreal world made no noise and laid down no touch and she'd lost her sense of direction. Up, down, left, right, all swung around her like a carnival ride.

Yet blood stained the ground. A hand lay in the dirt next to her feet. Burners gorged themselves on a five course Shifter meal.

Behind her, deep in the courtyard, two SUVs, their doors flung wide, sat at an angle to one another.

Ping.

A sound.

They were out of sync, the tan vehicle faster than the black. *Ping Ping.*

She'd moved from silent visions to talkies. But the sounds swung with the unhinged directions and made her want to vomit up not just her guts, but her lungs and her heart, too.

On the other side of the courtyard, a lean man with hair auburn like Rysa's, eyes blue like the sky, thundered a seer through the courtyard. It felt familiar, like her mother's chimes-in-the-storm, but it blasted forward. This man's seer rode a train into the future, and like a train's whistle, it dropped low as it moved away, drawn out into hammers beating on metal in the center of a thunderstorm.

A dark-haired, dark-eyed woman knelt at his feet. Her seer shifted higher, compressed as it approached the present. Hers, cymbals.

Faustus. Ismene. Her mother's brother and sister. Her uncle. Her aunt. People she'd never met, but she knew, deep down, were family.

L'avenir et le passé du Premier Jani. 'The future and the past of the Jani Prime.'

French? Rysa's gut tangled into a tighter knot. If French froze her in place inside this world whipping in funhouse circles, could she find Marcus?

Ping. Ping. Ping.

Faustus slapped Ismene and she cried out, but no sound left her mouth. Rysa read Faustus's lips: *My sister is a whore.*

Ping.

A whisper in her ear: "*Qui est Premier Jani Triade maintenant, mon Père?*" 'Who is the Jani Prime Triad now, Father?'

Rysa jumped, but nobody stood next to her. Yet they were here, invisible like Dragon, two brothers and their sister.

Family, but not her uncle and aunt. These three would have been consigned to the kid's table with her during holidays, whispering in French, all snarky, because they were older.

Her cousins. And they were better.

Power oozed from the French words whispered in her ear. These three would steal her toys and tear her holiday dress because they could, and no one dared say a word about it.

These three, they knew how to wage war. They filtered fate through strategy, and they were not to be trifled with.

Her cousins—*the* Jani triad. *Les Enfants de Guerre*. The Jani Prime wasn't so Prime after all.

Faustus slapped Ismene again. *Whore.* But it was the same slap, replayed. This place was an afterimage, a memory. Rysa watched what she didn't know how to access later—the moment her mother's triad died.

"*Je l'ai cousu.*" Next to Rysa's ear, the female laughed. 'I stitched it.'

"*Les Brûleurs sont illisibles. Papa ne sait pas.*" 'Burners are unreadable. Father didn't know.' The future-seeing brother kissed Rysa's cheek.

Rysa screamed, but no sound left her throat. She staggered, but the vision twisted into hot reds and ripping teeth. *Ping.*

"*Nous allons la trouver, cousine. Celle que nous avons manquée. Puis elle ira* à son *triade.*" 'We will find her, cousin. The one we missed. Then your mother will go to her triad.'

Chicago, the attacks in Wisconsin, were all inciting events designed to throw the present into chaos and force the last member of the Jani Prime out of hiding. Had Rysa been a side effect like the nausea her pill gave her? Was she to be something *Les Enfants de Guerre* threw up all over the world?

"*Oui.*" 'Yes.'

The vision swung. The slaps reset. The pings grew louder.

Noise exploded into this unreal world. A severed arm hit the side of the tan SUV with a dull smack. It slid down, wet and sucking, and thudded into the dust.

Burner giggles echoed from the four corners of the enclosure.

Rysa grasped her ears, trying to block it out. Too loud, too grating, she felt as if she'd see the spots again. But this time, when they popped, they'd rupture her eardrums.

She knew the real intent of locking her to the Burners: It removed the threat of her Prime seers. One *Enfant* laughed. Revulsion wafted off another. They'd deal with her mother. Then they'd deal with her. They were, after all, the children of war.

The female's fingertip touched Rysa's nose. "*Imaginez que vous êtes en sécurité*." 'Pretend that you are safe.'

But she wasn't. They'd find a way in. They'd rip open her soul and let in cockroaches to suck it dry.

Ping Ping. Ping. Marcus. Where was Marcus?

Ping Ping Ping. The dings erupted into full music and the resonant beauty of the past filling the courtyard, a bubble of safety between her, the blood, and her cousins.

The vision wavered. Faustus and Ismene froze in mid-slap. The SUVs flickered. Right next to Rysa, so close she heard their heartbeats, one brother held Marcus by the neck.

This brother, the past-seer, flinched. He pressed his temple. "*Bâtard. Je vais percer votre intestin, vieil homme.*" 'Bastard. I'll pierce your gut, old man.'

Marcus, young and handsome and not at all an old man, his thick black hair cut short and his body lean and strong, his eyes bright with intelligence, grinned as he grasped her fingers.

The past-seeing brother of *Les Enfants de Guerre* looked down at their joined hands. Fear registered in his eyes.

Dust swirled. The wind howled, a deafening scream reverberating between the buildings. The vision of Faustus and Ismene hiccupped.

Marcus stood to the side of her uncle, his head low, his iron eyes predatory.

But Marcus held her hand.

When the dog attacked, when she was a child, her mom stepped between Rysa and the black hate hurdling across the yard. Her dad caught the animal in mid-lunge, his big arms contracting under his shirt. Both her parents danced and the dog slammed against the concrete patio. It broke and a wet crack echoed off the yard's fence.

The dog whimpered once.

Now, in her vision, talons slammed *Les Enfants de Guerre* into the dirt. They sloshed, wet, and for the moment, broken. Wherever their real bodies squatted forcing this attack, all three vomited.

But they didn't whimper.

The Marcus holding her hand touched her cheek. "Thank you."

19

Rysa's scream echoed through the house. Ladon held her on his lap, his arms tight around her shoulders to contain her thrashing limbs. Above her, Dragon smashed against the ceiling. Plaster fell, white chunks dropping into her eyes and Ladon's hair.

"Dragon!" She pitched off Ladon's legs, "We're out of the vision! It's okay. Stop!" He'd smashed the War Babies. He'd gotten them out. He'd followed her into her blackout and pulled both her and Marcus out of its depths.

The beast calmed and his body draped over the couch. He touched her cheek and her shoulder. A big eye looked her over, his head so close she breathed his heat.

"Marcus guided him into the vision." Ladon's entire body leaned into hers, a shield against any new threat. "We heard French." A growl rolled from both the man and the beast. "The War Babies." Another growl, louder than the one before.

A wave blasted between Ladon and Dragon. The beast roared.

"Where are they?" Ladon let go and slammed his fist into the floor. A crack echoed through the room when a floorboard shattered. "They're dead!"

"They killed my aunt and uncle and they sent the Burners after my mom. Everything that's happened was to make sure that they'd be the Prime triad." How could anyone knowingly unleash so much death?

They'd bound Rysa to the Burners so she couldn't become a threat to their power, but they didn't understand what they'd unleashed.

The Ambusti Prime. She was a thermonuclear bomb they'd accidently

detonated because their talisman—their filter—was war. And war justified
all weapons.

She'd pant if she didn't hold it together. Pant like some terrified
poodle and fall onto all fours, her tail between her legs.

Ladon's focus shifted suddenly from the room to her. He ignored her
commands for distance. Ignored them and wrapped his body around hers the
way Dragon had when she activated.

She scrunched against his chest.

"They won't hurt you." His words rumbled through the room, low
and vibrating as they mixed with a deafening growl from Dragon.

Marcus appeared in the hallway leaning on Harold's shoulder. He
shuffled, his steps unsure. "I don't know where they are. Not physically.
They could still be in France, for all I know."

Harold's face reddened. "You let them in on purpose? You had
a seizure!" He helped Marcus to the chair but kicked at Ladon before
Marcus's backside hit the cushion. "Get out!"

Ladon caught Harold's leg. "You touch her and I will snap your knee.
You will shriek for months. Do you understand, *pedes*? No one touches her."

Harold had been kicking at Ladon's ribs, not Rysa's arm. But Ladon
didn't care.

"Ladon, let go." He'd break Harold's leg with the sheer pressure of
his grip. Gently, she pulled his hand away.

Harold staggered back. "Don't come back here! You kill him too and
I'll hunt you, you bastard! I don't care if I'm a normal, I'll slice you open
and—"

"Harold!" Marcus sat forward in the chair. "This is not the Dracos'
doing. I set myself out as bait. I knew they couldn't resist." Pain radiated
from him like he'd been stabbed.

But Marcus gripped the chair arm with the same conviction Rysa had
seen in his younger self's eyes while they were in the vision. The sickness
might take its due, but he'd stand against the War Babies until the day he
died.

"Only they'd have the gall to inflict the damage they did in order to
force Mira out of hiding."

"You knew it was them?" Ladon hit the floor again. Another crack reverberated through the living room. "Why didn't you say?"

Marcus closed his eyes. "Daniel predicted they'd unleash ruin on the world."

Rysa stiffened. Her. He meant that they'd unleash *her*. She'd bring ruin down on everyone.

Marcus pointed at her. "Only one Prime per family." He waved his hand in the air.

He didn't mean the burning. He focused in on her cousins' original intent—getting her mother. It took them twenty years to cut through her mom's cloak. Now they wouldn't let up until they accomplished their goal.

Marcus's hand shook. "Abilene, Texas, twenty-one years ago. *Les Enfants de Guerre* destroyed a Shifter medical facility. Set Burners on the place. No one knew that they'd murdered their own father and aunt."

Harold knelt next to the chair and touched Marcus's back. "The healers stopped helping after that."

Marcus's fingers jittered over the torque around his neck. Three cables braided around each other, each strung with a dragon hammered from entwined gold and silver. The beasts lined up across Marcus's throat, tail to snout. "Ladon-Human divided our insignia. Fashioned us each equal parts. I've worn all three since my brothers passed."

Both his hands shook. "*Les Enfants de Guerre* activated on a dagger. A terrible piece, said to have belonged to Alexander the Great himself." Marcus stroked one of the little dragons. "I saw Daniel." With a deep inhale, he sat tall in the chair, his head held high. "It's my time. This was fated long ago."

The other Marcus in the vision had been his identical triplet brother, Daniel. But he'd died a century and a half ago.

Rysa flew across the room. This couldn't be happening. She couldn't cause Marcus's death. Seeing Daniel wasn't a sign he should die. It couldn't be. "That doesn't mean—"

He touched her shoulder. "You must go. They will protect you." He nodded toward the door.

Ladon stood and dusted his knees. "Go south. I will call Dmitri."

"We will stay here," Marcus said.

"No! You go south! Dmitri will help." Ladon pointed at Harold.

"You take him to Branson. You pack all your weapons and you get on the interstate. Stay with Dmitri's clan until Dragon and I grind that unholy triad into paste."

Harold ignored him. "Damn it, don't say it's your time." He pushed at Rysa but she wrapped her arms around Marcus's chest.

She tried to hold the sobs in, to keep them under control, but it didn't work. They jumped out of her chest. "I won't let you die!"

"Harold!" Ladon bellowed.

Harold pulled away, his gaze darting between Marcus, Dragon, and Ladon. Skin reddening, he opened his mouth to yell something, but Dragon knocked his shoulder.

"We cannot protect you. You will be in more danger if you come with us. Go now, while they're distracted." Ladon extended his hand to help Harold stand.

"What…" Dazed, Marcus blinked, but Rysa didn't feel his seer. He waved between Harold and Ladon. "It will be fine. Rysa, do you see it? Everything will be fine."

She wiped away tears. "Fine?" He wasn't making sense.

Harold looked between Ladon's extended hand and Marcus's face. Inhaling sharply, he nodded and gripped Ladon's wrist.

Ladon hauled him to his feet.

"…Yes…" Confusion washed over Marcus's features. "Shifters." He pointed at Ladon.

Harold touched Marcus's forehead. "He's got a fever." He looked up at Ladon. "Dmitri damned well better help."

What did she do? She'd hurt him.

"It is time for you to leave." Marcus gripped Rysa's arm. "Be careful."

20

Ladon, phone in hand, watched Harold pull out of the driveway. He took Marcus south, to Dmitri's clan, their old truck crammed full with as many of their belongings as Dragon could fit inside. He'd put Harold's swords under the driver's seat, along with two of his guns.

Dmitri yelled vulgarities through the speaker of Ladon's whining smartphone. Ladon glowered at the phone as if his stern look could worm its way through the device. Threatening did no good. Nor was it necessary. Dmitri understood what was at stake and he'd provide the support Ladon required. "Are you done?"

The Russian fell quiet.

"And find Sandro Torres." He hit the off button without finishing the conversation. The War Babies were as likely to go after Rysa's father as Marcus. Just to be thorough. Just to cause as much agony as they could.

Rysa waited on the bumper of the van, half a shackle in her lap. The beast concentrated his flame and heated a link he'd cut from the chains—his third attempt—to a dull glow. A couple of taps and it rounded to fit her wrist, this time without shattering. She paid no heed, staring at the now empty porch swing, her chin in her hands, silent.

The beast nuzzled her side. An ache vibrated to Ladon, a brief flitting through her ever-present connection.

Ladon wanted to offer comfort, but boundaries needed to be reestablished. Respect shown. So he stayed back.

Dragon quenched her new talisman bracelet in water from the hose. She slid it onto her wrist when the beast held it out, her face expressionless. Then she handed him the shackle half and turned away, her wrist and the burndust surrounding it dropping against her thigh.

When she came out of the Texas vision, she'd allowed him to trace his fingers over her skin, though she'd declared a need for distance. And she'd calmed his fury before it erupted onto Harold, for which he was eternally grateful.

She'd helped him as much as Dragon had helped her.

He tossed the phone into the van. They'd find Mira. His gut told him she wasn't yet dead—the Burners wouldn't harm her until her system cleared of dust, and like Rysa, no Fate could see her. It'd take careful tracking, but he and Dragon would find her before the War Babies.

He'd give Rysa back her mother, alive and able to help her daughter gain control her escalating abilities.

When Marcus guided Dragon into her vision, the beast heard the grinding, hellish fire that scorched her mind with every seer flare. Heard the noise, seen the overwhelming detail, felt her world spinning.

Mira had not lied—the pain worsened.

And now, every twitch or hiccup she made raked Ladon's mind, body, and soul. When she crawled into the van and buckled her seatbelt, she stared out the window. A flat echo of defeat bounced from her to Ladon and Dragon.

"Rysa?"

She turned in her seat, glancing at him, but her gaze dropped away. He wanted to lift her up and settle with her in the back of the van, offering the touch she needed until this cloud lifted. But his muscles tensed. She'd feel his desire to rain a Roman retribution onto her cousins. It would drop from Dragon's talons like acid from a Burner's finger.

And she'd push him away.

"Are you ready to go?"

She nodded and looked out the window again.

The beast curled his neck around the seat and laid his head on her lap. Dragon offered the comfort Ladon could not.

Instead, he drove.

They stopped in Mankato. Her new talisman bracelet clinked against the window when she stroked a finger across the glass.

He pointed at a big box store on the other side of the parking lot. Her t-shirt and sweats twisted around her body and she looked uncomfortable. And Dragon wanted food. "Do you want to go in?" Shopping might cheer her up.

"All I see is fire." Her forehead pressed against the window. The pressure made the skin around her eyes lighten. "My seers whip around and I don't know what to do."

"Stay with us." The words surprised him—she needed to stay. She was too vulnerable otherwise. But they snuck out, an impulsive flaring of a desire both he and Dragon had wrestled with since the beast laid her on his blankets in Minneapolis.

All Ladon's muscles cinched with a sudden fear that her back would stiffen as it had when he touched her hair. Or the way it did when he'd wrapped his arm around her waist and leaned against her body.

Her reactions had yelled volumes even as her swaying hips whispered enticements. He still felt confused.

But now, if she batted away his words, the world would deflate again. Colors would separate and lay down, unwilling to fight or care. He and Dragon would go back to Wyoming, sleep, and listen to the echoes inside their home.

Her breath fogged the glass. "I want to help find my mom. If they find her first, they'll kill her. When the dust wears off and she's visible again, you won't know where to go without a Fate to help."

A shallow inhale rasped into his throat. She didn't say "go away" or "I'm done with you."

You are a Prime Fate, Dragon signed. *We will listen to your instructions. Correct, Human?*

Ladon exhaled, thankful for Dragon's quick answer. "Yes."

She sat up tall and a little bounce straightened her back. "Really?"

Seeing her bounce was more of a reward than any thank-you. Every time her body moved in cheer or excitement, her eyes took on a glint of the openness he'd seen when she was in her visions. The hint made it real, and maybe, if he was lucky, obtainable.

He wanted to take her hand so she'd feel that they spoke the truth, but he pulled the key from the ignition instead. "Of course. You're smart and you have the best heart of any Fate we've ever met, better even than the

Draki Prime." More of his words toppled out.

She blinked, her lips parting. His neck tightened and he looked away. When he glanced back, she greeted him with the most beautiful smile he'd ever seen.

His world slammed tight around her. He saw only her face, heard only her voice.

A shudder ran up her spine and she shivered. A small blush crept up her neck. "Oh." She looked away, not saying anything. But a hint of her smile reflected off the glass next to her face.

He'd made her feel good. Not with a touch but with a soft moment. He'd reversed some of the hell which had dropped into her life.

Ladon wanted to do it again. To kiss the delicate skin at the nape of her neck, to whisper reassurance and hold her until the fear lessened. He wanted her to know, more than anything else, that she'd be okay.

Dragon pulled forward, blocking Ladon from Rysa. *Do not think about sex*, he pushed. Then he backed up, curling a warning flame at Ladon.

I must vent before entering the building, the beast signed, so Rysa understood. *I do not want to overheat.* More flames curled as he cooled himself.

Rysa tapped the dashboard, obviously grateful for the distraction. "So that's why he breathes fire."

"One of the reasons, yes."

She peered at Ladon for a long moment. He held still so as not to jolt her again, no matter how much he wanted to push aside the stray hair on her forehead.

"Let's get him some food." She popped open her door and stretched her legs.

She'd rolled the waist of Harold's ridiculous sweats over and they sat like a thick belt around her hips. He walked around the front of the van, his gaze following the line of her waist.

"Dragon's right…" Rysa's eyes closed and she pointed off to the side. "There!"

Ladon chuckled. Burner chaos might cloud her abilities, but she was still Prime. "Very good. When you're confident about him, you can practice on me."

She slapped his arm. A delectable pout pushed out her lower lip. "Like I could miss *you*." Then she bounced away, following the beast.

If she had stayed next to him, he would have pulled her close, distance be damned.

She hitched up Harold's too-long sweats, her hips sashaying as she passed through the sliding doors. Dragon scaled the wall and scrambled along the girders overhead and the giant cutout bumblebees and sunglasses and picnic tables hanging from the ceiling swayed.

"How long can he stay up there?"

Her jaw's perfect line invited a kiss to the delicate spot under her earlobe. "Thirty-two minutes." But he stayed back, careful not to damage the new trust they were building. He felt buoyed by the new-but-delicate confidence she radiated now that she realized they wanted her help.

"That's not very long."

The incessant whine of the cell phones in the store would drive him out before then, anyway. He pulled a cart and twirled it with a dash of grandeur, to entertain Rysa. An older woman with a big bosom watched from the produce section, an apple in her hand and a scowl on her face. Ladon winked.

"Food first?" The beginnings of a new smile threatened as she watched him maneuver the cart.

I want oranges.

She glanced up at the ceiling, her brow furrowing. "Does he eat anything other than oranges?" She set two big sacks of the fruit in the cart. "Oh! Cara Caras." She snapped open a thin film bag. "They're at the end of the season, but they still look good."

Did she hear me?

Ask her. Ladon watched her lovely fingers pick up another Cara Cara fruit. She looked at it, then set it down.

I do not think so.

Besides Ladon and Sister, no one heard either of the dragons, except for one Shifter, centuries ago. Rysa didn't respond. Maybe it was her seers.

I will continue trying.

She waved a Cara Cara under Ladon's nose. "These are the best oranges. He'll like them."

"Anything you pick out, he will like." Dragon would eat kumquats if Rysa asked him to.

I dislike kumquats and kiwis. If Rysa asked, I would not eat them.

Yes, you would.

"You need to eat, too." Her shoulders squared as she set the fruit in the cart. "Don't think I haven't noticed." This time, a finger waved under his nose.

He jammed his hands into his pockets to keep from stroking her arm. "I don't get hungry when I'm fighting."

"Well, you're not fighting right now, are you? And vodka and moldy pizza don't count." She pointed at the leafy vegetables. "Spinach? Kale for Dragon? Maybe some salads. Do you good."

I told you the drinking would upset her.

Ladon frowned at the ceiling.

"He's chastising you, isn't he?" She dropped all manner of salad into the cart, along with a loaf of bread. "Come on. I need clothes."

In Women's Apparel, she yanked a pair of jeans off a rack.

"Won't fit." He pointed at a different display. "Those." He'd run his hands over her hips enough to have a good sense of her proportions. This time, he gripped the handle on the cart.

Her eyebrow rose. "Is that so?" The wrong jeans went back onto the rack as she asked.

"Yes." It took considerable effort to keep his gaze from dropping to her belly. He tossed a couple of t-shirts into the cart instead.

Color touched her cheeks as she looked away. She'd been blushing a lot since they stopped. He wanted to nibble on her ear and feel the heat against his lips, but also to stand between her and all that caused her discomfort.

The jeans he'd pointed out landed on top of the shirts. "Not just black stuff, Mr. Monochrome." A couple more colorful items fell into the basket. "I need underwear."

An image of her in thin underthings jumped into his mind and he clenched his throat, fighting a groan.

"Intimate Apparel is over there. So is Footwear." She pointed, either oblivious to his effort or choosing to ignore it. "Could you get me some shoes? Size 8. And socks. But not all black ones." She gave him a little shove.

He walked away, doing his best to focus on his task. She couldn't stomp a Burner with anything they had here, so he chose garish athletic shoes.

Perhaps the new clothes would make her feel better. Her fingers gliding over the skin of his shoulders would make him feel better. Her kisses would calm his raging mind. He'd do the same for her. Take his time. Find all the spots on her neck and along her rib cage and evaporate her anxiety like dew from her skin.

You are thinking too much about sex.

Ladon glanced at the ceiling. Dragon refracted, his tail swishing when he moved across the girders. The beast didn't want Rysa to feel discomfort. Not from the hell chasing her and most definitely not from any action on Ladon's part.

Across the aisle, she tossed several bra and panty sets in a variety of styles into the basket. The lace shimmered through a rainbow of hues as if she'd decided to wear Dragon against her skin.

Stunning Rysa, the Fate with a heart as beautiful as her body. She deserved all the respect he and the beast could provide.

At the registers, Ladon packed the food into two bags as Rysa put her clothes in two others. In the lot, Dragon crawled into the back of the van and she handed over their purchases. Ladon leaned against the door, watching her stretch and twist to transfer the bags.

"Aren't you going to help?"

"You're done." He twirled the cart and gave it a shove toward a corral. It hit true and straight, nesting into another.

"Show-off." Her lovely lips pinched together, a tad bit of mischievousness twisting them ever so slightly.

Dragon snorted.

Rysa reached for the beast, her fingers spread for a gentle touch as they moved across the van's threshold toward Dragon's head. "You're a show-off too, you big, wonderful lug."

Ladon reached for her. He reached to lift her up, to hold her close.

To give her everything she needed to hold onto the happiness he saw on her face.

"Rysa," he whispered as his fingers glided past her talisman, up her forearm and to her elbow.

Her gaze dropped to his fingers. Her face slacked. Shock from her seers hit him hard—he shouldn't have touched her. She must be seeing him as forward again.

He let go. "I'm sorry. Beautiful—"

Her abilities flared across the parking lot, a combined music so breathtaking it broke into Ladon's vision. In the van, Dragon rolled over, his hide sparking.

"Oh...." She tripped, her hand grabbing for Ladon's shirt. "What's happening...?"

The siphoning locked on and they staggered against the bumper. The edges of the world fuzzed.

Control it, Dragon pushed.

Their flow sputtered. Ladon forced air into his lungs and steadied his mind so Dragon's attempt to moderate her vision didn't unravel.

"Rysa?" He pulled her into the back and laid her down, then slammed the door. He touched her arms, her hands, assessing. She felt cold again, like she had at her house. He picked her up, cradling her against his chest.

Dragon's hide barely moved, all his concentration on Rysa.

Another wave blasted from her seers and her nails dug into Ladon's arm.

"Rysa?"

A vision has her.

Pain echoed from her body to his. A new twitch arced across her fingers. He twitched, mirroring the movement.

If she had another uncontrolled vision, she might not wake up—and the only help Ladon had access to now traveled south to Branson.

To the Shifters.

Ladon laid his palm on Dragon's neck. *Could one help?*

The beast wagged his head. *I do not know. How?*

He didn't know, either. But something said *Shifter* and in particular, *enthraller*. Ladon could almost see—

Do you feel that? Ladon pushed. *It's coming from her seers, like at her house in Minneapolis.* He couldn't quite see, as if he had to squint because the images were too bright. And too loud.

She twitched again.

"Phone!" Ladon waved at the front of the van. Dmitri's bar teemed with enthrallers. They enticed good tips. One could come north. Meet them half way.

Dragon held out the phone. *I will take her.* The beast extended his hand to cradle her head.

No. Ladon dialed with one hand. She stayed where she was. "Dmitri!"

The Russian swore at him.

"I need an enthraller," Ladon growled.

Dmitri paused.

Rysa coughed.

"Now." The bar was too far away. "Who's nearby?" But Ladon knew—a brief memory flickered in his mind's eye: A woman dropping a necklace onto his palm.

A very particular, very unfriendly woman. Dragon blew out little rings of flame.

Dmitri said her name.

Ladon swore in a variety of languages. "You call her. Then call me back with a location." He disconnected the call.

Penny. Another one of Ladon's many mistakes. But if Penny was Rysa's only option, so be it. He'd stomach that hell for Rysa.

I will take her.

No. Ladon's arms wouldn't release. What if she didn't wake up?

You must drive. Dragon gently, carefully lifted away Rysa.

Dragon lay her down and Ladon wanted to pick her up again but instead he covered her with the blanket, tucking along the side, and touched her forehead. No fever. But he still felt her seer's fingers.

He needed to drive. He'd have to go up front and leave her in the back of the van where he couldn't feel her skin for a fever.

He exhaled. Dragon had her. Ladon fumbled for his keys as he dropped into the driver's seat. They'd go south, toward where Penny operated. If—

Human.

He looked up. Rysa caressed his shoulder and wiggled onto his legs, wedging herself between his abdomen and the steering wheel.

She is still in a vision, Dragon pushed.

The chill of her skin bit into Ladon's. "Beautiful." Why did he put her down? He wrapped his arms around her to give her all his warmth. "You need to rest. I found someone who will help—"

Her lips glided over his, her arms tight around his neck. A kiss—a real kiss, one full of purpose and intensity—touched his chin and silenced his words. The tenderness of the next kiss held all the trust and intimacy he'd seen in her eyes. Her mouth caressed his, wanted his, her body pressed tight against him.

"Rysa." Her name expanded from his throat and out to his chest and limbs. It moved into the quiet moments of his life and into his deepest worries. She melted all the what-ifs and brightened all the dark corners. Her touch calmed his world.

Somehow, even in this vision, even with her demands of distance, she wanted him, his touch, his attention.

Or she will. The future jutted into the present again and pressed her body against his.

But he couldn't lift her off his lap. Turn her away. Be strong like he should. She tasted perfect, felt perfect. Rysa, a woman who, somewhere inside her, accepted him, even though she was a Fate.

Ladon returned her kisses, accepting this gift he didn't deserve.

Her fingers wove into his hair and traced the slope of his ears. She moved, squeezed between him and the wheel, her hips swaying with her kisses. He could lay her on the blankets and express everything inside him. Stroke her hips and breasts and kiss every inch of her skin.

Let the inevitable bind her to him with a physical need so strong that when her world righted, she'd understand why he wanted her to stay.

He pushed aside the thought. He couldn't ask for a future she might never want, inevitable or not.

She kissed his cheek, holding tight to his chest. "Thank you," she whispered.

His head filled with an overlay of caresses, of kisses, beyond what he felt now. The future danced on his mind and all the possibilities of her staying wrapped around his mind the same way her arms wrapped around his neck.

A wave of color and texture pushed from Dragon. The beast nuzzled her cheek, his emotions mirroring Ladon's. The future touched the beast, as well. Her laugh would fill the silence of their van and give Dragon a new voice for his words, one strong and beautiful.

She moved like she was awake, kissed like she was awake, but the vision had her. The kisses were a promise of a gift that neither he nor Dragon may ever know.

"Rysa, can you hear me?"

"You are right." She whispered the words into his ear, barely a breath.

"What? Rys, I don't underst—"

"When I hurt you, please come for me."

She had said the same words after the fight at her house. He cupped her cheeks, kissing her again with every ounce of his resolve. "We will." Even if she walked away, they'd come for her. Now, tomorrow, centuries into the future, it didn't matter. They'd be there for her. Always.

"I'm sorry you have to see Penny again." Rysa's eyes closed.

Then she slumped against his shoulder.

21

A deep memory: Most people thought Daniel and Marcus the same, but to Ladon they were as different as night and day.

Marcus held the Shifter against the tavern's table, his knife at the base of the man's skull. "You did not sense him?"

Ladon wiped the blood from his cheek. "No."

Daniel spun his daggers. Light flashed off the blades. He turned in a circle for everyone to see, his expression predatory, and the tavern's normals cowered.

Marcus pressed the point of his knife into the Shifter's skin. Blood oozed. "Will this kill him?"

Ladon squatted next to the would-be assassin. Far Eastern. "Is this your real face, barbarian?"

The Shifter spat and cursed in a language Ladon did not recognize.

The clans were changing. First the new families who made others do their bidding and now assassins he could not sense.

Ladon stood tall. "A blade into the head is often enough."

Marcus twisted the dagger. More blood dripped down the man's neck.

The melody of Daniel's future-seer played along the edges of Ladon's awareness. "The Emperor is angry. You and the Dracas claimed his tribute." Daniel sneered and tapped his temple. The circumstances of the Draki Prime's activation, though years passed, continued to heat the brothers' behavior.

Ladon mimicked Daniel, tapping his own temple. "I did not claim tribute."

The future-seer chuckled and drove a blade into the assassin's thigh.

The man's high-pitched scream grated through the little tavern.

"Besting his cutthroats will make the old fool livid." Daniel twisted his blade.

Marcus's past-seer harmonized with his brother's. When the triad used their seers together, the three rang true. They were young but worthy of their Prime designator.

"You should have asked for five times your payment, scum." Marcus pressed his blade deeper.

Daniel pulled his dagger and wiped the Shifter's blood on the man's tunic. The assassin's wounds closed but did not fully heal. He'd live, but the agony would rake his body for days.

Marcus's seer rippled again. "Three others. Outside."

They wait by the stables. Dragon's bulk would have destroyed the tavern's walls, so he had climbed the oak tree towering over the low-slung building.

Ladon gestured at the entrance.

Daniel's seer sang. He clasped Ladon's forearm, his brow crinkling. "Women."

The assassin laughed.

The Emperor of Rome's corpse sent women to murder him? Ladon guffawed. Women did not want to murder him. At least not at first.

Daniel's iron eyes darkened. "Women will be our ruin."

"Not me, dear brother." Marcus gestured at Ladon. "Him, most definitely."

Daniel ignored them, his seer pulsing and his eyes distant. "Your beautiful fate will find you one day."

"You are the only beautiful Fate here, Daniel." Marcus kicked the assassin when he tried to escape.

Archers, Dragon pushed. *I must vent.*

"Skewer him to the table." Ladon pointed at the Shifter before waving at Daniel. "Arrows, my friend."

Daniel did not respond.

Ladon stopped, his sword half-drawn.

Marcus rammed a poker through the Shifter's shoulder. The man, now pinned to the table, screamed. Daniel shivered, his gaze traveling between the Shifter and his brother.

"Women." He frowned as he slid his dagger into its scabbard and drew his own sword. "Take care with your fate, Ladon-Human. Only your fate will stand between you and your ruin."

22

The nasty thing in Rysa's head wanted to kill her. Ladon said she'd passed out—he didn't say anything about her *kissing* him—and she'd popped awake when he yelled something Russian and foul-sounding into his phone.

He turned off the freeway onto a cornfield-lined county road and accelerated harder than the van liked. The engine groaned and the phone landed in the cup holder.

Marcus's charms wore off at the store. Just like that, out of nowhere, she blacked out, kissed Ladon—*kissed him*—and now her nasty writhed like a pissed off squid. Flashes and sounds and now smells—she didn't tell Ladon about the Burner stink infesting her nose—bubbled around the edges of her peripheral awareness. Who had a peripheral nose? An endless stream of *Wait, what's that smell?* made her jerk her head side to side like a crazy person.

She spent twenty minutes ranting about randomness and jumping up and down in the back of the van, jerked around by phantoms. Dragon pushed himself as far as he could to one side to protect his tail from her spazziness.

Ladon hadn't pulled off. He watched her in the rearview mirror and yelled more Russian into his phone.

They passed through a little town with an ugly pink one-story hotel, a strip club, and a huge farm implements store-warehouse. The van slowed to the required thirty miles per hour. Rysa stared out the back window, transfixed.

The entire town lived within a thousand feet of the highway, as if the road pierced it like a bullet and carried all its muscle and bone down the asphalt. The town distorted but hadn't yet burst.

Rysa's whipping tentacles picked up hate and defeat and a lot of booze. Then, as they moved across the town's boundary, the vision vanished. Her nasty abruptly pulled in. Rysa stared, dead still, out the front of the van, her mind a vast blank landscape.

"Rysa!" Ladon waved his arm around the seat.

The tip of Dragon's tail flicked in front of her eyes. The van suddenly lit up, as if the beast had turned on an entire dive bar's worth of neon.

"Sit down!" Ladon pointed at the passenger seat. "Before Dragon rolls the van because you've forced him up the wall."

Her feet moved, dancing against the increasing speed of the vehicle, and she found herself dropping into the seat. The seatbelt pulled across her front, her hand guiding it, and snapped into place.

Even at her worst ADHD moments—when she'd pace back and forth in the hall outside her fifth grade classroom, or when she'd disrupted her Health class in high school and had to go to the office, or when she had to drop her calculus recitation section her freshman year at the U because her teaching assistant couldn't understand her when she talked too fast—she never felt this disoriented. Never.

Something she didn't catch flickered through Ladon's eyes. "We're almost to the rendezvous. You'll be okay. I promise." He lifted his hand from the steering wheel and reached for her, his fingers out and gesturing for hers.

He wanted to hold her hand. She was totally out of control and he still wanted to hold her hand. Was this because she kissed him? A sense of *committed* bounced between him and Dragon. Then their energy washed across her—not over, sort of parallel—and she felt *committed* again. Like fate had them by their necks and they had no choice but to help her.

It took every morsel of self-control she had left not to unhook her seatbelt and curl into a ball on the van's floor, right there in the front, between the dash and her seat.

She hadn't said anything about the kiss, but she remembered it—and in particular the feel of his stomach against hers. The power of his muscles alone made her want to weep. And his mouth. She'd faint if she kept thinking about it. Stubble against her lips never felt so good. Tom's stubble hurt and Ladon's hurt too, but in a way she liked.

Which made no sense. Stubble was stubble. But the way he held her against him, and the way he moved his lips, made their kiss warm and brilliant and very, very good.

She'd kissed a god. He drove down the little country highway like Apollo, but in black. What was up with the black, anyway?

He pulled back his hand and something new played across his face. She'd missed her chance. She could have taken a sun god's hand.

Hurt bounced between him and Dragon. She'd hurt him.

She'd do it again. No escaping that. It was as inevitable as them having sex. She'd hurt him real bad. A sudden sense of *fate you cannot escape* blanketed her perception of the world. Ladon turned gray—his skin, his hair, his clothes.

It vanished.

A whimper popped out of her throat like she'd just gacked up a hairball. How much randomness could flip around in her head before it exploded? Or was her mind *imploding*?

"Beautiful! Look at me."

"I'm sorry!" She leaned forward. "I'm going to puke."

"Please don't throw up in my van!" He looked totally freaked out. She'd never seen him so freaked out.

She'd freaked out an immortal man who she was pretty damned sure had literally seen everything a human could see. "Why are you so good to me? I'm a problem. I'm—"

"Rysa! Stop! Don't say that." A massive pulse moved between him and Dragon.

The beast craned his neck around the seat and laid his head on her lap. Her nasty yelped—she heard it—and her seers stopped whipping. Stopped, laid down, and passed out.

And as fast as the rant started, it stopped.

She wrapped her arms around Dragon's head and pressed her cheek against his crest. He did something, like when he stopped her cousins in the Texas vision. He calmed the chaos. "What did you do?"

Ladon stared at the road. "He's been trying."

She picked up *We've been trying*. Not the words, but the concept.

Commitment came from both of them.

She didn't know what to say. They did so much for her.

Ladon pointed at the glove compartment. "Your meds are in there. If you want them."

Her stomach lurched but she kept her head bowed over and on Dragon. "I'll puke for sure." Words spilled out, too fast again and too numerous, a reflection of her body's full rejection of the meds. They always had made her feel sick. Now, she'd be throwing up within twenty minutes, just like at Marcus's. And probably having ultra-intense visions that screamed "Come mess with my head!" to every megalomaniac Fate on the planet.

"I'll puke all over the van and Dragon! You don't want me puking on Dragon. I don't want to puke! I don't want to take them."

"Okay, okay. You don't have to." His confusion didn't ease. Now his lips bunched up. "Dmitri said the next exit. Penny will help."

"Why didn't you call her yourself?" He'd been waiting for calls so he could yell more Russian into the phone. Driving, yelling, then driving some more.

"Not a good idea." He shook his head and his grip on the steering wheel tightened.

"Why?" But her seers flicked the knowledge into her mind as soon as the question passed her lips: Penny might not be the most powerful enthraller, but she knew things about Ladon. Intimate things. And talking to her directly wasn't the wisest idea. "Oh my God she's your ex-girlfriend!"

A new vision-flash: The seventies. Dragon, a car, hate sex in a field of corn so tall it dwarfed Ladon. "I didn't need to see that. I didn't want to see that!" Or smell it.

Now Ladon looked like he'd throw up.

"How many ex-girlfriends do you have? I don't want any more visions like that!"

Another very quick, polar-opposite flash: Ladon flirting with her in the Women's Apparel section of the store in Mankato.

She'd seen gray before, like a shroud. Now he gleamed like Dragon, happy and very much alive. Ladon, the magnificently hot, sun god flirt.

Something bounced between Ladon and Dragon and the beast raised his head so fast he almost smacked it against the roof of the van.

"I do not flirt!"

Rysa's mouth dropped open. "You heard that? I said that out loud?" Imploding or exploding, it didn't matter. She'd die, right now, right here, from embarrassment.

He didn't look at her. He watched the road instead.

She watched the fields pass by, not saying anything. Her cheeks burned. If she opened her mouth, she'd make it worse.

A truth bubbled up from her nasty: Two days and she'd defeated an immortal. This time, it didn't take her ten days to scare off a guy. Two must be a personal record for her.

She acted like… she didn't know what she acted like. But it wasn't tolerable to anyone and she just lost Dragon. She'd just lost Ladon. She had no control and when this was done, he'd walk away. They wouldn't even be friends.

His cheek twitched. "You told me not to touch so I haven't touched." His lower lip very quickly, very briefly, pouted out. "Mostly."

Neither of them spoke for what felt like an eternity. Jagged patterns flashed over Dragon's hide. Rysa watched the Iowa corn. They pulled off the road onto a narrow gravel lane and Ladon inched the van along.

"We're here." His voice blurred as if he didn't care anymore if he had an edge. He put the van in park and pulled the key from the ignition. Exhaling, he nodded out the front. He still wouldn't look at her. "I'll go out, so you can change."

She looked down. Harold's ratty sweats crumpled over her thighs.

When she looked back, he'd already pulled the door handle. But his hand moved toward her tentatively, his fingers curled under like he wasn't sure what to do.

When she touched his knuckles, his hand unfurled. Their skin met, palm to palm. He squeezed. Then he was gone, out the door, before she could say anything.

***

Ladon pressed his back against the cold exterior of the van. Inside, Dragon picked up the unending stream of jarring, slashing seer bursts from Rysa. Every time it happened, she cringed.

Her abilities—she called them her "nasty"—wrapped around his connection to Dragon and alternated clutching and siphoning. The frantic whipping had almost overpowered his concentration while he drove.

He and the beast, they didn't say anything. Adding weight to the burden Rysa already carried wasn't something he'd do. She needed help— Penny's help. Dragon's help. *His* help. And he'd give it freely, no matter how panicked she became.

They'd stopped briefly, outside of Mankato, after she'd passed out on his lap. He'd sat next to her while she lay on the blankets and waited for Dmitri to return his call. Each time she twitched or moaned, he touched her shoulder or hair or cheek.

He'd woven a leather thong around a *Legio Draconis* insignia as he sat with his back against the driver's seat, to keep his hands busy. While he tied the knots, she'd rolled toward him and, in her unconsciousness, pressed her cheek against his thigh.

He didn't move again until his phone rang. He couldn't. Not after their kiss.

He threaded the thong through the chain of her mother's talisman. Made for her something to represent the good in her life, to balance the damned Burner fire. And he waited as Dragon cycled calming hues over both him and the beautiful woman who slept against his leg.

He now carried the bracelet in his pocket. A gift he wondered if she'd accept, overwhelmed as she felt.

Inside, Rysa stripped off Harold's sweats. Dragon turned away to give her privacy, but the dragons had another sense, a sort of perceiving that operated separate from their vision. He and Sister detected it but never fully comprehended what it was. They still didn't.

His brother-in-law, with his scientific mind, once said he figured it was akin to how octopuses sensed the background they hid against. The dragons' hide saw as well as mimicked. They had to, or they couldn't vanish.

A human brain couldn't comprehend the information their hides produced. Ladon and Sister felt its effects, but didn't understand.

Ladon had managed to adapt some in the twenty-three centuries he'd lived with the beast. Dragon-perceiving flitted in and out of his consciousness, sometimes like the after-image of a scene viewed in bright sun. Sometimes as a tactile doppelgänger of Dragon's body as his coat mimicked the texture of a pattern. Often as a phantom second world that overlaid the first.

Rysa floated just outside his awareness, her dragon-sensed form lovely but ethereal and inaccessible. The beast learned the smoothness of her skin to a level of detail Ladon could never feel. His hide saw her curves and angles and the precise connections of her muscles and tendons. He learned how she moved. How she breathed.

A ghost of Rysa drifted to Ladon, as brilliant and perfect as the woman herself.

In the van, the beast stroked her back. *She weeps.*

Ladon felt her ghost touch the delicate skin under her eyes.

Someone like her, someone so beautiful his breath hitched when she smiled, should not wipe away tears.

Headlights turned from the narrow county road onto the gravel of the field access.

The engine of Penny's 1967 Chevy Impala purred, modern and smooth, like it'd been recently rebuilt. She'd painted the car at least twice since the last time he saw her—the surface gave off slight distortions—though she'd kept the original oxidized-mineral tint. But the finish glistened like glass and Ladon suspected she'd had the side panels bullet-proofed.

Five dragon lengths away, Penny parked her Impala crosswise to rows and rows of corn seedlings. The headlights blinked out and the area dropped into evening shadow.

In front of him, an enthraller strong enough to make Rysa think she had her visions under control tapped her fingers on the well-maintained dash of her retrofitted classic automobile.

Ladon stood tall, feeling Rysa pull a new t-shirt over her head. She and the beast would soon roll out the van's back door and she'd stand next to him, feigning calm, though not strength. She was stronger than she realized. Stronger, he suspected, than both him and Dragon.

He'd get her the help she needed, even if that help did not look happy to see him.

Not happy at all.

23

Penny squatted in front of the Impala, her knees flexed and her weight distributed in that peculiar way women wearing heels knelt.

Ladon glanced down at her boots. Laced leather, reinforced toe, obviously custom-made. And the two-and-a-half-inch blunt heel she preferred.

It hurt like hell when kicked into a nose.

She'd aged at the rate Ladon expected. Like most enthrallers born around the time of the Civil War, she looked to be about sixty. Maybe a little older. The severely short hair didn't help. Yet she still moved like an athlete.

A piece of sunbaked bone stuck out of the gravel and she pinched it with precision before lifting it to her nose. "Raccoon."

Some enthrallers like Penny—not many—could take as well as they could give. Fates may not be able to read Burners, and the bastards were poison to all Shifters, but a good enthraller could track them fifty miles out.

If they were fast and strong enough, the enthraller tended to get caught by "the calling"—the Shifters who patrolled and protected their kind, no matter their own desires.

Or their own proclivities. Last year, Ladon met a sixteen-year-old morpher boy who'd been activated young so his family could shape his body-altering abilities to suit Burner hunting. He'd run away. Now he worked for Dmitri, crunching numbers and fiddling with the whining electronics in the back rooms of The Land of Milk and Honey.

Ladon suspected the young man was the true source of the Burner tracking app on his phone.

In front of him, Penny stood. Her blouse glowed in the evening light, well-tailored and formfitting, as was also her preference. Styles may change, but the basics of Penelope McFarlane Sisto did not.

She glowered, her lips a thin line. "A Fate, now, Ladon-Human?" She shook her head. "Never expected a surprise out of you."

Why do you care? he thought, but held his tongue when he felt a blip from Rysa's seers. Irritating Penny helped no one.

Penny glared at the van. "When is she coming out? Let's get this over with."

Rysa asks for a moment. She sat with her back against the passenger seat, hiccupping. Dragon placed his head on her lap and cycled through every calming light and pattern he knew.

Ladon wanted to open the door and jump into the back. To hold her like he had after their kiss. To keep his promise that they'd always be there for her.

But he couldn't shake the feeling he'd only make things worse. "When she's ready."

Penny sniffed, her eyes narrow. "Clean your van. It smells of Burners, vodka, and sad little Fates."

He stepped toward her. A fast movement, and not too close, and he did it without thinking.

Penny held her ground. "There's a triad in Wisconsin Dells. They emigrated from somewhere in Eastern Europe about five years ago. The pawn shop on the edge of town is theirs."

Ladon did not step back. He crossed his arms. Shifters liked tourist havens such as The Dells and Branson. They tended to be attracted to transient economies. But Fates preferred to confine themselves to affluent urban areas. Better security. "Fates so close to Shifters?"

"They're breeders. Not very powerful. No one knows what their talisman is." Penny shrugged.

"So this makes your behavior okay, Penny? Because some of your friends are Fates?"

Her voice took on the magical tones of a practiced enthraller. One who knew, all too well, which resonances to soften and which to calm both Ladon and Dragon. "Darling, I do this for you. You know that, right?"

Her saccharin grin looked a little too Burnerish for Ladon's tastes.

"It would be wise, Penelope, for you to remember with whom you speak." Practiced or not, only a few enthrallers could control Ladon or his sister. Penny was not one of them.

She sighed, a grand exhalation of her many decades of pent-up annoyance. "I can't give her something she doesn't already have. You know that."

Healers changed. Enthrallers coaxed. If Rysa didn't have the capacity to control her abilities, no matter how Penny modulated her voice or what pheromones she breathed from her lungs, it wasn't happening.

But Ladon wouldn't mention this to Rysa. She needed to believe.

And so did he. Stomaching the thought she might be caught forever in this cycle of misery wasn't something he'd accept.

If Penny's enthralling didn't work, he'd take her to Dmitri. They'd stay in Branson as long as it took for the Russian to figure out how to heal her out-of-control abilities.

If something like this could be healed. Ladon frowned. He'd concentrate on the good they could do now, not the what-ifs he had no control over.

"She's not royalty." Penny's eyes narrowed. "You tell her to come out. I won't waste my time waiting for a Fate, no matter her lineage."

In the van, Dragon raised his head.

"What do you know?" Ladon moved again, this time placing himself between the van's door and Penny.

"Only a Jani Prime would be arrogant enough to buy a house in Minneapolis using her real name, though 'Torres' was a bit of a surprise."

Ladon shrugged, not taking the bait. "It's a common name."

Penny held her face flat and unreadable. "Are the War Babies in the States?"

The Jani triads had caused plenty of havoc for Shifters over the centuries, but the War Babies made it sport. Ladon wondered how many times other than the Texas attack they'd snuck in and out of the States without him knowing. "Probably."

Penny sighed again, but this time she sounded tired—and old. "Rumors are that the War Babies were responsible for Abilene."

Ladon didn't answer. Best to let her talk it out of her system. He'd learned how to handle this bit of her personality a long time ago.

"They killed a lot of healers. We didn't have many to begin with, you know." She walked back toward the Impala. "Enthrallers, too. They set medicine back a hundred years." She paused. "And they're after your new pet?"

"She's not my pet, Penny. No more than you were."

She snatched a rock from the ground and threw it at his head. It hit the van, just above the taillight, and bounced into the field. Ladon stared at the new dent.

Her finger pointed accusingly at his nose. "What's the best way to stand against the War Babies? Recruit a Dracae." She looked him up and down. "And God knows your sister will have nothing to do with your little Fate."

He'd talk sense into his sister, no matter what Penny insinuated.

"So the poor little Fate bats her eyelashes and acts all scared and here you are, saving the damsel in distress."

It wasn't like that. Rysa needed their help.

The back door of the van opened. Dragon rolled out, his big head first looping around Ladon as he jumped onto the gravel. He shook as he landed and a low growl rolled from his chest.

Ladon turned to the van. Rysa stood on the bumper, her hands on each side of the door frame. She'd changed into the jeans he'd picked out and a lighter-colored t-shirt.

She didn't look at Penny. She looked at him. And he saw only pain in her eyes.

Pain he felt. Pain that had pushed through the ice of his life. Before America, a wife bled to death, a baby boy never breathed, and the Draki Prime were murdered. He and Dragon lumbered away, their guts in their hands, across an ocean and into the arms of his sister and her pretty Irish Shifter companion.

He wasn't sure how much of that century and a half they'd spent with Penny. Or what they'd done any of the other moments. He'd have to force the recall. Because when the world is flat and colorless there's no value to making a life worth remembering.

On the bumper, Rysa looked down at his hands. The strap of one of her rainbow underthings peeked out where her shoulder met her neck. He wanted to brush aside her hair and kiss the little hollow where the strap lay. And feel her cheek against his when she smiled.

That would be worth remembering.

"So you're the Fate who's got the Dracos tied in knots." Behind him, Penny snorted. "He's not worth it."

Rysa's gaze left Ladon. She stared over his shoulder at the other woman and the pain turned hard.

"How much vodka are you drinking now, Ladon-Human? Two, three bottles a day? He says it doesn't affect him, but that's one of the lies he tells himself to get through the day. Isn't that right, lover boy?"

Ladon turned toward Penny. The sneer on her lips said more than any of her insults.

He knew exactly what she was about to say. But he couldn't stop her from saying it.

The sun's last rays bounced off a lonely bank of clouds, spreading reds and purples across the western horizon. Rysa breathed in the humid Iowa air. Both the van and the Shifter's turquoise muscle car sat on some farmer's gravel road, noses pointed toward the crappy two lane county road.

They were, quite literally, in the middle of nowhere.

Dragon, stretching like a giant cat, rolled out first and stood between Ladon and Rysa and Ladon's ex-girlfriend. He shimmered softly, casting just enough light to temper the long evening shadows.

Penny looked old, like she was about to retire, or just had, and dressed like a cop from a detective show—tailored blouse so white it glowed in the light of the sunset, tailored mid-rise boot-cut jeans accentuating her still-thin waist, and black leather boots with a bit of heel, but not too much. Rysa suspected she had a blazer on the back seat of her car.

The Shifter spit insults at Ladon. Rysa smelled the bile. It sat in her nose and tongue like some sort of phantom memory. It tasted like 'hate'—like a command to hate.

Penny leaned against the hood of her car, watching Rysa with eyes that spit just as much anger as the pheromones wafting from her.

She said something about Ladon not being worth it.

Someone as old as Penny should have a better sense of "worth it." Even if Rysa had ruined any chance with him, he and Dragon were "worth" more than anyone she'd ever met.

Penny said something about vodka.

Rysa jumped down and stood next to Ladon. She touched his elbow to say thank you. To let him know she appreciated what he did, even if Penny didn't. He looked down at her hand.

Penny's sapphire gaze darted between Ladon's face and Rysa's fingers. Each time her eyes dropped, she sighed. Not a loud sigh, or a defeated one, more of an inaudible groan. Her body made the motions of a sigh—the contraction of the stomach, the drop of the shoulders and the tightening of the neck—but Rysa didn't hear it.

Penny sneered and 'spite' hit Rysa's tongue. Too sweet and too salty, it made her gag.

Penny raised her hand and a crocked finger pointing first at Rysa, then Ladon. "He used to kill your kind, Fate. Slaughtered them in the streets. Cut them down like the rats you are."

Penny's sneer said it all: Rysa was supposed to gasp and cover her mouth, maybe faint, too, for good measure. Put on a grand show to justify Penny's ill-will.

Rysa had already driven a wedge between herself and Ladon. She wasn't someone he might care for, so Penny could say anything, exaggerate everything, and it wouldn't change *what-will-be*.

But the inevitability of sex still confounded Rysa. Would it be pity sex? A one night stand decades from now when this was over? She hoped it wouldn't be hate sex, like what she glimpsed with Penny.

She wouldn't be able to handle hate sex.

If she became the weird random thing fate wanted her to be— the Ambusti Prime, her mom called her—the Burner Fate incapable of controlling herself and who burned cities, he'd hate her.

"Are you going to help me or not, Shifter?" The 'spite' she tasted coated her own words.

"Rys?" Ladon touched her elbow, her wrist, her fingers. He tried to learn from her skin again, to listen to what her body told him. "Beautiful, are you okay? You're acting dazed." He sniffed the air. "Penny!"

"I'm not doing it! *She's* the freak, not me, you fool." Penny's voice carried much more information than simple words. Her voice carried 'fear.' "I'm not doing *anything* to her!" She stepped toward her muscle car's door. "Fucking Fates. You're worse than Burners." She reached for the handle.

Dragon placed a hand on the door. He didn't growl, or flash, but he put enough pressure on the car that it rocked upward. A loud creak erupted from the underside.

Penny's voice modulated. "Dearest heart, it's okay. I brought you oranges. I have a whole bag. Just for the one I love."

Dragon swung his head between Penny and Rysa, then back to Penny. He lifted his hand off the car to sign. *Are they Cara Caras?*

A brief wave of 'puzzlement' rolled from Penny. "What are those?"

My favorite.

An almost inaudible *Heh* came from Ladon. "Do what's been asked of you, Penny."

The whipping in Rysa's head started again: For a split second, Penny's car looked as if someone had poured gasoline on the hood and set it ablaze. Rysa heard the crackle, smelled the acid. Felt the heat.

Her entire front screamed like someone had pressed her against a hot stove. She looked at her hands. No blisters, no fire. But it crawled, the burning. It crawled over the car and she felt it as if it crawled on her.

Rysa screamed.

Ladon swung her into his arms. "Penny!"

Rysa heard Dragon growl. She saw a flash, and Penny appeared in her field of vision.

"I won't help a Fate! I won't—"

The metal of Penny's car shrieked. Dragon dragged his talons down its side, gouging deeply, and curls of turquoise paint dropped onto the dirt.

"Not my baby!" Penny shook her fist at Dragon. "May the old gods eat your soul, you foul beast!"

The fire in the vision—and Rysa's skin—sputtered.

"You want to keep the roof, you help her *right now*!" Ladon yelled like a general.

"I hate this," Rysa whispered. Was she really on fire? Was that stupid car on fire? Did that bitch really shake her fist at Dragon? Who *did* that?

Another gouge. More car curls hit the gravel.

"Stop! Stop!" Penny's hands wrapped around Rysa's face. She leaned close as her voice took on the same magical information density it had before. "You are clearheaded and in control."

'Calm' and 'clear' wafted into Rysa's nose.

I'm clearheaded. Rysa inhaled deeply. *Stop whipping!* she yelled at her nasty. *I'm in control.* Not you. *No more burning!*

Ladon dropped her legs. "We felt that." But he kept his arm around her waist. "Are you okay?"

The tentacles folded away. She still felt them, but they listened. *Stay.* Weird as it seemed, she pointed an imaginary finger at the imaginary nasty thing in her head. It seemed the best way to deal with it.

For the first time, it heeled.

Penny backed away but Rysa's nasty yipped. Rysa grabbed the Shifter's collar. "Say 'You will *always* be clearheaded and in control.'"

Penny clamped her mouth shut.

Behind them, Dragon leaned onto the muscle car's hood. It groaned.

"Okay! You will *always* be clearheaded and in control!" Penny slapped away Rysa's hand.

Dragon lifted his talons.

The bitch ran for her car, swearing loudly at both Ladon and Dragon.

24

As soon as Penny pulled away, Rysa's seers popped a vision into her mind: One very perplexed farmer wondering if he'd been visited by aliens. She didn't know if it had happened, or would, but the prudent thing to do was to not be around if he came looking.

Ladon helped her into the van and they pulled off the gravel road onto the county highway. She should feel better. When the vision of the farmer came to her, she controlled it, and even though she smelled his aftershave, it didn't overwhelm her, and she stopped it when she'd gleaned what she needed.

"You're okay now?" Ladon looked her up and down. "You look okay."

She nodded instead of answering, knowing she'd say something stupid if she opened her mouth. Something like "I want to kiss you."

"Do you want to rest? You should rest. Then practice. Your seers shouldn't come uncalled. Your talisman might be chaos but it's the filter, not the camera." He nodded, obviously more for himself than for her. "You may be the Ambusti but you're still a Prime and with practice and dedication, it won't feel nasty anymore. It won't control you."

Did she infect him again through their connection? He talked fast and a lot more than usual, like her.

"You'll be okay. Nothing's going to hurt you. Nothing."

She wasn't so sure about "practice and dedication." But Ladon and Dragon seemed willing to help. Maybe she hadn't completely scared them off.

Maybe they could be friends. But if she did something stupid, she'd ruin it. So she tried very hard to smile and hold still. "I can't believe Penny shook her fist at Dragon."

After a long moment of staring at the road, Ladon chuckled.

I have had many fists shaken at me. Dragon dropped his head onto her lap again.

She couldn't bounce in her seat while he held her in place. She scratched his eye ridge.

"Fists, sabers, an entire coliseum's worth of swords, a couple of trebuchets, pistols, machine guns and oh—" Ladon glanced at Dragon. "— Do you remember when that Shifter shook an entire tree at us? A whole tree. Strongest Shifter we've ever met. That's rare." He smiled at Rysa.

She'd melt if he kept it up. Right here, in the passenger seat of his van. She'd turn into a puddle of Rysa and that'd be the end of it, so she hugged Dragon to distract herself. "I can't believe she called you a foul beast. Who calls you that?"

Dragon pulled back so she could see his hands. *I have also been called a foul beast many times.*

"You are not a foul beast. You're beautiful and wonderful and you're *special.*"

The pulse of light from Dragon might blind the oncoming traffic, if there'd been any.

She was talking too much again. She bit hard on her lip and slapped her hand over her mouth. What did she just do? She'd tried to be careful, but no, she had to babble. Her mouth just ran and ran and Ladon would start sighing any minute now.

But he didn't. He gripped the steering wheel while pulsing information to Dragon. The beast put his head on her lap again and they drove in silence toward a glow on the horizon.

"Do you want to stop? I think we should stop." Ladon pointed up the road.

The outskirts of Council Bluffs manifested up ahead. Random suburban streets jutted out of the cornfields like the ground had a rash. A shopping center loomed just off the road.

"Are you hungry? I'm hungry. There's an app to find places to eat." Ladon pointed at his phone where it rested in the cup holder.

Happy for a distraction, she picked it up. The screen came to life. "It's on? I thought it gave you a headache."

"It does." He shrugged.

"You don't need a headache, you know." Not because of her.

An app window popped up. She tapped at the screen. "Is this thing tracking local cell phone calls?" He had spyware on his phone. "This is seriously illegal. You know that, right?"

A cocky grin appeared. "So is having three assault rifles and a barbed whip under the floor. And two handguns, three swords, and seven daggers."

Dragon's hand appeared between the seats. *Eight.*

"*Eight* daggers." Winking, he shrugged again.

"Does it pick up state trooper calls?" She tapped again and the "key terms" search box appeared.

"Already is. It's monitoring everything within six hundred miles."

Sword popped into her head along with *train* and *unauthorized vehicle.* She tapped in the words without realizing what she was doing.

"There's a grocery store." Ladon pointed at a sign. "We can get Dragon dinner."

She returned the phone to the cup holder. "You're okay with it on?"

"It's fine. We should let it be, in case." He pulled off the highway and turned toward the mall. "We can tolerate some whining, right?"

Dragon grunted.

"There's one of those big electronics stores." He pointed through the windshield. "You need a new phone. For emergencies. We'll put you on our data plan." He nodded toward the store. "Or Derek will. It's not a problem." He pulled the van into an open space near the rear of the parking lot and shut off the ignition.

Share a data plan? Heat blazed across her cheeks and she squirmed, unable to hold herself still.

Ladon inhaled sharply and glanced at Dragon. "We have something for you." He dug in his pocket.

Her heart skipped. What if he had a key to another car? Was he telling her to go on her way?

"We thought you might want to wear your mother's talisman. It should help you see her, when the dust is out of her system." Her mother's bracelet draped off his fingers. "Now that your seers are calm, you can start feeling for her."

A black leather strap wove through the chain.

"As soon as you sense anything—anything at all, no matter what or when—you tell us. We'll go straight away."

Tied into the leather were two entwined dragons of silver and gold.

"We stopped the chaos of your talisman from completely randomizing your seers and we will stop the War Babies from taking your mother. I promise."

"Oh." He said something about her mom, but she didn't really hear. The emblem drew all her attention. "What is it? It's gorgeous." Squinting, she peered at the detail worked into each beast. Braided ridges rose along their backs. Six talons graced their hands. "They look like the dragons Marcus wears."

"It's a *Legio Draconis* insignia. The man who forges my weapons puts them in the hilts. My *nunchaku*, as well." His fingers danced over the edges of the insignia. "We thought you might like one. As a balance to the burndust." His fingers touched the link around her wrist. He paused for a moment, touching the metal.

The little dragons astounded beyond any piece of jewelry she'd seen, much less owned. "He makes them for you?"

Very gently, very carefully, Ladon touched her skin. "I smith them. When we're home. The dragons always touch the metal as it cools, to bless the emblem." Below the link, he clasped the chain. Working quickly, he tied the thong. "There."

Ladon fashioned the insignia with his own hands. She should be happy to have her mom's charm, but this—the little dragons warmed her soul as much as the beast himself. "It's for me?"

"Yes."

"This is why you wanted to stop?" He wasn't going to kick her out of his van.

He looked puzzled. "Yes."

He wasn't mad about her out-of-control behavior.

Ladon stroked the back of her hand before nodding toward the store. "That, plus Dragon's hungry."

A seer-tentacle reached out, responding to his touch. But it didn't whip in the gross way her seers had before. It mimicked Ladon's touch, stroking the river of energy between Ladon and Dragon.

What if she started siphoning again? Her nasty might have calmed down, but she didn't understand how her abilities worked, or what separated them, or if the siphoning was something else. She yelled at it in her head. *Stop!*

But Dragon reached out to *her.*

Her whole body tingled as vivid globes with a distinct citrus scent appeared in her mind. Brilliantly colored like the sun, and with a perfect, ripe texture she felt with six fingers. They fit in her hand—*his* hand—the way a grape fit in hers, but he flipped more than one in his palm, checking their rinds for variations. A swipe of a talon and Cara Cara juice sprayed into the air.

"Oranges!" Actual oranges, like she held them herself. "I saw oranges!"

Ladon's eyes gleamed as bright as the beast's images. "He's been trying."

Dragon nuzzled her side and flashed more oranges into her mind. *Rysa can hear me now that her seers have calmed.* He knocked Ladon's shoulder as he signed, as if to say *Told you so.*

Another flash with Cara Caras, and also kale. "You're amazing! And hungry."

Ladon scratched at his messy hair. "Phone first. Then dinner. You can practice while we eat. Do you feel up to shopping?"

"I think so." She kissed Dragon's eye ridge and laughed when he sparkled. From outside, the van must have looked like someone inside was setting off flares.

She tapped her cheek, examining Ladon's faded black t-shirt, as she popped the latch on her door with her other hand. "Why do you always wear black? I'm buying you something plaid."

Ladon hopped out and rounded the back corner of the van to open the door for Dragon. "Why would you do that?"

The invisible beast rubbed against her side as they waited for a couple of teenagers to walk by. She leaned toward him to keep her footing and was sure she looked quite bizarre to anyone watching. "Because the monochrome is, well, monotonous." Though the ominous overtones suited him. It balanced the messy hair.

"I don't like plaid." Ladon frowned. "Highlanders wear plaid."

"What's wrong with Highlanders?" She poked at his shoulder.

His lips bunched up.

"You're embarrassed." She smirked. "What did you do?"

Dragon pushed an image into her head: Ladon, drunk, holding two mugs of beer or mead or whatever Highlanders drank in one fist, swinging his arm and bellowing like a fool. He slapped Dragon, goading the big beast into compliance. Dragon, annoyed, covered himself with a complicated plaid pattern as much to shut up his human as to prove his mimicking skill.

Rysa doubled over laughing.

"Dragon pushed it to you, didn't he?"

An outline of a dragon hand flicked Ladon's shoulder. He staggered to the side, frowning at the air next to him.

"I saw it!" Rysa snorted. "He's still irritated." Tears clung to her lashes. "Okay, no plaid."

Ladon pointed toward the store, smiling like a little kid. "Let's go."

"Were you wearing a kilt?" Surprised by the image, she doubled over again. More laughter erupted.

"No."

"Yes, you were!" She'd seen it in what Dragon pushed to her. "How did you get a black kilt? Aren't they all plaid?" She followed Ladon through the lot, skipping over a pothole. "Is it true what they say about kilts and—"

"I will not talk about Highlanders." He marched off toward the building.

"Do you still have it?"

On the sidewalk, he turned toward her again. "What?"

"The kilt."

He tapped his elbow. "No. But I do have my claymore."

"What's that?" Dragon nudged her forward and she moved toward the entrance.

"My really big sword."

Laughter burst out again and she bent over in front of the entrance, right in the middle of traffic. "Well, I would hope so." It felt good to laugh. Snorting again, she shook her head. "Really big, huh?"

He stood in front of the store smiling his brilliant smile, handsome and wonderful and happy.

"You know…" More laughter bubbled up. "… there can be only one."

He pulled her toward the doors. "Only one what?"

"Oh, we need to get you some movies."

Ladon had managed to lift some of her gloom. She accepted the insignia and now she laughed. He made her happy.

Dragon hung from the wall inside the main door. *It is noisy in here.*

Ladon tugged Rysa toward the inner door. "We need to hurry. Dragon says it's loud in the store."

They stopped next to the carts. Her scent curled around him, a layered bouquet that held his senses. Her skin glowed, a vision of the jasmine and mist-under-the-moon he pulled in with each inhale.

She looked toward Dragon's spot on the wall, her hand still in his, the perfect line of her jaw accented by the tilt of her head. She didn't move away.

She likes us.

Ladon glanced at the wall. Happiness flowed from the beast in warm waves of color and pattern.

But Penny's words still echoed in his mind. He'd fixed this moment, given Rysa this small joy, but she'd ask sooner or later. Her brow would crinkle and she'd say "Wait…" and his past would register. She'd want him to explain. And all the promise he'd seen in her eyes would vanish forever, only to be replaced by disappointment and anger.

Now, next to him, she peered down the aisle. "The cell phones are behind the cameras."

A step moved her inches away. He pulled her back, wanting this moment to last. Wanting not to think about when she'd drop her gaze and mutter that he wasn't someone she could be with.

Rysa looked up, her beautiful face in the present, in the *right now*, happy for the first time since they'd met. The world brightened. She wasn't in a vision. She wasn't seeing a future that might not come to pass or a past he couldn't escape. She saw him, and she smiled.

It took all his effort not to pick her up. Not to kiss her neck and her cheeks and her lips and do his best, in the present, to make sure her smile never faded.

An electronic whine hit his skull like someone threw a rock at his temple—a customer with an open cell phone walked by. The pain yanked his mind back to the glaring harshness of the damned store.

"Are you okay?" Rysa glanced around. "All the cell phones?"

He nodded and dropped his head to her shoulder as he sought the comfort of her closeness. Her fingers moved up his arms and cupped his biceps.

"Give me your credit card. I'll get a prepaid phone and meet you outside. It won't take long." She tapped his elbows.

She wanted to go into the store without him? He'd have to let go. And this store stretched deeper than his connection to Dragon.

"Don't make that face. I'll be fine. There's not a single Burner around."

The aisles did look clear. Neither he nor Dragon sensed any Shifters or Fates. "Are you sure?" He'd be happier if she had a phone not linked to her current number.

"It's bad enough you've been driving around with yours on. Plus, the faster we're done here, the faster we get dinner." As quickly as she said the words, she smoothed her fingers over his stomach.

The full force of what had been brewing since Minneapolis exploded from the skin of his belly up into his chest. He pulled her into a tight embrace. Every moment they'd been together, every ounce of joy she brought to both him and Dragon, moved from his lips to hers. The kiss, quick but intense, was meant to share it all.

Color deepened across her cheeks. She pulled back but didn't let go. "Ladon!" Her gaze darted about and she touched her chin. "You...*oh*."

"Kissed you?"

"I didn't think..." She bit her lip.

"What?" He hadn't thought someone could look both completely happy and utterly embarrassed at the same time, yet she was. Maybe he should kiss her again.

A grumble of irritation rolled from Dragon. The beast felt left out, hanging on the wall and invisible. Ladon glanced over.

By the entrance, the employee in charge of dispensing faint-but-holier-than-thou sneers huffed and said something into her earpiece.

"You're going to get us kicked out," Rysa whispered, her eyes still huge and her hand still on her chin, like she didn't know what to do.

It is noisy. My head hurts. I want to leave.

"We'll get the van. Pull up front and wait for you. Then we'll get him his fruit and us some take-out." Under his hands, her hips swayed ever so slightly.

She might ask about his past, but tonight he'd prove his intent. So she'd know, now and always, what she meant to him and to the beast.

She nodded, biting her lip again. "I need your card if I'm going to buy a phone."

Wallet out, he offered the plastic. He'd have Derek put her on his account. Get her a card of her own. "We'll be right out front."

Letting go of her hips took more effort than killing a Burner. More effort than fighting a class-one morpher. Carrying her out to the van would be like a morning stretch, his face turned to the brightness of the day, even if he kissed her the entire way and relied on Dragon to navigate the potholes.

She kissed his cheek. Softly, her perfect lips pressing his skin with what he could only describe as real, true affection. "Don't run off."

He'd stay with her like this for the rest of the evening, if he could. This close, touching this way. Knowing that he could make her happy. "We will always be here for you."

Her lips rounded. "Oh."

But her smile returned.

25

L adon kissed her. In public, in a store, in front of people. He stepped forward and kissed her on the lips in a way that said he wanted more than friendship. More, not less. More.

He kissed her like he'd kissed her when she was in the vision.

Thinking wasn't happening. And if she used her seers, she knew *exactly* what she'd see. Her back would arch and she'd moan in the store, in public, in front of the whole world.

She might anyway, the way he was looking at her. And if he kissed her again, she'd melt—a response just as embarrassing as an orgasm.

A moment to calm down, maybe get her mind under control, is what she needed. A moment without his sun-god scent driving her insane.

So she gave him a little shove. "Go on. I won't be long."

The next kiss landed as a gentle touch to her cheek. "You need us, call to Dragon." Bits of concrete fell as Dragon dropped off the wall.

Ladon's swagger made her tingle again. She watched his black jeans frame his exceptional backside as he walked away.

A little bounce escaped as she watched him walk through the sliding glass doors, even with all her effort. How fast could she find a phone? Something simple with prepaid minutes and no extras. She needed to stay on task. And to breathe. If she was too hyper, he still might not want her around.

No, they'd have dinner. She'd practice her new-found control. And maybe some more kissing.

She grinned as she walked into the store. First, the phone. Usually, phones were up front, but not in this place. They were behind the music players and across from the movies. Perhaps she should pick up a DVD player for Dragon, but not movies about bad dragons, because he'd brood. Maybe turn gray. That, she *didn't* want to see. The players were tucked away with the car stereos for some stupid reason and—

She pulled her attention back to finding a phone. Should she text Gavin? The Feds were likely tracing calls to his number. Guilt prodded. He worried about her. She grabbed a phone off a shelf and turned it over in her hands.

"A Fate's seer sure is grating."

Rysa spun but the big Shifter grabbed her arms. Taller than Ladon, wider too, he held her wrists with an iron grip.

"No screaming." His voice modulated the way Penny's had. "No running."

Dragon! she yelled in her head.

The Shifter snickered, one corner of his mouth higher than the other. His flat nose bobbed under his receding hairline.

"Why are you so ugly?" she spit out. "Can't all Shifters morph?"

He slapped. The sting trailed across her cheek. The lady at the end of the aisle gasped. The Shifter pointed at the woman, but his eyes stayed on Rysa. "Go away, normal."

The woman blinked and backed out of the aisle.

"That witch Penny Sisto was right. You got a mouth." He yanked Rysa toward the back of the store. "Do you have any idea how valuable you are? You're an accessible Jani Fate."

He sniffed her hair. "You smell nice. Got a good rack on you, too. No wonder he likes you. Is he taking you to his hidey-hole in Wyoming? You know he lives with his sister, right? You want into that? Talk about dysfunctional."

"Shut up," she croaked. But with her new control, she found some will to fight his commands.

He stopped and she bumped into his smelly side. "Impressive, sweetcheeks. Fate's got some immunity, huh? Don't run into many who can resist. A couple of other enthrallers. A few of the healers." Shrugging, he tugged her toward the store's back room.

"Let me go." The words clung to the roof of her mouth. Part of her wanted to spend the rest of her life with this ugly Shifter and his bad breath.

His massive shoulders danced when he laughed. "Is your boyfriend going to beat me up?" The backroom door swung when he dragged her through. "I walked right by you two when you were doing your cuddle-bunny routine by the doors. He didn't sense me—"

Two hands wrapped around the Shifter's head. Surprised, he reached under his arm toward a gun, but the fingers poking into his cheeks jerked.

She expected a snap. Something sounding like a movie noise, sharp and faintly metallic. But the Shifter's neck broke with a wet grinding scratch. A gurgle followed as he tried one last time to breathe.

Ladon stepped back, his face solidified cold. The Shifter's body flopped at his feet and rolled onto its side. The man's eyes bulged, his legs convulsing.

Ladon shook off the hardness, a wave moving from his core to his neck and face. He stepped over the Shifter and took her arms, checking for wounds. "Did he hurt you?" His palm glided over her shoulder as he checked her eyes. "Did he give you specific instructions? Tell you to hurt yourself if you got away?" His gaze darted around the storeroom. "Were there others? Were you able to fight his control? He's likely a high class-two. Even low class-two enthrallers are dangerous."

Ladon killed a Shifter. Snapped his neck. Right in front of her.

A crack appeared in the back of her mind. A big crack, glowing with the fire behind it, and a hot glare poured over her seers.

"Rys, are you okay?" Ladon pointed at a loading bay. "Dragon says we need to leave."

"You killed him." Were the Shifters monsters, like the Burners? Cruel and terrible. Penny was a total bitch, but—

"Rysa?"

Was this okay in his immortal mind? She stared at the Shifter on the floor.

His boot knocked the Shifter's shoulder. "He's okay." He swung her into his arms and carried her off the end of the loading dock.

Her throat constricted like a tilt-a-whirl whipped her head too fast. "Is that what you did to those Fates?" The words scattered across the pavement, broken shards dropping as the calm she'd felt minutes before shattered.

His stone face flitted so fast she almost missed it.

"No one touches you." He gripped her fingers so tight they hurt. "No Fate. No Burner. No Shifter. They don't come near you!"

A stereo growl reverberated through the loading dock. It issued from them both, Ladon in front of her and Dragon, invisible, somewhere to the side.

"Rysa, get in the van. He'll call his friends when he wakes up." He caught her arm to help her into the back.

She pushed him away. "I'll get in on my own."

Dragon rolled in behind her and slammed the door, leaving Ladon alone on the asphalt.

26

That Shifter could have killed you. If he had told you to die, you would have died. Dragon signed faster than normal. Discordant patterns jerked across his hide in uneven intervals. The incident in the electronics store disturbed him as much as it disturbed her.

Ladon drove and, once again, yelled Russian into his phone.

Dragon's colors darkened. *Human is angry. The Shifters must show respect.*

She'd scream if she didn't calm down. Her abilities fizzled again—fire danced on the periphery. A hint of acid hit her nose. Flames licked at her eyes. Heat touched her skin. The Ambusti part of her Fateness used her confusion to reassert itself.

Clearheaded and in control, her ass. A swarm of burning cockroaches scurried around in her head and clicked just outside her field of vision.

She held a shudder. The bug image wasn't helping.

Dragon touched her shoulder. *Your mind is sizzling.*

So? she signed back. Her seers always dropped random crap into her awareness. Rysa Torres, the Chaos Fate. A monster.

Human worries. I worry, as well. Dragon's hide mimicked the wall of the van. He vanished for a split second, then reappeared, his head swinging toward the driver's seat. *We do not understand why you reject us. You called to us. We felt your terror. Human cannot tolerate when you are in danger.*

The van stopped. Black poured in through the roof vents. Ladon must have taken them out of town for it to be this dark.

Up front, he grunted and tossed his phone to the side. The door banged open at the same time as he reached under the seat. Then he stalked away, the door slamming hard behind him.

"Where's he going?" She peered out the windshield. In front of the van and surrounded by trees, a large picnic shelter and a playground sprawled over sand and asphalt.

Human must calm down. He is upset. Dragon's patterns cycled so fast they blurred.

Rysa pushed open the back door and hopped out. Ladon stomped around the playground clutching a bottle of vodka so tightly she thought it might shatter in his hand. Grunting like he had in the van, he whipped a rock at the jungle gym. It skipped across the slide, dust billowing off the plastic. A loud crack resonated through the park when the rock struck the slide's wood post.

He took a swig when he saw her walking toward him across the playground sand. "Are you going to yell at me again?"

"You're drinking?" He worked off snapping a Shifter's neck with vodka? So Penny wasn't just some bitch with an attitude. What she'd said held truth.

And she'd pointed a claw at Ladon, sneering. "He used to hunt your kind."

Rysa shuddered.

The crack in the back of her mind brightened for a split second. She forced herself to ignore it. She didn't go through hell with Penny just to lose the benefits of that witch's enthralling in less than a day.

Ladon's glance toward the picnic shelter caused an upwelling in the energy pulsing between him and Dragon. The beast must have moved out of the van after she'd stepped out.

Ladon flexed his biceps the way he did when Dragon chastised him and took another pull from the bottle. "I did what needed to be done."

"Killed a monster?" Shifter, Fate, or Burner, they were all monsters.

The vodka sloshed when he thrust the bottle forward. "He's not dead! They wouldn't put someone in my path who couldn't handle a neck twist."

Twenty-three centuries and he must have all sorts of rationalizations for his behavior floating around in his head.

His eyes narrowed. "This is about what Penny said. About me hunting Fates. It's why you asked if 'that's what I did to those Fates' at the store, isn't it?"

The air behind him shimmered. Dragon had moved under the jungle gym and now leaned against the slide.

Ladon glanced over. "We knew you'd ask, sooner or later." The bottle clinked when it bounced against his belt buckle. "I'm not a legate anymore. I don't have men under my command. Or people to protect. The concept of justice has changed. The rule of law of the Roman Empire is not the rule of law you were born into."

Her seers flickered: She saw his face, hard and cold and far more frightening than any moment she'd seen in the short time they'd been together. Ladon, a god of war who terrified everyone, including war's children. Dragon, his head low, his hide showing nothing but fury as he pranced behind his human.

Ladon rested a palm on the invisible Dragon's shoulder. "I have no progeny, Rysa. No woman I've loved has birthed a living child." His biceps flexed again, but he leaned into the beast. "Most pregnancies ended before my companions realized they were with child. Very few quickened. Even fewer came to term. They were all born dead. Sometimes they killed their mothers."

The woman who'd died the same night as the Draki Prime—the flash kicked Rysa in the gut. "Ladon—"

He shook his head and held out the bottle. "It's how things are. It's been the same for Sister. She's lost all her babies."

Ladon looked down at his feet. "Except one. Her daughter was born in a *Legio Draconis* tent under a snow drift on the edge of the Empire's northern frontier. My sister held in her arms the only breathing child born to either of us, then or now.

He smiled, the memories momentarily brightening his features. "She returned her family to Rome, me following. I had a niece. I wanted to see her grow. One morning, her father lifted her to his shoulders. They left the villa for the market, both happy and laughing. She was five years old, vibrant and so fast she could climb the flank of a dragon before you drew a breath."

A ghost of another smile flitted across his face. Even after the long millennia, thoughts of his family must still affect him deeply. But death and more death filled his life—and it settled in Rysa's chest like a demon determined to steal her air.

"Fates cut down both father and daughter outside the gates of our villa." He looked down at the sand again. "And Fates suffered a swift and severe retaliation."

He threw another pebble at the slide. The plastic cracked with a loud snap.

"All your grandfather's descendants who did not hide found death at the end of our swords. Invisible dragons rendered more than one triad to pulp in the public squares. Ripped tendon from bone for all to see. The normals thought gods had descended from the heavens.

"We emptied Rome of Fates, except for the Jani Prime. They knew not to cross our paths."

He leaned his forehead against the beast's neck. "Your uncle Faustus eluded me. He was complicit and I vowed vengeance. So I dragged his daughter from their villa and cut her throat. The girl didn't fight."

Vodka sloshed down his throat. "It had all been some damned Parcae game. Both girls were sacrifices." He held the bottle to the sky. "I was the knife the Fates wielded to call the gods down upon Sister and me."

Rysa touched her lips. A child for a child. Ladon had taken the life of a girl who would have been her cousin as revenge for the murder of the only living descendant of the Dracae.

"Her triad mates were twins. Your aunt's children. They killed themselves. The Emperor frothed and your uncle got his way—we were driven from Rome, Sister and I. Vanquished to the frontier. In the following centuries, we rarely returned. We commanded the *Legio* and kept our distance."

He'd consumed most of the vodka and now stared at the remaining liquid swirling inside the bottle. "I stopped hunting Fates after that. No more children have died at my hand."

His eyelids drooped. Every gesture moved in slow motion. His fingers gripped the neck of the bottle but twitched in a slow cadence. His breath moved shallow and deliberate. Ladon stood a frozen statue, a body reflecting the past. "I'd spent four centuries as Roman military. It was me and I was it. I *was* justice. I enacted what was expected of me. But Faustus's daughter did not cause my niece's murder." The bottle rested against his leg. "I can't undo what's done."

Dragon inched forward and waited between them, his big head a shadow swinging back and forth.

She felt as if rocks sat at the back of Rysa's mouth. Her body wanted to force them from her throat, but they weren't hers. They were purely Dracae.

"Sister stopped hunting Fates when the Draki Prime joined the *Legio*." Ladon kicked at a pebble. "They saved your kind, Rysa. Daniel, Timothy, and Marcus. They gave us a reason to leave the Fates alone. They were the tribute paid to the dragons to stop a war."

He looked up at the stars. "Now you know," he whispered. "You know what kind of man I am. What happens when the fury escapes. We are no better than Burners.

"So if you want to leave, we'll understand. We'll stay back. Keep you safe from a distance until we know both you and your mother are okay. Then we'll leave you alone to live your life."

He rested his forehead against Dragon's darkened hide. Flattened versions of waves and shapes flowed by his face.

"Your ability to see images from Dragon, the visions about us that you've had, the connection we feel—these things can't cloud your judgment. You need to make your own decisions and follow what your heart tells you."

She'd seen the joy in his eyes when she asked about surveying. The concern not only for her, but for her mom, and for Marcus and for Harold, too. The care he showed Dragon. The respect he offered her.

She'd felt his joy when he kissed her.

He'd left war behind, civilizations ago. Now, he wanted to work with the land. To help. He wanted forgiveness, even if he'd never ask for it.

She extended her hand.

The bottle dropped to the sand. He moved so fast he was inches from her before she inhaled, his fingers weaving around hers. She kissed his knuckles. When his grip unfolded, when he stroked a fingertip across her cheek, she turned her lips to his palm.

He scooped her up, his thigh between her legs and his face buried in the curve of her neck.

"Rysa," he whispered. "Don't leave."

27

"Ladon." She kissed his brow, the bridge of his nose, her arm around his head, her fingers in his hair. Her other arm reached for Dragon, her palm caressing his snout.

The beast hummed and the shadows infecting his patterns dissipated. Dragon became a mirage of brilliant radiance. He nuzzled Ladon's shoulder, then Rysa's, then Ladon's again.

"It's okay," she whispered. "It's okay."

Her body slid slowly down his front. His lips pressed gently up her neck to her jaw and chin.

"Every morning I wake determined to be the best man possible." The relief of the weight lifting from his shoulders brightened his eyes and skin. "I know can, now. I've felt that I can. From your seers. From you."

Electricity crackled under his hand and danced on the tips of her nerves. He kissed her palm. His tenderness flowed up her arm and all her fears dropped from her body like ice breaking under the sun.

"Ladon."

He breathed life into her world.

He smiled as the focus of his kisses traveled across her thumb, her knuckles, her nails. His lips settled onto the inside of her wrist and drew at her skin as if he drank. She shuddered, the sensation sparking up her arm and down to her fingertips. Her awareness of her own body swelled and she felt every inch of her flesh in high resolution.

Ladon released her wrist. His jaw nuzzled her arm as he moved his lips to the tender spot where her neck met her shoulder. He brushed aside her shirt's collar and kissed up the curve of her neck to just below her jaw.

Her body concentrated on him—his fingers as they traced her shoulder. The muscles of his core and chest as he held her against him. His scent. The brilliance of his eyes. His kisses. When his lips glided across her cheek, every inch of her body shivered.

He kissed the corner of her mouth, a soft touch much gentler than the kiss to her wrist. His fingers traced the lobe of her ear and down the delicate skin of her hairline.

Rysa wanted this moment, this tenderness, this, only this, in the present without the future or the past interfering. Her nasty flexed, drinking in their river of energy, but it didn't siphon. The crack in the back of her mind dimmed.

Ladon's embrace tightened. Dragon's colors filled her eyes. She wanted to soothe their minds, to take away their hurt, to give them all they needed. Now. Right now.

A kiss, a real kiss full of need and desire and focus, found her lips. She pulled him closer, kissing him harder. "Now, Ladon. Please."

His muscles rippled under her palms. Nothing else mattered, only his hand on her breasts and his lips traveling across the crook of her neck. Just him. Only him.

He pulled back enough for her to see his face. "Are you sure?" Another bone-melting kiss met her lips before she could answer.

She could argue with him. Babble words about character and fate and how he was done with war. But she called her seers instead, quickly, and looked for exactly what he needed to hear.

And exactly what she needed to say: "You can touch."

He kissed her with an intensity she hadn't expected and pulled her so tight against his chest she sucked in her breath. He lifted her high and buried his face against her collarbone. The tension in his shoulders released. His breathing deepened. Ladon enveloped her as his body accepted what she offered.

Three steps and he pressed her back against the van's rear door. She fumbled open the latch, grinning when his hand threaded under her shirt. As she scooted in, she rubbed the inside of her leg against his side, her ankle massaging the erection straining his jeans.

A low, deep sound rolled from his chest and his mouth descended to her nipple, his teeth nipping through the fabric of her shirt and bra. Heat washed through her body. Her back arched and her focus tightened to the tickle of his breath as he trailed nips over the delicate skin between her breasts.

But he stopped, holding most of his weight off her. "Rysa." He glided a finger over her abdomen. "There's still a chance you might get—"

Not tonight. "We're fine." She pulled him down on top of her and wiggled her hips against his.

He nibbled on the top of her ear, relief loosening his chest, and massaged her breast. Pinching her nipple hard, he rolled it as he breathed in her ear.

She ached like she'd been in the sun too long, a baking that needed release. It coursed out to her limbs, strengthened by Dragon's joy as he spun into the van. The beast settled, wild rainbow colors playing along his hide.

Dragon scooped her against his chest and Ladon's kisses trailed up to the soft spot above her breastbone. She stuttered in response, overwhelmed by the perfect rhythms of his body and the brilliance of the beast's lights.

Ladon yanked her shirt upward with his teeth at the same time his fingers tugged at her bra.

"It's been a while." She tangled her fingers in his hair. "I—*oh!*"

He pulled a nipple between his tongue and the roof of his mouth, pinching and sucking the right amount to fold a spark of pain into the penetrating pleasure. Another moan ripped from her throat and both her thighs rubbed against his sides. He chuckled as he bit, flicking his tongue as he unhooked her bra.

The fabric of his t-shirt teased, denying her access, and she yanked it over his head. She tugged on his diamond of chest hair, delighted when a deep *ah* pushed from his throat. Every one of his abdominal muscles contracted separately, each muscle skirting his chest and under his arms vibrated under her touch.

Next to her shoulder, Ladon splayed a hand over Dragon's hide. His eyes flicked to the beast. He licked between her breasts as he unzipped her jeans. "We're going to make you feel better than you've ever felt."

His kisses, his touch—she already felt more alive than she ever had in her entire life.

A low half-rumble, half-growl rolled from Ladon as he caressed her belly. She lifted her hips and he tugged at her jeans. Kisses stroked her thigh as he stripped off the fabric.

He caressed the side of her knee, in the hollow, at the perfect pressure and angle to send dazzling flashes of pleasure up her leg. At her calf, he nuzzled down her sock, playfully kissing her shin.

Her jeans hit the back door of the van with a loud snap.

She scooted up and he pressed her against Dragon with all his body weight. The thunder of his heart and the pulse of his blood washed over her. When he kissed her, his tongue darted into her mouth, touching hers with the briefest flick.

She wrapped her limbs around his torso. She wasn't going to let go, let him get away, to move his body off hers. But he shimmied down, his kisses moving lower as he followed the line of her rib cage. Delight fired into her chest and between her legs when his tongue flicked into her bellybutton.

He curled his thumbs around her panties and, as he kissed along her waist line, pulled them down. The lace fluttered to the floor after it hit the door.

Ladon kissed one inner thigh as he strummed the other. She moaned, not wanting him to stop, not wanting to be apart from either of them ever again.

His fingers moved upward and tugged on her auburn curls.

He licked his lips, a gesture that sent shivers all the way to the roof of her mouth. So very sure of his skills, bravado winked across his face.

Her head fell back, her body rising toward him, wanting the blinding pleasure he offered. "No one's ever—" Dragon's colors filled the van, flooding her senses. "*Oh!*"

Ladon's tongue found her most sensitive spot and he lapped at it, playing with it, like a predator played with a kill. Intense waves of pleasure flooded through her with each stroke and she pushed her hips upward, unable to stop herself. He chuckled, a low growl, and wrapped one arm around her middle.

Heat filled every cell, every corner and every curve. Her limbs trembled. Ladon's tongue encircled and flicked at the same time. An orgasm broke free, stronger than any other she'd felt in her life. Thoughts stopped and her vision blanked. Her body lost all sense of itself.

Ladon's rhythm changed. He matched the ecstasy bursting from her core and fueled another surge as intense as the first.

A low, deep moan rolled out of her, floating away on the final tremors as Ladon kissed her thighs again, grinning.

She pulled on his shoulders. She wanted to feel his weight and his body on hers. "Come here."

He slid off his jeans and leaned into her, pressing the full length of his hard erection against her belly. Every ounce of the need echoing through their bodies flowed through his kisses, his mouth slick with her.

She wanted him to feel the same power as the orgasm still pulsating inside her. To feel his body respond to her the same way she responded to him.

"Not yet." His gaze said that he wanted to plunge into her, but he didn't. He stroked her cheek instead, kissing her gently.

His shoulders tensed and his eyes lost focus. Dragon's hide glinted as Ladon pushed his palms into the beast's patterns. Their energy collapsed around her, the river contracting to a torrent. Its power concentrated into the short space between them—the space she occupied.

Visible electricity flashed across Dragon's skin, over hers, and onto Ladon. Every hair on her body stood up. A moan ripped from deep inside, the pleasure as penetrating as the orgasm.

"For you," Ladon whispered.

Her body surged in slow waves. Their power clarified everything and the world became a blend of spectacular sensation. Dragon's colors and the textures of Ladon's body merged with the force of the desire in his eyes. The rhythm of his heart and the barely visible matching beats within Dragon's patterns colored the scent of rain in the air.

Everything inside her opened. Every need, every fear, every moment of happiness and pain and longing, opened to Ladon and Dragon. Her cheeks rounded. She gave to Ladon the same brilliance he gave her.

Behind her, Dragon shifted into rich purples and burgundies.

"Beautiful." A rumble washed from Ladon's body all the way to her bones. "I'll earn what you give us." He kissed her top lip. "I swear to you."

Then her bottom lip. "I swear."

She stroked his cheek. Past, present, and future, he had. He did. He will.

Another rumble flooded over her body. It rolled not only from his chest as he leaned his forehead against her temple, but also from Dragon's chest to her spine.

She couldn't speak. The torrent rippled her body but the rumbles warmed her soul. And when Ladon gripped her hips, if she could have rumbled too, she would have.

She jumped when he moved into her, the pleasure and the pain twining together. He was bigger than Tom and it almost felt like her first time. But her body called to his, wanting him deeper.

"Are you okay?" He stopped, only a little inside her. Before she could answer, his mouth covered hers and all his need flowed from his lips to hers.

"Don't..." she breathed, returning his kisses, her arms tight around his neck. "Don't stop."

Nodding yes, he slid an arm under her bottom. He moved her onto him slowly, in soft, swaying movements.

Ladon filled her perfectly, fit perfectly, in her, against her, his arms tightening, touching, his mouth not releasing hers. His pelvis swayed in rhythmic pulses. Each sent a wave of joy through hers, and she answered, her voice staccato, her limbs jittering.

Another orgasm, amplified by his mouth on hers, tore through her body and broke into her vision. She yelped, pulling on his shoulders.

"Rys." He pressed her into Dragon as he traced her temple. "Beautiful woman." His pulses turned to strokes and he pulled her down with each thrust upward. *Beautiful... Rysa... With you.*

This man, this beast, their energy tight around her, his body against hers, in hers, he moved with purpose. She was their purpose and they wanted this—*he* wanted this—as much as she did. To let go of *alone*.

He kissed her again as his pace quickened. He didn't move like Tom or demand or grunt when he shifted her hips but breathed in when she breathed out, his chin grazing hers, soft reflections of language flooding from his throat. *Perfect woman...*

She kissed his neck, holding tight, her own pleasure keeping her from speaking. Fresh, real, it increased with each thrust. She stroked his back, gripped his shoulders, touched his arms. "More… Ladon…" Her body knew only him, understood only him, and his passion flowed through her, filling her soul as he filled her body.

The muscles along his spine tightened and his fingers dug into her shoulder blades. His back arching, he sank into her. His orgasm jolted through his muscles, and his body rocked against hers. She responded in waves of elation that met his, stronger than the ones before.

Dragon rolled backward. Rysa yelped, her hands twisting into the beast's coat. His starbursts expanded, brightening, and her eyes filled with brilliance as he carried his humans upward.

"Ladon!" She held tight, her forehead inches from the van's roof.

Ladon grasped an open vent to hold them steady. Still inside her, he continued to move, their legs entwined, his face intense. Secondary waves of frenzy rocketed through her oversensitive body and he responded the same, a quiet gasp moving from his lips to her ear. Another orgasm, one mirroring the beast's pulsing patterns, flooded his body.

The starbursts calmed. Dragon rolled again and Ladon dropped onto the blankets. With his face against her chest, he held her steady as she slid down between him and the beast. She pressed close, one hand on Dragon's snout and the other on Ladon's arm.

They wanted her touch. They wanted her in their lives. Ladon, his body calming, kissed the curve of her ear. There was no other place she wanted to be.

They tangled together, Ladon leaning them against Dragon. The beast shimmered in the gentle tones which calmed her chaos, his big head on the blankets next to her thigh. She rested in Ladon's embrace, soothed by the rise and fall of his chest and the gentle touch of his hand as he stroked her back.

How many minutes passed, she didn't know. Nor did she care. This, now, with them, let her breathe like a normal woman. Let her accept the comfort Ladon offered and the wonders Dragon presented without her fears and her issues and *monster* stomping on her life.

Ladon's kisses traced her hairline and his fingers caressed the little dragons on her wrist. "You're all we need." It lifted from his throat, clear and warm and with the full force of the energy curling around her.

She sat up. His eyes and skin gleamed. Confidence pulsed between the man and the beast and Dragon touched her hip. He harnessed it all— their lights, what they felt—and pushed it into her mind. Rysa saw strength and steadfastness in shapes of structure and weight.

Dragon showed her what she gave to them.

"Oh, Dragon." She hugged his head and he puffed out a small flame.

Everything would be fine. She had them and her world would be fine.

She kissed Ladon with all the passion they'd just shared. "We have a lot to talk about, don't we?"

He pulled her back into his arms. "And plans to make?" He traced her cheek.

They'd find a surefooted path, one they'd navigate together. She smiled. "I think so."

He exhaled like he'd been holding his breath. A quick grin danced over his lips. He tapped along her hip as he considered options. "Should we go? I don't like being out in the open like this." He moved away, only an inch or two, and reached for their clothes. "There are restrooms in the picnic shelter, if you want. Before we leave." He pointed at the door.

The crack in the back of her mind brightened. Ladon handed over her bra and panties, not noticing her unease.

"We could find a hotel." He smiled as he stroked her arm.

She squeezed his fingers, determined to hold the weirdness in check. Her Ambusti Prime status dropped sudden and annoying blasts of Burner chaos into her life. But she had control and she'd tame it. She had the help she needed.

Dragon nuzzled her shoulder and Cara Caras danced through her senses. "He's still hungry. We should stop."

Ladon felt around for his socks. "We'll get food. And I vote hotel. I'd like to sleep in a real bed tonight. With the most beautiful woman who has ever walked this earth right here." Grinning, his brilliant eyes warm and happy, he pointed at his side. "And your head right here." His finger moved to his shoulder.

"Most beautiful?" She tossed a sock at his head and chuckled when he made a show of fumbling it.

"Like no other." He pulled his sock on. "America's finally given us a reason."

Dragon opened the back door and rolled out onto the asphalt. Images of *itch* flicked to Rysa. The beast wanted a good rub against the big tree next to the picnic shelter before they left.

"A reason for what?" she asked.

Ladon pulled on his other sock, watching her watch him. "To remember. To pay attention. To plan."

Dragon ambled away.

For a moment, a split second, for no reason at all, Rysa smelled fire.

Ladon patted his pocket. "Have you seen my keys?" He turned his back and leaned away, toward the front of the van.

The energy they shared stretched like taffy. It pulled away from her mind like silk lifting from her skin and for a split second, she felt naked and exposed.

Vulnerable.

Sudden glare flooded into her head like fire reflecting off ice. It yanked her mind sideways, a threat so terrible it clamped onto all of her attention.

Death filtered into her nose. Death by fire, death by acid. She'd never smelled death before, but she knew immediately what the stench meant.

She was going to hurt them. It poked from her seers, sharp and so ice cold it sucked away every ounce of the warmth she felt in Ladon's arms. Like a flood of cockroaches, the thought poured into her seers, through the crack that had been enlarging since the Shifter terrified her in the electronics store.

It swept in, a fountainhead of ice bugs crawling on her skin, fueling an acid death.

"Two days together." Ladon patted the driver's seat, not looking at her. "And you're already taking better care of Dragon than I ever have."

She stiffened. Her calm shattered like it had been stabbed. Everything she felt seized solid and turned dense and unbending.

The future forced through a new vision: Ladon, rigid and in pain, blood soaking his t-shirt. His agony raked her body.

The control had been an illusion. Her seers lashed out, snapping and screaming and she'd cause Ladon's death. The truth of *what-will-be* cut, a knife her nasty couldn't block. Every one of her muscles contracted.

"Two days," she muttered. Snaring them like this, so fast—she should have known better. Impulsive and stupid, she'd wanted him and his body and she'd just put the best part of her life in mortal danger because she couldn't pay attention.

"Rysa?" A rigidness constricted Ladon's abdomen and he grimaced. "Love, what's wrong?" A groan pushed out of his chest. He leaned forward and dropped a hand to the floor.

She bolted for the door. Their future held death and it was her fault. The burden of her actions solidified into an evil, serrated knife attacking her physically, as if someone else wielded it.

Her temples throbbed. She was a monster. She wouldn't cry.

She had no right to ensnare them this way. She'd trapped them inside of something they'd never step out of willingly. A net over their lives, that's what she was. She held them to the dirty ground.

Her feet landed on the parking lot. All she saw was blood and burning.

She slid on the grit as she ran away.

28

"Rysa!" Her seers buzzsawed across his mind, then vanished, silenced.

The door of the women's restroom slammed against the wall. Dragon forced his front through before it closed, but she backed away. She huddled inside, refusing to acknowledge either of them.

Is she in a vision? Ladon pushed. Yanking his t-shirt over his head, he dropped off the bumper. *Do you know what's wrong?*

The beast's back end stuck out the door. *Her seers are silent. She will not respond to my questions.* Dragon mimicked the restroom building but his tail moved in a clipped arc across the asphalt walk. His hide sparked with random flashes. He was a dragon-shaped cloud of churning fireflies between Ladon and the door.

She'd muttered "two days." What if the flare he'd felt had been her future-seer? *She won't tell you why she cries?*

No. A pause. *She attempts to pull away.* A punch of fear hit Ladon before the beast reined it in. *She is good for you. She must not leave.*

"Rysa!" Ladon ran to the shelter. On the edges of his perception where her seers caressed his consciousness, the music diminished. It backed away like a terrified animal retreating into a den.

Muffled sniffles pushed from inside the building.

"What did you see? Don't pull away from us!" Agony flitted across the surface of their connection. "Tell me what's wrong!" If she'd seen the War Babies, she'd have said something, not run away. Whatever it was, *he* did it—will do it.

She hiccupped. "You're the second man I've been with."

Second? Was this about that boy? The one who hurt her? He slammed his fist against the door's frame. He said "two days together" and her past-seer must have fired a terrible memory into her present. Part of him breathed again—she hadn't seen the future. What tore at her wasn't some stupid behavior *he* might do. The past idiocy of others he could deal with.

I'm going to find that boy, he pushed to Dragon.

Why?

The beast would not approve of his answer so Ladon ignored the question. *Will you move, please?*

She won't allow me to touch her, but she won't allow me to leave, either.

What did that little punk do to her? "Rysa! Come out!"

A sob echoed through the wall. "I'm… I'm…" She trailed off, not finishing.

She signed 'I'm bad for you.'

"Bullshit!" Twenty-three centuries of companions and wives who watched him from the corners of their eyes, always with a twinge of tension. They didn't think he noticed, but he did. Not one of them trusted him. Not one touched his connection to the beast.

And now memories of some damned normal made Rysa think she was bad for him?

He didn't care about her attention problems. He didn't care if others found her anxiety issues irritating, either. He only cared about the woman and the joy they'd found together. "Finding you was the best thing that has *ever* happened to us!"

"It doesn't matter."

"Yes, it does!" He'd find that boy and smack the life out of his pathetic head.

Then he'd snap his damned normal neck.

You will not.

"Why?" Ladon shouted.

Another sob. "Because… because…."

Because you promised Rysa you would earn the joy she gives us.

Ladon hollered, fists clenched. The pain in her voice fired through every one of his nerves. No one caused trauma to his woman and got away with it. "What did he do to you?"

"What are you talking about?" The sobs subsided.

She has moved closer but she still refuses to allow me to touch her.

"That boy. The normal who hurt you."

She paused. "Why?"

"Why? You've locked yourself in a restroom!" A growl crept out of his throat.

"He has nothing to do with this!"

"That's it!" Ladon smacked the building and knocked loose a brick. "I'm going to find him. He's going to apologize. Down on his knees, his forehead pressed to your feet. He's going to beg for your forgiveness." The punk would offer a sincere apology. He'd mean every word of it or he'd lose fingers. Maybe a whole hand. Dragon could cauterize the wound.

"No, you are not!"

"Yes, I am." He paced next to Dragon's tail. "Do you think I will tolerate this? You crying in a park restroom? Hurting this way?"

"Ladon! You can't!" Anguish spread her voice thin.

All of his attention pointed toward Rysa. No more thoughts of revenge. No more pacing. His hearing pinpointed to her breathing. His vision to the edges of the door.

"After what just happened, I can't let this be." He'd promised she'd be safe. Past, present, or future, that nothing more would stalk her.

"He's dead." More sobs. "He wrapped himself up in my life and he went home and his car got hit by a semi on 94 outside of Janesville. He died and his cousin died, too. They died in the snow on a freeway in Wisconsin because I had a bad feeling and he wouldn't listen when I asked him to please wait half an hour before he left."

The little bastard hurt her, ignored her pleas, and ended up dead. "Beautiful, I'm sorry." Served him right. But his stupidity killed part of her, too. "It wasn't your fault. Your seers weren't active. You couldn't have stopped him." Even dead, his ghost tore open wounds.

"Gavin decided my freshman year that he wanted to be part of my life, and what happened to him? The Burners almost ate him. I almost brought ruin down on him, too."

Damn it, why wouldn't she let him in? He smacked the doorframe again. "Rysa, you cannot think any of it was your fault."

"I'm a goddamned *Fate*!" Her sobbing increased, the volume rising. "I'm a Fate who can't control her impulses and... and..." She trailed off, her sobs becoming harsher.

She backs away from me.

"You can't... Love, you can't think this way." She'd lose herself in it.

"Ladon, leave me alone." Her words edged bitter and broken through the wall.

She is hyperventilating.

He heard the terror in her voice. The difficulty breathing. "Rysa?"

A pause. "I should have waited. I should have made sure that..." She hiccupped. "That you and Dragon would be okay."

"Move." He leaned against the beast, fear binding his gut. This wasn't about that boy. Her future-seer showed her something that frightened her so deeply she pushed them away. "Please."

Dragon backed out of the door.

"No! No! I've tangled you up with me and—" She bolted around Dragon.

"Rysa!"

She skidded, her arms around her chest, the sobs as strong as before. Dragon leaped over her head and landed between her and the trees. He circled, his head low.

A rasp pulled up from her chest and she bent over, her arms crossed over her belly. "I see what's inevitable now. We... we can't..."

"Rysa..." He stepped closer, but she backed away.

"I know now what kind of..." She looked away. "I'm sorry I snared you. It can't be anything more than just sex."

"*Snared* me? *Just* sex?" Those four words sliced him open from chest to groin.

She didn't believe that. She couldn't believe it. Her head hung and a rasping hiccup pulled from her chest.

Her terror crushed down on his ribcage. She'd lose herself to this. And he'd lose her. "Damn it, Rysa, look at me!"

"No."

Dragon reeled, invisible, as confused as Ladon.

"That was *not* just sex!" Anger flickered. "You didn't think it was just sex before your seers flared." Underneath, is this what she thought of herself? "With you, it will *never* be just sex! Never."

Dragon crept forward but she pushed him away. If she dropped too far, these thoughts would kill her. She'd cut herself off.

"It doesn't matter what I believe. Or what I want. I'm a Fate and I'm your death."

He wrapped his arms around her though she pushed against him, too. "No you are not. You're not my death. You won't be. Ever. You touched Dragon and color returned to his world. You touched me and I came back to life. You're—"

She twisted away. "I don't have control. I thought I did, but I don't. Penny gave me something fake."

"No, love, she could only coax out what's in you. So it has to be there. You have what you need."

Shaking her head, she pulled her arms tighter. She pointed at her temple. "There's been a hole since ..." She slapped the side of her head. "... since Dragon smacked my cousins. The future flooded through. It ripped open and I see fire and I see you dead, Ladon! I'm your death!" Her throat constricted like she wanted to scream, but nothing came out.

She hit the side of her head again.

The War Babies must have gouged her mind during the Texas vision. *Do you feel it? What they did?* They damaged her and it manifested now.

The cretins would bleed out at his feet for this.

Dragon sniffed Rysa's head. *Her seers feel wrong.*

The Draki Prime's seers had been a trio of instruments, tuned perfectly. The War Babies' seers thundered like a storm, discordant and violent. But the Jani Prime, the triad of Rysa's mother, they'd been in the middle: Cymbals in the wind, chimes, and hammers on a metal drum.

Sometimes Rysa's seers siphoned. Sometimes they added. But they always sang when they touched Ladon's mind and they always embraced.

But not now. Her music clanged. Her touch hammered. Her seers felt not as if she'd lost control, but as if her control had been stolen from her.

"Rysa, come here." He extended his hand.

Daniel could override other future-seers, Dragon pushed. The beast surrounded them both, blocking all views from the trees and the lot entrance.

Centuries ago, Ladon watched Daniel shape the future into a weapon and thrust it into the minds of a triad who didn't have the experience to fight it.

"Rysa." Ladon swung her into his arms. "We need to get you back to the van. Now." His vision charted every corner and shadow of the park. "You're not safe out here."

She sobbed against his chest but she didn't hit him again. "I won't hurt you. I should have waited. I'm impulsive and I should have remembered and made sure you would be okay."

He stopped half way to the van. "That's not you talking."

Choked whispers buried her words. "I was eleven when my dad left." Another sob. "I hurt the men I love."

Everything in his soul slammed against his chest. Everything he felt, everything reverberating to him from Dragon, every kiss, every touch that had spoken more volumes than any word.

Every single moment he'd spent with her welled up.

He dropped to his knees on the damp pavement, his arms cinching tight around the woman who had become his core the first moment he saw her. The woman whose touch righted his world.

The men she loved hurt *her*. But it stopped now, here, in this park.

We must leave, Dragon pushed.

Each tree rustled, distinct and separate. The illumination from the road blinked, dipping slightly with each passing car. Dragon backed away, running silent. After centuries of practice with the Draki Prime, the dragons had learned to hide themselves from both Shifters and Fates, including Primes.

Because only one explanation accounted for what was happening. Only one, and it wasn't *Les Enfants de Guerre*.

No matter how powerful they were, their future-seer, Metus, wasn't Prime enough to inflict this kind of damage. In all Ladon's twenty-three centuries, he knew of only two Fates other than Daniel who could create an injection: Janus, his fellow Progenitor and man from whom all Fates descended.

And Janus's son.

A dark sedan with tinted windows spun into the parking lot, its tires squealing.

Ladon didn't need Fate abilities to know who it was.

29

Rysa pressed her palm against her temple. Her seers erupted flames against the ice bugs clicking in her head: She saw Ladon covered in so much blood it dripped from his arm. She smelled his pain. She felt Dragon's mind shred as his human bled out.

She couldn't stop it. Fire and blood and dissolution. Her seers felt stuck on.

"I should have made sure." She should have stopped herself. Thought things through. But no, she acted impulsive and stupid because a wonderful man wanted to be with her.

She curled into a ball against Ladon's chest even though she should run. She should leave and take her burning ADHD as far away from him and Dragon as possible.

"Fight it. Hold on." Ladon tensed under her palms. Every one of his ligaments stretched as his body reflected her torment.

Dragon stepped over his humans, his body a shield between them and the sedan. He flashed in microsecond bursts of angry reds and oranges. After-images filled Rysa's eyes and she squinted. For a blinding split-second, the pavement turned dust beige and the sky flame blue.

"Don't trust your seers." Ladon nodded toward the sedan.

His connection to Dragon arced across her consciousness as they tried to calm her spasming seers. Splendor mixed with blood and death. Dragon's memories rushed through her consciousness: Her touch on his snout. The wonder in her eyes when he held her above the asphalt. *Hello.* And he blazed more beautiful than any other creature on Earth.

The memories burst to vapors.

Ladon lifted her into his arms. A new symphony played out in the tactile sense of his skin and the tender voice of his words: *Beautiful*. It echoed in her head, clear and crisp. *Beloved*. Under the pain in her skull, her seers grasped one thin filament of possibility: Ladon, content and entwined with her. His lips on her forehead. Her head on his shoulder.

"Put me down!" Her tears soaked his t-shirt. It was a wish. It could only be a wish.

"No. This isn't you." His chest tightened under her cheek as air whistled through his clenched teeth. "By the gods, we feel it. We feel what's happening to you."

The beast mimicked the gray world and the speed of information transfer flowing around her increased.

"We will not leave you." Ladon's arms stayed like steel as he dropped her feet to the pavement. "We will get you through this."

The sedan's door swung open. A tall man unfolded from the interior, his expression flat. The expensive suit he wore draped beautifully, but it looked unkempt. Singed.

She knew who he was. She'd seen him in the Texas vision. Auburn hair, similar to but lighter than hers. Wiry and strong, like her mother. Eyes so blue they flashed in the park's one light.

Her uncle Faustus.

His skin looked red, as if he'd spent too much time under a heat lamp. Fingers twitching, he adjusted his cuffs.

"How can he be here? He's dead."

Ladon enfolded her, his arms tight around her belly, his chest pressed against her back, his chin against her cheek. "He lied. He's good at it."

The War Babies faked the vision. Stitched in the present a fake view of the past and made it look as if the Burners killed her uncle in Texas.

Twitching again, Faustus stepped forward, then back, toward the sedan. "So you recognize your family? Good. Good." A quick growl popped out of his throat and he slammed his fist against the top of the car. "You're a good Jani child. A good one."

"Burndust," Ladon said. "He's snorting burndust to stay invisible."

The dust did the same things to his body that Rysa saw in her mother when she ingested the implosion. The shuddering. The anger. The damage.

He wouldn't feel the effects of the sickness in his joints either, no matter how much they hurt.

"Why did Ladon-Dragon vanish?" Faustus scratched his chin.

"He's deciding if he should kill you."

Faustus frowned and walked forward. He stopped about five feet away, his eyes narrow as he studied Rysa. He clapped, the sound pulsing through her head, before pointing at Ladon.

"You want to stay with him, pumpkin? He kills me and your mother drops dead from the sickness." He sniffed and tapped his cheek. "She's not *that* strong. No. She'll drop where she stands. Stood." Another sniff. "That pathetic Burner will gorge himself on her flesh before she cools." He shook his head, his disapproval registering as a dramatic frown. "Damned Burners show no respect."

"Get out of her head."

Her uncle was in her head? *Fire* was in her head. The entire world burned.

She'd seen this, at the house—the burning world—and she'd forgotten because she let her feelings for Ladon and her out-of-control abilities and the War Babies threatening her mom take over. She forgot because she couldn't pay attention. But the world will burn. People will die. And she'd cause it.

Faustus laughed and leaned forward, his hands on his hips. "Why? She needs to see what's coming." He whistled and pointed at Rysa. "She's the catalyst. She's the one who will harness their chaos. She's the Ambusti Prime."

"Get out of her head. *Right. Now.*" Ladon growled, the sound pushing from his chest to Rysa's shoulder blades.

Faustus sighed, a grand exhalation of air accompanied by the wide sweep of his arms. "Pumpkin." He extended his hand. "Let's go. He's not what you think he is."

An ignited world gurgled in the back of her throat and she couldn't keep anything straight. "You're a liar. You beat my aunt and your children murder and I won't go to the Burners! I know what will happen and I won't be their tribute."

She buckled forward but Ladon laced his fingers with hers, his grip so tight it hurt, and held her back, against his chest.

Faustus paced to the left and grimaced before pacing back to the right. He bounced on his heels, jolting again. Another burst of his laughter filled the park. "Tribute? Please. Parcae are not *tribute*. We are the measure of civilization. The shapers of purpose. All our sacrifices move forward what must be." He pointed at Ladon's head. "Did *he* tell you that ridiculous story?"

Neither Rysa nor Ladon answered.

Faustus guffawed. "Of course he did! Still a simpleton, I see. You share two brains. You should be a genius. But there's not much in either head, is there?"

Ladon didn't respond. He stepped in front of Rysa, his body a wall between her and Faustus. She watched her uncle over his shoulder.

Faustus jabbed a finger into the air several times before he waved his arms. "You're the damned ghouls' savior."

The Burners will eat her. Tear her body into little pieces and pass around a bowl full of Rysa so they all got a mouthful.

Faustus paced again. "What the hell are you going to do with your life? Use your seers to cheat on exams? Become a park ranger? Have visions of lions and tigers and bears? Or are you going to lay a finger to the winds of time every evening—" He licked his finger and held it out. "—as you drive home to your suburban hovel?" His finger poked at Ladon. "One must know exactly what dinner to cook for him each night."

"I won't go to the Burners!" she screamed. Her life was her own. Ladon had told her when she activated that her life was her own.

Faustus laughed. "You're *Parcae*. We are the living equivalent of the Fates. We do not now, nor have we ever, lived for the simpering desires of the petty." He clapped loudly and skipped in front of the sedan. "What are you going to do, pumpkin, the first time your seers take the measure of a man and you know you must cut his threads and send him to his death? Will you wring your hands and blubber like a housewife? Fate will have its due, young lady. Fate *always* has its due. Your purpose is to give its glorious clarity to the world."

His bared teeth held more heat, more viciousness than a Burner's. Predatory and precise, her uncle's goal was to make her a weapon.

No. Her seers showed the truth: She was to become a weapons *factory*.

Her uncle's future-seer danced like hammers on metal. "Yes! Now you see. You're to be their lovely center. The one who gives them purpose! Someone needs to. Your aunt couldn't do it."

The flood from the crack in the back of her mind raged into her chest and her belly. The nauseating truth clicked into place: Ismene was *half* dead. Dead enough to cause the sickness for her mother and her uncle, but not dead enough to hold still. "How?" Rysa yelled. "How did Ismene become one of them?"

"They got her. I couldn't stop it." He jigged around, pointing at the stars. "No one can predict what Burners will do."

Was it an accident?

Her brain clicked again: Fire over land and sky. Fire in her veins. Fire burning every nerve to nothing but anguish and she'd only care about her hunger. Stripped of her humanity, her Fatehood, she'd be fire uncontrolled.

Faustus shrugged. "Ismene's blood made them useful. Regular Burners couldn't set off a mall. I made the best of a bad situation. Do you know how hard it is to herd those damned monsters? And I had to have enough of her children to get the job done. Had to find the pumpkin." He waved at Rysa. "Imagine my delight when I realized *you're* the Ambusti Prime. The Jani are the best. The best."

"But the world burns." If she went to the Burners, she'd cause it.

Faustus shook a fist at random bits of air. "I've seen the truth for a century and a half, niece. The same things you're seeing." He paced again. "It's not you that causes Hell on Earth." Faustus reached out his hand. "Our role is to stop it. You need to come with me."

Under her palms, Ladon's core tightened. He turned in her arms and touched her cheek. He didn't plead. He wouldn't plead. But she saw need. Need and ferocity and promise.

Everything she wanted stood in front of her, offering everything he had.

Faustus stared, his gaze steady over Ladon's shoulder.

Ladon didn't turn toward her uncle. He focused on her. "Where is Ismene?"

Faustus jigged in a circle. "How the hell should I know? She's a Burner." He danced forward, his eyes narrow. "Come out from behind him and act like the Parcae you are. Do the job fate's given you."

Ladon's hand moved between their chests and he finger-spelled: *Run. Van.*

Faustus's gaze darted to their vehicle as his seer thundered through the parking lot. "Stay here, Rysa. You need to come with me. We have work to do." He tilted his head, his gaze boring a new hole in her skull.

The spike in her head inched deeper. She grabbed her forehead, a shrill groan grinding between her teeth as she pushed back.

Ladon whipped around but kept his hands behind his back and gripping her waist. "Faustus!"

Her uncle's attention snapped to Ladon, but he mirrored her movements, touching his own forehead. A low groan rolled from his throat and he squinted. "She can't do that. No one pushes back."

What-will-be seared: Burner venom morphing her body into something caustic and violent. It will ravage as it scorches, a deluge of fire and transformation roaring from cell to tissue to organ and out through her veins.

Twisted and angry, she'll create an army.

Her children will be like her, the Fate singular, and hold past, present, and future. She will give them the order of the universe, the opposite of their Burner chaos. Her blood will calm their ragings.

They'll be stable and overpowering.

The agony of the vision knocked her backward. She couldn't ignite into something soulless and malevolent that was meant to birth demons.

It couldn't happen.

Faustus stroked his chin. "I always knew the Jani Prime would bring about the cure."

"No." She'd create an army so incendiary neither Ladon nor his sister could stop it.

"Get out of her head!" Ladon bellowed.

Faustus walked toward them. "She's seeing what all the Primes have seen for the last century and a half. I just opened the spigot." His wrist circled in little twisty motions. "It's not the Burners who end the world." He halted inches from Ladon. "Who else makes fire?"

Who else—

The realization hit like her head had bounced on the pavement.

She was just another attack, another weapon in a battle fought in a very long war between the Parcae and the Dracae.

Rysa, the weapon of dragon destruction.

Another deep growl reverberated from Ladon's chest. "Take care with what you insinuate, Faustus Aurelius Jani."

Her uncle poked at Ladon's chest but he pulled back before his finger touched. "Every powerful future-seer on the planet sees it. I see it. Her cousin Metus sees it. Oh!"

He pointed again. "All of Timothy's descendants see it! And that ponce Daniel? It was the last bit of knowing his brain made before my boys gutted him."

Something was terribly wrong. This wasn't right.

"Leave me alone!" Rysa screamed.

"Come, pumpkin." Faustus extended his hand one last time.

Ladon's stance changed. The mention of Daniel turned his back as hard as granite. "She's made her choice. She won't go with you." The words came out deep, with the authority of the ages filling all his pauses.

Faustus sighed another grand exhale. "Get in the car! No more playing house with Ladon-Human. It's time you grew up and faced your responsibilities. You're Parcae. We do what we are meant to do."

Behind Faustus, the air shimmered.

Dragon swung a large metal pipe, fire pouring from his mouth.

Her uncle's future-seer thundered toward the beast and Faustus avoided the flames, but the pipe cut a gash along his forehead.

Faustus dropped back, dazed, blood streaking his hairline. "Ladon-Dragon!" More thunder on metal. "There you are. I know where you will be."

His posture cocky and arrogant, he dodged more of Dragon's stabs.

Rysa saw Dragon's instructions. Her body froze.

The pipe flew like a javelin toward her head, a shrill whistle screaming through its length. Ladon twisted, one arm behind his back and around her, the other at his shoulder.

He caught the pipe, his grip less than a foot from Rysa's nose.

Ladon's back rippled as he slammed the pipe into the asphalt.

A crack blasted through the park and sparks showered their feet, the pipe grinding deeper. Holding it like a pike, Ladon leaned forward, his focus on her uncle.

Rysa backed away.

Right now, in front of her, Ladon's body manifested the opposite of the gentle touches they'd shared before.

He poised to kill.

He didn't want to be a warrior anymore, to fall to the expectation that he'd do battle. Yet here he was, between Rysa and her fate.

For an instant, it frightened her more than her uncle's attacks.

She'd stolen Ladon's options and now the violence of his past reared into his present. He called on an expertise he wanted to leave behind. All because of her.

Faustus sneered.

He threw a knife, fast like a Burner. But unlike them, her uncle wouldn't miss. Her nasty took control and her rigid body jerked to the side, but the blade nicked her upper arm.

She fell to the pavement, a new fire erupting through her veins. Her nasty pulled in her seers as it desperately tried to protect her fraying consciousness.

Ladon slammed Faustus to the ground.

Her uncle rolled and landed in a crouch. He sneered, his fingertips drumming the asphalt.

He laughed and pointed at Rysa's temple.

Another future dagger pierced a new wound and she stiffened, her muscles unwilling to move. She tasted death, all death: Ladon in blood. Dragon, his hide gray and lifeless. Herself, a bullet in her chest.

Dragon's ghost-form shimmered against the dark sky as he lifted Faustus off the pavement. The beast's hide bristled, his fury that Faustus harmed his humans stood as a solid wall in the emotions flowing around Rysa.

He flung her uncle at the sedan as a brilliant white flame burst from his mouth.

Faustus contorted midair and landed on his feet, dropping out of the fire. A haze billowed off his suit jacket, but he'd escaped unharmed.

Ladon's arm drew back, the speed and control of his muscles perfect, and the pipe launched like a missile.

Faustus lunged to the side but the pipe caught his jacket and speared it to the pavement. His shoulders wiggled and he yanked, but Ladon twisted his arm before he freed himself.

Faustus laughed. "She's going to become what she's meant to be. She's Parcae. You can't fight that."

Ladon slammed Faustus against the ground. "She will have the future she wants."

"A litter of Dracae pups? That worked *so* well for your other women, didn't it? Better she become a Burner."

Ladon punched. Faustus spit out a tooth.

The world rocked like a canoe and Rysa pitched to the side. She'd drop, slam her head on the pavement, maybe shatter her elbow, but Dragon's invisible hand laid her down.

"Your boyfriend's going to die in a rain of blood and fire, pumpkin, and you're the cause." Faustus chuckled, more a gurgle than a laugh, and pushed against Ladon.

Rysa pulled herself to her knees. "It doesn't have to happen. I won't let it." She'd pay attention, even if it killed her. She wouldn't become something evil.

Faustus struggled. Ladon held him down. "We're Parcae! Control is irrelevant."

"Your visions are wrong." Ladon slammed Faustus against the pavement again.

"*All* Parcae are having false visions? You *are* an idiot." Faustus grunted. "Of course, it might be the Dracas. But I think it'll take both of you to cause the damage we see."

"If I stay with them, if I see it coming I can help them. I—"

"You can't stop what's due with kisses and hugs! Please, child. Dragons are feared in European mythology for a reason."

Ladon punched again.

"I see what you will do!" Faustus licked blood off his lip. "Your kind is more dangerous to this world than all the Mutatae and Parcae combined! You can snap my neck but others will stop you. It's fated."

"It won't be them!" Blood dripped down Rysa's arm and her stomach churned. The visions flared. She squinted, knowing only burning and death.

Faustus chuckled. "She has you wrapped around her little finger. When she turns Burner, you won't hurt her. The beast won't, either. My dear sister and her impeccable present-seer. She's the best."

Ladon smacked Faustus's head against a window. Glass cracked.

"Her army will end you. You won't defend yourself!" A small gun dropped from Faustus's sleeve. He pushed it into Ladon's ear. "Silly me. Forgot about this. I blame the dust. Heh."

Ladon stiffened.

"Maybe I should kill you now." Faustus frowned. "But martyring you would cause your sister to rampage." Faustus pushed Ladon off. "And we know what happens when one of you rampages, don't we?"

Backing toward the driver's door, Faustus snorted, his future-seer hammering. "Tell you what, pumpkin. I'll give you more time with the Dracos, how's that sound? So you can say your good-byes. Then we'll talk again."

Faustus saluted with the gun. "She was born for a purpose." Then the driver's door banged closed.

And the future banged in Rysa's head.

30

Memories that weren't memories blotted out everything Rysa saw and heard. Her body shook with jolts and spasms. Her gut knotted. Three seers snapped between past, present, and future and the Jani Prime overrode *Rysa*. Too fast, too intense, the emotions frothed.

Her body ebbed in venom and flame.

Sensations flowed from the present-seeing tentacle of her nasty Fate abilities: One War Baby hit her mother and another made burndust. The third tortured Billy by breaking his bones.

Mira tried to run into the prairie with the snorting buffalo but the past-seer slapped her hard and grinned under his expensive sunglasses.

"Mom!" Rysa's cheek stung like the past-seer had hit her.

Ladon picked her up off the gritty pavement. Her uncle had driven away but she and Ladon and Dragon were still exposed, still out in the open, in the middle of the park's asphalt parking lot.

"What are you seeing?" Ladon asked.

Her mother's rage punctured every nerve in her body. Rysa cringed as she mirrored the flailing pain of her mom's present. "Stupid Eurotrash triad! *Ah!*" She thrashed in his arms, more Mira than herself.

A different sensation hit, felt by her past-seeing tentacle: Faustus hitting Ismene. Rysa tasted blood in her mouth.

"Put me down! Worthless damned Dracos! All you two have ever done is strut around and look pretty." Ismene's or Mira's anger spit out the words. Rysa didn't know which.

Ladon ignored her yelling. He carried her to the van and set her on the blankets. Dragon followed, slamming the door.

Her mother seethed somewhere far away. Rysa tried to contain it, but Ismene also foamed across the threads of the Jani.

Rysa tasted metal and hammers.

Ladon covered the knife wound on her arm with a towel. "Keep pressure on it."

She blinked and pressed on her bicep.

A jug of water gurgled as he ripped off the top. With a damp paper towel, he dabbed at the cut. "We need to stitch that."

Her mother forced her way into Rysa's vision again. "Bison." Lots of angry bison. Her mother put up a fight near a herd of American Bison.

His brows knitted. "Where?"

A "Welcome to South Dakota" sign flicked through her seers, but the sky was bright. "They entered South Dakota this morning." She shook her head. "Tomorrow morning. I don't know."

"We fix this first." He pressed the towel against her cut again.

She slapped at his hand. "Let it bleed! What difference does it make?"

He leaned back. "Try to focus, Rysa."

"I can focus." Mira and Ismene might flicker in her consciousness, but her own past also flooded in.

"You're like all the other guys. You smile and then get mad when I talk too much and can't sit still. I'd think watching my boobs move up and down would be fun." She flopped against the floor.

"When have I treated you that way?" He stopped dabbing, anger and hurt playing through his eyes. "I haven't! I never will. I'm not some pathetic normal."

Rysa stared, caught by the memory of his stubble against her skin. "You taste good." She stroked his stomach.

He grabbed her wrist. "You're out of control."

"You can get whatever you want just by walking into the room, can't you?" Bloody fingerprints trailed across his t-shirt when she slapped him again. "Ladon-Human, the gorgeous sun-god, and his amazing Dragon."

He groaned, refusing to answer. He pressed clean gauze against her arm.

Her mother's memories flickered like cards in an animation. "You're a good man. Better than any of the Jani."

She remembered her mom staring at her little stuffed toy: "He's a good dragon, but you know that already, don't you?"

Rysa muttered her mother's words. "He's special because he's *Rysa's* dragon." What they meant, she didn't know.

Ladon glanced at Dragon and a pulse moved between them. "Tell us what you're seeing. No matter what we feel, we can't help if we don't know."

A jolt snapped through her limbs. Dread clicked and locked, thick and smothering. She leaned forward, gasping.

French words pushed aside her English: "*Les Enfants de Guerre ont ma mère*," she groaned. 'The War Babies have my mother.'

Ladon's face blanked.

The van came back into focus. "What's happening?" The pain from the cut throbbed up her arm to her shoulder. "My mom's gone. I can't sense her anymore."

Hot agony rippled from the wound and she leaned into Dragon.

The dread, dark and heavy and viscous, smeared over the world. "I'm going to hurt you. I'm going to—"

"Stop! You can't fall into that pit." He pulled her to him. "Do you trust us?"

As hard as his features were, his eyes still boiled with turmoil. "We won't burn the world. I swear to you, we won't do that." He touched his forehead against her cheek as Dragon poked at her arm. "It's a trick. We'd have to be Burners."

Her seers thumped with images of blood and fire but she leaned her head against Ladon's shoulder anyway, unable to stop herself. "I see it coming." She'd bring their death.

Ladon kissed the bridge of her nose. "We need to stop what's happening to you *right now*. I'm taking you to Dmitri."

The tears welled up as the pain reverberating between her head and arm intensified.

Ladon cupped her cheeks. "You need to sleep."

She nodded. "What about my mom?"

"We'll get it sorted." He glanced at Dragon before touching her wound. "Dragon will stitch your arm."

If she ran away and found a hole to curl into she wouldn't become the catalyst her uncle saw. "I can't be that. I can't become that."

Her mother returned: Mira hit a War Baby. Rysa winced. "She's fighting them."

But the vision flicked away and left only a ghost.

A sob yanked at her chest. Foreboding pinned her arms and legs to the blankets. Her entire body shook. She was going to drown in waves of murder, gulping for air.

"Rysa!" He gripped her shoulders. "Love, look at me."

She gulped again, scrunching closed her eyes.

"Look at me!"

A barrier dropped. Dragon's hide and body froze motionless. He stopped, poised over the med kit, his talons retracted and his hand-claw shaped in an odd cascading pattern over the bandages and medications.

New images broke: Cara Caras. Sensing her body's rhythms when he touched her hip. The brilliant rainbow of joy because she understood his signs. The intense bonding he felt when his humans made love against his chest.

Ladon lifted her onto his lap. "We feel everything that's happening to you." Tremors moved through his fingers as if Dragon had transferred all of her anxiety to him. "Don't let the visions take you. Stay with us."

The hold released and the panic inched back.

Dragon tapped Ladon's shoulder and he tilted his head, listening. "He's going to give you something to help you sleep." He set her down and glanced at the beast. "Give her an eighth of what I need."

I must stitch your arm. Dragon held the pill to her mouth and helped her sit to drink. She swallowed the water and the pill without a fight. Lying down, she watched him pull antiseptic and a needle from the medical kit.

Ladon stroked her forehead. "We need to leave."

Agony bristled through her arm. Groaning, she rolled back and forth. "We'll be okay." He kissed her cheek.

The pill made everything stand still and move fast at the same time.

Ladon jumped down to the seats. He pulled the phone from the cup holder and dialed a number. "I'm not calling about Sandro Torres, Dmitri." A pause. He dropped into the driver's seat. "We need a healer experienced with Fates." He glanced back at her one more time. "I'm bringing her to you. She's been attacked."

Ladon pulled the phone from his ear. "Then ask Marcus! He can guide you. He—" Another pause. "What do you mean they're gone? How the hell did Harold steal—"

His head dipped and his hand rose like he was pinching the bridge of his nose. "No. It's not the sickness. It's—" He glance back at her again. "Then you find someone. Now."

Russian yelling poured out of the phone. Ladon pulled it away from his ear again. "You find a class-one healer and you find one now, do you understand?" Another pause. "I don't care if they work for him," he growled. "Let him try. If he comes near her, I'll kill him and every member of his little cult."

Rysa reached for Ladon one last time before her consciousness dropped below the blood and fire.

Inside the dream, Rysa's back slammed into iron-hard clouds. The metal vapors billowed with dust and chains and wiggled into her nose. Inched into her ears. Filled her throat with acid grains. The clouds gripped her wrists with pulleys that twisted knives into her skin. Her back bruised against the dust, her kidneys savaged.

Apparitions rode the updrafts. They bit with dream teeth she felt but couldn't see, and slapped with hands that couldn't possibility hit.

She should fall. Drop free, tossed in the dream gravity.

Everything inside her body coiled. Every joint, every bone screamed. Dream hands wrenched and she crashed against the clouds.

Gravity should pull her to the park's asphalt. Yank her chest and snap her legs on the monkey bars. Twist her pelvis and snarl her neck in the swings. It should do what needed to be done.

Glowing splatters hit the grass and clung like dew, blistering green to gray-brown sickness. It rained from Rysa's body, rolling along her arms in acid droplets. Each drip adhered to an elbow, a finger, the tip of her nose. Surface tension sucked at her skin, but the drops weren't shackled, like her. Gravity grasped.

Fire rained down from her skin.

Her nasty shrieked. It wanted to unfurl and show itself, but it would ignite if it got too close. So it vanished like Dragon, gone invisible to mimic the burning world.

Below, the beast would catch her when she fell. He caught her once already. She'd melt his patterns and scorch his bones when she dropped, but he'd catch her again.

Ladon shouted but the storm overrode his words with dream hammers and drums and chimes so loud they dripped acid into her eyes. She couldn't see his intent, or *what-was-is-will-be*.

She should have seen that the burning dust would strip his skin from his body. She should have felt she was the center of the storm. Its engine of knives and pulleys.

Dream gravity yanked, but the burning world held her high.

Droplets fell, but she did not.

From above, Rysa dissolved the lives of the man and the beast who adored her, body and soul.

31

Rysa bolted upright. Phantom weight tugged her wrists as if the dream shackles still pulled her down.

The nightmare flicked through her vision: Ghosts pinned her to a storm while she dripped acid onto the world below.

She hugged her knees, her forehead on her thighs, counting in and counting out, trying to find a tiny shred of control. At least the van's roof blocked the clouds from pulling her into the sky like some alien abduction victim. The dream couldn't steal her away.

Sun flowed through a lone tree outside and in through the vents. The world had become dappled in bright and white. Alone in the van, she watched the light play through the interior like phantoms of the patterns on Dragon's hide.

A breeze moved through the open windows and out through the back door. It should lift from her skin the tingle and ache left by the dream. It should warm her body and she should breathe easy and be happy and find Ladon and wrap her arms around his chest and feel his heart beat against her cheek.

She should know she hadn't brought his death.

How much of what she saw had been placed in her head by her uncle and how much had been her own seers cracking under pressure? She didn't know. Telling past from present from future took more attention than she could muster.

The floodgate had been opened and now she understood the context of her talisman: Rysa, the Parcae whose purpose was to shape the Burners. Her fate lay in her status as weapon and as the bringer of Dracae death.

Her bicep ached and she touched the cut. The bandages constricted under her ripped sleeve.

She was dangerous, deadly, but Dragon didn't care. He tended to her anyway, even though she'd bring ruin to both him and his human.

The breeze carried Ladon's voice into the van. She sat up, listening.

"Are you going after her?" A pause. "South Dakota. Rysa saw bison." Another pause. "*Les Enfants.*"

A shadow passed by the driver's-side door. "No one gets near her." The shadow moved back the other way. "I could have said the same thing to you when you took up with Derek."

The shadow flickered. Ladon must have jerked the phone away from his ear. "And he'd be dead now if I had."

The top of the van creaked as a growl rolled in from above. Dragon must be on the roof.

The volume of Ladon's voice dropped. "Yes." A longer pause. "I can't control when it happens any more than you can."

The rumbling. They'd offered her a part of themselves last night. And she'd accepted.

What had she done? Faustus was right. If she turned Burner, they'd never bring themselves to do what was necessary.

She cringed and pressed her palm against her temple. *I'm going to hurt them*, she thought.

Dragon's head swung down. He stretched in his neck and gently nuzzled her shoulder. She sat still, too tired to push him away.

"I've got to go." Ladon's shadow moved toward the driver's door. "We'll be there in less than an hour." A pause. "Don't be like this. I need your help."

The phone clicked.

Dragon puffed out little flames as he undulated in. Under her pain she felt his symphony. Dragon's mind worked in patterns and colors, textures and shapes. He thought with the lights of his hide and when he talked with his hands he translated what he could.

But he moved slower than he should and his hide had dulled since last night, and his patterns had lost complexity.

"You're tired, Dragon. I can tell."

Yes. I must sleep.

"We will get you someplace safe."

A bit of understanding popped into her mind from her seers: Twenty-four to thirty-six hours, he'd sleep. Deep, like a stone, unmoving and unwakable.

He wouldn't rest, though, if he felt she was in danger.

We are close to home.

"Where are we?" They didn't take her south, to the Shifters?

Ladon crawled in through the driver's door. He knelt on the step, a hand on each seat, watching her.

Outside of Rock Springs, Wyoming. Human drove all night.

"All night? Didn't you sleep?" She looked around, trying to assess if Ladon had taken any blankets.

The van was clean.

Gone were the pizza boxes and the stray clothes and the empty coffee cups.

The bottles were gone, too. Leaning over, she lifted the lid of the storage compartment behind the driver's seat.

Empty. *All* the vodka had vanished.

Ladon didn't say anything, but instead touched her cheek.

Dull as it was, Dragon's hide sped up. *We will not lose you*, he signed.

Her seers laid bare their anguish when they lost other women: One, long ago, murdered. The second—her name had been Charlotte. He never named their son. Ladon held her in his arms as her life seeped away.

He and Dragon shattered. Each color and pattern that was Dragon dropped away. Every action and response that was Ladon unraveled. Nothing remained but brutal anger.

No more vodka. No killing Shifters.

They weren't going to lose her, as well.

The pain in her temple flared. If they stayed with her, they'd see her ignite and become the one thing which could kill them: The Queen of Ghouls.

White light flashed through her vision and she crunched over.

Ladon pulled her to him. "I watched Daniel do the same injecting, once. He overwrote the other Fates' abilities to control their seers, as if he had a remote control."

He closed his eyes. "Sixteen centuries and he only did it once. The triad he did it to were Timothy's children. His nieces and nephew. They…" He trailed off. "He couldn't control what they saw, only when they saw it. Like what's happening to you."

Daniel broke their camera's shutter mechanism. "Like he took away their talisman," she said.

Ladon nodded. "Yes."

The link around her wrist clinked against the little dragons of the insignia. Not that her talisman helped that much to begin with. She'd been dealing with random obnoxiousness from her seers since she activated.

But this was worse. Every vision hurt. Her teeth rattled. The stench of Burners clung to everything. She felt as if both her mind and her body were being eaten away by random bursts of acid-coated ADHD hell.

She knew most people had little tolerance for her issues. That, on a good day, her talking too much and her bouncing annoyed most everyone around her. The burndust-laced talisman on her wrist magnified the worst of her problems.

Her attention hurricane was now filled with fire.

But now the spike her uncle drove into her head felt as if she'd stopped being Storm Rysa. She'd vanished into gale force winds and she was now just simply Storm Death.

Hers. Ladon's. Dragon's. Everyone's.

Yet Ladon and Dragon refused to abandon her. They refused to walk away, even for their own safety.

They thought she had the strength to handle the pain.

"We'll find a healer who can help. I promise. But first you need to be someplace safe from your uncle."

The Shifter in the store had said something about Wyoming. "Are we going to your home?"

He nodded. "You'll be okay."

But bloody anguish popped into her mind again. She shuddered, pulling away. "How's a healer going to help me?"

She needed a functioning talisman and a calm mind, not a cut mended.

He held tight. "I've seen Shifter healers regrow a victim's leg. I've seen them cure the Plague. And once, I saw a healer lay her hands on the head of a madman and make him whole. The strong ones, the class-ones, if they know what to do, they can work miracles. And I swear to you, I will find one with the skills needed to stop what is happening. You can't hurt like this."

A healer made a madman whole. But could a healer make a Fate whole? And she doubted they'd find one who cared enough to help.

Ladon kissed her cheek, his lips lingering. "I should have been watching for Faustus. If the War Babies had truly seen you as a threat, the Burners would have eaten you, not put on the damned shackles."

"This isn't your fault." Her uncle did this. Not Ladon.

He leaned them against Dragon. The colors under their cheeks deepened and Ladon touched a swirl on the beast's hide before he stroked down her arm.

Each finger touched before weaving into hers. "Last night didn't happen because you're impulsive or because your family manipulated you into it."

But they had set her in his path. They'd manipulated all of them and used her inattentiveness. Her mother may not have understood why she did it, but she did it anyway.

"I don't think Mira had any idea that Dragon and I would become so... attached to you."

Another scorching vision of flame seared the back of her eyes. She refused to cringe. "It doesn't matter. Faustus will get his way. All the powerful future-seers see the same vision. We can't fight that."

"Yes, we can." He sat up. "Fates do not always get their way."

No, Ladon and Dragon would be dead. Fates, Shifters, Burners had all tried. She felt it reverberate across the weave of his life. Both Ladon and his sister had outfought or outsmarted everyone who had ever tried to do them harm.

She didn't know if it would work this time. She'd become something new. A Fate-Burner hybrid designed to be the ultimate combination weapon to destroy the Dracae.

Ladon's nostrils flared, his expression arrogant. "You will have what you want." A quick nod at Dragon and he kissed her temple. "And so will we."

He'd become so tied to her that when she dropped to the bottom of Hell, he'd drop with her. Dragon, too.

They'd never escape.

"We will buy a house in Minneapolis when this is done and both you and your mother are safe. You can finish your education."

He grinned, kissing her again. "Dragon and I, we will mow the lawn and install track lighting."

"Ladon, please don't." She needed to know that they could escape.

He held his breath. Pain flitted through his eyes and his jaw tensed. "I don't have to buy—"

She touched his chin. "It's not that." He offered so much: Every night, she'd sleep snuggled against his side, the rhythms of his body soothing, the brilliant energy he shared with Dragon perfect as it traveled over her skin. She'd wake to the warmth of Dragon's touch and to Ladon's smile. He'd touch her cheek. Then he'd offer a "Have a good day at class," and a "Dragon packed you an orange with your lunch."

The life she wanted.

But no matter what he believed, she didn't see it. "I need to know you'll be willing to take care of... me... if you need to. And that you'll be okay when it's done."

"Don't say that. Don't—"

Rysa cut him off. She felt like a thief. She stole his strength and gave nothing but the promise of death in return. Ladon and Dragon were everything she wanted. They were everything she needed, but it didn't matter anymore. It never did.

She was a Fate. A goddamned Parcae. The future would have its due and what happened here was nothing more than a ripple in the coming lake of fire.

She could shield them, though. She may wound them, but she'd keep them alive. "If you're with me, he will hurt you."

He slapped the floor. "You are not toxic!"

This wasn't about her. This was about the future in her head. "We need to focus on what's relevant—"

"*You* are relevant!" The same pain she'd seen earlier sparked behind his eyes.

"I can't let this be. We will not walk away from you! You're part of our lives. You're the best part. We don't care about prophesies or Faustus's threats or damned Fate power games. We haven't cared for a very long time. All we care about is that you are safe and the spike is healed."

He touched her temple. "We care about *you* because we—"

"Ladon, don't." She wanted to kiss him until the anguish in his eyes vanished. She wanted Dragon to feel it, too, and for his hide to glow in starbursts.

No matter what they believed, she was dangerous.

The Parcae blood in her veins made her toxic. "We can talk about this later. We need to get through what's happening first. Alive."

He closed his eyes and leaned his forehead against her shoulder. Dragon touched Ladon's back and nuzzled Rysa's side.

"How much of this fatalism is you?" Ladon whispered. "How much of it is your Parcae abilities? Or did Faustus shove it into your head?"

What was he talking about? "I'm being realistic."

Ladon snorted. "You are being stubborn."

"I've dealt with shit like this all my life. I know when—"

Ladon kissed her lips and forehead. "I know."

"Ladon…"

A pulse moved between Ladon and Dragon.

Ladon touched the beast's neck. "He's telling me not to argue with you. He says he's too tired and that your visions hurt you too much."

Leave it to Dragon to make practical sense of the situation.

Ladon stroked her cheek. "It doesn't change how I feel. Nor does it change how he feels." He patted Dragon's neck. "We will get you through this. Both you and Mira. I don't believe she was complicit in this. It wouldn't be the first time Faustus has used a sister for his own gain."

Some of the weight lifted. Even if they had to pop her Burnerized body, they'd help her mother.

"I'm going to take you to Sister. She's going to watch over you while Dragon and I find a healer." He leaned forward and kissed her neck. "And fetch your mother."

A seer-made vision: Another dragon, but not her Dragon. Smaller, sleek. Angry.

She pressed on her temple again. "Your sister's not happy about helping."

"I can handle Sister." He stood up, moving toward the front of the van. "You are more important than her irritations." He grimaced as he dropped into the driver's seat. "I need coffee."

She lay down next to Dragon.

Ladon glanced back before putting the van in gear, worry darting through his eyes.

32

They parked outside the main entrance to Rock Springs's hospital. A sprawling, one-story building, it housed several local clinics, as well as the emergency department. Construction dominated the back of the building—the hospital looked to be doubling its floor space.

Rysa's seers had calmed while they drove. For the entire half hour, Dragon rested his head on her lap and she fretted over the danger she'd put them in, but, thankfully, without any burning visions.

She didn't pick up any more from her mother, either. But the War Babies were smart enough not to strip off her mom's flesh. Nor would they murder her. If they did, they'd kill their own father, but it didn't mean torturing Mira to prove their superiority wasn't a possibility.

Ladon took her hand as they walked toward the hospital entrance. Dragon ran by and scaled well-worn dragon holds behind the landscaping.

"Sister-Dragon's on the roof." Ladon pointed at the little chunks of brick as they fell behind the decrepit evergreens.

This part of Wyoming was drier than Minnesota, a semi-arid place with many more grays and browns than Rysa was used to. Her childhood in California had been green and gold and the vastness of the Pacific. Minnesota had been fresh water and deep green trees with winter snow banks so tall they blocked sightlines. But here, the mountains and the sky commanded all and the trees cowered next to the buildings, clinging to the human population like domesticated pets.

She liked it. Even through the pain in her skull, she felt at home. The mountains began here. Real mountains, not the smoothed-out cores of the

Mesabi Range near Duluth, in northern Minnesota. California had it too, at your back when you looked out over the ocean. The massive presence of the land.

It fit Ladon and Dragon.

The beast's ghost-form refracted before he disappeared over the edge of the roof. AnnaBelinda had been pulling into the hospital parking lot when Ladon called. Derek's blood disorder made him grit his teeth and refuse to eat so Ladon's sister brought him down to the hospital.

Ladon stopped at the check-in desk and flashed an ID card.

The lady offered a cordial nod to Rysa. "ID, please."

Her driver's license was in her backpack. On the floor of the coffee shop in the basement of the Continuing Ed building. In Minnesota.

Ladon leaned over the counter. "Julie, she left her wallet in the van. She's with me." He winked and flashed a brilliant smile.

Julie smiled back, charmed. "What's your name, Miss?"

"Lucinda Thomas," Rysa said, using her middle name. Not having her real name in a database combed by law enforcement agencies seemed like a good idea.

Julie typed something and her computer printed off a name badge. "Next time, bring in your identification, okay?"

Ladon peered down the hallway.

"Same room as always, Mr. Drake. 1367E." Julie pointed in the direction Ladon looked.

Ladon flashed his brilliant smile again. "Thanks." He nodded to a waving nurse as he led Rysa down the hall.

A woman, small and lithe, wearing a black t-shirt and jeans much like Ladon's, her wavy black hair pulled into a ponytail, ran from the room and jumped into his arms.

"Brother!" she squealed. She hugged him and dropped back to the floor.

"Sister."

AnnaBelinda's uncanny eyes darkened when she looked at Rysa. Hers were light brown like Ladon's, but flecked with green instead of gold. "So you're the source of the trouble."

Ladon scowled.

The dragon woman scowled back and rolled her eyes. "Come on Derek wants to say hello." She looked Rysa up and down again. "You stay out here."

"Sister," Ladon said, his tone hard-edged. He tightened his hand around Rysa's.

Icy annoyance crackled from AnnaBelinda. Her mouth opened to respond, but she snapped it shut and walked back into the room instead.

Inside, Derek played solitaire on a table next to his bed. He was about the same height as Ladon, his biceps as defined and his shoulders as broad, but he had sandy brown hair. An IV tube snaked across the bed and into his arm above an ugly bruise. He gazed with crystal blue eyes at Rysa from across the room, but she couldn't tell his age. His face looked both young and old, as if he'd seen more of this world than he should have.

Ladon's and AnnaBelinda's expressions carried a detachment, a sort of immortal irony. Derek, though, understood death. Tom's cousin had had the same look when he came home after three tours in Afghanistan.

A broad smile brightened Derek's face when he saw his brother-in-law. Some of Ladon's tension fell away as he smiled back. These two men showed a closeness Rysa would have hoped for if she'd had a sibling.

"Ladon!" Derek back-slapped his brother-in-law.

Ladon pulled two chairs next to the bed and presented one to Rysa. She sat and Derek offered his hand. AnnaBelinda grumbled at the foot of the bed.

Derek ignored his wife and nodded to Rysa. "You are the Fate?" His Russian accent colored his resonant voice. Maybe he was an enthraller like Penny.

"I'm Rysa."

AnnaBelinda scowled. She shifted her weight and glanced at the ceiling. Annoyance poured from Sister-Dragon above.

Rysa had never met anyone with a smile as charming as Derek's. Not even Ladon could match its brilliance. If Derek wanted to be a movie star, all he'd have to do is wink.

He shifted in the bed, sitting straight, and Rysa saw the tip of a dragon's tail winding across his shoulder, under the hospital gown. It looked like an old tattoo, not very colorful, and faded. He had another dragon on his ring finger, partially hidden by his wedding band.

How did he get tattoos with his blood disorder? Everything in this new world was turned upside down.

"You have caused quite a stir, if you didn't know." Derek's eyes narrowed and his gaze flicked to Ladon before another smile highlighted his perfect teeth. He scratched his arm near the IV site. "There are new Shifters in town."

AnnaBelinda rolled her eyes, shaking her head.

"I told her to ignore them. Maiming isn't wise right now." He nodded toward Rysa.

AnnaBelinda snorted. Rysa understood these Shifters were an irritation, but one not normally ignored because, as she learned in the electronics store, they were dangerous. When Rysa dropped into Ladon's life, she complicated things for his sister in ways that must have hurled an already on-edge woman over a cliff.

"We have a situation which must be contained." Derek leaned toward Rysa. "I know Shifters." He frowned and sat back. "They whisper of the families and the Prime triads. The Shifters stay away. Mostly."

Rysa nodded.

"I know your family had something to do with the attack in Abilene twenty-one years ago. The Shifters are still angry." His lips thinned.

"I don't want anyone to get hurt because of me." She'd upset the delicate politics of Fates and Shifters and now anyone trying to help her had a target on their heads. No wonder AnnaBelinda was upset.

AnnaBelinda grimaced behind Rysa. She felt it, picking up the energy Ladon's sister shared with Sister-Dragon.

Derek sat back, his gaze steady on his wife even as he addressed Ladon. "You look like hell, my friend. Go home. Brother-Dragon needs sleep. As do you." He watched AnnaBelinda tic like she wanted to pace. "They will let me out this afternoon. *We* will find Mira. Isn't that right, *rodnoy?*"

"No. Not a Jani Prime." AnnaBelinda stood behind Ladon, feet planted, her body tense. Scowling, she refused to look at Rysa. "And I told you on the phone that I will not have a Fate in my home." Her body shifted into a slow alignment with Rysa. "I don't care if you've inserted yourself into Brother's life. I don't trust you."

Of course you don't trust me, Rysa thought. *Why would you?* But Rysa's nasty raised its head, digging around the edges of AnnaBelinda's belligerence. Rysa shouldn't trust *her*. Unlike Ladon, her fury never cooled.

Derek pinched the bridge of his nose. "Why don't you wait in the hall for a minute, Rysa." His face showed real concern. The suggestion was meant to protect her from his wife's ire.

Ladon's jaw tensed. "She stays with me." He pulled her closer.

AnnaBelinda whipped a gesture at Ladon that Rysa didn't understand.

Rysa squeezed his fingers. "I'll be okay." Dealing with his sister's hate would be easier for him without his Fate girlfriend breathing the same air.

He shook his head. "But—"

"I'm fine," she lied. Her head throbbed. AnnaBelinda's hostility beat in a painful rhythm. "There are chairs right outside." She'd wait for them to stop yelling. Then she'd make Ladon go home. Dragon needed sleep. He couldn't fight. He'd get injured, or worse, killed.

She'd had faith in her mom's ability to survive. That as a Prime present-seer, she'd get away or manipulate the Burners into an action revealing their location. But also that Ladon's sister was like him—someone who woke every morning intending to be the best person possible. Rysa had hoped AnnaBelinda would take this burden from his shoulders. That, as his sister, she'd help.

But AnnaBelinda believed all Fates deserved what the future forced down their throats. If Rysa's mom escaped, so be it. If she didn't, well, that wasn't AnnaBelinda's problem.

If Rysa sighed at the wrong moment, if she flinched or pouted or let down her guard for one second, Ladon and Dragon would disappear into the Black Hills of South Dakota. They'd track her mom. Not sleeping. Not resting. They'd drive themselves into the ground before they'd let her lose her family, all because his sister refused to help.

They'd die. Burned, frozen, she didn't know. The world would lose a dragon and cause the other to rampage, like her uncle foresaw. She'd serve her purpose as the weapon who killed the Dracae.

She stood up, giving AnnaBelinda a wide berth as she walked out into the hall. Maybe luck would hold. Maybe Ladon might talk some sense into his sister. Either way, he was done searching for the Jani Prime. Rysa would cut off that path to ruin.

"Why did you bring *her* here?" AnnaBelinda spit the words at Ladon, venom coiled around *her*. The disdain ripped at Rysa's gut as she stepped into the hallway.

"Will you calm down? You know damned well what's at stake." The harshness of Ladon's voice added to Rysa's anxiety.

AnnaBelinda swung her arms around. "Just because you're sleeping with her doesn't mean she's trustworthy. She's a time-bomb! Maybe things are fine now, but she'll be the death of us all."

AnnaBelinda slammed the door.

A time bomb. The death of them all. AnnaBelinda wouldn't put a knife in Rysa's belly, but she'd drive her into the back country and leave her there to die.

AnnaBelinda would do the same to Rysa's mom. She'd track Mira, but not well, and she'd miss opportunities. When Dragon woke, he and Ladon would take up the slack, but it'd be too late. And he'd never speak to his sister again.

Another path to ruin.

Rysa couldn't catch her breath, and she bent forward, attempting to hide her spasms from the nurses who walked by. She stood up, pacing, and stared at the door. AnnaBelinda yelled something and she heard Ladon yell back. Then more yelling, this time from Derek.

The hospital hallway closed in. Claustrophobia welled up, stuck as she was in a corridor smothered under hate from a woman who should be her friend.

Ladon and AnnaBelinda yelled at each other but the entrance glowed with the midday sun. Fresh air, warm and clean, beckoned from outside. Walking down the corridor, Rysa passed the reception desk and nodded to Julie, but stopped, backing up.

She needed a pen.

"Julie." A can decorated with construction paper and macaroni pinwheels rested against the computer. "Did your daughter make that?"

Julie blinked. "Umm, yes."

Rysa nodded toward the room. "Ladon told me." She didn't know why she lied. Her nasty wanted a damned pen.

Julie glanced at 1367E. "You two serious?" She leaned forward, her eyes wide. "He's a good guy. He's in here all the time visiting Mr. Nicholson when he comes in for treatments." She tapped the side of the pen cup. "He probably won't tell you this, but he and his sister paid for the new wing." She nodded toward the construction. "He's so down-to-earth I doubt he'd let on... you know..." She nodded toward the construction again.

Rysa focused on the pens. Julie's words rolled by without registering as Rysa's fingers pulled a marker out of the can. "Can I borrow this? I'll bring it back. I promise." She had no idea why her seers had a desperate need for the pen, but she figured she'd better listen.

Julie shrugged. "Sure thing."

Forcing friendliness, Rysa smiled and saluted with the marker. "Thanks again."

Julie nodded before turning to a nurse. Rysa felt them watching as she walked toward the entrance, their lips twittering as they glanced down the hall at 1367E.

Rysa caught her breath at the door. The bright sunshine beckoned. Everything floated by, skating on a thin film, flattening the world. Something told her to step through the entrance.

Outside, the hospital loomed behind her, anchored to the sky. She filled her lungs with the clean air, her head clearing.

Her nose pricked. Surprised, she searched the parking lot. She'd caught it on the breeze, faint but obvious: the unmistakable tang of Burner.

33

Derek leaned forward after Sister slammed the hospital room's door. "Anna! You don't know her. Mira is her only family."

Sister paced, not answering. Her behavior was worse than anything Ladon did when she took up with Derek. All he'd done for her over the centuries, and she treated him this way now?

Rysa had nothing to do with what happened two millennia ago. This hate, it reared its head every few centuries. Took ahold of his sister and wouldn't let go. He'd long suspected her antagonism toward the Shifters was a displacement of her hate of Fates more than a real fury.

Sister glanced at the ceiling, listening to Sister-Dragon.

Brother is angry, the other dragon pushed.

Ladon's lip twitched. Dragon wasn't taking abuse from his sister. Neither dragon brooded or nitpicked, but Sister's attitudes had long ago infected Sister-Dragon. She'd poke at her brother and make him pulse grating irritation into Ladon's mind.

"Damn it!" Sister threw a plastic bin at Ladon's head.

He caught it just above his shoulder. A snarl sat at the base of his throat as he crunched the plastic into a prickly ball.

"Stop!" Derek articulated each syllable of his next sentence, voice low and specific, his accent punctuating the words Ladon knew his sister needed to hear. "No one deserves to lose their family to murdering ghouls."

More enraged, Sister glared, but didn't answer.

"Then it is settled." Derek's gaze stayed locked on his wife's face. "You take Rysa home. Rest. You and Brother-Dragon cannot fight as tired as you are. *We* will find Mira of the Jani Prime and we will return her to her daughter. Alive."

Sister looked away, silenced but still angry.

Rysa has gone outside.

Ladon bolted for the door. *Why did she go out alone?*

You and Sister-Human were yelling.

He growled at Sister before he realized what he was doing. Her eyes narrowed. She'd heard Dragon, too.

Something is wrong.

Sister stayed behind as he ran into the corridor.

Billy waited at the edge of the parking lot, his hands tucked into his nylon jacket. His red cross-trainers stood out in the dry grass and his orange t-shirt nudged from under his collar.

She should do something, but Rysa couldn't remember what. She should tell someone there was a Burner out here in the parking lot, between the cars.

He danced a little jig and ran across the median to the white clinic building on the other side of the asphalt.

"Billy!" Dodging vehicles, she chased him into the lot. "Where's my mother?"

He stomped on the gravel in the rock-filled bank and cocked his head at the weird Burner angle. "Where's the lizard king?"

Lizard king? Something nagged at the edges of understanding. Something capable of bracing her against cracking into a million shards. Something to give her the will to stand on her own feet and know if she fell, it would catch her.

But she couldn't remember.

"I'm supposed to tell you something." Billy scrutinized the cars. An arm snaked out and he singed a print into the lustrous finish of a big pick-up. "They drive a lot of trucks in the mountains." He sniffed and scratched at the tip of his nose. Little sparks popped off his skin. "Harder to steal a truck."

"Is my mom okay?" She walked forward and flared her hands as if she approached an angry dog.

"They took Lizzy."

A memory tried to surface but slipped under Billy's mumblings. The world felt edited and the edges of her context trimmed. She remembered her mom, and Billy, and that she was in Rock Springs, Wyoming. These were the central clues in her game of life. Nothing else registered.

"Where is she, Billy?"

His head swiveled, his red-tinged eyes dancing. "Didn't you hear me, Fate bitch? They took Lizzy." Coiled like a snake, he seethed, as if waiting for her to twitch so he could strike. "Your mum begged us to take her. Said she'd help us get away if we helped her find the other one." His face heated and he jabbed his fingers in the air as if he were firing pistols. "I told her they promised us Shifter snacks and she'd better get us at least three or I'd eat her! But they caught us and took Lizzy."

"Billy." She held up her hands. "Who took Lizzy?"

"The girl is creepy. Even *I* can tell she's creepy." He bopped on his toes and bent forward, his voice lowering. "You pissed off their pa. That's what one of the boys said. I can't tell them apart." His gaze flitted across the lot. "The big horse-dog's not going to snap my neck, is he?"

What horse-dog? "Billy, please."

"They all thought together real hard and they saw your mum." He twirled around. "They were real cocky about it. Rubbed your mum's face in it, they did. Something about 'practicing' and 'focusing on consequences' and being 'the best.'" His fingers smoldered as he air-quoted the words. "Wankers."

He tapped a cheek and little wisps burst into the air. "We were with buffalo—bison—mean ugly cows." He shrugged. "They're big. Not tasty like you."

"Where is she?"

"They'll snap your mum's back!" A light popped from his mouth when he gritted his teeth. "That's what I'm supposed to tell you. Won't kill her. Not technically."

The War Babies. And she'd followed Billy away from the hospital building.

"I don't like them."

The editing increased and her nasty struggled, its confusion growing. It should have control of her seers, of the tentacles, but it didn't. It fought anyway, and it guarded something important.

"Come here." The pen felt as if it vibrated against her palm.

"Why?" Billy scoffed but walked toward her.

"Give me your hand." She moved closer and held her breath against his Burner stench. It pricked her eyes, but she had a task to complete.

Wiggling it out of his pocket, he jutted his hand forward. She twisted it so he could read her words when he looked down.

She wrote: *I will listen to Rysa.* On his other hand: *Bring Mira to Rysa.*

His eyes stared, unblinking, at the words. "Why the hell did you write on me?"

"Get my mother, Billy. Bring her to me safe and alive." Billy was the only one. No one else would help. No one knew where to search or cared to track or gave a rat's ass about her mother's spine. Only this Burner and his random loathing. *Why* had been trimmed, set aside as not important in this stage of the game.

She pushed the pen into his palm and backed away.

His lip curled. "I hate Fates," he muttered. "I hate all of you."

"Billy, please."

His red eyes closed to slits. "I'm going to skin her. I'm going to eat her myself." He pointed at the roof. "Tell your boyfriend I hate him, too."

The Burner's head angled and he planted his feet. Then he darted across the hospital drive, up the hill opposite the entrance, and vanished around another building.

Something changed. The overwriting grew stronger. The world flattened. Maybe this had always been her life. No color, no interest, the best of everything in the past. She dropped to the ground, her eyes blank.

She should tell someone. But she couldn't remember who, only that he was important.

They stepped around a large vehicle next to the clinic outbuilding: two males and a female. Identical, both with auburn hair and blue eyes, the men looked like Faustus. They moved in the same cadence as her uncle. But both were stocky and vicious, taut muscles obvious under their tight-fitting black clothes.

The female walked at the point of their triangle, her dirty blonde hair pulled back into a severe ponytail. It swung behind her like a hammer, its entire length wrapped in leather cording.

Around their necks they wore a dagger split vertically in three, each segment wrapped in a silver coil. The female carried the middle, the segment cut around a jewel as red as a Burner's eye. The two males carried the sides, each with one half of the blade guard, the dagger's divided point aimed inward, at their present-seer sister.

She didn't look at Rysa. Her cloudy eyes didn't focus, dead in their sockets.

This Fate was blind.

Yet the female knew where everything and everyone stood. She had a sense of the environment far beyond anything Rysa's seers comprehended. Her ability blipped like radar as it touched Rysa. It squirmed through her uncle's injection and replaced her world with the blind present-seer's.

Large guns poked from holsters on their legs and short swords from scabbards on their backs, except for the male on the right, who held his blades. Blacker than anything should be in the bright sunlight, the blades reflected nothing. They sucked away all sense of their existence. Their appearance alone sliced a hole in the universe.

The other male stared at the roof of the hospital, his arms crossed over his chest. He pulled a pair of expensive sunglasses from a pocket and covered his eyes as he studied the building. He pointed toward Rysa and tipped his head before muttering something in French.

The female nodded to her brother and walked toward Rysa. "*Venez, ma cousine, nous avons du travail à faire.*"

'Come, cousin, we have work to do.'

34

One male fiddled with Rysa's bracelet and muttered French insults when he couldn't undo the leather's knot. The other fired rapid syllables in his brother's direction. The first grumbled and wrapped her wrists and all—chain, thong, and talisman—in duct tape before pushing her into an SUV.

She frowned at her hands and watched the foothills pass by. She should have told someone she was leaving, but the world was in French now. No one would understand even if she tried.

The woman's unblinking eyes stared and she rested her palm on Rysa's shoulder. *Les Enfants de Guerre et la cousine.* Sleepy, maybe Rysa would dream in French.

The road bordered a broad swath of railroad tracks, the exit a long curve the driver took too fast. Rysa leaned into the blind present-seer. The three muttered to each other in strange inflections and vanishing consonants.

Wizards and demons, maybe. '*Magiciens et démons, peut-être.*'

Something pushed at the spike in Rysa's mind and watched the woman, hiding from her, dodging and filling the holes through which the French world poured.

"Are you my family?" Rysa asked. 'Êtes-*vous ma famille*?' She knew another way to talk, but she couldn't remember what to do. Something about her hands.

The man in the passenger seat stared for a moment before answering. "*Oui.*" 'Yes.'

The rail yard flickered. Shipping cars dwarfed the SUV, blotting out the sky in a clipped rhythm of dark thrown by a car, fire thrown by the sun into a gap—dark, fire, dark—as a train passed.

Her entire life, she'd seen trains from a distance. Long, winding chains of unbroken power, they moved away without a care. A train carried what it wanted into the future and nothing could block its passage.

The blind woman's hammer-ponytail hung over her shoulder, precise and controlled. Her dead eyes looked at nothing but her face concentrated.

Magiciens et démons. Et les dragons, peut-être.

The woman clamped fingers around Rysa's neck. "Stay calm." Her resonance off, her voice sounded as if it called from inside a metal drum.

The driver removed his designer sunglasses. Pulling the keys, he murmured to the woman and her grip on Rysa's neck released. "We're going for a ride on a train, cousin." *'Nous allons faire un tour sur un train, cousine.'* He pointed at a sleek, silver passenger car waiting not far away.

The man in the passenger seat oozed out his door, his muscles tight and perfect for killing. He concentrated like the woman and Rysa felt clanging and electric static, like lightning striking metal, roll through the SUV.

The driver watched Rysa in the rearview mirror, his lips pale from the pinch of his mouth. The man outside slapped the window and the driver swore, French vulgarity dropping like sand washing through gravel. The lock clicked open and the lightning man jerked Rysa into the slow strobing shade of the rail yard. She stared at his face. The moving shadows striped his feature in French.

"*Il peut nous trouver encore.*" 'He may find us yet.' More lightning pounding across metal. "*Les Dracas ne suivront pas. Elles sont en colère.*" 'The Dracas will not follow. They are angry.'

Out of the SUV, the blind woman cupped Rysa's cheeks. "I cannot look while I hold her. She fights and I am fatigued." Her fingers dropped and she clutched Rysa's arm.

"Hmmm…" The driver rounded the front of the SUV and a new thunder much like the other man's clattered across the gravel, but it struck *backward*.

Rysa should understand how they did these odd things, but the words eluded her, the concepts overwritten. Nothing worked and these three dragged her into dark-fire, dark-fire.

"*Les Dracos sont dans l'amour.*" 'The Dracos are in love.' The man with the sunglasses pointed at Rysa and smirked, his scorn jutting his jaw forward.

Les Dracos sont dans l'amour. Why did he point at her? She couldn't remember who *Les Dracos* were.

"Perhaps we use this, brother Metus? *Non?*" His sunglasses bobbed in his pocket when he crossed his arms.

"We have orders, Timor," the woman murmured.

Metus's shoulders wiggled and he adjusted the swords on his back. More ninja cowboy than French killer, he whistled as he hooked his thumbs into the waistband of his pants, his feet apart.

"You wish to infuriate him more?" The lightning rolled from him again. "He is already a danger." Metus clutched Rysa's chin. "As, I fear, are you."

Why was she a danger? French spun around her. French words, French ways. But somewhere underneath, something fought to bring back *Rysa.*

Timor shrugged. "I will check the crew." He strode off, the hilts of his swords poking above his head. Normals stared, but he ignored them.

"We leave as soon as possible." Metus touched the woman's cheek. "How do you fare, Adrestia?"

She tapped Rysa's shoulder. "She is strong, but I am stronger."

Adrestia seemed to struggle as if she lifted a heavy weight over her head. What if she dropped it? Would it shatter on the gravel, all the Frenchness falling from its surface like a candy shell?

Maybe if Rysa yanked hard enough, Adrestia might drop the heavyweight candy jawbreaker with the *en amour* center.

Metus nodded. "Yes, you are. You are stronger than all of us. You are stronger than our aunt, dear present-seer."

A constricted curve shaped Adrestia's mouth, tightening her already taut cheeks. "And you are stronger than our father, dear future-seer."

Metus glowered over his shoulder as he watched Timor walk away.

35

Dragon sensed *French*. A word here, a sensation there, all in French.

Les Enfants de Guerre snuck in using Faustus's damage and Adrestia hijacked Rysa's seers. They'd taken her from under his nose.

The shattering threatened—the dissipation that could drop both him and Dragon into the uncontrollable rending and violence that he couldn't—*wouldn't*—let surface again.

Ladon picked up his damned phone. Maybe he'd get lucky. Maybe a normal called in something. He shouldn't mess with it while he drove, but if he adjusted the—

The app pinged a hit: An unknown group with swords drove into the Green River Rail Yard. Rysa must have set up the search terms. When, he didn't know, but he gripped the phone, staring at the screen.

Every emotion he felt for her flooded his body. He smiled.

Tires squealing, they pulled into the Rail Depot parking lot. And there, behind the building, Ladon caught the glint of guns belted to legs and scabbards over shoulders.

He and Dragon vaulted out of the van, Ladon strapping his own scabbards to his back as he ran. Dragon, invisible, scaled a rail car and jumped from the top to the next train.

Ladon angled his shoulders and leaped forward. One boot slid across the greased metal of the coupler connecting the cars. Shifting his body weight with his other leg, he flipped midair and righted himself against gravity.

He landed in a crouch halfway to the next line.

The next train moved. His connection to Dragon oscillated as the train pulled away and the beast jumped from car to car. Ladon's senses took in the precise angles and speed of the metal boxes. A smaller step, a slight pause, and he hurdled the coupler between two cars.

His boot hit a safety bar and he launched himself with a twist. Rotating around the oncoming corner of the next car, he pulled his head and shoulder back. The dirty metal grazed his arm and a sudden sting clipped his skin. He landed, a small weld of blood appearing on his bicep.

The beast vaulted from the top of the train car, his already blistering anger heated farther by Ladon's injury. Dragon landed half way to the next rail line, a deep growl rolling from his invisible form.

The War Babies turned toward Ladon and Dragon in unison, their three-point triangle surrounding Rysa in front of a silver passenger car attached to the end of a waiting train.

Metus raised his gun. Never a good shot, Metus's aiming skills and future-seer abilities argued, as they did for many Fates. Ladon's perception zeroed in on Metus's hands. The Fate twitched and Ladon ducked, the bullet flying by his ear.

Behind Metus, Adrestia pressed against Rysa's back. Timor ran forward and pulled his gun, also aiming. The true threat, Timor's weaponry skills outstripped both his father's and his brother's. Guns, bows, slingshots—the past-seer's precision rivaled Ladon's.

But past-seers could not read *what-is*, or *what-will-be*. Dragon smashed Timor into the gravel. The beast whipped the gun over the rail car.

Metus's seer rattled—he targeted the space over Timor's body.

Ladon ran up the back of the SUV, one boot pushing against the window as the other landed on top of the vehicle. Reaching over his shoulder as he jumped, he lifted a short sword from the mechanical arms of his scabbard.

Metus swung toward Ladon, the pulse of his future-seer rotating with him. Ladon twisted in the air, the bullet missing his side. One boot hit the hood of the SUV. He rammed the other into Metus's breastbone.

Ladon landed in a crouch between Metus and Rysa.

Flame shot from the invisible Dragon, his anger pounding through the entire rail yard, but Ladon kept his eyes forward, on Metus.

Distracted, the future-seer glanced toward Dragon. Ladon threw his short sword. Metus dodged and pulled his own, whipping it at Ladon. Bending left, Ladon caught the hilt. As dark as midnight, the blade reflected no light. Sharp, its cutting edge all but disappeared. Ladon flipped it around and laid his new toy against his scabbard.

The edges of his perception jarred.

Rysa hooked in. "Let go of me!"

Pain fired through every fiber of Ladon's body, her siphoning stretching their limits, but he willed their connection tighter, ignoring the million needles raking his nerves.

Dragon couldn't. He volleyed pattern and color to Ladon, unfiltered by any language. The beast's sudden hysteria burst through Ladon's vision. He tried to shoot back calm, but Rysa drew too fast. Fatigue jigged inside the beast and he couldn't slow the siphoning.

Ladon planted his feet to keep from swaying. He wouldn't stagger. He would not allow Metus to see him weakening. Rysa battled to overpower Adrestia's hijacking and by all the gods he and Dragon would give her what she needed to do it.

Rysa's gaze locked to his. "Ladon!"

Adrestia clamped a hand over her mouth. The siphoning vanished. Behind her, Dragon skidded on the gravel.

"No!" Ladon dropped to his knees. She almost freed herself. If they willed her more—

Adrestia spun Rysa toward Timor. She pulled her gun, her present-seer blipping toward Dragon as she backed toward Rysa and her brother.

Behind Ladon, heels scuffed on the gravel. He ducked, swinging around, and slammed Metus's head into the ground. Future-seers lost advantage in close quarters. Their ability delayed their responses by a microsecond and in hand-to-hand with Ladon or Sister, it meant their death. Better to dodge, as Faustus had.

Metus clucked and grabbed for Ladon's leg but Ladon kicked at his face. Metus rolled, Ladon's boot scraping his cheek.

The future-seer's features hardened. "*Fâché, maintenant, n'est-ce pas?*" 'Angry, now, no?'

"Your seer finally working, *connard?*"

Metus swung his other short sword. Ladon kicked up with both feet as the blade passed by his arm and slammed a boot into Metus's gut. Revolving in the air, Ladon finished the back-flip, landing in a crouch. Metus slid across the gravel, the night blade dropping at Ladon's feet.

The sword had opened a hole in his t-shirt and skimmed off the bottom half of his chest hair.

Too close. The night blade clinked against the gravel and he caught the hilt, lifting his second blade as he laid Metus's other onto the scabbard.

Dragon boomed from the top of the passenger car.

"You're an idiot, Ladon-Human." Metus sneered.

Timor and Adrestia had Rysa.

Ladon broke for the train but it accelerated west, toward the river. His gut heaved, the pull too strong as Dragon moved away.

Metus, behind them, started the SUV.

36

L adon unlocked the van with the remote, the alarm sounding the familiar *whoop whoop*. Dragon rolled into the back as Ladon slid into the driver's seat.

The rail service road paralleled the lines. They'd pace the train faster on concrete than on the dirt next to the tracks. Slamming the van's gearshift into drive, Ladon accelerated out of the parking lot.

They needed to cut off the train before it left town, but Metus intended to cut them off first. The future-seer sped alongside the train, the SUV slipping on the gravel, moving fast to stay between the van and the train's engine.

She fights, Dragon pushed.

"There they are." Ladon pointed at the train as it rattled along picking up speed. Three miles beyond the yard, the tracks crossed a wide overpass spanning the road. From there, the line looped over the Green River and headed west. If he reached the overpass first, he could get to the tracks.

They'd get Rysa back.

Long-buried memories of other loves—other women who had called up the rumbling from Ladon's soul—punched into his consciousness like a sledgehammer. The blunt force knocked into the real world and Ladon gripped the wheel, trying to breathe through it.

They'd needed him too, but he'd failed.

Not this time. Dragon wasn't going to cut down Rysa's burned corpse. Ladon wasn't going to hold her while she bled to death.

Rysa wasn't going to slip away.

Two different pasts overlaid the present. Ladon's chest ratcheted and for an instant, the memories drowned everything else.

Dragon touched his shoulder. *Rysa calls to me.*

Reality snapped back and Ladon forced the memories down. Even after the long centuries, they still made splinters of his bones. But now, *right now*, he wasn't going to allow the same horrid future to destroy Rysa's life.

The part of her abilities she called "her nasty" called out, pleading for help, but neither he nor Dragon understood what it needed. Ladon slammed his fist against the driver's door. The plastic cover next to the handle cracked. The damned Burner chaos distorted her link and they couldn't will to her what she required.

A quarter mile ahead of the overpass, the road slowly dipped under the concrete span before curving away on the other side. Retaining walls terraced the sides of the road. A fence blocked access, but if he jumped the curb, the terraces led the tracks.

Metus had a solid lead and was a good ten dragon lengths closer to the overpass than the van. Ladon steered hard toward the fence, but Metus accelerated again, and the SUV turned toward the road.

The vehicle burst from the gravel next to the line and over the first low retaining wall and onto the road. Sparks flying as it bottomed out.

Metus's future-seer would lay bare any plan Ladon made. He'd counter. Getting the van through the fence and onto the terraces wasn't going to happen.

So Ladon accelerated past the access point, praying speed would be enough to get them around Metus and close enough to scale the concrete in time.

The train's engine crossed the overpass. Twenty lengths back, the passenger car lumbered forward.

In front of the van, Metus slammed the SUV into reverse, the transmission screaming, and backed toward the overpass, attempting to block the road to keep them too far away for Dragon to jump.

Ladon pulled the parking brake, spinning the van. The overpass and the concrete block of the retaining walls flew by. He clenched the wheel, his gut twisting. Dragon gripped the van's wall and used his weight to counter to the spin.

The van stopped a dragon length from the overpass, the back end toward the span. The SUV screeched to a halt sideways between the van and their goal.

Dragon burst out the back and rammed all four limbs into the roof of the SUV just as Metus dove out the driver's door waving his big semiautomatic.

A glass shard had opened a gash across Metus's forehead. He wiped at it with his pistol hand, and coughed out a choked grunt. "Your big lizard's dead!" His good arm aimed the gun at Dragon.

The beast ignored his threats and vanished as he leaped for the overpass.

Ladon yanked the dagger he carried under the driver's seat and whipped it at Metus's knee. It hit true and the Fate screamed. The bullet flew wide, bouncing off the van's exterior, and Ladon ducked.

Metus's expression warped. Smugness overrode his obvious pain as his future-seer clanged between the vehicles.

His seer pinpointed Dragon's most probable location. He swung the gun back toward the overpass.

Ladon burst forward. He'd smash his heel into Metus's face—but he wouldn't be fast enough. Metus would squeeze the trigger before Ladon reached him.

He'd hit Dragon.

A massive, six taloned hand appeared over Metus's head. He yelped, his body stiffening in shock. Hand latched on and the digits pulled Metus's shoulder from its socket. The gun dropped, the Fate screeching like a rodent caught in a wolf's jaws.

Ladon pulled back, his boots skidding on the asphalt, but his nose and chest smacked into an invisible neck anyway.

A new roar cascaded off the retaining walls as light danced from Sister-Dragon's snout, down her back to her tail. Her head swung around and she snorted. *Metus is not a good future-seer*, she pushed.

The dragons had called to each other. They had hid their intent so deeply and played an improbability so remote Metus had no idea the other dragon approached.

And neither had Ladon.

Sister-Dragon dropped her head. Ache seethed from the beast, her connection to Sister stretched tight. Ladon searched for his sister's double-axle RV. She'd parked on the other side of the overpass, behind a fence and up the hill.

She dropped off the retaining wall on the other side of the span, gun out.

Ladon laid his hand on the other dragon's neck. They hadn't abandoned him. "Thank you."

Go, Brother-Human. We will deal with Metus.

Dragon clung to the overpass walkway, the train passing him by.

The underside of the span was more than a full dragon length above the road bed.

Ladon ran for the SUV and vaulted, one foot hitting the vehicle's hood, his other the roof. He pushed off, all his strength propelling him for the span overhead.

He lifted a night sword from his back. With both hands gripping the hilt, he tightened his core and willed all his strength into the blade.

It sliced into the concrete, silent and purposeful. Ladon hung from the hilt and the blade slid down, a long gash opening in the overpass supports.

He braced his feet against the structure and extended an arm to Dragon. The tracks creaked and the train thundered, but the beast threw him true. Ladon's boots found purchase on the roof of Rysa's passenger car.

Ladon lifted the second sword from his back as he dropped. Dragon landed and the car quaked, his talons folding around a side. A metallic reverb shrieked from the roof until the beast stabilized.

Ladon punched the sword into the metal.

He pulled it forward, his arms working to their limit. The blade cut through sheathing and insulation. Wires sparked, heat rose, electricity arced across the gash. Ladon twisted the blade, drawing it at an angle to the first cut.

Rage boiled from Dragon, fueling Ladon's own.

From below, Rysa tapped in, but she did not siphon. Instead, she added strength and calmed fury.

Ladon's joints quieted and his muscles strengthened. His perception steadied—his mind countered the vibrations of the train instead of using them to fuel his anger.

She'd freed herself. She'd met the War Babies seer-to-seer and beat them back. But if Adrestia regained control, Rysa might lose hers forever.

Ladon and Dragon fired pride through their connection. They'd give her everything they had to help her to maintain control, even if it weakened them. Even if they suffered because of it.

Dragon's talons scooped under the roof. It buckled, the stability of the entire car compromised by Dragon's strength. Ladon dropped through the hole but the beast backed away, unable to fit through the ragged gash.

Adrestia held her temple against Rysa's and her gun pointed at Ladon. Timor backed toward the car's door.

"You hurt them and I'll feed you to the Burners, you—" Rysa stopped in midsentence, her eyes glazing.

Adrestia sneered. "*Je ne serai pas battu, Dracos.*" 'I will not be bested, Dracos.'

Ladon mimicked her sneer. "*Vous serez morte bientôt, Adrestia.*" 'You will be dead soon, Adrestia.'

The present-seer yanked Rysa to the side. "*Le dragon est entré par la porte—*"

Dragon erupted through the door. The beast reared over the seats and the two *Enfants de Guerre* rolled under the beast.

Adrestia pushed Rysa toward her brother, her gun swinging for Dragon. The beast's foot smashed down and present-seer's head cracked against a seat.

Timor yanked Rysa's taped wrists over her head, a long knife at her throat.

He'd slice her. Maybe rupture an artery. Because of the three members of the War Babies, Timor was the one most likely to cut their losses. The one who didn't give a damn about the future.

Ladon flung himself under Dragon's belly, his feet aimed at the past-seer's legs. Timor kicked but Ladon grabbed his boot. The train rocked, Ladon slid, and Timor rolled on top of Rysa.

The blade stabbed the car's floor next to her ear.

Timor punched.

"Let her go!" Ladon wanted to rip Timor's arms from his torso.

Timor pulled Rysa to a crouch, their backs to the open door.

"*Reculez!*" 'Stay back!' He yanked the blade from the floor and pressed it into her neck while his other fingers dug into her midriff.

Rysa's head lolled. Her lip bled. But the car filled with the vibrating power of her Prime abilities.

Blood spread across her belly. She stared, her eyes as blank as Adrestia's, unaware of the darkness spreading across her shirt.

New wounds. Rysa manifested another round of attacks on her mother in the same way she had at the house.

"*Qu'est-ce qui se passe?*" Timor grunted, holding out a bloody palm. 'What is happening?'

Adrestia panted, Dragon's foot holding her to the floor. "*Brûleurs.*" 'Burners.' "*Vous n'êtes pas Parcae.*" 'You are not a Fate.'

Her present-seer fired. "*Sorcière.*" 'Sorceress.'

Timor's stance changed to a menacing, fatalistic scoff. His eyes showed confusion—the future he was supposed to help bring about no longer made sense. Somehow, the wounds on Rysa's belly were outside the fate *Les Enfants* were bound to when they stole her away from the hospital lot.

"*Vous êtes déjà la Reine des Brûleurs.*" 'You are already the Queen of the Burners.' Timor wrenched Rysa to standing.

She grasped for Ladon with her taped wrists. The past-seer's fingers rose from her waist. They trailed over her breasts and a slow blink fixed a cruel leer in his eyes. Around her outstretched arms and over her throat, he traced her body until he clutched her jaw.

Timor jumped backward through the door onto the bridge over the Green River, Rysa in his arms.

Dragon roared, his hide exploding in violent bursts. He didn't wait. He didn't listen. He flew over Ladon's head, his body contorting out the opening. He landed hard on the tracks and the entire bridge shook.

Rysa didn't fight. She didn't pull. She stared into space, her eyes glazed and her body limp.

What this new vision was doing to her, neither Ladon nor Dragon understood. The Burners hurt Mira. Rysa bled and Timor yanked on her neck. He hauled her to her feet, cursing in French.

He tugged her up the guardrail.

"Timor!" Ladon landed in a crouch on the bridge's wooden walk. Standing slowly, he raised his hands.

A line of sparks moved up Dragon's snout as it appeared next to Timor's cheek. Flame curled. His sounds blended with the exiting train.

Timor had pulled his own death to the surface and it now showed on the beast's hide, in his giant eye, and along the full extension of his talons. *Les Enfants de Guerre* would have their war and Dragon would slice them each into slivers.

"*Faites la retraite, Ladon-Dragon!*" Timor hissed. 'Back away.' The blade cut shallow into Rysa's throat and a hint of blood touched the metal.

Long ago, Daniel had pointed into the courtyard of his manor as the young Jani triad disembarked from their carriage, laughing and playing, as children do. "We need to kill them now, my Dracos. Before he activates them."

Ladon should have listened.

"Let. Her. Go!"

Timor laughed. "Did you know Adrestia's had a crush on you since we were children?" He shook his head. "My poor sister. All this time, she thought you'd never want a Parcae woman."

Dragon snorted and inched closer.

Timor yanked on Rysa again. She moaned, still in the grip of her vision.

"My father's never thought us good enough to stop you. He says she's the only way. I told him to use a rocket. Hit your van when you're out in the open and little bits of dragon would rain from the sky." He grimaced like he smelled Burner. "But no, he said the world's not as simple as *our* context." The past-seer's expression blanked. "Maybe he should have listened to me." His eyes closed as he dropped into the water, Rysa in his arms.

Flames poured from Dragon as he dove. Ladon ran up a support and flipped over the guardrail, diving feet first.

37

A ll that had dripped from her place in the clouds filled the river.
Gravity finally pulled her down. Now she drowned.

Water flooded her eyes, her nose, her mouth. It screamed into her
ears. The river snapped shut and Rysa's vision of Billy stripping flesh from
her mother bubbled away.

She'd brought this on herself. Billy punished by hurting her mom
and blood filled the spaces around her eyes. Her uncle punished through *Les
Enfants* and gravity bound her to her purpose.

Her hands pulled against their bonds. The real world teased, ten feet
above. Rysa's life melted into the mud at the bottom of the river.

No air. Nothing.

A new vision unfolded.

In the dark, clarity caged Adrestia's false world and contained her
uncle's damage. Agony transmuted to terror. It fired like a Burner's acid
through her limbs and pushed against the river's current:

Dragons.

Burners.

A haze, orange and thick and burning, blistered the sky.

The river thundered like the seers of *Les Enfants de Guerre* and Ladon filled
his lungs to dive. The current pulled and he kicked, gauging its tug and the
distance and speed Rysa moved downstream.

Dragon searched the murky water for any sign of Rysa's form. The
beast felt her disorientation but couldn't see her. She floundered, somewhere

on the bottom of the river.

Timor surfaced. Ladon ignored him but the past-seer latched onto his shoulders. Bracing against Timor's trunk, Ladon punched a right jab directly into the past-seer's nose.

Timor bounced, but didn't let go.

Ladon wrapped an arm around Timor's leg. Everything but his fury submerged, like the river submerged Rysa.

She'd die if he and Dragon didn't find her.

Rysa would die and Timor would cause it.

Ladon's body worked on its own, acted on its own, and every moment of anger, every minute of rage he felt for the siblings erupted.

He snapped Timor's femur.

The past-seer thrashed as Ladon dove.

Water rushed around Rysa as she sat in the mud. Water wrapped her senses in thickness and muffled her life to nothing.

Is this what the other Fates saw? The sky burning and the Dracae roiling in the flames? Ladon, bloody at her hands. Burners taking cities.

Ambusti Prime. She couldn't let it happen. She'd die first.

She'd let the acid take what it felt it was due.

If she cut the threads of her life it might be enough. She wouldn't be bound by her fate if she passed away to nothing.

But someone spoke to her in colors and begged her to please go up. To please, please breathe air.

The beast whispered and showed Rysa the sky and the stars and told her to reach.

The muddy water filled Ladon's eyes but he saw her first, on the edge of Dragon's lights, her face turned down. She didn't fight. She didn't try. The river had her.

Dragon lifted her into the air. She tried to gulp but her body buckled over, her eyes rolling back into her head as the beast set her on the dry ground.

Ladon scrambled up the bank. Dragon laid her flat and Ladon wiped her hair away from her mouth. He forced three quick breaths into her lungs. She coughed, water gurgling from her throat, but she breathed for herself. Rolling onto her side, she vomited river water.

"Love." He pulled her into his arms as he tore off the tape binding her wrists.

She heaved again, more water pouring from her mouth.

"Ladon." She twisted in anguish and clutched at his arms and chest, but she lived. "You should have let me die."

What did they do to her? She couldn't think such things.

"I saw it! I saw what's coming. What the other Fates see. I can't hide. You should have let me die."

"You can't think that." He kissed her forehead and her nose as he tried to stop his fingers from shaking. Her cheeks tasted of the river and her breath was dirty and sour, but he didn't care. "Don't say that."

She hiccupped and her arms pulled him close even as her words pushed him away. He responded, kissing her again and again.

She shivered. The threat of a horrid future tore at her mind and that damned Burner harmed Mira. Despite her strength, it might be too much. Overwhelmed, she'd give up if he didn't find a way to help her.

He'd seen other women fade away. Lose everything they were and everything they could be.

"My love." He kissed her again, wiping away the river. "We will not let what you see come to pass."

Ladon lifted her and climbed the bank. He should let Dragon carry her, but he couldn't let go.

He wouldn't put her down. Not now.

Not ever again.

38

Sirens approached but Ladon held her and kissed her cheeks and checked her wounds no matter how many times she tried to wiggle free.

Dragon-images poured into her chaos: Anger, frustration, AnnaBelinda's huge RV pulling away all pulsed from Sister-Dragon. Jagged bursts of color and pattern cracked like ice from an exhausted Dragon.

Their cacophony rained down and Rysa curled into a tight ball where she sat in the back of the van.

She pushed Ladon away. Pushed Dragon away. She backed into a corner and sat with her arms around her legs on top of the bin where her shackles clanked when the beast's weight rocked the vehicle. Sat and pulled a blanket over her head and blocked all their attempts to calm the chaos. They couldn't. Drawing them in only made it worse.

Rysa Lucinda Torres, the Parcae monarch of the Ambustae breed. A time-bomb.

"Rys…"

Dragon pushed Ladon toward the driver's seat. Then he laid down his head at her feet and the dragon-noise stopped.

He didn't sign. Puffs rolled, but he couldn't seem to muster the energy needed to translate his thoughts into something a human could understand.

She'd drained his reserves. He should have left her on the bottom of the river.

"Headlights." Ladon pointed up the road.

Dark images of Mira crackled through Rysa's seers. Billy had licked broad swaths across her mother's belly but the damned Burner had listened.

For the first time since Ladon and Dragon pulled her out of the river, she actually felt air move into her lungs.

At least her seers gave her this one good thing. "It's Billy." She moved between the seats. An old sedan angled down the bank of the road, parked facing the wrong way so its headlights glared into the van.

Billy killed the lights when Ladon pulled off. Long shadows spread down the road as her eyes adjusted. The late evening sun set off the dry Wyoming brush and it glowed in high relief.

Palm prints lined the top of the car, a scorched and ratty pile of junk just like everything a Burner touched. A duct-taped sheet of plastic covered a broken back window. It snapped in the breeze, catching the sunset in a distorted arc of bleached-out orange.

"He has my mom."

Surprise darted across Ladon's face.

"He was at the hospital. I wrote *Bring Mira to Rysa* on his hand." She tapped the tender skin on the back of her wrist next to the insignia and its leather thong. The tape residue stung.

"You didn't tell me?"

Her strength to be indignant had drowned in the river. "I forgot."

Ladon scowled, his gaze returning to the car. "He cooperated? Why?"

No point in using her seers. Burners were unreadable, and Burner fire now locked her abilities into an endless nothing anyway. "I don't know." But her mom lived. "She's in the trunk."

Ladon's head tilted while he talked with Dragon. "Stay here."

She pushed off the blanket. He had no right to keep her in the van. "She's my mom."

He slapped the back of the passenger seat. "No Burner gets near you, Rysa!" His neck reddened. His exhaustion must be fueling a fire not unlike the chaos eating at her mind.

"He won't hurt me." She didn't want to argue. Why would Billy hurt her? She'd be his queen soon.

Ladon stood, a hand on each seat. "You should be in the hospital. You might have water in your lungs. Internal injuries. But you won't let me take you and even if I did, he can't wait on the roof." Ladon pointed at Dragon. "Neither of us could go in with you."

She knew what would happen. Hospital staff would poke at her, asking too many questions: Why so much blood? What were you doing in the river? Why are you going to let the world burn, young lady? Don't you know you have a duty to perform?

She pressed on her temple.

"You're wincing again. Dragon and I, we know exactly how deep into your head that bastard drove his spike."

A hard edge thrust through their connection and for a brief moment, the world took on a crisp focus. Ladon's male mind ignored all elements he found irrelevant to the current danger. What he did pay attention to, he saw in spectacular detail: Every minute movement of her body. The time it took for her to react. The feel of her seers. Dragon's exhaustion. His own disquiet.

He'd fix everything. No doubt played in his expression, only the rock of his century's-old confidence. And right now, that meant keeping her in the van, with Dragon, where he knew she'd be safe.

Even if her mother was in the trunk of a Burner's sedan.

If she snuck out the back, she could steal the car, strand Billy in the wilderness, and run away. She and her mom could go into hiding again and—

"I'll find you." He didn't say anything more. He didn't cross his arms over his chest or flare his nostrils like he did when his arrogance surfaced. The only movements he made were to say those three words.

He would, too. He'd find her and kiss her until she melted in his arms. And he'd never escape her snare.

He lifted the tread of the top step and pulled out a large knife that caught the last evening rays of the sun in blinding flashes. "Stay here."

He was out the driver's door, walking toward the car, before she could answer. The blade flipped between his hands, glinting like a strobe light.

Rysa crawled toward the back door. She'd stay next to the van, not go near Billy, but she'd be outside if her mom called to her.

Dragon grasped her waist. Not hard, no pressure, but he didn't let go.

"My mom needs me."

An image flowed. Dragon made real a concept. He gave it color and texture and spread it through all the parts of her brain that perceived the world: All colors at once. The sensations of skin on skin. The tactile feel of his coat. The knowledge that her details—the ones they perceived in high resolution—were the correct details for their lives.

So do we.

She did for them what her talisman was supposed to do for her.

"Let go of me." Faustus was right. They'd never fight back. The inevitable roared into the present and they'd let it steamroll right over them. All because she'd been inattentive. Impulsive. Threw caution to the wind and let two days be enough. "Please."

No, he signed. *Please stop hurting Human.*

Billy lurched out of the driver's door. Hair shaggier than in Minnesota, his jacket frayed and warped, the bastard looked dirty. The paint on the car's roof melted into a welt under his palm. Less control, a stronger smell—he needed to feed.

Mira hadn't been enough.

Ladon twirled the knife. "Let her out of the trunk or I pop you right here."

"Your woman told me to do it!" Billy threw his arms forward and pointed at his wrists. The words Rysa wrote on his hands were still visible. The lines smudged across his skin like they'd been traced again and again.

Ladon tapped the trunk. "Let her out. Now."

Billy leaned through the car's window and the trunk opened.

Mira's wounds hadn't healed like Rysa's. She lay on her side, her midriff wrapped in an old sheet. Dirty strips of fabric pasted her forearms.

Damned Burners.

The crack of Ladon's punch boomed between the vehicles. Billy staggered into the road as he clicked his jaw back into place. "Stop hitting me, you goddamned brute!"

"Run, Burner."

"But—"

Ladon slammed the knife into the roof of the car. "Run so I can deal with you over there." He pointed into the brush. "Don't want to ruin the finish on my van. But I will. If I have to."

Shoulders straight, Billy pointed at Mira. "I turned the other one! Me. In Texas! She said if I told you, you wouldn't kill me."

Mira moaned and touched his elbow. "He did. He was going to help me find my sister but *Les Enfants* found us first." Her fingers dropped back. "Maybe she can stop Faustus. I can't."

"You turned Ismene?" He scooped Mira out of the trunk as he glared at Billy. Her heart beat strong, though she moved in and out of consciousness.

"Fates are *so* tasty." Billy sniffed the air like a bloodhound. "Not as tasty as her pup smells, though." He licked his lips again. "I smell her on you. She's got this sweet and sour scent—" He stepped forward, his eyes on the van. "—like her special center is just waiting for me to lick the layers away."

"You do *not* touch her!" Ladon roared. Fury threatened to submerge the world again, like it had in the river. Damned Burners. Damned Fates. Dragon's exhaustion folded into Rysa's pain and the temptation to punch Billy into a quivering pile of ash all but took over Ladon's awareness.

Billy backed against the car. "Stop yelling!" His eyes darted around and he clutched his throat. "Where's the dino-dog? He snaps my neck and I won't tell you anything!" Snickering, he rocked back and forth on the balls of his feet.

Mira moaned. Shifting his shoulder, Ladon positioned her against his chest and released his other arm from under her knees. He reached for the knife.

"Hey! Leave the machete where it is!" Billy squeaked and backed away. "I remember what happened in Abilene, okay?"

Ladon relaxed his grip on the knife's hilt.

"Fates captured a bunch of us. Set us loose on this compound. Good times, it was." A dreamy look came over his face.

Mira dropped her legs but still leaned against Ladon's chest. Billy's attention snapped to Mira and he pointed, his fingertip glowing. "That tight-assed brother of hers was beating senseless this pretty, dark-haired Fate. Angry, he was. She screamed and he slapped and said that if she stayed he'd kill her, even if it brought the sickness down on him and their sister." His finger wiggled at Mira.

So Ismene was in the compound of her own free will.

Back straight, Billy snorted. "I'd never turned anyone before. Didn't know how. Normals are easy, compared to Fates. Shifters always die, but a Fate, oh, if you can concentrate and know how much venom to inject and when, you can turn one."

"Faustus helped," Mira moaned.

Billy clapped. "Told me to listen and he did that thing they all do and I injected the right amount at the right time and poof!" He snapped his fingers, sending up a sick cloud of vapor. "The world's first Burnerized Fate!"

Nothing a Fate did was ever an accident. Faustus had used his sister as a dry run for what he planned to do to Rysa.

A soft whimper rose from Mira as she clung to his side. Faustus destroyed his own triad because he believed it's what fate told him to do. Crippled Mira. Murdered Ismene, if not in body, in mind.

Billy twitched, a walking corpse like Ismene. "Can I go? I'm hungry."

"No more killing, you damned ghoul." If he dropped Mira in the van, he could pop this Burner in the brush.

Astonishment flicked across Billy's features. "Do you think I want to?" he yelled. "Sometimes I remember who I was! My blood might pop in my head and I don't always know what the hell is happening, but if I think real hard I remember being a person, instead of… instead of…" He twirled, his fingertips glowing. "*I* made women happy, you goon. Girls knew my songs! Some still do. *I* don't."

"So? Now, you feed. Now, you explode." Ladon pulled the knife out of the roof.

Billy waved a wild gyration of his arm. "One recognized me. Middle-aged, she was. Chubby around the middle. Tasty." Billy glanced at Mira. "But I couldn't."

He didn't feed?

"She *knew* me. *I* don't know who I am, but *she* did."

The Burner had stopped himself. For a woman.

The bastard was still a danger. He'd forget. They always forgot. Unless… "Billy, do you have the pen?"

The Burner scoffed but he pulled it from his jacket's pocket. Ladon added "No killing" to Rysa's words.

"Thank you." Billy stared at the back of his hand. "Tell the princess I'm sorry for shackling her."

Ladon nodded at the car. "Go. Before I change my mind."

Billy drove away, heading south, toward town. Mira's seer flicked like a bell chiming in thunder. "You were good to help him."

Ladon glanced at her closed eyes as he swung her into his arms. The present-seer of the Jani Prime, a woman more dangerous than any Burner, bent her arms around his neck.

Relief should relax his muscles. Rysa was about to get back a parent. But his senses still piqued for war and the world jumped in high definition.

A memory jolted: Daniel gripped his sword's hilt, his eyes glazed by a vision: "Women will be our ruin."

Not *women*. It had never been women with Ladon. Always one. One body against his in the darkest hour of the night. One kiss to his cheek. One place he found his center.

Mira held as tightly to him as she could muster. In the van, Rysa stood between the seats, watching him through the windshield. Her open hand moved from her lips in a downward curve, palm up. *Thank you*, she signed.

Seeing her like that, her face a sea of emotion so complex Ladon couldn't begin to understand, Daniel's other words emerged. Clear and crisp, Ladon heard the future-seer as if he whispered in his ear: "Your beautiful fate will find you one day."

His beautiful Fate. Twenty feet away, Rysa watched, blinded by misery. He'd give her what she needed to stop the pain. She was no one's tribute. She was no one's ruin.

Not his. Not Dragon's. Not the world's.

Not her own.

39

Outside the van, the mountains looked as if they mimicked the night. Out there somewhere, behind a curtain, they blended into the dark.

Rysa wanted to feel, to know the returning sun and the stillness replaced by walking and running and laughing. To know the curtain could be pulled back.

She wanted to see Ladon's eyes gleam again. To feel his living body against hers. To know the darkness she dropped onto his soul could be cleared away.

He drove, slowing when the potholes became too deep, and they moved through the forest into the mountains.

Rysa tugged Mira's bracelet from the leather thong around her wrist. The clasp clinked against the little dragons, but she worked it around the knots without dislodging the insignia. The silver wedding band dropped onto her palm when the chain pulled free.

"Here, Mom." The charm draped around Mira's wrist. The ring, she slipped onto her mother's finger.

Mira's eyes opened for the first time since Ladon laid her on the blankets. She lifted her wrist. "I had a choice: Keep it so I could use my seer, or leave it, to make it harder for your cousins to find me. The little pricks did anyway."

Mira's thumb rubbed against the underside of her ring. Her other hand wrapped around her knuckles as if protecting the silver band. "I miss your father."

"Oh, Mom." Rysa hugged her mother, offering what comfort she could. "Ladon has a friend looking for him."

Her mom's seer blipped. Rysa sensed that she would have chuckled if she weren't so exhausted. "Your father's a good man." Her brow furrowed and her seer blipped again.

Mira stroked Dragon's crest. "I remember the toy dragon you had, honey. You loved that little beast." She rolled slightly, moving away from Rysa and toward Dragon. "I should have learned sign language so that I could talk with you, Great Sir, but I always knew it was more important for Rysa than me."

Dragon didn't raise his head, though a puff curled from his mouth. Little flashes popped along his hide but moved slowly from his crest to his tail.

"You need to know I never faulted you or your sister for what happened. The Primes were all bound to a war waged by our Progenitor. We all suffered horribly because of the arrogance of my father." Stiffly, Mira extended a hand, but quickly pulled it back. "We Parcae are bound to our fate. Those bonds are... difficult."

Mira sighed. "I am truly sorry, Ladon-Dragon. It's paltry, I know, but I offer it to you. I should have offered it then. To you and your family." She pulled a blanket to her chin. Her eyes closed and she rolled onto her side, drained by all her words.

"Mom?" Rysa touched her cheek.

Sleep took her again. She'd offered what Rysa couldn't give— forgiveness. Dragon puffed again and draped his hand over her mother's hip.

They rode in silence, Rysa stroking her mother's arm, Dragon watching, until Ladon pulled into a large, barn-like building and the van stopped.

He opened the back. He stood in the door watching her mom for a long moment, then inhaled deeply before squaring his shoulders. "We need to transfer." He pointed at one of three flatbed trucks facing a large door at the rear of the garage. "I can't take the van on the mountain roads."

Rysa took his hand. "She means it." At least her mom could give them some solace. *Her* presence only offered a future of pain.

He kissed her temple as she stepped off the bumper. "I know."

Another van almost identical to Ladon's, as well as several ATVs, waited along the sides of the building. A disorganized kitchenette full of boxes and folded-up cots occupied another bay.

Rysa helped her mother into the back of the new vehicle. Ladon coaxed Dragon over and the beast climbed onto the back of the truck, coiling around Rysa and Mira. A door in the rear of the garage opened and they drove into the Wyoming night.

The sky gleamed bright, the stars overhead brilliant. Rysa touched Dragon, his hide dull, glimmering only a fraction of his normal luminescence. He should be beautiful beyond anything she could imagine, like the sky above. Beautiful and happy and unaffected by the terrors of the world.

But instead he lay almost comatose next to two Fates.

She pulled back her hand.

They turned onto a switchback. Ladon crept along, his body forward in his seat, as he watched every bump and rock. The road switchbacked again and he pulled the truck under an overhang. Maneuvering around a corner, he backed into a cave and stopped behind a wall of rock blocking all sightlines from the outside.

Rysa crawled out. The sheer granite walls all extended into blackness above. Solid and certain under her fingers, the stone sat still, not budging or closing in or do anything at all. "Is this it?"

"This is our front door. You'll both be safe inside."

"Safe" had been gutted when she activated and ripped down to a word defined only by other words, with no real core of experience. It had become a Trojan horse with an exterior of calm but filled to the brim with memories of everything but safety.

Dragon climbed into the overhead gloom. His head and forelimbs swung down and he lifted Rysa by the waist. She teetered, disoriented by the sudden pull, but he set her on a ledge and nuzzled her hair. *Wait here,* he signed.

He set Mira next to Rysa and she leaned against the wall, her eyes half closed.

A tunnel extended into the rock, ending in a warm glow. Ladon handed up their supplies and Rysa helped Dragon pack them into a pull cart sitting on the ledge next to the tunnel.

Ladon jumped up to the ledge. Mira moaned when he lifted her into his arms. He stood silent for a moment, looking down at her. "This way," he said, then he carried her into the tunnel.

Dragon followed, hooking his tail around the handle of the cart as he passed by. A squeak echoed off the rocks each time one of the cart's wheels hit a divot or pebble. The sound blended into the gloom like some weird ghost-cry of a long-dead mouse.

Rysa walked between them, shuffling in the dark. After a moment they came to a big brass door, one round and studded with rivets, and set into the rock. Coated with a brown and green patina, it looked like an old bank vault. Her seers blinked, still drowned in flames but hinting at treasures inside.

Ladon set down her mother and jumped to another ledge. He rounded a corner and the door popped open with a hiss. Dragon ushered her through, followed by Ladon with Mira.

They entered into a huge kitchen area. To the right, a dining area opened into a library. Details were difficult to pick out in the gloom, but Rysa made out bookcases and shelf after shelf of equipment filling the alcove, some of it odd and covered with gears and handles, much like the vault-door.

On the far side of the kitchen, the walls extended upward at least four stories and curved into a dome. Doorways dotted the wall's surface much like a Pueblo cliff town. A large spiral path snaked up the side, curling around and around, a dragon path disappearing into the shadows.

Cabinets in the kitchen area blocked her view of the other side of the cave. But a few more steps inside and she stopped, her jaw dropping open.

Hanging above it all, opposite the wall dotted with doors, hung a colossal rosette window like the ones in the churches of Europe. Patterns very much like those that flowed along Dragon's hide swirled outward from the center of the glass. They looped and danced until they washed along the edges and against the intricate metalwork of the piece's solid frame.

The whole window shimmered in greens and golds and blues like waves lapping a shore.

The window was the most beautiful thing she'd ever seen, outside of Dragon's lights.

Ladon walked by, carrying her mother into the cave. "This way."

Fabrics draped furnishings and mirrors reflected the soft starlight glow filtering in through the giant window. Rysa picked up a sense of color, of jewel tones and shimmering metallics. Pillows, blankets, candles, the whole place exuded comfort and serenity.

Deeper in the cave, garden plots spread from the kitchen area into the gloom. The scents of growing fruits and vegetables wafted to her, all warm and inviting. Farther along, past a curve that hid the other end of the cave, she heard a waterfall and what could only be the spinning of a waterwheel.

The dragons built this. They carved the rock and planted the gardens and fashioned the marvelous, hypnotic window.

She felt the stars move behind it. All the stars that had greeted her as they drove under the Wyoming sky came together to speak as a choir through this mesmerizing work of the dragons. It sang of secrets her fate may yet destroy.

Ladon stopped in front of a wooden door that towered over his head. "My rooms. The entrance to Dragon's nest is inside."

Rysa pushed open the door but stopped inside the frame, gawking. "That's..." She pointed over her shoulder. "That's a *tree*."

He chuckled. "I thought you might be distracted."

Her mother's mouth gaped. "By the gods, Ladon-Human. I'd heard stories. Is it...?"

Ladon walked under the tree, Rysa and Dragon following. The room stretched deep into the rock to a large arch at the back. The tree dominated the center, its crown brushing the dome above.

A massive bed sized for a dragon and a pair of humans filled an alcove carved into the side of the room. Fabrics draped over supports surrounding the bed and swayed in the light breeze drifting through the room.

Dragon ambled by and crawled onto the bed, backing into the corner. Ladon set Mira down next to where the beast waited and touched his snout.

"The tree is a descendant."

Mira rolled onto her side. "The olive tree. It's an offspring of the one the Progenitors awoke under, all those centuries ago."

"Progenitors?" Rysa looked over Ladon's shoulder at the tree.

"Five of us—seven, including the dragons—awoke under the tree. As we are now, we were then." Ladon pinched his eyes closed for a beat. "Sister and Sister-Dragon, myself and Dragon, your grandfather, the first Fate—" He paused, glancing at her mother. "—the mother of all Shifters, and the man who infected the first Burners."

Ladon and Dragon—they *were* gods. And Rysa was the weapon meant to bring them to their knees.

Mira touched Ladon's arm. "The mountain took it. The first tree." She laid her head down. "I remember. *Mons Vesuvius, non perdet animam Dracae.*" Her eyes remained wide, her mouth slack, as she stared at the tree. She looked reverent and honestly humbled.

All her life, Rysa had never seen her mother quieted by anything. "What did she say?"

"Vesuvius could not destroy our soul." He pointed over his shoulder. "I need to get him settled."

Mira moaned, her eyes closing. If Rysa could heal her mother, she would. She'd fix what Billy did, no matter the damage it caused her own body.

Ladon pointed at the arch. "The baths are through there. There's a private one inside the corner."

Mira's breathing calmed.

"She's asleep." Rysa touched his arm. "Vesuvius." Two thousand years suddenly took on a crushing sense of proportion, as if time, too, was a mountain.

Ladon pulled a blanket over her mother. "It happened a long time ago. In another life, for both her and for us." He nodded toward Dragon before stroking her cheek. "I'll be back in a minute."

A quick squeeze to her fingers and Ladon moved away, across the bed to another arch at the back of the alcove. He paused for a moment, silhouetted in the soft, reddish glow from what must be Dragon's nest. Then he and the beast vanished, Dragon first, up the side of the rock.

The central nesting shaft angled into the rock and reached to within a dragon length of the mountain's surface. Ladon swung onto a ledge and followed

Dragon up the craggy wall. Littered with alcoves and boulders, the dragons moved debris and rocks throughout the shaft, sometimes carving new holes and at times filling others. They came in here when their humans slept and dug the entire night.

The shaft's ventilation structures funneled air into his and Sister's rooms and cooled the apartments. The dragons had engineered the mirrors to give their nest the dim glow of ancient light and it oscillated little between day and night. The moon's brightness filtered through anyway, throwing deep shadows throughout the recesses.

Dragon's hide glimmered in the shadows of a mid-level alcove above the arch leading to Ladon's rooms. The beast turned in a circle and pushed a boulder out of the way.

Ladon rubbed his crest. "You sleep. She's safe here." No matter what that spike did to her mind, he'd keep her safe while Dragon slept.

Dragon nestled Ladon's side. *Yes*, he pushed. He backed away and circled again, searching for a comfortable spot to rest. He coiled into a corner, his hide turning dark and his coat stony as he fell into sleep. His body blended into the cave wall, his respiration slowing. If Ladon hadn't known where he was, he'd be impossible to find.

Ladon stretched, his perception contracting as their flow dropped to a trickle. When Dragon slept, Ladon had the freedom to move as he pleased, though he needed to be within range when the beast woke. Dragon might sleep a full thirty-six hours this time, as exhausted as he was, so Ladon would have time.

He dropped off the ledge and caught a handhold. Dropping again, he landed in front of his door. He looked up at Dragon's sleeping spot. He'd have the situation straightened out with Rysa by the time color returned to Dragon's hide. He'd have a plan.

Through his door, Mira slept ten feet away, on the bed. Rysa, though, was nowhere in sight.

40

A bove her, the olive tree's upper branches brushed against the dome. Leaves stroked the stone and touched paintings. In the boughs, birds danced.

A tree rustled in the home of gods.

This place calmed her seers. It pulled all her attention to the physical world. The dome that touched the sky, the walls that sheltered the world, the waterfalls that sang like chimes in the breeze. Inside this mountain, life darted above her head and the earth caressed her feet.

Fire might spill back into her mind and she might find herself on the ground rocking back and forth but for now, the fabrics draping Ladon's bed and the soft rustle of his tree soothed the spike.

Ladon said that there were baths through the arches. She should clean up and rub her muscles, then return and lie down next to her mother. Sleep for a while, before it all came screaming back.

She pulled off her river-soaked shoes and walked toward the back of the room. Her toes curled into the clover under the branches and she paused for a second, feeling the ground touch her skin. She had wanted this before everything fell apart. She'd wanted a future with real air in her lungs. Real dirt under her feet. A life free of trouble for a mind that flitted between animals and trees and all the different lands and rocks and rivers.

But she was locked to the Burners now, and her reality was the talisman around her wrist.

A tunnel opened into another large cavern. About half the width of the main cave and with a ceiling the same height as Ladon's room, it still dwarfed her senses. Humidity touched her skin like a kiss and the scent of fresh rain, her nose. A soft shimmer of moonglow danced across the surfaces and white marble statues shone in the silver light. Hanging plants trailed over walls and onto tables. Couches and chairs dotted terraces and lined walls. Giant, unlit candles filled alcoves in the rock and waited for attention on several tables.

Behind it all, water cascaded over a cliff three stories tall. It rushed, not roaring but singing, and filled the entire cavern with a gentle, flowing sound. The water poured into a long pool flowing into several channels, some moving deeper into the cavern, some to private areas.

The gardens out front, his tree, the painted dome and the wall of cascading water all made her eyes widen and her lips round. Ladon had given her paradise. For a moment, she gaped, buoyed by the splendor.

But she'd set it ablaze.

"Love." Ladon wrapped his arms around her before she could respond. Surprise jolted her back to the here and now. He'd snuck in as silent as a cat and now gently kissed her cheek. "I took off my boots."

"Promise me you'll care for my mom until she's healed." The jolt loosened everything and fire ripped at her head again. It'd ruin this beautiful place.

"Of course." He didn't let go when she tried to break away. "How are you feeling? Does your chest hurt or—"

She couldn't do this. She couldn't be this close to him.

He watched her face as if a monster was about to crawl out of her nose. "No one gets in unless we open the door. No one will hurt you or Mira while you're here."

"But—" She was a Fate. A Parcae. That monster had gotten in with her, a specter which now haunted every place she walked.

The inevitable broke to the surface. Her lips parted just enough for each shallow breath to keep her body alive. How could she fight her future?

His calm vanished. The questioning ceased. Everything she'd seen when he pulled her out of the river rushed into his eyes.

"Rysa." He cupped her cheeks and stroked her hair. "Don't drop into a hole so deep you can't get out. I thought when you saw this…" He waved at the cavern. "… you'd understand. That you'd trust me. Show some confidence."

Confidence? In her or in him? "There's nothing you can do." If anything, this place reinforced the concept she'd become a weapon in a war between gods.

"I've seen women lose their will before. Sister did the same thing when Shifters came for Derek." He swallowed. "That face, I've seen it right before women died. Right before I lost them forever."

If he didn't lose her, *he'd* die.

"You can't think the way you are right now." A growl rolled out of his chest. His eyes pierced; his senses sharpened for battle. He must see the baths in high relief and hear every noise within the cavern. A bat flitted around the ceiling. Water gurgled as a breeze tickled their backs and rustled the plants.

For an instant, wrath played across his features.

"You should have left me in the river. Cities burn. Whole cities, Ladon. If you rampage, or if my super-Burners riot, it's still my fault. I'm the cause, either way. I'm the Ambusti Prime. I'm chaos's tribute."

"Rysa!" he yelled. "Killing yourself will not stop this! Don't think that. Don't *ever* think that!"

Her eyes darted to the tunnel to his room.

"Don't run away from me!"

Ladon and Dragon were everything. They were better than she deserved. But she wasn't strong enough to force her way beyond the damage in her head.

She backed away. "Fate will have its due. Fate always has its due. I'm sorry." He tried to pull her close but she dodged his arms.

"Why are Fates like this? 'Fate has its due' is bullshit!"

"It's true."

"What about Metus? He didn't see Sister-Dragon coming. Your seers are not infallible."

She didn't respond. It didn't matter what he believed.

"Beloved, listen to me." He caught her and held her close. "Please."

She stiffened. "Don't call me that." Every time he spoke that word, he tightened his bond to her. Every time he touched her, he dropped deeper into her hell.

His body tensed the same way it had when she'd told him before not to tell her how he felt. "Why?"

She tried to wiggle free but he wouldn't let go.

"Tell me why."

She shook her head.

"Why?"

He'd ripped the top off a train for her. He'd destroyed Burners for her. If he said those three words, he'd solidify his actions and he'd die. "Don't. Please."

"I love you."

Her breath lumped into a hard pellet above her heart. He shouldn't do this. She pushed at his arms but he held tight.

He stroked her cheek. "You need to hear it. You need me to say it and it's the truth, Rysa. Dragon's loved you from the first moment you touched his snout. I can't live without you. I haven't been able to since Marcus's." The jumbled line of his lips mirrored the inflection of his voice.

"You can't know that. You can't be sure. No one—"

"Yes, I can! I'm old enough to know the difference between infatuation and desire and honest love. With you, I've finally found a reason to walk this earth. We absolutely, utterly *love* you."

She'd more than snared him. She'd jammed the hook so deep into his throat that if he pulled it out, it would drag his innards with it.

"I'm leaving, Ladon. Now. Right now." He'd take care of her mother. If she vanished into the wilderness, maybe he'd take care of himself.

Groaning, he swung her legs up and jostled her in his arms, his anger disorienting her balance.

He tossed her to get a better grip when she came down. "You are the most willful woman I have ever known. You are more willful than Sister and I thought that was impossible. You are willful to the point of extreme irritation."

"Willful? I'm not some damsel you need to rescue." She slapped his shoulder.

He flared his nostrils. "You slap like one."

Her mouth dropped open. "Put me down! Stop acting like a caveman!"

"You stoop to your uncle's manipulations and it's your decision…"

He scowled and tossed her again. "… but when I lay bare my heart I'm a caveman who's oppressing you?"

"Damn it, Ladon—"

"I am sick of you not trusting your own strength." He tossed her again. "And I am sick of you saying cruel things to push me away. I don't like it and you're going to stop doing it." A small tic moved across his cheek.

She hadn't realized how much her words injured him.

"I've spent centuries with women. I know exactly what you are doing and it still cuts me. You do it and parts of my soul break off because you are the center of our world. You are the center of everything and I love you."

"Ladon—" If she kept him at a distance, he'd not hurt as much if she became a Burner.

"You feel the same way I do. You told me, in the park. You said 'the men I love.'" His nostrils flared again, his mouth twitching. "*I'm* the man you love. *Me*. I know because of the way your soul opens when you look at me. In how you respond when I touch you." His lips set into a hard line. "I brought you to three orgasms our first time."

Her mouth rounded. "Put me down."

"Not until you tell me how you feel. Tell me what you want. Tell me the real future, not the one your uncle forced into your head."

"Ladon, it doesn't—"

"Yes it does!" He swung her legs around so she faced him and scooped a hand under her bottom. "Tell me."

She shook her head, refusing to look at his face.

Three quick steps and he pressed her back against the stone wall next to a settee, between the end of the long piece of furniture and an alcove full of huge pillar candles. "Say it." His mouth traced her jaw and her earlobe. "Damn it, you're going to admit it. This weight you carry will kill you if you don't push it off. You are no one's tribute."

She didn't have the strength to argue. Not with him.

"You are not alone." His lips traced her ear. "Dragon and I will help you. We love you."

He ground his hips against hers in a slow, tight circle. This moment with him pushed back her uncle's injection. Her nasty focused her senses on his warm scent, on the way his lips trailed over her neck, on how his teeth tickled her skin.

Before she saw the inevitable, when she believed that she was only locked to the Burners, she let herself feel the tingle when he stroked her arm. To enjoy his company and to talk about field work and caves and the land in the places they'd lived. But also to talk about her education and what she wanted to do and her life before all this happened.

Though he was immortal and he'd seen everything and lived through more than she could imagine, he wanted to learn about her as much as she wanted to learn about him.

He kissed her with enough force to pull her breath from her body. "All the lies about us ending the world infuriate me but the thought of losing you turns my blood to ice." He touched her temple. "So you are going to tell me what you want. Not the other Fates. *You.*"

She wanted to finish school and work a real job and clear the flowerbeds while he mowed the lawn. Most importantly, she wanted Ladon and Dragon.

She closed her eyes. Her voice disappeared and only her mouth formed her words. "You and Dragon, you mean more to me than anything. More than my own life."

"Dragon has two humans. You are my mate and nothing's going to change that." He kissed her again, his free hand finding a breast. "I know you love me. Say it."

"It doesn't matter." What she wanted, what he wanted. The Jani triads of Empire and Strategy overran her Burnerized life.

He pulled his chest back but continued to hold her against the wall with his hips. "It mattered when you didn't let me tell you how I feel."

She sniffled, confused.

"It mattered because words hold power. They change possibilities. They change what will happen," Ladon said.

"Words aren't magic." Voicing a wish didn't change *what-will-be*.

"It's not magic. It's will. Dragon and I choose you." He kissed her again, his body holding her steady.

Will. Something the Dracae had in spades. They moved the

unmovable and carved this beautiful home into a mountain. They had the strength to battle the inevitable.

Maybe… maybe he was right. Maybe they could bring her through this. "You choose me?" His will manifested in the small circles his fingers drew on her skin and in the trickle of energy tickling her senses even as Dragon slept.

"Yes. We choose you. I choose you. And I will have what I want, fate be damned."

The threads rewove, altering. His strength flowed through his touch and pushed back the pain in her skull.

"Dragon and I, we will give you the life you want," he said. "Always."

Her terror melted, and with it, the hold on her soul. "My love." Her lips met his in a brilliant kiss.

He tugged at her jeans, his response instantaneous. Groaning in frustration, he pulled back, searching for the zipper.

She wanted his skin and his hands and his mouth on hers. She yanked at his t-shirt and he fumbled it over his head. He twisted her shirt and seams gave way, threads splitting across her belly. Up and over her head, its tatters landed on the floor next to his.

He ripped at her bra. "Off!"

She unhooked it and he whipped it away.

Lifting her again, he held her with his mouth at her chest and her bare back against the cool granite.

"Tell me." His animal need took over. "Say it!" His tongue found her nipple and her back arched.

"I want you alive and in love with me." More dread evaporated. She had a *dragon*, for goodness sake. A dragon who could stand against anything.

"Say it again." His mouth devoured hers before she could answer. "I want to hear you say it. I want to know you mean it." The zipper on her jeans released and he tugged the fabric down her hips.

"I mean it. I—*oh!*"

He grasped the fabric of her panties and yanked. They split, ripping into several pieces as he pulled them off her feet.

"Swear it!" He unbuttoned his jeans and she pushed them down. "You will not die. Do you understand, Rysa? We will not lose you."

He entered her and she bucked against the wall. A deep moan pushed from her core and her nails dug into his shoulders.

Shudders rippled through every one of her muscles when he thrust deeper and he responded in kind, every part of him vibrating.

"Tell me how you feel. Tell me the truth." He thrust again as he nipped below her earlobe.

She couldn't speak. No words formed. She kissed him instead.

Holding her hips, he dropped to the edge of the settee, thrusting as they landed. "Tell me!"

Every inch of her skin against his felt alive. Every kiss traveling over his chin and neck bonded them tighter together. Their need building, he flipped her onto her back and pulled her thighs up toward his chest. He moaned and his pace increased.

His gaze intense, she could see he wanted to say more, to demand a response again, but no more words left his throat. He said it all with his body: his need, his love.

His hurt.

"I'm sorry for the terrible things I said." Was this what it meant to be Parcae? To inflict on others what fate demanded because that was just how it was? Many of the behaviors Tom had done to her—the cutting off of her emotions and the little, mean things to force her away—she'd done to Ladon.

It didn't matter what fate dealt out. She'd never again say words that hurt him.

One arm wrapped tight around her hips. His other arm flexed as he lowered her to the pillows. "You are not... going... to leave us...."

"I'm not. I won't. Ladon!" The orgasm flooded through her, her fingers twisting into the pillows. Her nasty dipped in, not siphoning, but sharing.

His eyes fluttered and his lips parted. The deep, dragon rumble erupted from his chest as elation burst through all his muscles. His core contracted and his back arched. He dropped down, unable to hold himself up.

"I love you." Her voice filled the void she'd forced between them and she opened herself to everything he and Dragon offered.

"I love both of you. I love the man and I love the dragon and I choose you. You are the fate I choose. You. Only you, for as long as you want me."

He groaned, the one sound his throat released.

Another spasm, as strong as the first, rocked through his body and she kissed the spot on his chest that made him resonate.

His core contracted again, the pleasure radiating in tight bursts from his abdomen to his limbs. Slow waves moved across his skin and through the rasping moans pushing between their renewed kisses.

He halted mid-inhale as another spasm played sideways through each distinct muscle of his stomach and chest. Jaw tense, his back arched again.

"Ladon!" She clenched his hair, her body reflecting the spasms rocking his.

"I... *oh*..." He kissed her deeply.

His climax still pounded, and now it rumbled. The sound filled the cavern, echoing to her ears moments after it flooded her body.

The first time it happened, in the van, it had warmed her soul. This time, it warmed everything, including the harshness of the spike and the coldness she'd forced between them.

Pleasure twined with love, colored with burgundies and violets, and a new orgasm rocketed to all her cells. She lost all sense of the world, of time. Ladon's love filled all of her and when he touched her cheek, she opened her eyes to the bright and real joy filling his.

"This is our truth."

She kissed his forehead and traced the slope of his ear. "Yes." Their truth. Hers, his, and Dragon's too, when the beast awoke.

Ladon's breathing steadied and he moved out of her but stayed entwined, his legs wrapped in hers and his arms tight around her waist. Kissing her jaw, he tucked his face into the crook of her neck.

This man and the beast bound to him were worth fighting for. They were worth pushing against the future and taking on the inevitable. If she lost, if the fate forced as a spike in her head came to pass, she'd have this time with them. "Yes, it is."

A flash: another crater. She winced. This time, though, she tightened her arms around the man she loved.

He kissed her temple. "I will fight every Fate and I will destroy every Burner who threatens you. And I will find a Shifter who will return your control."

Her eyes closed but she traced the lines and planes of his face. She wouldn't lose them. Fate be damned, they were the future she wanted, no matter how badly her uncle's injection hurt.

The spike still distorted her seers and menaced both her and Ladon with death, but she breathed here, now, in the present. "Thank you." She could fight. "Thank you, my love."

Her eyes joyful, her body naked and exquisite, he led her deeper into the baths. When he pulled her under the shower fed by the waterfall, she bounced, her happiness palpable. His smiles didn't stop, didn't decrease even with her excitement, and she kissed him, wide-eyed at his response. When he smoothed his hand over her waist and settled his fingers into hers, she caressed his hands, and wrapped her arms tight around his chest.

The water cascaded over their shoulders and they washed the river from each other. Her expression opened to him again, her face giving him everything he'd seen when she was in her visions: union, intimacy, friendship. Passion. And a pure, purposeful tenderness meant for only him.

They made love again. He held her against the stone wall, her hips balanced on the shower's ledge. His voice left him but he whispered, unable to stop the words that rolled from his heart: Love you. Beautiful one. My beloved. My mate. Mine.

Yes... It flowed from her, melding to him. *Yes.* And when she kissed the spot on his chest, he rumbled with such fierceness the sound drowned the rush of the cavern's water.

Love you.

Now she slept with her back to him, a borrowed pair of Derek's pajamas ballooning around her middle. Mira slept on the other side of her daughter, her back also to Ladon.

He nestled closer. All of Rysa's physical wounds had healed. The cut on her arm was nothing more than a thin line. He'd pulled the stitches in the bath. Billy's last marks looked like they'd been healing for weeks, not hours.

So had his. The cut from the fight with the War Babies had all but vanished. No welt, no line. Nothing. He healed much faster than a normal, but after less than a day, he should be able to see a mark.

Ladon raised himself on an elbow and peered at Mira. Rysa had cleaned up her mother in the van, bandaging every place that the damned Burner had licked her skin. Ladon couldn't see her wounds. Yet her color had returned and she snored softly, in a sounder sleep than pain should allow.

He lay down against Rysa's back, close enough to feel her warmth but far enough away she wouldn't awaken.

She shivered. He tensed, his fingers flaring over her hip.

His senses focused on her and all he saw—all he perceived—was that his woman hurt.

He'd make it right. Come morning, he'd speak with Mira. Hearing Dragon, manifesting her mother's wounds, extending her health to others, all reinforced his questions. Time to ask about the other half of Rysa's family, and in particular Sandro Torres.

Ladon closed his eyes and leaned his forehead against the nape of her neck. The pain would stop. He'd give her what she needed to fight the spike.

And something told him he didn't need Dmitri to find it.

41

L adon sneezed. Sunshine flicked through the tree's branches and onto his cheek. He rubbed at the spot, fighting wakefulness. The familiar lack-of-Dragon that numbed part of his awareness when the beast slept sat on his mind. It slouched like a determined cat sitting on his leg and dug in its claws when he tried to push it away.

He ignored it, focusing instead on thoughts of his lovely Rysa and the feel of her exquisite breasts. The soft skin between them tasted as perfect as the woman herself. The little stuttered breaths she exhaled when he kissed her nipples held his attention like no other woman's. He'd spend all day exploring the tender smoothness of her body.

Chart every inch and tally every reaction he caused with a gentle kiss or a quick nip.

He rolled over. No one else slept on his bed.

Sitting up, he scratched at his belly. From the intensity of the light and the angle of the reflections falling on the tree, he guessed he'd been asleep for ten hours. Rysa and Mira must have decided to let him rest. Which was a shame. He'd rather wake surrounded by women, even if one was his love's mother.

Maybe they'd gone to the baths. He listened as an oriole called from the tree's branches. Deep in the cave, the hydropower generator hummed. Birds tweeted in the ventilation shafts. But no sounds of activity rose from the rear cavern. They'd probably gone out to the kitchen to find something to eat or to get Rysa's clothes from the pull cart.

Though watching her hips sway in the too big pajamas would be a nice distraction for the morning. He'd follow her around the whole day, grinning and rubbing his chin against the slope of her neck until she sighed, even if Mira frowned at him.

Ladon pinched the bridge of his nose. Randiness when he walked into the kitchen would only embarrass Rysa, though her blushes did tempt kisses. Maybe later, he'd sneak her away for an hour or two. Suggest a nap.

He allowed himself one quick groan. He awoke with a diffuse desire pumping through his veins most mornings, but now that desire had focus. A very clear and perfect focus.

Still, he should do his best not to embarrass her. The cool stone floor under his toes should help. As would a cold shower.

Maybe he could entice Rysa to join him.

Another groan and he looked up at painted swirls covering the dome. He had work to do. Allowing himself to be distracted by his own wants in no way fixed Faustus's damage.

He'd find a healer so when Dragon awoke, they could fetch help immediately. But first he needed Mira to answer his questions.

Sister and Derek should have been home last night, though no roars or threats to Mira's life had disturbed his sleep. He'd left messages but Sister hadn't responded. Her irritation about a Jani Prime in her home most likely had Derek sleeping in the RV and wishing for his hospital bed.

He'd use the Sister-free peace to cook the women breakfast. Perhaps he'd make a frittata with basil from the garden and fresh eggs from the coop. Acceptance and a friendly gesture might help Mira to be generous with her answers.

Ladon padded across the cool floor and swung open the door. The hinges squeaked, the iron halting as he pushed. He'd install a new counterweight system so the massive wood panel glided. Scratching at his stomach again, he peered at the rivets on the latch. With Rysa living here—

The tang of Burner hit his nose in full, clawing fury. He pressed his back against the stone wall, his eyes searching the main cavern.

Shifters and a few Fates had tried to get in since Sister and Sister-Dragon began excavation more than two centuries ago. The entrance vault kept them out. The ventilation system's fortifications confounded everyone but the dragons. No one got in.

Not unless invited.

Did Billy damage Mira's mind? But a Burner couldn't sustain thought long enough to brainwash a Fate. She'd done this on her own.

Ladon's senses primed to detect movement, breath, blood flow. Somewhere near the mouth of the cave, Rysa gasped.

Every muscle uncoiled and he ran toward the kitchen, his bare feet gripping the stone floor. He stopped just out of sight of the cabinets, his breath still. Whispers spilled from the sink area. He heard a tug and a push, followed by Rysa's stuttered breathing.

He crept along, silent in the shadows. Rysa stood in the bright light flooding the kitchen, her back against the table. She shook, her eyes blank with a vision and her fingers bent into claws.

Behind her on the table, clutching to her throat a dagger forged from the same night metal as Metus's swords, crouched Faustus. Mira sniveled in the corner.

"Ladon-Human," Faustus murmured. "It's about time you woke up." His seer danced with Rysa's, small movements here, another there.

Her nose bled.

"Let her go." Ladon's chest tensed. The more the bastard twisted the spike, the more damage he did. And the more pain he inflicted.

Faustus yanked on Rysa's neck. "No blackouts, pumpkin. Alert and in the moment is what we want."

Mira screamed a blistering string of Latin profanity and whipped a plate at Faustus's head. It slammed against the wall and shattered into a spray of ceramic chips.

Rysa slipped to the left but her uncle held tight. The bastard yowled, a bitter sound reflecting his effort to hold her seers at bay. "Mira, take the burndust I brought and quit your pathetic bawling."

Mira shrieked and hurled another dish. So she'd let him in for burndust, seeking it like some useless junkie. Ladon should have seen this coming. He shouldn't have offered trust, even with her apology. If the damned dust calmed the sickness, she'd need it now.

Yet Mira threw dishes. She let Faustus in, but regretted it. Damned Fates, never strong enough to fight their futures.

Maybe she'd find her backbone. Ladon picked up a dirty glass from the counter and flung it at Mira's head. If her present-seer showed his intent, she'd cooperate, dust-addled or not.

"Shut up, cow!" he barked, pointing at her as he released the glass.

Screaming, she ducked. Dramatic flailing followed, as he had hoped. Faustus's attention flitted to his sister.

Rysa jerked free of his grip.

Ladon lunged. Dagger up, Faustus sliced, but Rysa yanked on her uncle's arm. Off balance, he dropped the dagger, missing Ladon's stomach by a fraction of an inch. Ladon slid across the table and landed on the other side.

Rysa flung herself over the surface and into his arms. He picked her up, her clammy skin a shock against his, and set her down behind his back. Her entire body shook as she pressed her forehead between his shoulder blades.

"Help her!" Ladon bellowed. If Faustus didn't release the spike, he'd cause permanent damage, not unlike the ravages caused by the Parcae sickness. No healer could counter it, no matter their skill.

"You're the one addicted, you damned fiend! I didn't let you in for the dust." Mira leaned against a counter. "You're killing her." She buckled forward, panting. "Fix what you did, brother! How many of our triad's children do you have to send to their deaths? *Les Enfants* are shadows of who they could have been, all because of you. How many of our babies do you have to murder? Fix my daughter or I will gouge your eyes from their sockets!"

Faustus's future-seer thundered through the kitchen and he rolled his eyes. "No, you won't." He pointed at a plastic bag on the counter. "The dust will make you feel better. Stop the pain in your joints."

"You're going to die," Mira muttered.

"Quiet, dear sister." Faustus sneered and shook his head.

"I don't know what your seer has shown you." Ladon held Rysa against his back. "Whatever is coming is not my doing. Nor is it Sister's. You should understand that. All the Fates should understand that."

"*Parcae!*" Faustus scowled.

"I won't go with you," Rysa murmured.

"What was that, pumpkin? Did you have something to add?" Faustus leaned toward her.

Ladon twisted to stay between them.

"Oh, I think you will. The pain's so strong you'll do anything to make it stop."

"I'll die first."

Faustus's eyebrows arched. "Ha! You'll kill *him* first."

"Get out!" Mira shuffled forward. "Twenty centuries and I've always done what my seer told me to do. I shouldn't have listened this time."

"You know none of us has a choice." He jumped and latched onto Mira's neck. "I won't kill you, but I will snap a bone or two."

Mira hit Faustus with a full blast from her present-seer, a colossal wave of power rolling off her body. Ladon stumbled and Rysa let go, gasping as she fell to the floor.

Mira's elbow landed in Faustus's gut. "I hate you! You goddamned monster! I've always hated you!" She bent over, vomiting onto the kitchen's stone floor.

"Ladon!"

He spun just as the Burner punched. Encased head to toe in a wet suit, the ghoul looked ready for a dive into the ocean. He gave off a faint whiff of the Burner odor anyway. Huge and ugly, he hit harder than any Burner Ladon had dealt with before.

The ghoul punched again but Ladon ducked and rammed the Burner against the stovetop. The ghoul rolled and his fist came down hard on Ladon's kidneys. Ladon breathed through it and seized the stove's grating. He swung. Twenty pounds of metal contacted the Burner's jaw.

"Let go of me!"

Faustus hauled Rysa into the tunnel, but she kicked at his knee but he dodged and bounced her head against the wall.

She crumpled to the stone floor. Ladon's focus constricted to her, to the damage her uncle caused, and he willed her his strength. He'd will her his life, if he could. He'd give her everything.

She gasped, her back arching.

Ladon dropped the grating and sprinted down the tunnel. If he could get enough distance between—

The Burner slammed him into the rock. Mouth wide in a stiff sneer, teeth luminous, the ghoul pressed a palm against his own face and clicked his neck and jaw back into place.

His other hand sizzled around Ladon's throat.

The bastard blew an acid kiss.

Ladon coughed. His eyes blurred and he twisted against the ghoul's grip. "You're dead, Faustus!" he yelled down the tunnel.

Faustus wrenched Rysa's hair and dragged her away without a response. He offered no grunt or snigger or comeuppance, only his sour gaze as she screamed and kicked against his grip.

Ladon tried to lunge but the Burner held him fast. "Not so tough without the dragon, are you?" The ghoul laughed.

"Rysa! Fight!" Maybe she'd get away. She was strong enough.

Faustus hit her again. He pointed past Ladon into the kitchen. "Mira! Come!"

Rysa panted, clawing at his grip.

Ladon punched but the Burner hissed and banged his shoulders against the rock. The ghoul tisked, sparks flying off his teeth.

"Fate binds us, Ladon-Human." Mira shuffled by and down the tunnel. "I didn't mean for this to happen."

Rysa bit Faustus's wrist.

He hit her again. "Bite me one more time and the stone wall will be the last thing you see, you little bitch."

Mira hit Faustus's back. "She's your niece!"

The Burner scratched at his forehead with one hand while he fried Ladon's neck with his other. Ladon grabbed the rock wall and lifted both legs. He kicked, his heels shooting down into the ghoul's knees.

They both tumbled into the tunnel.

Ladon came down on top of the ghoul, one knee smashing into his face. The Burner's nose and jaw cracked. Wheezing, he threw off Ladon. Middle fingers jabbing the air, he bolted into the cave.

Toward Dragon.

Faustus dropped over the ledge at the entrance, Rysa with him. "Go save your beast, Ladon-Human," he called.

"Rysa!" The damned Burner didn't know where to look. Ladon would grind Faustus into pulp and then take care of the ghoul—

Mira's seer chimed through the tunnel, so strong Ladon cringed. She pointed over his head, her eyes wide. "Go!" she yelled, and dropped off the ledge.

Ladon skidded, turning on his heels, his body instinctively listening to the warnings of a powerful present-seer. How many times had he regretted pausing before listening to Timothy? He darted through the kitchen, picking up Faustus's dagger as he sprinted into the living quarters. The ghoul ran through the garden, moving fast. Ladon threw the dagger, praying that this one time he'd be good enough without the beast.

The dagger sliced through the Burner's spinal cord and lodged hilt-deep in his chest, the tip a dark point protruding from his breast bone. He crystallized, imploding into a point above Sister's salad vegetables.

The blast ricocheted off the walls and blew over a storage shed.

The plots lay shredded, a wide crater in their place. A fruit tree toppled. Benches caught fire. Six panes of the *draconis fenestra* shattered, the leaded crystal rained onto the library.

Ladon bounced against the cavern's rock wall.

He dropped to his knees. His home ripped apart. Rysa gone.

Her uncle meant to turn her Burner and Ladon let it happen. He let Faustus drag her away. He might have to take her life, exploding her newly-incendiary body, all because he couldn't take the chance of being too far from Dragon.

He needed to hold his psyche together, to keep his wits about him. If he descended too far, the beast would wake a hunter and smear flat every Fate within a thousand miles.

He couldn't. Rysa did not want him to become a monster like Faustus.

Something glinted on the cave wall. It flashed and he stared across the cavern at the spot. The threatening rupture of his control froze, entranced by the dancing light, and he stood up. His eyes focused as the spot flashed again. Walking through the shattered field and past the smoldering apple tree, he watched the glints of light. He continued walking, moving around a storage shed and the stream.

Mira's wedding band hung tied to a string, a note taped beside it. He pulled it off, turning it over in the reflected sunlight.

He unfolded the paper. Across the front, written in Mira's precise hand, was an address on the outskirts of Salt Lake City. An address, and three words: "You are right."

A new fear tumbled through his gut. Faustus couldn't see the possibilities beyond turning Rysa. Once the venom hit her blood, she'd vanish from his future-seer, cloaked in chaos. No one could read Burners. So he didn't know.

She wouldn't create an army. She never could. The venom would kill her.

Shifters always died.

He had no way of heading it off. Dragon slept and would for another day. They'd follow, but they'd be too late.

Ladon flipped the note over, fighting a need to shred the paper. Three more words were scrawled across the back: "Wake the beast." Followed by another four: "What makes you tremble?"

Ladon stared at the paper. He didn't *tremble*. Nothing made him *tremble*. But… he looked down at the swath of skimmed hair on his chest. He and the beast, they mirrored more than their energy.

A single chuckle rose from his throat.

He touched Rysa's spot before running for Dragon's nest.

42

The storm lit the building like a forties black and white horror movie. A giant boomerang seventeen stories tall, the building's top floors weren't finished.

The roof shredded the sky like the open jaw of a shark-toothed ogre.

Lightning flashed. Reflections thrust across the glass and brick surface in jarring, high contrast angles. And like an ogre, it dominated the land surrounding it.

Rysa leaned against her mother as they rode up the elevators at the center of the behemoth. When her uncle jerked them onto an open level, she stumbled forward.

"Let her go." Mira's present-seer hissed across the concrete deck of the unfinished floor. Her chiming had been subsumed by a faster, discordant vibration that rattled Rysa's teeth.

Faustus squinted and slapped her mother.

The spike in Rysa's head bled colorless heat into the void behind her eyes. About half way between Rock Springs and Salt Lake City, her uncle shut down her seers and her nasty yelped once before cowering under her consciousness.

She felt nothing.

Not the spike, or her pain, or any of the emotions that should be flooding her mind.

I'm normal again, she thought. Back to the hyperactive girl who failed school but aced tests. Who scared the other kids because she *knew*. Who hid with her toys and dreamed of a day when she'd swim in lakes and explore caves.

Back before Ladon helped her find the will to fight for the life she wanted.

Plastic tarps snapped and dust blew into her eyes when the wind gusted through the open walls.

"Let us go," Mira pleaded. "Please."

Faustus slapped her mom again, wiggling his fingers when he pulled back. "You don't see the visions. You don't know what they're going to do."

He wiped Mira's tears on his pant leg.

"You don't understand what you're seeing! How could you? You destroyed our sister." Mira waved her swollen knuckles. "You destroyed me. The future means nothing unless you understand its foundations."

"Is that so?" Faustus snorted. "Yet here you are, propelled by the same power that propels all Parcae." He grabbed Rysa's arm. "Let's go."

"No!" Mira swung at him. Faustus bent her wrist and she screamed.

"Next time, I break it." He waved at Rysa. "Only we were capable of dealing with this. No one else could maneuver the Dracae. Only the Jani Prime."

"I hate you," Rysa screamed. "You murdered those people in Chicago! The Burners were your tool. *You* did it. You destroyed Ismene's life. You twist and destroy everyone you touch."

Rysa tried to pull away but Faustus slapped her across the mouth. The sting pushed onto her tongue.

Mira spit at her brother. "I *sent* her to Ladon! When we were young, when we all served the Empire and his sister claimed retribution and you and Ismene paid dearly for our father's conceit, Ladon *never* treated me or Ismene like meat. Not once. He let us live when the Dracas wanted our heads."

Surprise darted across Faustus's features.

"That's right! He's always regretted what he did! The first time Ismene and I escaped from you? When the ash from the mountain fell? When you and Father schemed? We found him. He let us go! Ismene and I tried to hurt him but he made sure we reached the port. He's a better man than you. He's *always* been a better man!"

Mira tried to pull Rysa to her side. "I wasn't hiding from our sister. I was hiding from *you*."

Ladon only told Rysa about the girl. He didn't tell her that he'd protected her mom. But he wouldn't. Protecting is what he did. To him, it wasn't special.

Mira yanked Rysa's face around so they were eye to eye. "I do forgive him, honey. He's worth forgiving. I hope you can forgive me."

"Mom." Her mother never felt she had a choice.

Faustus's ice-cold grip clamped down on Rysa's bicep. Mira's pleading hands pawed, her eyes wild with a whirlwind of love and hate.

"It changes nothing." Faustus shoved Mira into a stack of sheetrock.

"You are as much Torres as you are Jani." Mira held up her bandaged forearm for Rysa to see. "Maybe more. Use it, daughter!"

Her mother's words made no sense. Rysa's dead emotions blocked any attempt she made at understanding.

Faustus wound an electrical cord around Mira's wrists and tugged her toward an open wall support. The cord snapped against the metal as he bound her mom's arms to the teeth of the building. "You're staying here."

"You're going to die!" Mira yelled. "You undo what you've done or you're going to die!"

Faustus dug his fingers into Rysa's back and pushed her forward. "So says the present-seer."

They walked from the elevators into the left wing of the building, around a gas-powered winch attached to a spooled cable.

Faustus snatched down plastic sheeting and the wind cracked it against his face before it tumbled away. He spit out dust. "You can hate me all you want. It will have no effect on the future. You'll birth an army. They'll follow you."

Twice Faustus pushed Rysa over pallets of concrete blocks and stacks of girders.

"I will not do this." Ladon told her that words held power. She'd use hers to find her strength. She'd snatch her control back. Her uncle interfered, but her seers—her nasty—were part of *her*.

Not part of him.

Faustus continued droning. "After a while, you won't remember hating me. You won't remember your mother. You won't remember sleeping with the Dracos. But you'll always be Parcae, and you will always go to your fate."

"Shut up."

He wrenched her wrist, blinking for a moment as if he couldn't speak. "You little whore. You let him touch you?"

She didn't answer. He pressed the insignia bracelet into her flesh and the metal dragons poked into her skin. She focused on the new twinge. It let her feel, at least a little.

Faustus shoved her forward. "When the time comes, the Burners will do what they were meant to do. The Burners will end fire with fire."

Inside a tool cage on the open edge of the deck, a man wearing a light blue cardigan and holding a pipe in his lips paced from mesh side to mesh side, muttering into the wind. He clapped when he saw Faustus. A cloud rose off his skin.

A Burner.

"Tell her to let me out!" The ghoul jigged around a generator.

Adrestia stepped from behind a stack of sheetrock. "It is not your station to demand anything, Bob." A ragged laceration on her cheek and the bruise around an eye bloated her face. She lumbered toward her father like a zombie Fate.

"I hope that scars up nice and pretty." Rysa signed *bitch* at her.

Adrestia muttered something in French. Faustus muttered back, sullen, and yanked Rysa toward the cage. The Burner sniffed and pointed with his pipe.

"Oh… she smells scrumptious." He sniffed again. "And different from you two." With lightning speed, he climbed the mesh. He hung from the top of the cage, the pipe between his teeth.

Adrestia hit the metal with a rod. "*Tais-toi!*" 'Shut up!'

Startled, Bob bit down and his pipe snapped in two. "Hey! That's my favorite pipe!" He dropped to the floor and smoothed the front of his cardigan. It crinkled and scrunched like a plastic tarp. "I don't have to be quiet if I don't want to. I'm doing you the favor here, not the other way around." The tarp-cardigan contracted into rows of permanent wrinkles under the heat of his fingertips.

He sniffed again. "I smell Dracae." Bob stepped back, his hands up. "One of them didn't follow you, did they? Because you promised."

"No. The Dracos-beast sleeps and the Dracas hate Parcae."

"I don't see why. Fates are delectable." Bob smacked his lips and did another jig.

Faustus narrowed his eyes. "Back away from the gate."

Adrestia hit the side of the cage again and swore at Bob in French. The Burner flipped her off.

"She's mean." He nodded toward Adrestia. "Where's the two who put me in here? One of them said you'd bring some Shifter for me to snack on when I was done." He clapped with sparks and a wispy smoke.

Rysa's seers were silent, but *what-is* pointed to this fate. She was about to be turned into the Queen of the Burners by a demented Mr. Rogers.

"This is not the future I choose." She needed to fight, not be an automaton like Adrestia. "That Dracae you smell? He took care of the other two—" Rysa pointed at her cousin. "—and he's going to take care of you, Burner."

Bob chortled and smacked his lips at Adrestia. "Can I eat the mean one?"

Faustus swung a wrench and hit the cage mesh so hard it dented. Sparks flew as the wrench slid down the wire. "Show some respect," he yelled.

Bob stepped back, his hands raised again, the cardigan reflecting hot-blue onto his teeth. "I'm just asking."

A gust blew through the open floor and picked up the Burner's stench. Faustus gagged. Rysa staggered back. Bob's teeth flashed like the lightning behind him.

Arms pulled Adrestia into the grid of the ceiling.

And the past rode in on the wind.

43

Adrestia disappeared before Faustus could pull her down.

"Burners! She can't see them." Faustus spun around, a gun aimed at the shadows. The gun flitted to Rysa's head. "This is your fault! Metus and Timor should have been with her."

"You sent them after me! What did you think Ladon would do? Ask them nicely to give me back?"

Faustus pointed the gun at Rysa's chest. "Your talisman's chaos. We didn't see the Dracas giving a damn." He flicked his gun at the darkness above. "Addy!"

Bob laughed. "Addy. That's a cute name for such... a... *bitch*!" He shrieked the last three words and hopped up and down, giggling like a fool.

Rysa dropped to the floor, her back against a wheelbarrow. "Fix what you did to me so I can use my seers."

Faustus punched this time.

Rysa tasted blood. She touched her mouth. He'd split her lip.

Pain raged through her head—it, too, might split. Pop like a damned Burner.

Maybe she should let Adrestia die. What did she care? After everything the War Babies had done, they deserved to have their present-seer eaten by ghouls.

But her mom hadn't raised her to be coldhearted. To be Parcae. This wasn't what Adrestia would have chosen, if she knew how to choose.

Rysa couldn't let Adrestia's fate strip her to bones and meat. "You trained them to be your attack dogs." Her seers clicked a small bit of understanding through the fog. "You had her killing by the time she was five!" He did this to them when they were *children*.

Faustus leaned against a stack of sheetrock. "Damned Ambustae. Where did they come from?"

"Let me out!" Bob howled. "I saw them first!" He climbed the mesh.

Faustus scratched his head and the butt of his gun rubbed against his temple. "We watched this place. Burners don't come to Salt Lake City. We were careful."

"*Papa*! Ça fait mal!" 'Daddy! It hurts!'

Rysa had spent her life dragged behind her attention issues, bruising and breaking every time she hit a sharp edge or a terrible divot. But, she realized, her issues belonged to her. They were part of her.

Ladon loved her anyway. So did Dragon.

And her mom.

Her father, too, wherever he was.

Faustus might have spiked her head but her abilities were hers. Her talisman didn't function, but her abilities belonged to *her*. And unlike her family, Rysa had had enough of being dragged by fate.

Her seers unfolded, snarling and reluctant to cooperate. The agony painted the concrete hot white, but a vision flared.

She didn't see the Burners. Not directly, but she sensed threads of *what-was*.

She doubled over. "Two have Adrestia. I can't—" She cried out and wiped at her nose. Blood. "Fix me!"

"No." Faustus future-seer sputtered. He lowered his gun. "Ladon and I, we're one and the same. We both do what we are meant to do, no matter the consequences. No matter who it hurts."

He thumped his chest. "At least I do it for the rest of the world." He gestured at the open side of the building. Another gust flipped his jacket over his hip.

The world was bigger than him. Bigger than his king-making talisman. Bigger than he could *ever* see. He could do all the douchebag rationalizing he wanted and he'd still be an idiot.

The Burner link around her wrist slid down and clinked against the little dragons. Rysa looked down at her hand. Talismans filter, but her dragon enhanced. The beast gave her calm when he laid his head on her lap.

The man gave her strength when he said "I love you."

Faustus's little mind was about to let his own daughter die.

She sprang at her uncle. He landed on his back, Rysa on his chest, a knee on each wrist. His gun clattered away.

His seer slammed into her mind. The injection twisted.

When she was between Ladon and Dragon, she felt their river of energy. Her nasty's arms—her seers—curled around it.

This close to her uncle, her nasty did the same to him. Rysa leaned her forehead against her uncle's the way Adrestia had leaned against her in the rail yard—and her nasty felt his end of the injection.

No whipping this time. Not snapping or flailing. Her nasty dug down to the root and yanked the spike out of her uncle's skull.

The world integrated memory by memory, point by point. Her mind stabilized, the crack at the back closing.

The ice bugs withered. Her nasty closed the holes in her psyche as fast as it forced out the spike.

No one would ever do that to her again.

Faustus's head bounced against a concrete support. "What are you?"

Rysa smirked as she pushed off him. "A better Fate than you, obviously."

Adrestia shrieked. "*Papa! Ils sont trop nombreux. Je ne peux pas les repousser!*" 'There are too many! I can't get away!'

Four Burners dropped out of the ceiling next to Rysa and Faustus. Two, big and ugly, threw bits of sheetrock at each other while they hopped away toward the central elevator. One, thin and potmarked, leaned against a support. His mouth spread in a pompous sneer, the reek drifting from him heavy—he was the unwashed teenage dork-Burner.

The one in front snorted and pointed her little finger at Rysa.

The child.

"Skankadoodle!" she yelled. "Your boyfriend ain't here so I'm going to chew you all up!" She jumped up and did a one-eighty in the air, pointing down the length of the building at the stairs as she landed. "Don't mess up, asswipes!"

The one closest to the elevators pulled on his lower eyelid with his middle finger.

The child jumped again and pointed at Rysa. Pellets of her past rained down: a slap, a black eye, a belt. Screaming. A tiny doll, its painted face rubbed clean to the plastic underneath. She hid from everyone. Then anger, and the world igniting when the dark-haired woman found her half frozen in an alley.

She'd been abandoned. Kicked from one terrible life to another. No child should have to live through that.

"You have a past," Rysa yelled. "I see threads."

The child glared at Rysa, her red eyes flashing. "Past? So?"

"You don't have to be like this." But maybe for her, *not* remembering was a blessing. Who'd want to remember that? She'd been a vessel emptied by a horrid life before she was turned. Ismene exchanged one type of blankness for another.

"You don't know anything, you smug Fate bitch. You're all the same. Keep out of my business or I'll eat you." She giggled and kicked Rysa's thigh. "Tasty little Fate skank."

Rysa tried to say something else, to reason with the child. But her head boiled and her seers roiled. A new spike tried to push in, flashing destruction and chaos. It grated, and not like the cold razor of before. This spike both burned and foamed.

Lightning flashed outside of the building. The wind whistled through the floor and over the open edge behind the tool cage.

The child laughed. "Mom's home."

44

A Burner woman lowered herself from the ceiling grid, a zipped-up hoodie bagging around her midriff. She held the grid with one hand, her arm flexing as she controlled her descent.

Only her chin, neck, and hands were visible, her face hidden inside the long hood. Doom bubbled off of this woman as she effervesced and the air exploded along the surface of her exposed skin.

Her boots clanked when they hit the concrete. A step and she ripped the lock off the cage.

Bob kissed her cheek. "Thanks, Mom."

Faustus had thought Ismene's children to be stupid and volatile like all the other Burners. Just a little less stupid and a little more volatile. Timor must have identified them by using the past threads trailing like kite tails in their wake. But the War Babies, like their father, had snouts full of conceit. Adrestia wasn't the only Fate blind to the obvious. Rysa's family had utterly underestimated what they were dealing with.

The Burners behind Rysa laughed. Bob pulled himself into the ceiling.

Rysa knew he'd eat Adrestia. Do it slowly, cooking her fingers and stuffing them in her mouth one at a time so she could taste her own flesh, the way he tasted her. She couldn't fight what she couldn't read. Her skin would sear and her tendons would rip as he savored her body. He'd melt her bones and snort her ashes.

Bob would be a new monster created more out of the idiocy of the Fates than the stupidity of the Burners.

Ismene watched him go.

She locked her hand around Faustus's neck. Her fingertips stroked his throat and she clucked. Sparks flicked off her teeth. The cooked-meat stench rising from Faustus's skin was as strong as Ismene's Burner tang.

She tilted her head at the Burner angle. "My dear brother." Her voice spun out viscous, like fireworks in honey. The pop and crackle of the explosions that burned away Ismene's life were sweetened by the Fate blood running through her veins.

She wisped her free hand, a shooing gesture meant to acknowledge Rysa, but her face stayed hidden in the long hood, and angled toward Faustus. "I had a sense of you. He thinks you're the final weapon in his little war to save the future." Sparks flicked off her fingers. "My brother's petite Enola Gay."

"I saw him hurt you. In Texas," Rysa said. He'd slapped Ismene the way he'd hit Rysa so many times since dragging her into the building.

Faustus gurgled.

"He called me a whore. Me. His sister." The tips of the fingers waving at Rysa alternated glowing and smoking, a hazy symphony tapping in the air.

"I'll help you," Faustus croaked.

Ismene let go and he rolled onto his side. He writhed on the concrete, a worm dried out by his sister's heat.

"You won't be alone anymore." Faustus pointed at Rysa, his voice as singed as his skin. "Turn her and she'll be like you. Then we can all be together again. We can be a triad."

"But you called me a whore, brother. Why help me?"

"I'm sorry! I was wrong." He flopped onto his back and closed his eyes. His hand slid up to cover the wound on his neck. "It wasn't your fault. That Shifter enthralled you. I should have killed him."

"You *did* kill him." Ismene kicked Faustus in the groin.

He heaved, his eyes bulging. "Ismene! She's supposed to be the Burner, not you. I see it."

Ismene spit fire at Faustus, a green cloud of vapors that stirred the air. She pointed at Rysa. "He sees your fate."

They stood in front of her, Ismene bent over Faustus with one hand poised, glowing, to cook his flesh. The other waved in a graceful arc toward Rysa. Faustus cowered, one arm up over his head.

The past- and future-seer of the Jani Prime played out a Baroque opera backlit by the lightning flashing across the edges of Salt Lake City. They posed; thunder crashed. He lied; she accepted. He hit; she presented her cheek for more. They followed their script.

"A triad again?" Ismene's gaze slid back to her brother.

"Yes, Ismene," he purred. "Let her take your place."

Ismene turned her face toward Rysa. Under the hood, her eyes glowed a horrible maroon-red, like scabs on fire. Rysa gulped.

If she didn't escape, her eyes would soon burn that way.

She tried to back away, but the child pushed her forward.

"I won't!" she yelled. "I'll hunt all your children, starting with this little punk." Rysa's context was chaos, and chaos she'd bring. "I'll hunt you. I'll hunt everyone! I'll be the best Burner who's ever walked the Earth. Better than the Progenitor. I'll be the *Reine des Brûleurs*."

"Let me eat her!" the child screeched.

"No!" Faustus sat up. "You're Parcae, sister! Do your duty."

Ismene grabbed her brother's hair. She pulled his head back, exposing his neck. "Come here, child." She wiggled a finger.

The kid bounded out from behind Rysa and over to Ismene. "Mom!"

Could Rysa run? Three other Burners waited between Rysa and the elevators. Maybe there was a staircase closer. But her mother was tied to the wall. Rysa slid her foot backward, praying for her seers to show her the way.

The greasy teen grabbed her arm and exhaled at her nose. She coughed, her eyes blurring, and he twirled her back toward her aunt and uncle.

"Did you miss me?" Ismene stroked the kid's head.

Her cap smoked under Ismene's grip, but the child didn't seem to notice. "Can I eat one of them? Please? Dick-boy was mean to me, but the skankadoodle smells super-tasty." She pointed at Rysa.

Ismene's seer spread like a thick paste. Faustus cringed. Rysa dropped to her knees. The child and the teen both giggled.

Five fingers fanned out over the little Burner's head. One hand twisted.

Burner necks snapped different from Shifters. Burners spurt and crackled like a car backfiring.

Ismene flung the body at an angle, around the tool cage and off the open deck of the building. The little Burner crystalized as she flew, trailing red dust. But rain bombarded the building and violent water attacked the edges of the deck. She vanished in a cloud of sparkles against the storm and the mountains.

Ismene hated the Burners, even the ones she made, just as much as her brother.

"*La Reine des Brûleurs, nièce.*" Ismene's gaze dropped to her brother. "What you are will be gnawed to nothing."

Ismene bit into Faustus's shoulder.

His eyes rolled back into his head and he tried to call out but nothing left his throat. Faustus's agony blazed through Rysa's seers, a wet clawing desperation not to die.

Ismene's wicked Burner teeth twinkled like diamonds. She'd taken a chunk of muscle from between her brother's shoulder and his neck. Her acid cauterized the wound but his collar bone showed, off-white and gouged. He dropped onto his side, thrashing.

"I must *feed.*" Ismene pointed at her Burner guards. "But unlike them, I remember. I feel. I see the normals and I remember." Her foot descended and Faustus's knee cracked. "He didn't know I wouldn't forget. Prime future-seer, but he can't read me. He never saw that I understood what he compels me to do."

Faustus stopped fighting. He lay on the concrete, stray rain drops settling on his ash-white skin, his body broken but not bloodied. Acid sealed it shut.

"He turned me into a ghoul."

"You don't have to kill him." But Rysa knew there was no getting around what her aunt saw as her own fate—and the fate of her uncle. They'd continue down this path, not fighting. Not trying.

"I was going to marry my Shifter. He was a morpher with some healing ability. They were working on drugs, applications of their abilities. Some were investigating a cure for the Parcae sickness. My brother killed him. Sent in Burners and murdered him."

"Ismene, I'm sorry," said Rysa.

"Not all of the Shifters hate us." Ismene knelt next to Faustus, stroking his hair. "You'd think they would have learned their lesson long, long ago."

She tilted her head. "If I consume him, will I become both past- and future-seer of my triad?"

Ismene bit into Faustus's arm. She ate, burning away his clothes and taking flesh and meat. His body vanished into his sister, meat and bone disbursed to pay his debt.

Rysa retched. The greasy teen breathed on her ear, increasing her nausea tenfold. She swung, not caring that his skin singed her fist, and punched him in the neck.

He snorted, surprised, and clicked his teeth. "We ain't supposed to hurt you." He grabbed her face, his palms thankfully cold, and moved in for a kiss.

Rysa kneed him in the groin.

He coughed, acid blowing into her face, and his fingers heated. She screamed, kicking again, and he let go. She had two hundred feet, tops, between her and the elevators. If she—

Ismene grasped her upper arm. Around her wrist she now wore two eagles, one of the past and one of the future.

Her aunt's seers locked onto Rysa's awareness. The disorientation overwhelmed, but it didn't foam. "You can be a weapon, if you choose. I don't care." Her diamond teeth flashed. "But can you rule them?"

Rysa's seers jarred: Ladon burning. *What-will-be* gleamed in a different pattern. "The future's changing. I can't see…"

"Of course it is, niece. I am Ambustae. I am Parcae. When the breeds cross, the world always finds something new."

45

E nergy surged upward from the base of the building. Energy she recognized. Energy she'd thought asleep.

Ladon and Dragon had come for her.

Rysa touched back and the beast called in colors brighter than the sun.

Ismene's seers fizzled halfway between the foaming of Burners and the clinking of cymbals in a storm. Bewilderment washed over her face.

"How can this be? His beast sleeps." Her grip cinched around Rysa's upper arm. Acid soaked through the sleeve.

Rysa's skin heated but she ignored it, her attention hyper-focused on the center of the building.

Ladon kicked through the stairwell door. He dodged to the left, avoiding the two Burner guards. Reappearing, he ran up a pallet, his armored jacket and gloves flashing in the lightning reflecting off the mountains.

Thunder rolled through the building.

Ismene's seers grated over Rysa like nails on a chalkboard but she didn't cringe. She wouldn't let her aunt hurt Ladon and Dragon. Her nasty reared up, a snarling guard dog Ismene couldn't dance around.

Her aunt slapped her face and her fingers left a new sting on Rysa's cheek. "Please, young lady. Have some respect."

Ladon's foot caught a guard. The Burner lurched backward but stopped, hanging in midair.

If Dragon snapped the Burner's neck, the building—

The entire floor flashed as another bolt of lightning flooded the area with white light. Rysa squinted, jerking against her aunt's grip as the thunder crashed across the concrete.

"Down!" Ismene threw her behind the tool cage.

The dead Burner's fireball spread around the mesh. Rysa stumbled and her foot slipped off the concrete deck.

Wind and rain buffeted. Sixteen stories below, asphalt gleamed like an oiled snake. If she dropped, she'd bounce. Every single bone in her body would turn to jelly.

Ismene hauled Rysa up the side of the tool cage.

The second guard barreled toward Ladon. He flew sideways into a column when Dragon rammed him from behind. Ladon whipped a brick at the ghoul's head, then signed obscenities.

"My mom kept me hidden for a reason. Let me go. Please."

A new snap echoed over the deck. The other Burner guard bounced off the concrete, imploding as he flew, only to fizzle away in the rain.

Ismene's scab eyes burned hotter. "Mira abandoned me." She looked away again. "She didn't help. She could have helped."

Ladon ran for Rysa. Behind him, the greasy teen lunged from the shadows, the end of the winch's cable in his hand.

Rysa didn't need her seers to know what he was about to do. "Dragon!"

The Burner locked the winch's hook around one of Dragon's hind limbs.

The beast roared, kicking and swatting at the ghoul, but he dodged. Grunting loud enough Rysa heard him all the way down the length of the building, the ghoul yanked on the power lever and ripped it off the engine.

The winch chugged to life.

The cable pulled Dragon back.

Dragon's hide flared. The Burner laughed, pointing, and danced around. But Dragon's talons extended. He wrapped his hand around the ghoul's head and slammed straight down, his shoulder twisting to grind the teen into the concrete.

The agony seething up Dragon's forelimb thudded to Rysa. It mingled with the beast's fatigue and slowed his responses. Yet he pushed down harder, grinding the Burner into the floor as the winch dragged him backward.

The teen's body spread into a thin trail. Wet bubbles hissed off the concrete, popping visibly even to Rysa at the end of the floor's deck.

Ismene pushed Rysa off the front of the tool cage and landed next to her, her head tilted. Rysa felt ghost-threads of both past and future spool from her aunt. Ismene sniffed the air, her eyes narrow.

Ladon jumped pallets and dodged equipment, his gaze locked with Rysa's. But he couldn't hide the agony of his stretching connection to Dragon. He slowed, his face stone.

Dragon flamed the engine. It kept chugging, the cable winding tighter. The beast smashed a steel bar down onto it again and again.

Dragon strained forward but Ladon couldn't come any closer.

"Leashed by your pet." Ismene's finger flickered when she tapped against Rysa's forearm.

Ladon stopped less than a dragon length away.

Rysa stretched out her hand. The wind carried his scent to her—she picked it out through her aunt's stench. She focused on it, calling it, wanting nothing more than for their fingers to connect. "You woke Dragon," she whispered.

"Your mother left a note." Ladon pulled her wedding band out of his pocket. "Told me what to do." He tried to smile as he touched his chest. "All these centuries and I'd never figured it out."

Ismene stroked Rysa's cheek.

The winch's engine coughed and stopped but the cable still wound around Dragon's leg, shackling him away from Ladon.

And from Rysa.

Ladon shuffled forward, his fingers extended. Pain coiled around his body. His jaw hardened to granite.

The closer he moved toward Rysa and the farther from Dragon, the more his light dimmed. Ladon turned phantom before her eyes, dying little by little so he wouldn't have to die all at once when Ismene Burnerized his woman.

Dragon's hide erupted in mad, desperate patterns, but they, too, were bleached. The hook around his leg held and both their bodies withered.

Their souls would crack and she knew where all the blood in her visions came from: Things Ladon thought long gone, horrors he thought controlled, would rupture. Their minds will tear into writhing bits of wrath and vengeance. And someone puts a bullet in his neck.

"Let her go, Ismene. You can leave. We won't stand in your way. She doesn't have to be like you."

"Maybe I don't want to be their queen anymore, Ladon-Human." Ismene seared a finger across Rysa's jaw.

Rysa refused to flinch.

Her aunt clucked. "She'll hunt. She'll end it all. For me. For you. For my sister."

"Let her go, Ismene." Even pale and bleached, fury reddened Ladon's neck.

"Ladon!" Rysa shouted. Maybe he could escape. Maybe he could control it. "Promise me you won't let the rage take you! That you'll do what needs to be done. Promise me *right now* you'll survive this! Because I need to know. I need to know you'll be okay."

"No!" His stone face turned ice cold. "Let her go, you damned Parcae witch!"

Ismene trailed a finger over Rysa's neck like a surgeon marking before surgery, her features as hard as Ladon's. "Murderer," she hissed.

"Please don't," Rysa whispered.

Ismene closed her eyes. Her lips parted. The interior of her mouth glowed and a nauseating, orange light built behind her teeth.

"You can't turn her!" Ladon yelled.

Ismene's mouth snapped shut.

He stepped backward, closer to Dragon. "She'll die."

Ismene's head pivoted, her eyebrows dancing with equal parts confusion and annoyance. "I'm the future-seer! I know what to do."

"Mira stitched her past." He pointed at Rysa. "Look! You may see *what-will-be* now, but you will always be the past-seer of the Jani Prime."

Rysa gritted her teeth and cringed under the onslaught of Ismene's frothing seer.

Dragon yanked on the cable. Ladon inched closer.

Foam ate away her mother's stitching and the veil fell away from Rysa's past. Her past-seer revealed a vision of Abilene, Texas, through her mother's awareness:

Rysa's father, his hazel-green eyes narrow as he watched the dusty courtyard through a high window. "You are the Lady Ismene's sister. Your safety is my priority." He'd snapped a Burner's neck and took a bite to his shoulder to keep Mira safe.

Sandro Torres healed their wounds and oscillated his pheromones and she knew the Burners couldn't smell them, as long as she stayed against his body.

But he lied. He didn't protect her for Ismene. He did it for Mira.

So Mira stitched. She couldn't save her sister. She couldn't save the Shifters who had taken them in, but she could protect this man from her brother and his malevolent spawn.

Sandro held her close. "Why does he do this?"

In the courtyard, Ismene's life bubbled away into caustic bitterness.

Mira buried her face in his chest and tried desperately not to hear her sister's screams. She'd have two weeks with him, on the run, before she told him to go. For his safety. But Alessandro Torres had been a warrior for a very long time and he refused. They would be, at least for a while, a family.

The vision clicked off.

Ismene screamed. "You are *half Shifter*?"

Rysa's father was a healer. A warrior.

She yanked against Ismene's grip. *Shifter*. She wasn't just a Fate. She was much more. They could plot and manipulate all they wanted, but she had always been more than the Jani Prime realized.

Rysa Torres, Fate *and* Shifter.

46

By the elevators Faustus had dragged them out of, Mira dropped out of the unfinished ceiling grid-work, a small figure at the center of the building. She cradled Adrestia, an arm around the other Fate's waist.

Ismene screeched. "You married a Shifter?"

Mira jerked as she set down Adrestia and a vicious, rasping shriek ground from her throat.

Burndust. Rysa's mother had snuck out of her uncle's bonds and inhaled burndust to power her body so she'd have the strength to pull Adrestia from the Burners.

Ismene shook Rysa. "I was supposed to have *my* Shifter. Me!"

Next to Dragon, Adrestia pitched forward, something big and heavy in her hands. The Burners had stripped much of her skin. Dragon sniffed at her head, touching her shoulder, and took what she offered.

Mira shrieked and ran hard for Ismene and Rysa.

The beast clamped the wrench onto the spool casing. Light burst off his hide as he ripped it open.

Rysa reached for Ladon. He glanced at her, his face hard with concentration. A roar billowed across the concrete—Dragon yanked the coiled cable off the housing.

Mira jumped a stack of girders and landed parallel to Ladon. Rysa's seers flared, her own future solidifying in the rock-solid line fueled by her mother's intent.

"Mom! Don't!" If Mira stopped, Ladon could get to them both. But her mom's dust-infested mind only paid attention to her Burnerized sister.

Rysa shoved Ismene. Her aunt's hand released and Rysa grabbed for her mom, hoping, this one time, to stop the inevitable.

She blinked. Time slowed. A gust pummeled Rysa's shoulders and whipped her hair into her eyes.

Dragon charged down the concrete.

Mira's arms wrapped around Ismene's waist and Rysa's mother and her aunt, bound together with shrieks and violence, flew off the side of the building.

Mira's and Ismene's combined screeches rose like the din of fire hornets and drowned out the storm. Behind Ladon, Dragon boomed, moving so fast he blurred. Rysa spun backward as her foot slipped.

Terror consumed Ladon's face.

In the same instant her aunt and mom fell, Rysa fell too, her feet betraying her body.

The storm and the lights of Salt Lake City reflected a terrible orange off the clouds above—a chemical-like orange that scorched the sky like Burner fire. But this time, Rysa wasn't shackled. This time, she was both Fate and Shifter.

This time, she found her control.

Just above her, Dragon sailed over the side. Ladon jumped too, frantically coiling the other end of the cable around his chest and shoulders.

Ismene grabbed Rysa's arm. Her Burner rage fried through the fabric of Rysa's shirt and the cotton smoldered. Her mother howled just out of her reach, her own skin sizzling as she held tight to her sister.

Ladon's boot hit the top of her aunt's head and she jerked back, releasing Rysa's arm.

"Ladon!" Rysa screamed. "Get Mom!" Even if she fell, even if—

Dragon snatched Rysa to his chest and she gasped, the sudden pull disorienting.

"Mom!" She gripped the beast's coat as tight as she could. Ladon and her mom were in free fall. Dragon had her, but—

They bounced against the building and spun away from Ladon and her mother. The beast ground talons into the glass and they swung back.

Ladon lunged for Mira. She twisted around Ismene's waist, shrieking and raking her nails across her sister's face. Little bursts popped off

Ismene's skin. Her aunt howled, swinging her arms wildly. Mira knocked her forehead into Ismene's chin.

Ladon clutched the cable with one hand and grabbed for her mother with the other. He snagged her upper arm and yanked her hard from Ismene.

But Ismene's flailing arms caught Ladon. He tried to push her away but a gust hit and they all slammed into the wall.

Dragon couldn't swipe at her aunt. He held Rysa and they were too far away. The beast pushed against the building, trying anyway, but Ismene's anger honed in on Ladon, her fury pinpointing the curve where his shoulder met his neck.

She hooked onto his back, legs kicking at her sister clinging to his side, and one arm snaking around his head so fast he couldn't respond.

He hollered, his neck straining, but she couldn't twist it. He was too strong. Hope jumped into Rysa's throat. Maybe—

They suddenly jerked to a stop—the cable must have caught something on the floor above.

Ladon looked up. His shoulders strained—he concentrated all his effort on holding her mother against his side with one arm and the line with the other. Ismene hung on his back, tendrils of Burner hell puffing off her anger-heated skin. Her clothes smoked. Ismene's stench was so strong Rysa smelled it from where she clung to Dragon's chest.

A hate-filled snort popped from Ismene. Ladon knew what she was about to do, his expression betraying that he understood but couldn't stop it. He wasn't going to let go of her mother so he could knock off her aunt. He wouldn't let Mira die just to save himself from a Burner.

Shock streamed off Dragon and his talons gouged into the glass. Images flickered into Rysa's mind: Ladon on the ground, his arm shredded. AnnaBelinda, her body ashen, unconscious in the dirt. Ladon, his face torn by a mace.

Terror that this time his human might not survive.

Ismene yanked down the collar of Ladon's jacket and exposed the muscles at the base of his neck. Her mouth glowed bright and sickly orange.

Dragon bellowed. They couldn't swing closer.

Everything Rysa's uncle set in motion was about to combust through Ladon's veins.

Ismene bit.

Ladon roared. Agony fired through their connection and punched Rysa like a fist in the gut. She coughed, holding to Dragon as he jerked under her clenched hands.

A vicious shriek screamed from the floor above as whatever held the cable broke under their weight. They dropped again, but this time the cable wouldn't catch on anything. This time, they'd plunge to the ground.

Rysa and Dragon slammed into the building as he snatched for the other end of the line—the end that wrapped around Ladon's shoulder.

The beast's hide flashed against Rysa's face and she jolted, squinting. But she held on.

So did he. Ladon, her mom, and Ismene had dropped fast and now swung below Dragon's rear limbs and tail, but he twirled the line around his forelimb. He had them and they wouldn't slam into the pavement. She wouldn't lose them both. She wouldn't lose Dragon as his mind shattered.

Flames poured out of the beast. He couldn't hold them all. He—

Something new flowed *from* her. Something that allowed her to will the beast everything she had. Something strong. "Dragon, hold on." She'd give him all she had.

His hide calmed.

Below them, Mira's palm snapped upward into Ismene's nose. The Burner spasmed and let go of Ladon's back. Ismene plunged toward the asphalt below.

Her mother's and Ladon's weight yanked on Dragon's shoulder, but he held on.

The talons of his other limbs gouged into the building. They slid downward.

Ladon's boots clambered along the glass just below them, his end of the cable looped around the shoulder Ismene bit and his other arm wrapped around her mother. He groaned and Dragon's hide responded in glaring, painful spears of orange and red.

Rysa spread her fingers wide. She was Fate. She was Shifter. She was as much Torres as she was Jani, and her father's blood coursed through her veins. She could heal Dragon and strengthen his muscles. Reinforce his joints. If she fired her abilities through their connection, she could calm

Ladon's wound.

Her nasty unfolded and revealed its true shape. Her perception grew, tripled, quadrupled, and she knew the positions of the building, herself, Dragon, Ladon. Her mom. They fell, sliding along the building's surface, but a new heat coursed outward from Rysa's core.

She knew what to do and how to do it. Her body rippled up and down, becoming active. Becoming Shifter.

Her healer augmented from a well she didn't know she had and it touched every cell, holding down Dragon's fatigue and the venom in Ladon's shoulder.

Some color returned to Ladon's skin and he gripped Mira closer. His boots danced on the steel and glass, searching for anything to stop their fall.

Dragon slipped and a talon separated from his foot. Pain fired like flames across gasoline and burst out of his mouth as hot tendrils.

Rysa opened her hands against his hide. Her healer calmed his pain and dampened his leg's raw stabbing.

A new boom pounded up the rain-slicked side of the building. Light flashed, the glass reflecting a brilliance as strong as the lightning over the city.

Sister-Dragon climbed from below.

Dragon grabbed for a seam on the building's side but slid and lost his footing. They dropped until he dug in another talon and caught concrete. They swung back, slamming hard against the wall.

Dragon-ribs cracked. Rysa told his cells to stitch the bone. A gust hit and Dragon flung one leg out so as not to crush her against the glass. Rysa strengthened the ligaments in his shoulder to keep it from tearing out of its joint.

They had dropped far enough that they were below the glass and alongside the brick façade. Dragon swung again, rotating on one hind limb, and the pavement below came into view. They faced downward—Rysa hung upside down between the beast's chest and the hard brick.

Dragon skidded, the façade releasing with loud pops under his talons. Little bits of brick hit her face as they twisted on the wall. His back end slid but his front end stayed in place.

The pavement vanished and the night came back into view, slashed by the whipping cable holding Ladon and her mother

They were about to hit the ground. "Ladon!"

Sister-Dragon's head rammed into Dragon's side inches from where Rysa gripped his coat. They stopped suddenly, bolstered by the other dragon's stability. Rysa gasped and both beasts released puffs of flame. Heat rolled over Rysa's back and shoulders.

Sister-Dragon snatched the cable. The other dragon had Ladon and her mom and wouldn't let them hit the ground. They bounced against the brick, their fall countered.

Rysa touched the other dragon's snout, all her gratitude firing through her fingers to strengthen Sister-Dragon's muscles.

The building groaned. Dragon jerked as a swath of brick facing released. Rysa's body cinched—they were falling again toward the pavement.

She saw the sky above. Rain splattered against her face and she lost her hold on Dragon's coat.

She'd let go.

They'd almost made it. She was about to hit the ground and every part of her body was going shatter. She'd die. But Ladon and Dragon lived. And so did her mother.

Dragon's forelimbs wrapped around her body from behind.

He had her. She jerked backward, against his chest.

They rolled down his sister's back, the two dragon's ridges snapping against each other as Dragon flipped. Sister-Dragon's tail whipped and Dragon twined a forelimb in its length as the talons of his back limb caught the wall. They swung down, facing the pavement again.

They stopped, Dragon clinging to the building, the sidewalk inches from Rysa's nose.

A shudder ran up her spine. They survived. Sixteen stories, and they survived.

Ladon's feet hit the ground. He released her mom and Mira bounced with a thud against the building's wall. Ladon rolled to a crouch, his skin deathly white. He grasped his shoulder just out of Rysa's reach, blood oozing between his fingers.

Dragon flipped her up and set her on her feet. Disoriented, she leaned against his neck, as much to check his wounds as to steady herself. She needed to know he wouldn't die, right there, on the spot, from some hidden injury. He felt bruised, but alive.

But the venom eating Ladon's shoulder churned both her head and stomach. Blood soaked his t-shirt, his face the mask she'd seen in her visions.

Ladon was about to turn Burner.

AnnaBelinda smashed Mira against the wall behind Ladon. Dressed head to toe in black like Ladon, her eyes goggled, the dragon woman raised her plated glove to punch.

"Stop!" Rysa staggered forward but Sister-Dragon's big hind limb stepped off the building between her and her mom. "Leave her alone!"

"Sister!" Ladon barked.

Rysa tried to push by Sister-Dragon. "Don't hurt her."

AnnaBelinda dropped her mother. She leaped the beast's leg and wrenched Rysa's arm. "This is your fault!"

"Get out of my way." Her mom was okay but she needed to get to Ladon. Too much blood flowed from the wound. She sidestepped to wind around AnnaBelinda.

"No Fate touches my family." AnnaBelinda flipped her onto her butt. Her foot lifted to stomp.

Ladon groaned again, his entire body deforming. Dragon rocked back and forth, confused.

"I am a healer!" If AnnaBelinda didn't move, Ladon would die. "Get out of my way!"

"Dracas!" Mira screamed. "Let her heal him!"

"Anna." Derek pointed at the street.

On the center line, rain puffed off Ismene's convulsing body in little explosions of steam.

"This is not good." Derek pulled a big pistol from a holster under his jacket. "This is the very definition of *not good*."

AnnaBelinda stepped from Ladon and Rysa pressed her palm over the blood pouring from his shoulder.

47

Rysa knew every nuance, every cell and every tissue of Ladon's body. His life, his pain, his power.

The thing scorching into his being was about to transmute him into a Ladon-shaped fiend. It would look like him—mostly like him—but it won't *be* him. It won't beat with the heart of a man. It would drone with the buzz of a Burner.

And he'd set fire to the planet.

"Don't let me turn." The pain ripped from Ladon's throat as a loud howl. "I'll hurt you. I'll hurt Dragon. I'll hurt everyone."

Through the eyes of a nameless victim, the future gave her a vision more terrible than any she'd had yet: Ladon crouched on the rubble of a distant building. His eyes a burned vicious red visible to all, his imposed his will onto the Burner chaos in his blood. Slowly, his fingers curling into a tight claw, he set fire to a chunk of concrete sitting on his palm. Behind him, Dragon's hide swirled with the flames of a demon. Ladon roared and the beast jumped over his head, his speed and strength tripled.

Rysa gasped.

His Progenitor blood would be a thousand times more caustic than Ismene's. Ladon, the Ambustae-Dracae hybrid, would burn the world with an unstoppable flame.

This new vision wove itself into the familiar visions she'd had over the past few days: So sure of his interpretation, Faustus had caused this. He'd set into motion this one improbable future.

But Rysa's healer, working with her seers, knew how and where the venom changed Ladon's body, even if she couldn't read see the venom itself. Ismene's injection invaded Ladon's cells and altered his chemistry. It set every protein on the verge of ignition.

"I can get it," she whispered.

A new, phantom sensation hit her nose: The putrid rotting of Sister-Dragon's blackened corpse.

Rysa flinched but she didn't let go of Ladon. She wasn't going to let a horrid future happen. She'd pull out the venom out of his shoulder.

"It'll hurt you." Ladon doubled forward. "Let Dragon take care of me. You can hear him. He can bond to you. You'll both be safe."

"Don't say that. You don't know that." She cupped his face with her free hand and made him look at her. "You can fight this! We can get it."

Derek watched Ismene as he uncoiled the cable from around Dragon's legs. In the street, out in the lessening rain, AnnaBelinda and Sister-Dragon circled her aunt.

Ismene sat up. Steam hissed off her shoulders and she turned her face toward the clouds. A loud, vicious screech filled the air.

Sister-Dragon vanished. Mira backed away.

Dragon, still disoriented and swaying, stayed between Rysa and Ladon, and Ismene. Rysa fired her healer through their connection and the beast's hide calmed. He dropped his head low, staggering less, and nudged Derek closer to his side.

Rysa refocused her attention onto Ladon's shoulder. She cupped the wound, her hand heating, and used her healer to pull at his cells. The venom wiggled, but she worked to force it back toward the bite.

It danced in his vein as if mocking her, as if it knew exactly what it was doing, and it evaded every tug and grab she made.

Ladon howled again, his body stiffening. "I won't hurt you…"

"Then don't. Fight with me." Her palms heated to the point she felt as if her skin would blister. "Ladon, please. We can do this together."

Bits of the venom crystallized and exploded below his skin. He cringed, his lips curling. "I can't stop it."

The venom twisted and lurched around her attempts to yank it out. She had to focus, had to—

Dragon's snout touched her shoulder. An image pushed into her mind—sinuous tunnels, a layered maze. She couldn't see. "Dragon! Don't blind me. Don't—"

Veins. Understanding filled through her mind, a beautiful ballerina gift from her present-seer. Dragon was giving her the structure and pattern of Ladon's body. His arteries. The push and pull of his muscles. The windings of the injection.

Dragon's perception mapped. Her seers navigated. The venom snarled like a rabid animal, but it couldn't escape their combined efforts. It tussled with her, angry and random. It exploded parts of itself in an attempt to disguise its way. She blocked it anyway, calling its bluff.

Dragon bolstered her abilities and showed her the way. She followed his map, outflanked the venom, and stopped it cold.

She hooked it.

In the street, Sister-Dragon roared as AnnaBelinda knifed Ismene's side. Ismene countered, her hand wrapping the hilt protruding from her hip, and whipped the already imploding blade at AnnaBelinda.

Sister-Dragon caught the hilt and slammed the knife into the pavement.

The ground buckled, the shockwave rolling under Rysa and Ladon, but she held on.

Venom pooled in the wound, as red as Ladon's blood but phosphorescent and glowing. Rysa flattened her palm over it, drawing it out.

AnnaBelinda hooked her legs around Ismene's neck and flipped her to the pavement.

Ladon clutched Rysa's waist so tightly her ribs creaked. She couldn't breathe, but she concentrated, ignoring her own pain, and hovered her palm over his shoulder.

On her hand, four drops of red liquid rolled like scarlet mercury. Ladon fell back, gasping. He lived. She wasn't going to lose him.

A whine rose from the venom.

"It's imploding," Ladon croaked.

He grabbed for her waist again but her seers took control and she dodged, her fingers closing around the red liquid. Her palm spasmed. The venom's power stung as if electrified barbed wire wrapped around her arm, but it didn't feel hot. It felt ice cold, as if it sucked away all her heat.

Dragon swiped for her, too. Her seers flared and she dodged again.

Naked Burner venom would destroy Salt Lake City. Murder Ladon and Dragon. His sister. Smear her mother across the—

Mira had her, one arm around her shoulders and the other plunging a knife toward her free hand.

"Mom!" She held onto the venom. She wouldn't let—

The knife pricked. A weld of blood appeared on Rysa's ring finger.

Fate blood stabilized Burners. Calmed their chaos and gave them threads of past, present, and future. Shifter blood made them more of what they were. More volatile. More explosive.

Rysa was both.

The venom began to shrink into itself.

She poked her bleeding finger into the red bead of venom. It stopped, frozen, the whine momentarily silenced. Stunned, she yanked back, but a drop of blood stayed behind. The venom lapped at it, feeding like some damned animal.

Its color darkened. A ripple traveled across its surface.

But the whine started again, quieter and less frantic but still piercing. Still Burner.

Rysa knew the truth, even if she didn't want to admit it: Chaos could not be constrained. Slowed, yes. But not controlled. If it couldn't have Ladon, it would have her. Shifters always died. But so would the venom.

"Not you. It can't be you." Ladon didn't plead. He wouldn't. But she saw his need—and love so deep it still surprised her, even after all they'd shared.

If she let in the venom—if she licked it off her hand or let it in through the prick on her finger—Salt Lake City would still stand when the sun's rays broke through the storm clouds at dawn. But *her* mornings would vanish from the future. She'd never wake to Ladon's smile and his kisses and to him loving her with all the intensity she saw in his eyes.

She saw Ladon and Dragon shattering. They'd become the brutal anger she'd glimpsed before and there'd be bullets. "Don't make them kill you! Promise me. Ladon—"

"Not you!" Ladon roared. He clutched his shoulder as he staggered to his feet. "You do not have to be Parcae! You are not bound! You're not—" He dropped to his knees again, his pain too much.

She reached for him but he held her at arm's length.

"I will have what I want, Rysa! I will have *you*." His skin blanched again—he hurt and without her, he'd also die. "You're smart enough to fix this," he whispered.

Out on the street, AnnaBelinda slammed Ismene's face into the pavement. She pulled another knife, ready to pierce the Burner's heart. Ismene hissed, a sound very similar to the whine of the venom in Rysa's hand.

She looked down at it. Concentrated chaos might not be constrained, but blood-diluted chaos had been *contained* for twenty-three centuries.

Inside Burners.

"Stop!" Rysa held out the venom for Ismene to see.

Dragon lifted his sister-human off Ismene and her aunt bolted across the street, her gaze not leaving Rysa's hand.

AnnaBelinda shouted and punched Dragon's forelimb until he dropped her. He flamed, but she also ran for Rysa.

Derek stepped in front of his wife. "Honey."

Ismene stopped an arm's length away. "You're giving it back to me?"

Rysa called her seers. She didn't see Ismene but she saw the one path that didn't lead to burning. Or her own death. "You will contain it." She stepped closer. "And you will stop killing. No more, Ismene! You've caused enough harm."

Ismene's eyes narrowed and her back stiffened. "Why should I pay you a penance?" A finger pointed over Rysa's shoulder, toward Ladon. Ismene's face scrunched into a tense façade. "You forgave *him*."

Ismene was jealous. It bubbled off her with her seers. Jealous of the family the Dracae represented. Jealous Rysa had the man she loved and Ismene didn't.

Jealous and petty, just like a Parcae.

"Why?" Rysa's fist tightened around the venom. "Because you're no better than Faustus," she hissed. "Because I refuse to die just so you don't have to take any responsibility." She waved the venom at Ismene and its whine grew louder. "Figure it out! And when you do, I will forgive you, aunt."

Ismene pursed her lips into a defiant line. "I have no control over the

Burner within me."

"Then you ask for help and you accept what's given to you. But if you harm my mom, I will find you. The Dracae will be the least of your worries."

Mira touched her sister's arm. "Please, Ismene."

Rysa opened her hand. Ismene bent forward watching both Rysa and the liquid, her head tipped at the Burner angle as she listened to it whine. She glanced up, assessing Rysa. Her face changed, her eyes taking on an acceptance Rysa had never seen in a Burner before, and she licked the venom off Rysa's hand.

Her skin changed, calming, and a cooler tone moved from her lips across her face and down her neck. The rain no longer exploded when it hit her skin. Her Burner stench diminished, its acid notes clearing.

Her features lost some of the Burner gear-and-pulley strain, and she turned her eyes to the clouds.

Mira touched Rysa's arm. "I'll take her. I'll take Addy, too. We'll protect her."

Her mom wanted to take on the task of overseeing a Burner? "Mom, the sickness. Can you do this?"

Mira's seer flared. "For now, yes." She squared her shoulders and nodded at her sister. "There are other Jani triads besides the War Babies, honey. You have family. Both mine and your father's."

Rysa took her mother's elbow. "I won't be Jani, Mom. Not after Faustus killed all those people in Chicago to get to me." The burnmetal bracelet slid down her wrist when she held it up. "Not after everything he did. Everyone he hurt." She nodded toward Ismene.

"I understand." Mira bowed her head toward AnnaBelinda. "Dracas." Then to Ladon. "Dracos. The Jani family will no longer cause you pain. Of this we swear."

Ismene narrowed her eyes again. Mira's grip on her arm tightened and she looked down at her sister's hand before looking up at Ladon.

She nodded once, then turned away.

"Mira." Ladon pulled her mother's wedding band from his pocket.

All this time, Rysa had been both Fate and Shifter and she never knew.

Mira slipped on the ring. "Tell him I'm waiting." She took Ismene's hand.

"Mom?"

Mira looked back.

"Why didn't you tell me?"

Ismene's seers thundered. "If another thread had been followed, you would not have activated yourself." She lifted her arms to the heavens. "Fate or Shifter, you are the first. The Jani Prime *did* find the cure."

48

Her family pulled away. They'd leave her alone. Rysa didn't foresee Ladon or his sister tolerating any more interference from Fates.

She curled her fingers around Ladon's shoulder and covered the wound as she leaned against his side. Exhausted as she was, she'd have to wait to finish healing the bite, but the blood had stopped oozing. He hadn't turned.

Derek chuckled and shook his head. He slapped Ladon's other shoulder. Wincing, Ladon frowned.

Dragon blew a line of flame at the Russian's hat.

Derek looked Rysa up and down before poking his chin at the beast. "They pout when they don't get their way." He rubbed the tip of his nose with the back of his hand as he nodded toward Ladon.

Ladon signed something she didn't recognize.

Derek laughed again. "See?"

Frowning, she weaved her fingers into Ladon's. "What'd you say?"

He pulled her flush against his chest and trailed kisses across the slope of her ear. "We'll teach you Russian Sign Language." More kisses moved down the curve of her neck.

Rysa bounced on the balls of her feet. "Oh! When?" No boredom with them. And from the way he nuzzled her neck and held onto her backside, she guessed she wouldn't get a lot of sleep, either. Which was fine. Grinning, she nibbled on his earlobe.

His skin brightened.

Her grin turned to a smile, happy to see his color returning. "No fading away, Mr. Monochrome."

Dragon nudged Ladon and touched Rysa's cheek, his hide brilliant with burgundies, a rich glimmering reflected in the puddles and off the building's glass.

"He says that you need not worry. We're fine." Another kiss, gentle but deep. "You're with us."

And she would be, for as long as they wanted her.

Derek's phone rang. He dug in his pocket and flipped it to his ear. "Cousin!" He winked at Rysa. "You think her father is a Shifter? And why is that?"

Ladon chuckled.

Derek covered the phone. "Dmitri found a healer. Her name is Lucinda de la Turris. She's flying in from Spain." He listened for a moment. "Cordoba. Lovely city. She says you may remember her."

Ladon's eyebrows arched.

"What?" Derek scoffed. "He wants to know if it's true the de la Turris clan can hear the dragons. He says he's jealous."

AnnaBelinda snorted.

"*de la Turris*? It means 'of the tower.'" Ladon laughed and kissed Rysa's cheek. "Your father must be part of her clan. That explains your connection."

"My clan?" But she knew it wasn't the only reason she heard Dragon. Frowning, she looked at the bracelet on her wrist. Damned chaos blanketed all her abilities.

"Alessandro Roberto de la Turris, you say? Hmm." Derek gestured toward his wife and pointed at one of the neighboring buildings.

AnnaBelinda tugged on Ladon's arm. "We must leave. You need rest." The RV waited next to the low-slung offices.

The dragons sauntered ahead, knocking each other's shoulders. They dimmed their hides but continued to shimmer and their light caught something resting in a puddle a few feet away.

Ladon said something but Rysa didn't hear. She let go of his hand, drawn to the sparkle.

Her knees buckled. They both almost toppled to the pavement but AnnaBelinda steadied them, one arm around Ladon, the other around Rysa.

"We will call you back," Derek said to Dmitri. "No, no. I will call you back in about half an hour." He tucked the phone into his pocket.

Dragon's talon, the one which had broken free while they fell, refracted in the puddle. At least six inches long, all of the beast's colors played over its surface.

When she carefully laid it on her palm, it altered, blending with her skin and the night.

Rysa's sense of tentacles, of grossness and monsters, of *other*—they all vanished. "Nasty" no longer applied. She blinked, staring at the glimmer in her hand.

The past, present, and future became distinctly oriented in the same way that she knew up from down, back from front, and left from right. Her healer, her Shifter part, also oriented to her seers, in the same way she knew her hands from her feet.

For the first time since she activated, she felt whole. She might bounce still, and talk too much, and get distracted, but her new parts stopped whipping. They no longer hurt.

In the street in Minnesota, when she activated, she wore the burnmetal shackles. But she'd also been held in the air, in Dragon's forelimbs.

And no one knew what compounds were in his talons.

She pulled the burnmetal link from her wrist and whipped it across the street.

"Rys, what are you—"

An image of her mother's talisman bracelet flashed from the beast.

Ladon's eyes widened. "How can that be?"

All this time, her seers hadn't meant to siphon. They'd been using her Shifter connection to Ladon and Dragon to reach her true talisman—the beast himself. The chaos of the burnmetal she wore on her wrist had only disrupted her already frazzled mind and kept her from integrating properly.

She held the talon to her chest. "I'm…" She wasn't Ambusti. She wasn't locked to the damned Burners.

"I'm the new Draki Prime." The Fate-Shifter healer.

Ladon swung her into his arms. "You're ours," he whispered, his lips on her temple.

"Put me down! You're wounded." The bite might open if he carried her to the RV. He'd bleed again. "Caveman."

Dragon pushed through RV door first, squeezing his head through, then his limbs. He curled into the corner of the big bed filling the back of the vehicle.

Ladon chuckled as he carried her through the door and set her down next to the beast. "Ah, but it is an excellent cave. One suitable for both dragons and beautiful women."

Derek laughed as he went forward to drive, Sister-Dragon squeezing in behind him. "That it is, my friend!"

AnnaBelinda appeared, a med kit in her hand. "Ignore the boys." She smiled as she bandaged Ladon's shoulder, then checked Rysa's pulse. "Your heart's beating fine."

She pressed a palm to Rysa's forehead. "But you're feverish."

Dragon cupped her upper back. *Yes*, he signed. *Your temperature is elevated.*

Fevers were to be expected in the newly activated. The bed felt comfy and all Rysa wanted was sleep. She'd be fine, resting with Ladon and Dragon.

AnnaBelinda handed her a bottle of water. "Drink this." Then she wagged a finger at Ladon. "She'll need food when she wakes up. Shifters are always hungry when they come out of activation."

He nodded and kissed the top of Rysa's head. "I'll make sure she eats."

"And watch her fever."

Rysa sipped the water. She felt safe between Ladon and Dragon. She even felt safe with AnnaBelinda and Sister-Dragon, who glimmered like an ocean behind Derek. There was no other place she wanted to be but with them.

Ladon touched her shoulder and her cheek. "Thank you, my love."

"You're welcome." She cuddled close. "Will you really buy a house near campus?" She'd live with them, even though they hadn't been together long enough for that. But she knew they'd insist. She didn't foresee either Ladon or Dragon accepting any other arrangement.

He kissed her cheek. "And another later, if you decide to go to graduate school."

The level of commitment he offered shouldn't surprise her, but it did. "You know, in a couple of weeks you may decide you don't like me." She stroked his arm. "I can be demanding. And hyperactive." He hadn't been around her enough to start making the faces.

She felt her body pull away in the same unconscious reaction she'd had to every guy who offered affection.

She didn't mean to. Ladon wouldn't do that to her.

"Look at me." He cupped her chin. "*You're* not high strung." He sniffed as he nodded toward the front of the RV.

A giggle escaped before she caught it and he grinned as he leaned back and pulled her close.

"We are more concerned about you."

"Why?" Her seers didn't scream *bad* or *be scared*. Just the opposite. She saw only happiness.

"I will explain my entire twenty-three centuries and what I have done and why I did it." He paused, watching her face. "You can ask me any question and I will always tell you the truth."

"I know." After what he'd given her already, she wasn't worried. The wars he'd fought were in the past.

"Thank you." He kissed the top of her head.

Rysa settled, her head on Ladon's shoulder and Dragon's hand draped over her hip. They fell into a rhythm, Ladon breathing in as she breathed out, Dragon's patterns matching their respirations. His lights reflected off the walls of the RV and moved in soft waves as if pushed by a gentle breeze.

Her body embraced true calm for the first time since the Burners found her. She drifted off into sleep, her new talisman under her palm.

The stars and waves passing by her eyes shone like the future, strong and smooth. No fire haunted her soul. Rysa slept, tranquil, with only visions of sunshine and oranges filling her dreams.

~~~~

If you would like to be notified when Kris Austen Radcliffe's next novel is released, as well as gain access to an occasional free bit of author-produced goodness, please sign up for Kris's mailing list at www.krisaustenradcliffe.com.

Your email address will never be shared and you can unsubscribe at any time.

Word of mouth and reviews are vital to the success of any author. If you enjoyed *Games of Fate*, please consider leaving a review. Even one sentence would be useful for other readers.
Thank you!

~~~

Turn the page for the first chapter of *Flux of Skin*, book two of the **Fate ✦ Fire ✦ Shifter ✦ Dragon** series...

1

Bumps and divots and tactile non-sequiturs wrenched across Ladon's abdomen. The RV bounced and reflections of Dragon's patterns whirled against the ceiling and a damned dream turned his gut into a cauldron.

He rubbed his midsection. They'd be home soon. The Jani Fates may have put them through hell—he could think of a thousand safer ways to activate his beloved Rysa's healer abilities than the fight they'd just endured in Salt Lake City—but that was done. In less than two hours he'd be in his own bed, under the solidity of the cave's dome, his woman where she should be—pressed against his side and free of her family's torture.

Ladon wanted to sleep off his wounds in comfort and peace, all his nightmares be damned.

Yet a sour sense of foreboding grated at his insides. The fractured emotions of the dream still chafed his body raw.

Rysa lay between him and Dragon, asleep again. He rolled against her back and snaked an arm around her waist, his fingers splaying over her belly. He laid his forehead against the nape of her neck, breathing her in her mist-under-the-moon scent.

She sighed and rolled slightly, her body unconsciously molding against his. He shifted, closing the gap, and the sourness seeped away.

This, with her, filled more holes in his long life than any other moment he'd experienced. Yet he couldn't shake the thought the dream's menace was backwash from her Fate's future-seer. Her abilities saw something bad coming and through the connection they shared, so did he.

Except it felt familiar. It felt like *him*. Twenty-three centuries he'd walked this earth and rolling dread only pierced his gut before the universe decided to reduce his life to rubble.

Dragon's patterns flickered to warmer tones. Unease filtered through the river of energy Ladon shared with the beast. Or it filtered from him to Dragon. After over two millennia sharing a psychic connection, sometimes neither of them could tell to whom an emotion belonged.

We are safe, the beast pushed into his mind. A slow ocean of disconnected patterns moved across the beast's hide. *You must not worry. Rysa will be distressed by your mood.*

Ladon willed his muscles to loosen. Even if his body screamed to pay attention, to keep his eyes open and his senses primed, she didn't need to see his unease.

She sighed.

The beast nuzzled her shoulder. Yawning, she wiped away sleep with the back of one hand while scratching Dragon's jaw with the other.

Ladon forced a bright grin as much to bury his discomfort as to mask it from her. Even without her abilities to see past, present, and future, she picked up more than she realized. The beast was right—she'd sense his anxiety if he wasn't careful.

He stroked a stray hair from her forehead.

"Hmm… Where are we?" She scooted closer.

Before they left Salt Lake City, they'd both changed into some of his brother-in-law Derek's extra sweats. She cuddled against Ladon's side and the big-eared, big-eyed Russian cartoon character emblazoned across the t-shirt she wore stretched tight between her perfect breasts.

All his life and he'd never found a woman with such exquisite balance. One breast was slightly fuller than the other—just a fraction and not enough a normal would notice—but her other had a small mole on the center top. When she held her arms out to him, it formed a perfect line between her shoulder and her nipple and balanced the slight extra roundness of her other breast perfectly.

He traced his finger over the cartoon character's ear, gently circling the mole under the fabric.

Her fingers traced the grooves of his bicep.

Every inch of his skin, every muscle and every tendon, sighed under her touch. Four days they'd been together. Four days and his body only felt whole when she pressed herself against his side.

"We're almost to Rock Springs," he whispered.

Her fingers caressed his forearm, her touch light but warm. Her seers danced along the borders of his consciousness with the rhythm of her movements, tender but solid, in a lovely and sure cadence.

He let it flow over him. The music of her Fate abilities wove into the edges of his mind like her fingers wove around his hand. He breathed under the completeness of her caress—both mental and physical—soothed more than he should allow himself.

He glided his lips over her brow, then down the bridge of her nose to land a gentle kiss on the tip. Another kiss followed, a sweet touch of his lips to hers. Her jasmine and mist-under-the-moon scent curled into him, but this close, a hint of something new added a deeper note to her bouquet: 'Acceptance.'

Her Shifter half had brought more than healer abilities—she exhibited burgeoning close-range enthraller pheromones as well. Scents he could only smell when he was within inches of her body. Scents her body made just for him. Scents that said she loved him.

He could let his focus change. Concentrate on her skin and her touch and the wonders she shared with him. He could cover her with his body and kiss the sleepiness from her mouth. Give back to her all that she'd given him and let everything else fall away.

He nibbled her earlobe, nuzzling and kissing. The lumps lessened as he pressed himself against her and he felt, for the first time since opening his eyes, that maybe he'd only had a bad dream. A reaction to what had happened, not what will. He lay now next to perfection. What bad could happen?

She tickled the furrow between his abdomen and his hip and he squirmed, chuckling against her lips. "Woman, you will be my end." A rumble threatened to escape from his chest—his rolling dragon vibration that emanated from the spot below his heart. It had happened with other women, but never as loud as it did with Rysa, and never as frequent.

324

And she seemed to enjoy it. If they were quick, they'd be dressed again before Sister drove the RV into the all-night grocery in Rock Springs. He worked his hand up her thigh to the firm curve of her bottom.

A sly twinkle moved from her grin to her eyes, though she yawned and leaned her head against his shoulder. "You're going to have to wait until I feel better."

He pulled back. That's not what she said outside of Salt Lake City. She'd crawled on top of him, the activation of her Shifter half priming all her appetites, and rubbed against his groin until he couldn't take it anymore and flipped her on her back.

He pushed himself up on his elbow. She did still feel hot to the touch. He hadn't thought about it—she might take longer than other Shifters to come out of activation—but now he wondered. And she hadn't asked for food since they left—not even an apple or a drink of water in the five hours they'd traveled.

The dream's dread resurfaced and scoured a new trench across his stomach.

Behind Rysa, discordant patterns swirled across Dragon's hide.

Rysa rolled away. "I feel everything you two pulse back and forth between each other, you know." She rubbed the beast's snout. "I'm fine. I'm still activating, that's all. Who knows what kind of Shifter I'll be, huh? Since I'm an active Fate, too." A weak grin appeared—the corners of her mouth lifted, but nothing else. Ladon could tell she didn't believe her own words.

How could he have missed this? He'd been so wrapped up in his own desires, so amazed by the newness of her Fate-Shifter combination he'd failed to consider the potential danger of a double activation.

There were probably good reasons half-breeds were only activated as either Fate or Shifter. Probably very good reasons.

Rysa's skin had taken on the tone of ash. Her fever hadn't diminished and still flushed her face and neck, but a pallor had set over her cheeks and eyes.

He felt along her forehead with the back of his hand. She felt warm yet clammy.

"Ladon, I'm okay." Her brows knitted and the corners of her mouth dropped down. She looked like she did when she worried about *him*. "When my aunt gets here, she'll take care of it. I'll be alright."

She lied—fear sparked across their connection. Her aunt may be a class-one healer, but Rysa knew her double-activation was destroying her body. She was trying to conceal it from him.

"Rys, if you're hurting, don't hide it. Don't—"

Dragon flattened his digits and retracted his talons. *Lucinda de la Turris comes, Rysa*, he signed in American Sign Language so she understood, one big eye level with Ladon's face. *She is a good healer and will help.*

The beast pulsed calm as his big hand returned to her hip. *You are increasing her anxiety, Human.*

Ladon sat up. *She's sick.* Dragon's accusatory tone wasn't helping.

Rysa rolled onto her back, one palm on Ladon's stomach and the other on Dragon's snout. Anger flitted across her face. "Quit fretting! You're both worse than my mother." She rolled onto her front and closed her eyes.

Dragon's hide pulsed in his version of a frown and Ladon stared at Rysa's back, not understanding why she acted this way. It didn't make sense. He would do whatever was necessary for her to be healthy. He'd go anywhere and acquire anything, even if he had to fight every Fate, Shifter, and Burner on the planet to do it.

She knew that. She didn't have to ask.

"I'm serious." She buried her face in the pillow. "I'm not a doll. I won't break."

"But—"

She sat up in one swift, stiff motion. Her seers raked through the back of the RV, grating and dissonant, not rhythmic and musical like they should be.

Ladon squinted. No Fates' seers had ever felt so harsh against his mind. They'd turned rasping and violent so fast the surprise of the change hit him harder than the new rawness spreading through his mind. Something boiled away at her abilities.

The part of Rysa she called her nasty jigged along their connection as if it danced on hot coals. He felt it, almost saw it as a real, visceral extension of the woman he loved.

326

The energy he and the beast shared collapsed into a tight stream. Every other time they'd contracted their energy around her, calm settled her mind and pleasure eased her body. Her nasty drank deep and order would right her world.

But now, her breath hitched. A glaze clouded the moonlight of her irises and she blinked in a steady but unnatural cadence. "Put on your shirt."

He nodded as he reached for a t-shirt. Her face flattened like it did when she blacked out. But that shouldn't happen anymore. She had her true Fate's talisman—a talon Dragon had lost in Salt Lake City. She'd scooped it out of a puddle and Ladon bound it in duct tape and twine for her, to blunt its edge and hide its dragon-vanishing properties. She now wore it around her neck as a curve of adhesive tied with a square knot at her nape.

Her hand raised, rigid as if she lacked control, and her finger pointed toward the front of the RV. "Something's wrong," she whispered. "The road is stiff."

Stiff? Her seers pounded on the edge of his consciousness. What was happening to her?

Dragon's hand cupped her back. *Her fever rises.*

Divots poked again. Trenches deepened. Dread dropped from the sky and slammed into Ladon's body so hard his back felt as if it would snap.

She stared through the curtain at the road ahead, her eyes narrow. "Put on your boots. Now."

"Love, what are you seeing?" An instant of *fight* flickered along their connection. All edges delineated. All sound heightened. Her seers backwashed into his mind.

"Past, present, future—I can't see anything. The world is sharp and cutting. Hard and splitting."

Ladon pulled the t-shirt over his wounded shoulder. The Burner bite he'd suffered in Salt Lake City throbbed but he ignored it.

"Ladon…" Her eyes rolled back into her head. Her spine arched and her mouth opened wide, her breath rattling into her chest.

She dropped against Dragon's chest.

"Rysa!" All the muscles along Ladon's spine knotted. She didn't respond.

Dragon scooped her up and placed one hand on her back. He flexed his digits, fully retracting his talons, and reached for Ladon. The beast didn't need to touch his chest. Ladon already felt the torrents flooding off her body. They broke free like vapor boiling off too-hot skin.

She burned.

And Ladon didn't know what to do....

ALSO BY KRIS AUSTEN RADCLIFFE:

The **Fate ✦ Fire ✦ Shifter ✦ Dragon** Series:

Games of Fate
Flux of Skin
Fifth of Blood
Bonds Broken & Silent
All But Human

Coming Soon:
Men and Beasts

Science Fiction:

Itch: Nine Tales of Fantastic Worlds

Modern Erotic Love Stories:

The Quidell Brothers:

Thomas's Muse
Daniel's Fire
Robert's Soul

ABOUT THE AUTHOR

As a child, Kris took down a pack of hungry wolves with only a hardcover copy of *The Dragonriders of Pern* and a sharpened toothbrush. That fateful day set her on a path traversing many storytelling worlds—dabbles in film and comic books, time as a talent agent and a textbook photo coordinator, and a foray into nonfiction. After co-authoring *Mind Shapes: Understanding the Differences in Thinking and Communication*, Kris returned to academia. But she craved narrative and a richly-textured world of Fates, Shifters, and Dragons—and unexpected, true love.

Kris lives in Minnesota with her husband, two daughters, Handsome Cat, and an entire menagerie of suburban wildlife bent on destroying her house. That battered-but-true copy of *Dragonriders*? She found it yesterday. It's time to pay a visit to the woodpeckers.behavior.

CONNECT WITH THE AUTHOR

E-mail: krisradcliffe@sixtalonsign.com
Web ite: www.krisaustenradcliffe.com
Publisher: www.sixtalonsign.com/
Facebook Fan Page: http://www.facebook.com/AuthorKrisAustenRadcliffe

CPSIA information can be obtained at www.ICGtesting.com
Printed in the USA
BVOW06s0122020715

407180BV00006B/38/P